Critical Praise for

"**Straightforward and candid** . . . a story that must be told.
—*In Touch*

"**An often funny and introspective novel** . . . Downey is keenly aware of the controversy that his book has caused."
—*Outword Magazine*

"*The Moralist* is worth reading because it brings much needed light to a subject generally considered taboo."
—*Key West Celebrate!*

". . .this voice needs to be heard in these new dark ages for civil liberties."
—*Frontiers Newsmagazine*

"**Read it if you dare.** *The Moralist* is brilliant and outrageous. It is about things that matter: art, philosophy, politics, science, religion. Above all it is a love story, and one like no other. But be warned. Your settled notions of right and proper conduct could be blown sky high by this controversial oeuvre."
—Tom O'Carroll, author of *Pedophilia: The Radical Case*

"*The Moralist* . . . expresses a radical moral perspective that challenges contemporary ethical thought in an outrageous and funny way."
—Dr. Frits Bernard, author of the novella *Costa Brava*

"*The Moralist* is a stunning personal and political document. Rod Downey has created an antidote to the poisonous hysteria surrounding inter-generational relationships in today's society."
—Gerald Moonen, creator of the photographic collection *Image Dei*

"This daring book should be read by all who are concerned about building a healthier, more compassionate, more richly diverse society."

—David Werner, author of the internationally acclaimed community health care handbook *Where There Is No Doctor*

"*The Moralist* is an impressive statement about a kind of relationship that few have heard of. It should be read for that reason."

—Dr. Frans Gieles, educational specialist

Readers' Comments . . .

"**This book is so real it is destined to be burned!** Looking for a transformative experience? Read this book! . . .At last, we have the long awaited 'New Novel' of America! It should be enough to make Albert Camus salivate. Not only is it a book, it is a dare." —Montana

"**Downey tosses a torch into the fireworks factory**. A work of courage but deeply disturbing, *The Moralist* can change lives, and so should come with a warning label: 'Flammable: Handle with Care.'" —Texas

"The sometimes light-hearted treatment of the serious subject matter belies the importance of the underlying fusion of recent real events combined with outrageously funny fiction." —Australia

"Witty and truly refreshing. Rod Downey needs to be congratulated on a fine, fine piece of art." —Pakistan

"I have never in my life been so transfixed into another man's mind as when I have been reading this 'novel.' I see myself and many of my friends in these pages. This book makes me rethink much of my life." —Florida

THE MORALIST

a novel by Rod Downey

Copyright © 2004 by Rod Downey

All rights are reserved. This book or parts thereof must not be reproduced in any form or medium without the prior written permission of the author.

This book is a work of fiction. Names, characters, places, and incidents either are products of the author's imagination or are used fictitiously. Any resemblance to actual events or locales or persons, living or dead, is entirely coincidental.

ISBN   1 887650-40-7

Online: www.themoralist.com
e-mail: themoralist@prodigy.net

FACTOR PRESS
Post Office Box 222
Salisbury, MD 21803

To D.B.

Dulcissime
Totam tibi subdo me!
　　　　　—*Carmina Burana*

Aesthetics is ethics with an ass.

"Now you see it, now you don't."

1

Our life was a dream within a dream in this floating world, where our only certainty was fortune, no certainty at all, and our only purpose to discover beauty. Red found it in a boy named Jonathan Frame.

On his fiftieth birthday (Halloween), Red's arrested adolescence collided with his mid-life crisis. He gave himself a special gift: Minoxidil. His father and brothers were bald by the time they were thirty. But despite the "little wigs," as Michael used to call them, that had collected in the shower drain for twenty years, Red had somehow miraculously kept his hair; it had always grown back, until lately. The bald spot on his crown—the Minoxidil box called it a "vertex" with a photo of a man's scalp with a little pink yarmulke—was beginning to show. With his hair still dark, barely a silver thread in sight, his youthful appearance led most to assume he was at least ten years younger than his age, sometimes more, but now he was threatened by baldness and determined to fight the losing battle of age with every weapon at hand.

He shared this obsession for a youthful appearance with his boss Faye, the former child movie star turned corporate communications consultant, just behind Red in age but still dressed in the Peter Pan collars and Alice in Wonderland white leggings of a little girl. Her skinny no-hips, no-tits figure completed the look of eternal pre-adolescence. Even the blonde hair pulled back in twin ponytails matched identically the obnoxious New York rich girl she'd played in a Hollywood movie when she was fourteen. Fading framed posters and stills from the film decorated the office.

Red and Fay traveled together to the boardrooms of America, where they taught "media skills," how to keep the CEO's foot out of his public mouth. They were "spin doctors."

He liked Faye but was uncomfortable sitting next to her on the plane. The relationship was artificial and strained, the balance unequal. The boss held all the cards, and except for their mutual love of youth and an understanding of showbiz, they had little else in common. She was a conservative Republican businesswoman, he an artist and social revolutionary.

Luckily, most of the time, they sat in silence. A compulsive workaholic, she tapped away furiously on her laptop, as Red sipped a cocktail and read Gide. Traveling was a great opportunity to catch up on his reading. Canon only—Gide, Genet, Mann, Joyce, Nietzsche, Wilde, James, Dos Passos, Cheever—no airport bookstore junk. There was too much good stuff out there. You could never read it all. Life was too short for junk.

The flight attendant told Faye to put away her electronic device, so they had no choice but conversation. She leaned his way and inquired pointedly, "What do you do, Richard, when you're not working? How do you spend your leisure time?"

He had been with her agency for almost two years. She took a personal interest in her professional staff, so he was accustomed to personal questions, was surprised she hadn't asked sooner. "I read," he replied indicating the novel in hand, "and I write plays and fiction."

"Really? Well, I guess I shouldn't be too surprised. You're our best writer," she flattered him. "Have you ever had anything published?"

"A few short stories here and there in literary magazines," he answered cautiously omitting the rest of the sentence: "that specialize in boy-love writing."

"I'd love to read some of your work."

"I should warn you, Faye, it's provocative. I may be very discreet in my business life, but in my art, I don't pull any punches."

"Now, I want to read it more than ever," she smiled knowingly, confident it was nothing she couldn't handle. She was mistaken about that.

Red dreaded this request and hoped it was insincere, as it usually was. He had a rule: They had to ask twice. Once could be understood as politesse and ignored. Twice required a response, and what would he give her? His stories were all tales of pederasty. That would curl her ponytails. He hoped she would forget to ask again.

"Do you ever do any volunteer work?" she asked.

"Not really," he confessed. "Between my day job and my writing, there isn't much time."

"You know, I encourage everyone in our office to do volunteer work. It's important to be involved in the community, and I'm very flexible if you need to take time off during the day," she stated company policy, as the plane touched down.

Point taken.

A globular orange sun descended to a silken lavender sea. Red and Malcolm admired the view from the cliffs on a breezy afternoon in early spring. The two men stopped and gazed quietly at the vast silent panorama, too high up to hear the crashing surf below, only the persistent Pacific coast wind rushing in their ears.

Malcolm was seven years Red's junior, tall, lean and intellectual even to the Ichabod Crane nose between cool dark blue eyes with long fluttering eyelashes, more like a boy than a forty-three-year-old university professor. Also like Ichabod, Malcolm was a Yankee. They'd met at Harbour University twenty years ago, when Red and Theo were living together and working for the university, and Red was writing his first unpublished novel, *Seeing Red*, the story of Theo, his playwriting coach, mentor, and madman lover.

The book outlasted the relationship. Theo's madness got the better of him. He couldn't keep a job, ran up the phone bill, and medicated his mania with alcohol. Red sought refuge with his grad student buddy, who fell in love with the young writer. They met at the Flaming Peacock, the kind of raging, blown-out queer bar that only the disco seventies could produce. A giant papier-mâché peacock hung over the dance floor with flames of light shooting from its tail. The walls were niched with archways hung with beads. Behind the beads, a little cave just big enough for two with a cushion, pillows, and cup-holders, a mini-boudoir serviced by bar boys in silver lamé bikinis. Malcolm was waiting like a spider for his fly. Theo introduced them! Red gladly parted the beads.

The night was long and drunk, and Red awoke the following morning, his thirtieth birthday, with Malcolm in his bed and Theo nowhere to be found.

"Happy birthday," the young man grinned from across the bed with a glint in his eye.

"Are you my birthday boy?" Red inquired in all sincerity, naively imagining that the young graduate student was Theo's gift, this Theo's bizarre habit of creating rivals for himself, what he called "pimping for his lover."

At first, Red took this unusual habit as a sign of sophistication but later learned it was more an expression of Theo's jealousy and the engine of his mad drama. Living with it, Red learned the meaning of intrigue.

Malcolm was the beginning of the end for Red and Theo, and Theo knew it, hastening the inevitable with drunken violent scenes that drove Red all the more frequently to Malcolm's spare Nipponesque apartment where they drank whiskey shots and fucked.

One afternoon, at Reverend Bailey's Wednesday wine-and-cheese, the renowned reverend, who'd walked arm-in-arm with Martin in the sixties, asked Theo "Where is Red?" Red the quiet, snowy gull who dipped above the wreck of his larger-than-life lover. Theo answered loudly, so all could hear, "Hes off getting fucked in the ass by Malcolm Branson's big dick!" which was absolutely true.

When the news of Theo's shocking declaration got around, Malcolm's stock went up. To be the subject of scandal at a Reverend Bailey wine-and-cheese was a badge of honor among the queens in Asian Studies.

Over the next twenty years, the two buddies (or was it biddies?), who never became lovers but always were, hooked up again. Malcolm, now head of Asian Studies at Stanford, guided Red along the Big Sur cliffs overlooking the Pacific sunset.

"I wish I could share the beauty of this place with him right now," Red reflected, as the absence of the beloved stung his heart.

"You mean your little writing student?" Malcolm inquired.

"Yes."

"He's all you've talked about."

"Have I been that obvious? I hope I'm not boring you."

"Not your relationships with these boys are fascinating to me."

"Not 'these boys,' *this* boy."

"Yes, it's always *this* boy with you, isn't it?"

"Always."

"Are you in love with him?"

"Yes, I am." Red replied without hesitation. "But it's a unique situation. For starters, he was only eleven when we met."

"So you've finally gone and done it. You've fallen in love with an eleven-year-old! You've always said as you grew older, they got younger."

Red had often said that, and it was true—Malcolm twenty-two, Barry nineteen, Michael sixteen, Mark fourteen, Jonathan eleven—except for Theo, who was *his* older lover and mentor.

"He's twelve now," Red corrected him. "His birthday was Christmas Eve."

The Moralist

"You're Halloween, he's Christmas! Death and birth!"

"I love your sense of irony!" Red smiled. Malcolm's perspective was a strong blend of tough intellect and wry insight, like the rich dark coffee he often drank, no cream no sugar. "There's something magic between us. He's my destiny."

"Or you his," Malcolm added. "You are keeping a journal, I hope."

"Of course. At first, I was just making notes on our lessons. This whole teaching thing was new to me, so I was feeling my way."

"I'm sure you were."

"I had no notions in that department. Faye said I should do some volunteer work, so I signed up for the 'Authors of Tomorrow.' It's a school mentoring program sponsored by the Press Club for young writers. You don't pick the kid; you pick the story. They hand you a file full of stories to choose from, and you read through them, until you find one you like. You don't meet your student till the first lesson. I wasn't looking for love. I was looking for someone to teach."

"Isn't that the same for you?"

"You know me too well!" Red laughed. "Teaching him about writing inspired me to write. My teaching notes became descriptions of our sessions, so I put them together into a short story. I just sent it off to one of my boy books."

"With a few additions, I imagine."

"That's how it's done: Take the real life story and bump it. Now, I'm thinking about a larger work."

"A sequel to *Seeing Red*?"

"Exactly. I call it *The Moralist*."

"A nod to Gide?"

"Similar themes: ethics, aesthetics, sex, a critique of conventional morality, and who knows what else before it's over? Disaster, terror, death?"

"Is it a comedy or a tragedy?"

"I don't know yet. The story is still unfolding. It's a portrait of Red Ryder's moral and aesthetic landscape in the context of his love for a boy."

"Sounds familiar. In *Seeing Red*, you were the boy. In *The Moralist*, you're the boy lover."

"It's an idea I've had for some time, but I needed a story to give it structure. I think I've found that story."

"You've found love. That's what inspires you."

The exotic fable was neatly printed in pencil on blue-ruled paper by a child's hand...

THE BOY WHO TURNED INTO A DOG
by Jonathan Frame

A hundred years ago when there were sorcerers in the countryside of China—they have all been driven off now—a poor and dirty boy named Chan lay on the mat of his dirt floor hut and thought to himself, "If I became a sorcerer, then I could make myself rich beyond my wildest dreams." But what did he know about being a sorcerer?

One day as he walked down the road from his house, Chan noticed a little white booth on the side of the road with a red sign with blue letters that read, "Magical Herbs for Free."

"What kind of magical herbs would anyone give away for free?" the boy scoffed, but still curious, he stopped and stared.

A hunchbacked little old man, with one hand on his back and in the other, a red wooden cane, called out from the booth, "Step up! Step up, young man! Would you like some magical herbs?"

"What a weak old man," Chan thought, "I will take the magic herbs if he doesn't give them to me for free like the sign says."

"What's magical about them?" Chan asked, thinking he was clever by pretending not to act too interested.

"You are wise to ask," the old man flattered him, and Chan swelled his chest with pride. "They will turn you into a sorcerer."

"I can become a sorcerer for free?" Chan wanted to play it cool but could hardly hold back his excitement.

"You can have the herbs for free," the quivering voice replied mysteriously. The old man took his hand away from his back and opened his palm to reveal the three golden pills of royal ginseng that seemed to glow with a light of their own. "Take them," he grinned a toothless grin.

Chan moved quickly to snatch them from the old man's hand, but the crooked old hand was faster still and clamped its bony fingers around the boy's wrist like a trap.

"It takes more than a magic pill to make a sorcerer," the old man said, his eyes glowing with the same pale golden color as the pills themselves.

"Your sign says they are free!" Chan cried. The fingers relaxed. Chan jerked away his hand and ran down the road as fast as he could, squeezing the golden ginseng pills tightly in his fist. "I'm too fast for the old geezer," he laughed to himself.

When he got home, Chan swallowed the pills immediately, but he didn't become a sorcerer. He turned into a dog instead.

"Oh, no! The old man has tricked me," he cried and ran out of the house. "I have to find that old man to change me back into a boy again."

But when he looked for the white booth with the red sign and blue letters, it was gone. Chan wanted to cry, but all he could do was howl, because now he would be a dog forever.

Moral: The easy way is not always the best way.

The End

Good use of language, dialogue, complex sentences, setups and payoffs, a fable of character, the moral sounded like a fortune cookie. Red picked up another story, a delicate, descriptive piece about her life in America by an Asian girl, he deduced from the name. What a perfect contrast! Asian feminine description in an American setting, Occidental masculine plot in an Asian setting. A hard choice, but not that hard. He chose the boy.

The Martin Luther King Learning Place was the shining star of the crumbling urban school system of Dallas, a rare resource for the underprivileged kids who went there. Red sat at a sturdy pine table in the bright pine-paneled library awash in the autumn light that poured through the tall windows over children's constructions of wickayups and whales. Across the table sat the big, sweet, red-faced art teacher Mr. Moony, in charge of the Authors of Tomorrow.

"I think you'll like working with Jonathan, Mr. Rover," Mr. Moony suggested as they waited. "He's a very talented boy."

Red entertained no romantic notions of what might transpire. He was fully prepared to greet some goofy-looking kid, certainly not a young god. His attention was more focused on the business at hand, that he who had never taught children before in his life was supposed to teach some strange little boy how to be a creative writer. He hadn't a clue how he was going to pull that off and was having second thoughts about the whole thing. He wouldn't even be there, if it weren't for Faye.

Not that Mr. Moony noticed. He was proud to have a volunteer like Red, a writer from the real world of journalists, authors, and poets, working with the kids in his program. When the boy appeared at the door, the teacher stood and motioned to Jonathan with excited impatience.

Instinctively, Red stood, too, shocked at the boyish beauty before him, a skinny, pale, freckled kid with reddish-blonde sprigs of hair splayed out from beneath a blue baseball cap. A raggedy green flannel shirt hung loosely over his gray tee, grunge style. Baggy jeans with frayed cuffs dragged the floor. Fresh from band practice, he still clutched his recorder flute like a little Pan.

Mr. Moony introduced them. "Jonathan Frame, this is Mr. Rover."

Red took the boy's soft hand, smiling and gazing deep into the wide-open blue eyes. "Hey, buddy!"

"I'm pleased to inform you that your story has been selected for the Authors of Tomorrow," Mr. Moony announced. The boy's pale skin flushed. "Mr. Rover is your mentor. He's a writer from the Press Club, and he will be working with you on your story."

The youngster squirmed and bowed his head, nervously repositioning the cap over the brilliant thatch of autumn-orange hair. His cherry lips glistened against ivory skin, as he bowed his head and shyly whispered, "I'm surprised it was even chosen."

Mr. Moony smiled benignly, "Well, you shouldn't be. At the end of the year, we will publish all he stories in a magazine. You'll be a published author, Jonathan!" Rising to go, he added, "There's a prize for Top Story, too. You might be the winner!" Jonathan squirmed and blushed again.

Red called for his attention, "Jonathan? Do you prefer to be called Jonathan? Not Jack or John or Johnny?"

"Yes, sir," the blue eyes peeked up like a double sunrise. "It's my dad's name."

Red fixed them fast with his own fierce golden gaze. "All right, Jonathan it is, and I prefer to be called Red, not sir. My full name is Richard Rover, but my friends call me Red. Red Rover,' get it? Like the children's game: 'Red Rover, Red Rover, oh, won't you cross over?' Red like the color: anger and passion. Rover like a dog: curious, faithful, and a wanderer. Ruff, ruff," he barked, and a bright snaggle-toothed grin spread over the boy's face. "You have a dog in your story, a boy who turns into a dog. What do you think it feels like to turn into a dog?"

"I don't know," he shrugged and started to say "sir," but caught himself.

"Okay, that's your first assignment for next week." Red pointed to the blue-ruled page in his ring binder, "I want you to write a description of just exactly how Chan turns into a dog," Red instructed. "Does he act like this?" Red fell from his chair to all fours panting and barking and sitting up to beg, flopping his hands like paws. Jonathan giggled along with all the other kids in the library at the strange man's crazy antics. Red casually resumed his seat, as if a whole roomful of children weren't at that moment snickering and whispering about him. "What does he do? How does it feel? What does he see? What noises does he make? Write as much as you need to describe the complete transformation, but I want at least a half page. Got it?"

"Yes. . . Red." Again he wanted to say "sir" to the crazy man who was larger than life. But when Mr. Moony, who was tall, stood next to him, he'd noticed that Mr. Rover—Red—was short. He only seemed large, because he came from the world outside of school, the grown-up world he knew nothing about. Red wore a suit and tie and smelled like lemons and flowers.

His long dark hair was combed back, but when he was on the floor begging like a dog, unruly strands fell over his face, giving him a wild look that contrasted with his crisp, clean clothes. It was shocking at first, but then it was funny.

"I see you're a musician," Red continued, nodding at the recorder.

"I'm just learning," he allowed.

"A man of many talents."

Jonathan beamed and added, "I play bass in my dad's band, too."

"Your dad has a band?"

"Yeah, it's called Tarzan's Boy. We do blues, rock'n'roll, r&b. My dad's mainly a blues man, but I like rock'n'roll."

"Do you do gigs?"

"Sometimes in Deep Ellum and Lower Greenville. I can only play at the coffee houses. They won't let me into the clubs."

"What does it smell like?"

"Huh?"

"When you play a gig with your dad's band, what does it smell like?"

He rolled his clear blue eyes and grinned, "Coffee and cigarettes."

Red laughed. "Write about that sometime—playin' with your dad's band. Be sure to include the smell of coffee and cigarettes."

After sunset, a cool wind kicked up. Malcolm and Red returned to their tree house, a cabin raised on stilts among the branches. The sign in the rustic style of an etched piece of bark along the plank steps leading up to the door announced its name, "Los Innocentes." They exchanged glances and chuckled at the irony.

A fire in the stone fireplace and wine on ice were waiting in a room of rough-hewn planks finished and polished like Hepplewhite, and wraparound windows that displayed a panorama of mountains and sea. In the center, an elevated king-size bed was built-in. The only thing "rustic" about this sylvan retreat was the absence of a television. In its place was a private sound system with channels programmed for every taste. They put on some smooth r&b in the golden light of the blazing fire and sky.

"What about sex?" Malcolm inquired.

"Is that an invitation?" Red smiled, thinking it was.

"I was referring to your little Jonathan," Malcolm smiled back with that same unmistakable gleam in his eye.

"Penny asked me the same question."

"How did you respond?"

"I said I'm content to love and teach him as he is, and what will be will be. Plato was right: A boy has no sense until he has a beard, and that doesn't necessarily mean on his face."

"How do you know he doesn't? He's at that age."

"No, he's still a little boy. His voice is girlish. When he answers the phone, I can't tell the difference between him and his older sister."

"You're calling him at home?"

"And sending him faxes at school. They're delivered to him in class."

"So it's more than just meetings in the library?"

"Very much more. That's the story."

"Don't tell me things I don't need to hear."

"The school encourages it as part of the mentoring relationship."

"I doubt if they encourage that."

"I wasn't referring to that."

"But already you're making love to him as more than simply your student."

"Like you said, love, sex, pedagogy—it's all the same. But don't worry, I don't kiss and tell."

"No, you kiss and write."

Interrupting the teacher, the Hispanic lady from the principal's office poked her head in the classroom door to ask for Jonathan Frame. Before the boy could raise his hand, the teacher pointed him out, and the messenger delivered the message as all the kids looked on.

FAX MESSAGE: Please, deliver immediately to Jonathan Frame.

Dear Jonathan:

Before our next meeting, I wanta set some ground rules for our work together. I'm here to help you refine what you've already written. It's called "collaboration." I'll give you ideas, and you give me your ideas back. We leave some in. We toss some out. If you think something I say sucks, then I want you to tell me, "Red, that sucks." You're the writer, so you make the final call. You're gonna win the prize for Top Story, and that's a promise. —Red

Jonathan couldn't help but laugh out loud at the way Red wrote like he was talking to him with "gonna" and "wanta," just like he'd really say it, and writing "That sucks!" for all the ladies in the principal's office to see as it came off the fax. Red was cool. "Does he really think I can win Top Story?" the boy wondered. He was almost afraid to think so. Red promised. "He wouldn't promise, if he didn't think I could do it."

Annoyed at the boy's laughter, the teacher requested that Jonathan put away his note until after class, but the damage was done. Outside the classroom, the kids gathered around him with curious questions. He shrugged them off. "It was a note from my mentor in Authors of Tomorrow," he explained, and they dispersed, envying that they were not the recipients of hand-delivered messages from the principal's office.

Jonathan's dream

He was Chan. He swallowed the golden ginseng pills and gazed at his hands growing a coat of fur. His fingers shrank into paws. His fingernails stretched into claws. His nose and ears fell off. He tried to pick them up, but he had only paws where his hands used to be. He fell to all fours to use his mouth instead, only to feel new floppy ears falling over his face. He tried to stand up but couldn't. "I don't want to be a dog!" he tried to cry, but the only sound that came out was a pitiful whine. He tried to call out for his mom, but it only sounded like, "Woof woof." "So this was what dogs meant when they barked," he thought, because now he truly was one.

He grew angry. "The old sorcerer tricked me!" he thought. "I thought I was the clever one, but now I'm a dog! I whimper and run around the house peeing all over the floor! I'm not a sorcerer, I'm a fool!"

His mom walked through the door. He was happy to see her and ran up to her, hoping she'd pick him up and hold him in her arms. But instead, she screamed and cursed and grabbed a broom and chased him out of the house.

Alone on the dirt road, no mom, no home, he crawled under a tree and whined for the longest time, until he felt a gentle palm stroking his forehead. "There, there, little dog," a kindly old voice said, "I'll take care of you." He looked up thankfully at first and then with shock at the sight of the old sorcerer!

He growled and snapped at the withered hand, but the old sorcerer was too quick and laughed. "Where have I heard that laugh before?" he thought. He looked again into the sorcerer's piercing eyes that glowed like golden ginseng pills.

Jonathan awoke, his heart pounding. The dream was vivid and told much more than his story. He stumbled around in the dark of the tiny day-room that was his bedroom in the ramshackle cottage that was his home. Finding the light switch and his backpack, he took out his notebook and pencil and wrote down the dream. When he reread it the following morning, he realized he had completed his assignment, a description of the transformation into a dog, just as Red had requested, but he left out one detail: When he looked into the golden eyes of the old sorcerer, he saw Red.

"This is excellent!" Red declared with delight. "Now you're thinking like a dog! I like the part where his mom chases him out of the house. It reminds me of another short story called *The Metamorphosis* by Franz Kafka. It's about a young man who turns into a big cockroach."

"Gross!" Jonathan wrinkled his nose.

"What do you think your family would do if you turned into a cockroach?" Red queried.

"I guess they'd try to take care of me," he offered innocently.

"Perhaps, but that's not what happens to Gregor Samsa. It's more like what you've got here, where Chan gets chased out of the house. Gregor Samsa gets squashed like the bug that he is."

"But his mom didn't know it was him," Jonathan defended.

"Right, and if you turn into a cockroach, they'll squash you. You oughta read it sometime." Red wrote down the title and author in Jonathan's notebook. "I'll give you a reading list. You don't have to read it all right away, just anytime you think you wanna read something, or maybe as a school assignment." Red continued to read the boy's writing. "Now, this is a new twist. Your sorcerer wants to be the boy's kind master. You can build on this."

"I had a dream about it," he explained.

"Even better. Dreams can tell you a lot." Jonathan nodded, remembering the omission all too well. "So maybe your story doesn't end with Chan turning into a dog. Maybe that's just the beginning. Your moral says 'The easy way is not always the best way.' What if Chan thinks he is taking the easy way to become a sorcerer, but it turns out to be the hard way? That's irony. What if turning him into a dog is the old sorcerer's first step in training the boy to become a sorcerer? Why does the old sorcerer come back? What does he want?"

"Maybe he is lonely and wants to have a pet."

"But if he just wants a pet, why not get a pet, instead of turning a boy into a dog?"

"I know!" Jonathan's eyes burned bright with excitement. "Because Chan is still a boy inside. He's smarter than a dog. The old man wants to train him to do tricks, so he can become rich and famous!"

"Good. I like that. That's irony, too. Do you know what irony is?" Jonathan smiled sweetly and shrugged his shoulders. "Irony is where the opposite happens from what we expect."

"Like Chan expected to become a sorcerer, but he became a dog."

"Or he wants to become rich and famous, and he gets his wish. But there's a catch: He does it as a performing dog. It's like the old saying 'Be careful what you wish for. You might get it.' Maybe, that's the real moral of your story."

"Yeah, we read a story like that in English class called *The Monkey's Paw*."

"I remember that story. The wishes turn out all wrong."

"Yeah, it's cool and scary, too."

"So that's your next assignment: Write the rest of the story. What happens when Chan and the old sorcerer get together? Maybe it's like you said: The old sorcerer teaches him amazing tricks, and they get rich performing all over China, even for the emperor in the Forbidden City. Maybe Chan starts to like being the most admired dog in all of China. He likes the fine food and getting pampered all the time and being the center of attention. But Chan isn't really happy. He still wants to be a boy again. How can he get the sorcerer to change him back? Does he steal from the sorcerer? Does he trick him? Does he save his life, and the old man grants him his wish? Here's something else I want you to think about: An antagonist. Write this down." Red tapped the paper with his finger, and Jonathan took up his pencil. "An appealing character struggling against great odds to achieve a worthwhile goal." The boy dutifully scratched out Red's words in his notebook. "That's the definition of a good story. So Chan gets himself into a pickle, and his goal is to become a boy again. The great odds against him are that only the sorcerer's magic can make it happen. But what if you tighten the screws another notch? Maybe someone tries to steal the magic dog. Maybe someone does steal him. So now Chan's plight is even worse. He's kidnapped, and there seems no hope of becoming a boy again. He has an antagonist, the thief who steals him. Antagonist—that's a-n-t-a-g-o-n-i-s-t. It means the person who opposes our hero."

"Yeah, the bad guy!" Jonathan squealed.

"Exactly! The bad guy. The villain!" Red twirled an imaginary moustache and cackled demonically. The kids in the library twittered.

"But who could that be?"

"That's up to you. You're the writer." Red glanced at his watch. Their hour was up. "Your assignment for next week is to give your story a bad guy."

He led Jonathan out the library doors into the hallway lined with children's Holiday art. He extended his hand to the boy, who took it limply with a shy smile and admiring blue eyes.

"Thanks, buddy. I can't wait to see what you come up with."

"Thank you, si. . . Red," he replied proudly.

In half a second, Red gazed deep into the flame-blue eyes. He studied the young creature with freckled face, round protruding ears, and the ever-present tattered flannel shirt. Did he always wear it because he was poor or because it was his favorite and he wouldn't give it up, until it literally fell apart? It was well on its way.

Red had learned that his dad was out of work as a carpenter with a family to support, and felt the hurt of the kid's harsh circumstances. Jonathan smiled and turned to walk happily down the hallway.

Red continued his gaze. The flannel shirt reminded him of WJ, his best buddy in the first grade, standing among a crowd of children waiting for their buses in the foyer of the school. Red observed WJ from afar, how easy he was with his happy smile and circle of eager friends of whom Red was only one. He envied WJ's comfortable carefree manner, compared to Red's shy reserve. He wanted to be him.

Red turned toward the glass doors of the Martin Luther King Learning Place and stepped into a sunny autumn day.

"So it was love at first sight?" Malcolm queried.

"More like second or third. I was certainly taken with him at our first meeting, but it wasn't until I discovered his mind that I knew I loved him."

"But you knew he was smart from his writing."

"Intelligence isn't the whole story. There's also his innocence, the eager gollygeewow of a boy."

"Take out a clean sheet of paper."

"Oh, no," Jonathan thought, "a test." Which it was. Opening his notebook, he barely asked, "Is this a test?"

"That's up to you. I want you to try an exercise that helps you tap the free flow of your imagination. It's called 'automatic writing.' But first I want to tell you something very important. I do not intend to contradict what you have been taught by your teachers or your parents or your minister at church. There are certainly times when saying certain words is not appropriate, but for a writer, when it comes to what goes from here to here," Red touched his finger from the boy's golden red forehead to his pale soft hand still holding the pencil, "there are no bad words. When you're writing words on paper for yourself as your own personal expression, you can write anything ya want, anything. Okay? Remember that: There are no bad words."

"You mean like cuss words?" Jonathan asked sweetly in all honesty.

"Cuss words." How quaint, Red thought, as in "curse words," cursing God for your misfortune, as in the advice to Job, "Curse God and die." Or like the more modern-day version, "Fuck!" Sex was our god, so why not curse sex?

15

"Yeah," Red smiled in reply, "including cuss words. First, pick a letter from the alphabet, any letter."

The boy thought a minute, then suggested, "My story is about a boy named Chan, so how about C?"

"Very good. Write down the letter C at the top of the page." Jonathan did so. Red took up his pen and marked the ruled sheet with two spidery asterisks, one at the top and the other halfway down the page. "Now, I want you to write down whatever comes into your mind. It doesn't have to be sentences or even have any meaning at all. It can just be a string of words or phrases or impressions or anything that pops into your head. That's what's important. Don't edit it. No scratching out. No going back. Don't even read back over what you've written. Just keep moving forward, writing down your thoughts, your feelings, your fantasies, anything your creative mind comes up with. If you get stuck, if you have to pause for any reason, write down any word that starts with the letter C and keep going. Do you understand?"

Jonathan nodded.

Red stood up. "Good, and I'm not going to sit here watching you. I'll go over there and read a magazine." Pointing to the asterisks, "Start here and end here. When you finish, put down your pencil. That will signal me to come back."

As the boy began writing, Red rose and walked away. Deliberately paying no attention to Jonathan's efforts, Red sauntered over to the periodical rack and picked up a copy of *Boys Life*. It was amazing that the magazine of his own boyhood still existed, now with articles about scuba diving and mountain climbing, but not so different, even including the color comic-book pages, a modern anachronism that he at Jonathan's age once loved. *Boys Life* was the magazine of the Boy Scouts. All the kids read it, along with *Mad* and *Cracked* with their prepubescent humor, until they gave way to *Follies*, the girlie book Red and his buddies smuggled into their tent during Boy Scout camp-outs and masturbated over until the pages were hopelessly stuck together.

There was even a copy of *Life* Magazine on the library rack with a full-color photo layout of "today's generation," kids with skateboards, CD players, and video games, paraphernalia the kids of forty years ago had never heard of, when *Life* Magazine did the same story on sock hops, rock'n'roll, and as always, precocious sexuality, only then it was making out and going steady. Now it was condoms and AIDS.

The cute crew-cut boy in the black-and-white photo was Red's same age, thirteen. Sitting back on a sofa, feet planted firmly, thighs open, he expressed an easy sexuality in tight denim jeans and open shirt with rolled short-sleeves to expose a sleekly muscled arm draped around his steady girl with a flip do.

Red walked alone along the summer sun-baked gravel road. He liked to walk. A bike would get you there, but walking gave you time to think on a hot lush afternoon in 1961, returning from his summer job cleaning up around his dad's houses in the Atlanta suburb where he was raised surrounded by bright yellow skeletons of pine. The postwar building boom raged on, and his dad was making his fortune as a residential developer.

As he walked, Red recalled the photo, just as he did now in the library. Had his introspective nature changed so much? Not really. Except for the uncontrollable erection that strained against his cotton briefs then, so that every step was a moment of pleasure, that boy was still alive.

His sensuous walk was spiked with the poignant longing of envy, not to be like the boy and possess the steady girl in the picture—she was merely his ornament—but to *be* him. Like WJ at the bus stop, he wanted to be the boy.

So potent was this envious desire that Red dressed in denim and open shirts with rolled sleeves. He practiced curls with his brother's barbells to muscle up his arms. His goal was to recreate himself as the photo in the magazine, this the Eucharist of his hero-worship.

He walked past the school and cut across a field bordered by trees that grew along a meandering creek. Overgrown berms of old hay or manure dotted the fields, so that between them and the tree line was seclusion and a ready easy chair of soft wild grass and warm earth, the perfect spot to be alone on a summer afternoon, to lie in the sun and be the boy again, reading a Superman comic or a *Black Stallion* novel, his favorite series about a boy and a horse; odd this interest in horses in literature but little in life, except when he and his teenage buddies used to play cowboy hard-riding the hacks through the wooded bridal trails of Peachtree Park, bringing them back wet, until his gang was banned from the stable. Now his own daughter had become a horsewoman, almost from birth. Surely there was some connection there.

He made his way through the deep dry grass toward this favorite spot, only to hear a stirring before him and see a boy and girl spring from the mound and run into the trees. Red ran after them to catch a glimpse of who they might be, but they vanished. He had the place to himself once more, but it was no longer his alone. The lovers were still present, they who knew his secret place, who violated it with that knowledge and at the same time, consecrated it with their eros. He imagined them to be the young stud and his girl in the magazine. Only now the boy with his eager hard-on was making love to his girl in their secret, private place in the meadow. Red opened his jeans and allowed his solid erection to stand free. He imagined they were still there hiding in the trees, watching him squeeze it tight in his hand, as if trying to hold back the inevitable mad eruption.

Red glanced over at his student diligently scribbling away, boy-blue eyes intensely focused on the paper, unself-conscious like a child singing in the backyard. Human concentration was the essence of innocence.

"What kind of love do you feel for him? Agape or romantic?" Malcolm continued his inquiry.

"I'm not sure I make that distinction."

"I was afraid you would say that."

"Nietzsche writes that a man's sexuality reaches to the highest peaks of his intellect. It reaches to the depths of his morality as well, because it asks the question, 'What is good and beautiful?' Jonathan is a manifestation of beauty to me. This feeling of joy compels me to celebrate his presence in my life."

"But if your unequivocal love for him is sexual, your involvement with him becomes an elaborate seduction. You are content to delight in his beauty now, because you are grooming him to be your lover."

"Why shouldn't I?"

"Which? Delight in his beauty? Or groom him to be your lover?"

"Both."

"So you're a hedonist. You make a virtue of pleasure."

"Sure beats necessity."

Malcolm smiled, "Okay, but does that express a moral perspective?"

"The pursuit of beauty? What's more moral than that?"

"Aesthetics and ethics are two different things."

"I'm not so sure. You say sex makes the difference. I say love makes the difference."

"It's easy for you to say that now when he's still a little boy, but he will start to show an interest in sex, and what will you do then?"

"He already has."

Jonathan put down his pencil and caught Red's eye to signal he was done.

His mentor returned to the table and studied the verbal progressions, a mirror to the boy's own mind. . .

* big great beautiful humongous small tiny funny fun movies bikes bunny hop jumpin' curbs jumpin' ramps guitar fret chord cuttin' heads blues rock country RNB Muddy Waters Grateful Dead Willie Nelson Eric Clapton will you know my name if I saw you in heaven cool hot hangin' bad happenin' tight fine girl boy man woman love need desire *

"What does this mean: 'bunny hop'?"

"It's a bike trick. You lift up the front and bounce on the back wheel. It's called a 'bunny hop.'"

"Do you do bunny hops on your bike?"

"Yeah, I got a stunt bike at home. I can do all kindsa tricks."

"Sounds dangerous. Ever get hurt?"

"One time I crashed on my knee. It swelled up, and then my whole leg started turning purple. The doctor had to drain it. It hurt like hell!"

"You should wear protective gear, doing tricks like that."

"I know." Admonished, the boy retreated.

Realizing he'd said the wrong thing, Red changed the subject, "What about this phrase: 'cuttin' heads'?"

"It's like when two guitars go head-to-head to see who can play the best riffs," the boy explained. "Did you see the movie *Crossroads*?" Red hadn't. "There's this kid, he's a music student, and him and this old blues man go to Mississippi to a place called 'The Crossroads' where ya go to cut heads with the devil. If you win, he'll make you rich and famous. If you lose, he takes your soul. So the kid has this big scene cuttin' heads with this baddass rock'n'roller. It's bad! You'd like it, Red." He spoke his mentor's name without thinking.

"I'm sure I would," Red smiled in awe of the boy's eclectic mind, and also without thinking, he blurted, "Do your teachers know how smart you are?"

The boy blushed and squirmed and turned in his toes, stepping one ragged shoe over the other. "Never call the epic 'epic,'" Theo once cautioned, "It shies away."

Red later discovered the answer to his question. Jonathan's teachers knew very well how smart he was. In addition to Authors of Tomorrow, he was in TAG, Talented And Gifted, and MindQuest, where the kids put on their own play. Red began to grasp the minor role he played on the larger stage of Jonathan's life, a disturbing notion to a lover who wanted so much more. He saw how far he had to go and how difficult was the task before him, to move beyond this framework of approved education to the unique and special bond between them.

"I see these last words seem to focus in on the subject of sex." Jonathan turned bright crimson. "Are you interested in sex?"

"Sometimes," he squeaked out.

Red avoided further exploration. "Good, it's one of the two writer's great topics: love, which includes sex, and death. You wanta be famous? Keep a journal about everything you think on the subject of love and sex from now to about age twenty. That would be an instant best-seller. If you're too embarrassed or don't want to get caught with it, just write it all in third person and change the names. Turn it into fiction. Then no one will know for sure who you're really talkin' about, or even if you're telling the truth, which means you can make it as real as you want. 'Now you see it, now you don't.'"

"Huh?"

"It's what magicians say."

"Oh, yeah. I do magic, too!"

"You're quite the Renaissance man. You'll have to show me your tricks sometime."

After their session, Red stopped at Blockbuster and rented the video *Crossroads*. He mixed a vodka and tonic and settled into the ancient myth of the Old South about the demon and the blues man at The Crossroads, modernized with heavy metal punk. Red imagined Jonathan as the young rock-'n'roller. Did that make him the demon? Or was he the boy at The Crossroads taking on the demon society in the name of love? He smiled to himself at these multiple meanings he brought to the film, his eyes lit by the white warm light of the TV screen, basking in the boy's own nimbus.

2

Los Innocentes drank wine and fucked to the light of the crackling fire and the sound of whistling wind that rocked their tree house like a ship at sea. With the force of the night, Malcolm drove deep into Red, who came and came and came again.

"What do you like about fucking a man?" Red inquired during intermission, sipping wine with his friend and passionate lover, as the tree house creaked and swayed, and glowing coals cast dark red shadows about the room.

"I like masculinity. It turns me on."

"What about fucking? Fucking a man like a woman?"

"It isn't fucking a man like a woman. You certainly are not. It's fucking a man who loves to get fucked, and I love that. You understand. You fuck boys. How is that different?"

"Yes, I do love the masculinity of a boy, but it's different from that of a man. It's eager and playful and energetic and sometimes dominating and demanding, but at the same time tender and madly passionate. A boy wants to have fun, a boy wants to be loved, a boy wants to be a man, and he doesn't give a damn, not like he will, not like we all must eventually. Adolescence is a rare period when the boy is full of himself and takes his pleasure where he pleases. That's the difference."

"A boy would never know how to do what you did tonight."

"That's the other difference. That takes practice," he winked with his Cheshire cat grin.

"You are the most erotic fuck I've ever had. I've never seen anything like it. You're not even hard and you start cumming from the minute I'm inside you. I can see it in your face before it happens. Your eyes roll back, and you're overcome with pleasure, and then you cum again and again and again, without even touching yourself. The cum just flows out of you. It's amazing! It's not normal. Medical science should know about you."

"Only with you, Malcolm. Don't forget that. You're the only one I trust like that."

Aroused, "You make me want to fuck you again."

"You make me feel loved. Plus you've got a nice big dick. What a combo!"

"I've always loved you, ever since we met at Harbour twenty years ago. You know that."

"Yes, I do."

"So, now it's your turn. Tell me what it feels like for you to have that experience."

"The pleasure of feeling your ramrod moving across my prostate is like waves of pleasure. I imagine it's very similar to a female orgasm, as close as a male can get anyway. It's like cumming all the time."

"You *do* cum all the time. That's what's so incredible! I've never seen a man do that."

"I want more. That's what it feels like. Every time it happens, instead of being satisfied, I want more. That's why I think it's more female than male. Not acting out, but the sexual experience itself. The male wants the ecstatic release, and that's it. Mission accomplished. The female releases over and over again always wanting more to make sure she gets it. I am Tiresias. I understand why she-he declared that the female enjoyed more pleasure—because it goes on forever. Only one problem: No matter how many times she cums, orgasm by itself can never be fully satisfying for the female. The common complaint of women in sex is that her mate shoots his wad, rolls over, and goes to sleep, while she is left hungry for more. It's the answer to Freud's famous question 'What does a woman want?' She wants more. It's the logic of nature. The final female satisfaction isn't orgasm; it's motherhood. That's where men get it wrong. They believe a woman can only be satisfied by a dick. Not so. The dick is only the means to the ultimate end, pregnancy. When my pussy is hot like a woman, it can't be satisfied. There can never be a pregnancy. That's why no matter how many times I cum, I still have to jack off at the end. The male takes over to get off in the masculine way, so then I can be satisfied like a man. Then, I know I'm done."

"You must have had to overcome a lot of socialization to discover this."

"It took me twenty years."

"That's another difference between a man and a boy. A boy would never talk like that."

"No, he wouldn't talk about sex at all. He'd talk about his hopes and dreams and passions. Boys are natural poets. They speak poetry in their normal conversation, and I love them for that."

E-mail from the Boy-love Network (BLN)

Dear BLN:

I found this definition of "intergenerational intimacy" that I would like to share with you all. Perhaps, you can use it in your discussions with gay groups and the media...

"'Intergenerational intimacy' includes all non-coercive, two-way interactions in which a physically mature adult and a pre-adult in mid-adolescence or younger share interests, communicate with and trust each other, share responsibility for and power in the relationship, spend time together, and feel mutually fond of one another. Sexual contact is not assumed in this definition of intimacy, and if present, is regarded as adjunct rather than essential. By the same token, intergenerational sexual contact alone does not constitute an intimate relationship—though a sex-only relationship is not automatically assumed to be abuse."—*The Study of Intergenerational Intimacy in North America: Beyond Politics and Pedophilia*, Gerald P. Jones, Ph.D.

—Hawk, Boston

BLN editor adds:

Thank you, Hawk, for the helpful research. Your comments are always welcome. For those of you on the network who are not familiar with Hawk, he edits a literary magazine called *PAN* that includes essays and short stories about boy love.

Dear Hawk:

Where can I get a copy of *PAN*? I live in Texas where a lot of stuff is not available.

I am a writer whose short stories have appeared in *The Ganymede Reader*, which as you are probably aware, went out of publication when its publisher Ben Sheridan died. I'm currently working on a short story about a middle-aged mentor and his twelve-year-old writing student. I should have something to show you after the first of the year. —R², Dallas.

Red and Penny sipped wine by the rooftop pool of her high-rise overlooking the glittering Dallas skyline and arteries of the city flowing with light. The night was balmy in November. She posed before the panorama holding her gold-leaf stemware looking like a queen in her black St. John's knit jacket with gold shawl collar and cuffs, gold-threaded Escada skirt, bright blonde hair, and boobs galore. She was pushing forty but like Red looked younger, barely over thirty. They had been at first professional pals in the PR world of Dallas, but after ten years and even a few flirts, fast friends. He liked her bright, ballsy style that stood out among the shallow chaff of the Dallas social scene that surrounded her. She moved in the toniest inner circle, a poor little rich girl without a penny of her own, so she traded on her social standing, doing society PR to make a buck.

The provincial city of the plain was renowned for its flashy style and conspicuous consumption with little depth of intelligence or taste. Considering her socialite background, Penny was a rare exception. She'd majored in music at Trinity. In her twenties, she'd managed a rock band in Mexico City.

She described an excursion she was planning to escort the richest broads in Dallas on a tour of Paris, but the real purpose of the trip was to get hitched. Penny received a proposal a week from some rich, boring oil man or baron of business, all of whom were dying for a little sparkle in their vapid lives, not to mention the boobs. Boobs were big in Texas. But unlike her meretricious Russian Tea Room cronies, whose lives revolved around spending their husbands' money, who would have jumped at any of these offers and in fact had, Penny rejected them right and left. But now, as middle age approached and the old bio-clock was ticking, she was willing to give a more considered ear. An old beau had called to invite her for a visit. He owned a vineyard in the Bordeaux region. She was certain he intended to propose, and she intended to accept.

"Alan is good-looking, around 45, still has his hair, a little gray in the temples, and rich like I told you." Penny sipped her martini. "He's been after me for eight years. I told him no once, because I was seeing Eduoard at the time, but now that he's out of the picture. . ."

"Is he?"

"Oh, honey, he is definitely out of the picture!"

"You still see a lot of him."

"Because he is like my . . . *little* brother. I was hoping he would be my *big* brother, but I found out different. He's ten years older than I am, but he's a little boy. I think he's coming out of the closet! I do! Anyway, so *Alan* has been knocking on my door again, and I thought, 'Why not be the lady of Chateau Arles?' Cézanne painted it. I love wine, and I like Alan well enough. He's romantic and clever and good at his business. We were hot and heavy there for a while."

"I'd marry him just for the wine."

"He's way too old for you. You'd rather marry a boy!"

"The concept of marriage doesn't apply to man-boy relationships."

"But you say you're in love with him. Doesn't that mean you want to spend your life with him?"

"Do you love your onanist?"

"That's oenologist, and no, but I think he loves me." She finished her martini, thoughtfully gazing at the skyline. "I'm almost forty, Red. I might have been more picky ten years ago, but at forty, things change."

"Lady of Arles? You could do worse."

"You didn't answer my question."

"The answer is yes, I want to spend my life with him, but not like a marriage. I want to be his life-long friend, fan, and champion. If you call that a marriage, then so be it."

"It's strange," she reflected. "It's like you want to be both father and lover to him. It's almost like he's a god to you."

"I don't worship, but I do adore him. O come let us adore the son of the carpenter! He's a Christmas baby, you know, well, Christmas Eve. He'll be twelve."

"That is so young!" The booze and breeze were heady, and Penny was getting a little loose. "Please, be careful, Red," she slurred. "You had that other bad experience with—what was his name?"

"Mark."

"Yes, the one who was blackmailing you."

"I was trying to help him get on his feet."

"He was stealing from you and taking advantage of you, because he knew he could get away with it."

"He never threatened me."

"He didn't have to. You were helpless, and he knew it."

"Well, he's all grown up now, so I guess it's over."

"Don't be so sure. Are you still in touch with him?"

"Sometimes. He's a trucker. He drives an 18-wheeler all over the country. He calls me from North Carolina, Florida, Las Vegas, L.A. I wish him well. I loved him, and I'm sorry he self-destructed like he did. That's the trouble with loving boys—'Just when you think you know what you have got, it's what they're not,'" he quoted a lyric from *The Fantastiks*.

"I hope you learned from that. I don't want you to ruin yourself chasing after some little teenager."

"I would be ruining myself not to. It's harder to justify the abstention than the pursuit. Abstention is cowardice, and everyone knows it."

"But what is the goal of your pursuit?"

"His attention, his presence."

"His sex?"

"Under the right circumstances. What if he came on to me? Could I refuse him? Absolutely not. I'd love every minute of it."

"An eleven-year-old boy?"

"Almost twelve. They are very sexual at that age. I know I was. Besides, I could never reject him, if that's what he wanted."

"You scare me sometimes, Richard."

He wrapped his arms around her. Like most women, she just wanted a man to hold her close. "You're sweet to be concerned. I appreciate that. But this is all speculation. I'm happy like it is."

"I love you, Richard," she cried on his shoulder, "If you didn't love boys, I wouldn't be going to France."

"Here's another tip for good story-telling: setups and payoffs. All story-telling is setups and payoffs. You do this instinctively. It's already in your story. Chan wants to become a sorcerer. That's the setup. So he takes some magic pills to become a sorcerer, but he becomes a dog instead. That's the payoff. If you're telling a joke, the payoff is called the punch line. A man walks into a bar with a pig under his arm and says, 'Bartender, two martinis, one for me and one for my girlfriend.' That's the setup. The bartender says, 'I'm sorry, we don't serve pigs in this bar.' The plot thickens. That's called development. The man says, 'Are you calling my girlfriend a pig?' There's the wind-up, here's the pitch. The bartender says, 'I was talking to your girl-friend.'"

Jonathan didn't get it.

"Okay, it's not the greatest joke in the world, but you get the idea. Jokes are simple stories. They have a setup and a payoff called a punch line. Everything in your story should pay off in one way or another. There is an exception to that rule called a red herring, but I'll save that for another time."

The boy smiled again through orange bangs in girlish amazement. Red's ideas bombarded your mind like a hailstorm. You had to listen close all the time.

"Here's another version of setups and payoffs: action-reaction," Red continued. "When something happens, when a character does something, ask yourself, 'how do the other characters react?' You see it in the movies all the time. Somebody says something, and then you get all these shots of the faces of the people who heard it, so you can see their reactions. In cinematography, it's called a reaction shot. In theater, it's a take. In comedy, it's a double take. Do you know what a double take is?" Jonathan shrugged his shoulders. "I'll show you. Make a funny face." Jonathan did so, dramatically passing his palm across his face like a curtain to reveal a grotesque, wide-eyed gargoyle with tongue extended. "Okay, that's good. Hold that expression and watch me react to it." Red described his reaction as he performed it, "I look once. Yeah, okay, there's Jonathan. I turn away. But wait a minute, that wasn't Jonathan. So I jerk my head back in shock and surprise. That's a double-take." Jonathan couldn't help but giggle. Red played to the boy's laughter, mugging in amazement. "Gnong! Gnong! Gnong!" he exclaimed. Jonathan giggled again until his face was red. "That's how Burt Lahr used to do it. He was one of America's great comics. He played the Cowardly Lion in *The Wizard of Oz*. A good double take always gets a laugh. Actors and writers have been mimicking human behavior since the beginning of time. They've gotten so good at it, they even have names for it: setups and payoffs, punch lines, reaction shots, double takes. So when you're writing your story, think about setups and payoffs. If you set something up, ya gotta pay it off. Think not just action, but reaction."

3

Returning to the university the following night, Red and Malcolm attended an outdoor performance of one-act plays. The two men sat on folding chairs on the marble terrace of the Rodan Sculpture Garden, where the Stanford Players performed a selection of Chekov one-acts on a clear, cool California night among marble angels, athletes, and lovers. They seemed to observe the clever human performances like titans in the cool blue light of the blue moon contrasted with the hot amber light of the stage, the white Hale-Bopp comet blazing across a deep dark starry sky.

Malcolm lusted after the young lead. Red's mind wandered. He reflected on the current news story about the suicidal cult in the San Fernando Valley whose bodies had just been discovered. You'd think somebody would've raised a few questions: "Now wait a minute, let me get this straight. Ya took all my money, ya cut off my balls, and now ya want me to kill myself, so I can join the ET's hiding behind a comet. Are you working for the tabloids or what?"

The comet was herald for the new millennium, harbinger of calamity and death.

After the plays, Malcolm and Red stopped at a local pub for a late night snack. Malcolm had caught up with the young actor after the show, who had promised to meet them there. While they waited over crab cakes and a bottle of Napa Chardonnay, Red revealed The Philosopher's Stone.

The Philosophers' Stone

Answer the seven philosophers' questions and WIN THE TRUTH!

Yes or no, with no more than five sentences of explication or a short quote (please cite source):

1. Do you exist?
2. What do you know?

The Moralist

3. Are you God?
4. Is there a cause?
5. Do you have to be present for things to happen?
6. Do you have a choice?
7. Are good and evil real forces in the universe?

Malcolm laughed, "I love it! Ontology, epistemology, theology, teleology, phenomenology, existentialism, and ethics, all in seven simple questions! I assume you have the answers."

"Of course: Yes—I know that I exist—yes—no—yes—no but yes—and yes."

"'No but yes?' What kind of answer is that?"

"It's not simple, but I'll try to keep it short."

"Five sentences. That's the rule."

"On a day-to-day basis, we have the illusion of choice, just as we have the illusion of cause. Like Schopenheur says, the only real choice is to be, but that choice is not made by the ego in time and space. It is a choice only the true self, our cosmic eternal consciousness, makes at every moment of our existence. Three sentences. How's that?"

"Not bad, but you have to introduce this theoretical 'true self,' this 'cosmic eternal consciousness,' to make it work."

"Do you know you exist?"

"So it all comes back to ontology!"

"If you know you exist, or if you only allow that you know something exists, even if you can't say what it is, that is your true self, not your idea of who you are, but your sense of being itself. That is the ultimate *a priori*. Even if you answer 'no, nothing exists,' you're still confronted with the *idea* that something exists, even if that idea exists on its own with no source. The phenomenologists say, 'God is an idea thinking itself.' No matter how rigorous your systematic doubt, the buck stops at the question of existence. The only *a priori* donnée of all philosophy is 'I am,' or at least 'It is,' which is really the same thing."

"The words of Jehovah: 'I am that I am.'"

"Or Popeye." Singing, "I yam what I yam and that's all what I yam. . ." Malcolm joined in, "I'm Popeye the Sailor Man." Laughing, they touched their glasses in toast.

"So what do you call this? Your Popeye philosophy?"

"I call it a pleasant evening over wine and crab cakes."

"I'm not going to let you off that easily. What about the moral question? You say choice is subject to doubt." Malcolm was a hard-core existentialist. "But you also say good and evil are not, that they are real forces in the universe. How can you have good and evil without choice?"

"Ethics. That one takes a little longer."

"Okay, at least until my actor shows up."

"If he shows up."

"He said he had to stop by the drug store."

"To pick up some condoms and lube?"

"I hope. So?"

"As I said, choice is the province of being itself, not our ego as we commonly imagine. The illusion of ego-choice may be a useful working construct, but finally, all that truthfully can be said about our experience of life is that it's a story we're telling ourselves. It's irrelevant that the story is already written. The ethical question is, 'Why this story?'"

"Does there have to be an answer to that? Does that question even have to be asked?"

"Yes, it should be asked, even if we recognize that a comprehensive answer is beyond our grasp. If we could answer it, we would understand the entire design of our life."

"But we can't, because we don't know how it's going to end. Just like your book."

"Just like your actor."

"He'll be here."

"You're confident, but you don't know. We are so complacent in our present being that we must constantly be reminded what we don't know. We don't know what the future will bring, and we don't know if an action is good or not."

"So to recap, not only do we lack the capacity to choose, we have no way of knowing if the choices we think we are making are right. That seems to put ethics on pretty shaky ground."

"Only from the perspective of ego and moral principle. Blinded by the illusion of choice, ego wants to know, 'How should I act?' Ego wants 'to do the right thing,' as you often hear people say. I guess that's preferable to wanting to do the wrong thing, but it's no less deluded by our myths, the shadows of truth, which is why it's so often in error. On the other hand, if the issue of morality is viewed not from the perspective of individual ego but from the perspective of being, the moral question shifts from 'How should I act?' to 'How should my consciousness be?'"

"I'm not sure I see the difference. You seem to be drawing some distinction between acting and being."

"Yes, in the sense of being one's own story, as opposed to individual acts and choices, which are a Gordian knot of self-delusion. If I look at my existence as a story I am telling myself, the illusion of choice becomes part of the larger moral tale, where every choice is a moral choice. The only principle is to pay attention. Morality is an impulse that derives from being itself, a primitive, profound joy that is instantly understood with words like 'truth,' 'beauty,' and 'love.' The self seeks this feeling instinctively like an infant seeks its mother's breast to grow larger and stronger, and we need neither free choice nor moral principle to understand this. Morality is an appetite."

"You are a poet, Red, no doubt, but that and two bucks will get you a cappuccino. What good does it do you besides interesting conversation over wine and crab cakes?"

"That counts! It sure beats talking about the weather or the ball game!" Red grinned. He preferred critics to followers, and he loved Malcolm's Yankee practicality. "It changes everything," he continued. "Take our pleasant evening, for example. Imagine that this moment is nothing like you think it is. Erase the fog of ideas that you are a professor of Asian Studies, that I am your friend from Dallas, that we are in Palo Alto in a little cafe at the edge of the Stanford campus, that I am on vacation and have come to visit you, even that we met a continent away and have been friends and lovers for twenty years. Forget all that. Erase all that you remember about who you are and who I am! Imagine instead that you have manufactured this moment by the force of your creative mind for the sole purpose of having this very conversation, for me to communicate what I am saying to you now. This is your dream, and I have come here to give you this message." Red's eyes grew wide and staring, absorbing his friend and the cozy room, the clink of silverware and glasses, points of candlelight, and table talk. The vision flattened out onto a single dimly lit canvas like an unrestored Rembrandt. Malcolm's glowing face floated like the smile of Alice's Cheshire Cat. The vision was taking place as he described it. "In an instant, everything changes. The veil is pulled back, and we glimpse the truth that love and beauty, terror and horror, pleasure and pain are more than interior experiences. They are inextricably connected to the 'out there,' united with good and evil. It's not a way of acting or being. It's a vision of unity whose truth is immediate, compelling, and personal. That vision is the natural engine of ethics."

Amused and incredulous, Malcolm exclaimed, "That is the most solipsistic definition of ethics I have ever heard!"

"Another word for solipsism is mysticism, and the morality of the mystic ain't nothin' like the morality they preach in church. It takes guts to take the moral path. 'Strait is the gate,' like Jesus said, and it's not always 'doing the right thing' like everybody thinks. That's the easy way out. The real strait-and-narrow is following the moral impulse itself, wherever it might lead. That impulse is larger than moral principle and far more dangerous. The principled will condemn you for it, because it challenges not their truth but their authority. It's Jesus overturning the tables of the moneylenders. It's Jesus on the cross. Authority is the dirty little secret of moral principle. Authority is ego working in the world, and moral principle is its myth. Once you unmask this delusion, you see beyond the floating world and confront the nothingness of self face to face."

"So you're a mystic." Malcolm concluded.

"I have been for a very long time. I thought you knew that. All the world's a stage. The trinity of consciousness is producer, audience, and actor in the dream of life. As producer, our consciousness makes it all happen. As audience, we are as if among the dead, observing from outside of life, like Emily in *Our Town*. As actor, we are on stage making choices, but like the character the actor plays, we can't see that the course of the story has already been laid down. That's why Greek tragedy is the perfect emblem of both theater and life. Try as he may, the tragic hero cannot escape the fate of his circumstance, just as the actor cannot escape the stage, just as we cannot escape the story we have chosen to tell ourselves. The moral experience and the personal story are the same thing. To communicate the moral vision is to tell the story."

"Is that why your writing is always autobiographical?"

"Yes, autobiograph*ical*, autobiography with a mask."

"So why the mask? Why not just tell the real story?"

"Because, like you said, I don't know how it's going to end, and if I want to recreate my story as the dream that it is, it must appear as preordained, the tragic truth. The reader is the true self, the observer."

"So if the reader is your true self, what does that make the writer? God or actor or both?"

The handsome student entered the cafe and scanned the room in search of companions.

"Why, God, of course," Red replied, nodding toward the door. "There's your actor."

Malcolm turned to catch the young man's eye and waved to him. "Escaped from the stage," he added, as the young man walked over.

"But is he still an actor without his stage?"

"We shall see."

The bright young man had no notion why the old queens were cackling. "Please, excuse us," the professor allowed. "We were having a philosophical conversation."

Some private joke with his friend, the young actor imagined.

The man and boy sat side by side at the table in the pale gray light from the tall windows. It was late November, and the sky was painted with watercolor clouds. Red wore his suede jacket for the first time that season, Jonathan still in his ragged flannel shirt. The boy admired his mentor's sporting look. The jacket was long and loose, draped back from the neck around his shoulders almost falling off gangsta-style but more like a leather blazer with Red's dress shirt and tie, a contrast in textures, the soft nappy suede, the shiny silk tie.

Jonathan observed all of this, as he watched the man pouring over his latest installment of the story.

THE BOY WHO TURNED INTO A DOG
By Jonathan Frame

Part II

The old sorcerer fed Chan a bone. It was surprisingly delicious. He was terribly hungry, and it felt good to sink his teeth into the hard surface until it cracked.

"You will grow to like being a dog," the old man said knowingly. "I will make you rich and famous."

Rich and famous. Chan moaned at the thought that this was what he'd wanted from the start, but not as a dog!

The old sorcerer taught him how to do arithmetic and play the piano, things he hadn't been able to do even as a boy. Once he'd learned his lessons, the old man took him around from village to village to show off his talents—not just the kind of tricks dogs do, but amazing things, like answering questions from the audience by barking once for yes and twice for no. The townspeople marveled that he seemed almost human, which of course he was, only trapped in a dog's body. He understood everything they said.

Word of the remarkable animal traveled before them, so that soon the streets of each new village were lined with people eager to see their performance, even before they arrived. At last, they were invited to perform for the emperor in the palace of the Forbidden City, and the emperor was so delighted with what he saw that he declared the old sorcerer and his magical dog to be the permanent entertainers at the imperial court. Only the emperor and his nobles and their ladies would have the wondrous privilege to see this magical beast.

They had achieved all that the sorcerer promised. But Chan still hoped that the chance might come to take some more ginseng pills and return himself to his normal state, until the day that very chance came and he gobbled up an entire bottle of the golden tablets. The only thing that happened was that he got sick and vomited for three days.

The old man shook his head and said it was no use for Chan to dream of ever becoming a boy again, because even he did not have the power to change him back. Whether that was true or not, Chan accepted his fate and performed his tricks faithfully. Even if he was a dog, he was now a member of the imperial court and lived a life of perfect luxury.

But not everyone was happy with this new addition to the palace. The Royal Wizard did not welcome the prospect of sharing his position with this old charlatan and his mongrel. If the dog were as smart as he'd heard, then anyone could command him. So he plotted to murder the old sorcerer with a basket of poison figs and keep the dog for himself.

He stole into the old sorcerer's chamber, where Chan himself slept on a bed of silk pillows. But the foolish Wizard failed to heed his own reasoning,

The Moralist

for he still regarded the dog as a dumb animal and emptied the vial of poison over the figs in full view of Chan's watchful eye.

After the Wizard left the room, Chan struggled to knock the basket from the table before his master returned. He cleverly caught the inlaid ivory table's tapestry cover by a tassel with his teeth and dragged the basket ever closer to the edge until it toppled just as the old man entered to see his pet's latest trick.

The old voice shrieked, "You naughty Chan! Is this how you behave in the palace? You think you can eat figs now!"

Grumbling, the old man stooped slowly to gather up the fruit, but Chan was faster. He quickly lifted his leg and soaked them all in a yellow puddle.

The old man threw up his hands, "You spoiled dog! Do you think you can do anything you please?"

Chan barked twice and twice again. The old sorcerer recognized the sound of these barks from their act. "No . . . and no. Because you are not a dog. You are a boy in a dog's body," the wise old mind began to think, "and you saw something you weren't supposed to understand, but you did. Was there something bad about those figs?" Chan barked once, and with a series of yes-or-no questions, the old sorcerer quickly discovered the danger they were in. "We must leave the Forbidden City," he concluded.

Once a member of the court, no one left the Forbidden City, but Chan had a plan.

To Be Continued...

"I like what you're doing here," Red observed as he read the neatly hand-printed pages. "It has urgency. Do you know what it means when something is urgent?"

"Like you have to do it right now?" Jonathan suggested more boldly than in the past.

"Exactly right. The old sorcerer and Chan know the Royal Wizard won't give up, so they have to escape the Forbidden City. That's urgent. A good story has urgency and lots of it. Movies are a good example. Movies pile urgency on top of urgency. Have you seen the movie *Titanic*?" The boy shook his head. No, they didn't get to the movies very often, Red thought; he'd take the boy, if his parents would allow it. "The *Titanic* is a ship."

"Yeah, it hits an iceberg."

"Okay, now tell me, without even seeing the movie, what do you think makes the story of the *Titanic* urgent?"

"The ship is sinking!" he exclaimed dramatically, as if he were a passenger crying out in terror.

Red laughed at his histrionics, "That's right, but in the movie, they make it even more urgent than that. The story is about a young artist who falls in love with a rich girl, and her boyfriend doesn't like it."

"The antagonist," Jonathan interjected.

"Yes, exactly! He handcuffs our hero to a pipe as the water is rising. The girl sets him free, but then the boyfriend's henchman starts chasing him with a gun, as the water is rising. Now *that's* urgency, urgency on top of urgency! So what can you do to make your story even more urgent, so that things have to happen and decisions have to be made *right now*?"

"The Wizard finds out. He calls out the guards!"

"A chase! Yes! There's nothing like a chase to add urgency. Now everybody is after them. Movie studios used to have writers who did nothing else but write chase scenes? Why? Because once the chase is on, your characters can go anywhere and do anything. Chan and the sorcerer try to run away through the palace—into a banquet, into the kitchen, into a dungeon, over a wall, into the marketplace. They can hide in the harem with veils over their faces pretending to be harem girls," Red pulled the collar of his jacket up over his mouth and fluttered his eyes.

Jonathan giggled, "But Chan is still a dog!"

"That makes it even funnier! Then, they get to the top of the wall of the city. The guards are after them. What do they do?"

"What?" Enthralled, the boy wanted to hear the end.

Red shrugged his shoulders, "I dunno. It's your story. That's your next assignment. Write the chase."

4

The following morning, the professor and his guest headed for the hills again, an early nature walk conducted by a Stanford botanist in charge of the protected wilderness bequeathed to the university by the robber baron who founded the place. The lady botanist gave names and histories to the early spring wildflowers and animal feces in varying stages of decay in the arid northern California climate. Overlooking the sea, ancient oaks hung with Spanish moss wafting in the wind crowned the hilltop.

After the tour, the academics gathered for lunch under the courtyard arbor of a hillside restaurant. One of Malcolm's more outspoken colleagues Sheila, an anthropologist, was going on about the role of profanity in culture, her field of study. Red was fascinated by the way she peppered her argument with real examples like "fuck" and "shit" and "asshole" and "pussy," words that flowed from her lips with the most clinical precision over their garden salad with chicken strips and wine. It was all Red could do to keep from laughing out loud.

He wanted to tell her about his automatic writing conversation with Jonathan: "From here to here, there are no bad words." "Ya mean cuss words?"

"I've been teaching fiction writing to a twelve-year-old boy," Red began, but, glancing at his watch, Malcolm interrupted and hurriedly announced their need to go, obviously terrified of where this conversation between the pederast and the profanity professor might lead.

As the Miata curved through the hills back to campus, Red expressed his pique: "I know what you were doing back there. You should have more faith in me. I wasn't going to embarrass you."

"We did have to go. We have a date in town tonight."

"Well, they better be damn good company to pass up that opportunity. That was an interesting conversation."

"That's what I was afraid of."
"Ah-hah! I was right!"
"I know Vampyra all too well."
"Vampyra?"
"Pour a few glasses of wine in her, and there's no telling what she'll say."

Red conjured the image of Ed Wood's famous ghoul in her long black hair, ragged black gown, and Ripley-style fangs and fingernails. He laughed out loud, "Vampyra! That's funny! That's too fucking funny! But I beg your pardon, Vampyra isn't stupid, and she doesn't say stupid things. Sheila would have been fascinated by my anecdote. Of course, who knows what you might have told her about me! That's it, isn't it! You said something!"

"You see what I mean? As the sun sets, Vampyra rises."

"Vampyra is just getting warmed up. What lies have you been telling about me?"

"None. I've hardly talked about you, except today when you were present."

"Well, thanks! I talk about you all the time. All my friends know you, even those who've never met you."

"She's not exactly a friend, and her trash mouth notwithstanding, she would not have understood your point of view. The academics here are a pretty provincial lot. You'd think a fancy private university like this would draw a hipper crowd."

"I wasn't talking about boy love. I was going to tell her an anecdote about language."

"You would've found a way to work it in. These days, just the fact that you're hanging around with a boy that age is cause for suspicion."

"So you're afraid of what they might think of you with your pederast friend."

"I still have to live here after you leave."

"Are you ashamed of me?"

"No, I'm ashamed of them."

"You're always so careful of what other people think. What a Yankee you are!"

Feigning a mock Scarlet O'Hara, "Unlike you Southern boys, who just say whatever pops into your pretty little heads? Bullshit! Southerners are the most political people I've ever met. That's why the Japanese like Faulkner so much. It has nothing to do with sympathy for a defeated nation. They understand the politics of the South, because they are the same way."

The Moralist

Red smiled at his friend's insight. "Touché, and exactly the reason why you should have had more trust in my discretion. Can we stop by the campus bookstore for a few minutes? I want to pick up a few things."

"Gifts for the boy?" Malcolm inferred slyly.

"Souvenirs. We're not allowed to give gifts, except for Christmas and birthdays," Red explained. "But we are encouraged to 'share activities.' Last December, I took him to hear Izhak Perlmann at the symphony."

"He's a lucky boy. I would've given anything to have someone like you in my life when I was his age. You're his window on the world!"

Seven women and one man sat around the conference room table for the weekly staff meeting at the agency, Faye perched at the head. Red was the only rooster in this henhouse. Surrounded by straight, female, conservative Republicans, he was the Connie Chung of the agency, fulfilling a whole bunch of affirmative actions all at once: male, gay, liberal Democrat. In the eighties, Faye had worked at the Reagan White House. She thought Ronny was God. At the same time, a thousand miles away, Red had sat before the TV with his gay friends dishing the homophobic old fool who decimated an entire generation by relegating AIDS to "a gay problem." Now he was an Alzheimer's vegetable. Poetic justice.

Red particularly did not like Republican women in politics. They all had a thin, strained, waxy look with deep glassy robot eyes, like something out of *The Stepford Wives*, the scary, insane look of cruelty and sexual hysteria: Kay Bailey Hutchison, Susan Carpenter McMillan, Phyllis Schlafley, Laura Bush to name a few.

At least Faye did not fit that stereotype. She was more realpolitik than her ideological colleagues, a relief to Red. Once on one of their airplane travels together, she kicked back from her laptop and sighed with satisfaction, "I love power!" Smiling to himself, Red quietly shook his head, incredulous at the absolute accuracy of this self-revelation.

He was glad to hear it. He liked Faye in spite of her politics, and realpolitik was a point of view he could accommodate far more easily than the fanaticism of her right-wing cohorts, his mortal enemies who, given half a chance, would round up and gas every boy lover on earth. And they were doing everything they could to get that chance.

Before the meeting began, she leaned over to Red and whispered in her conspiratorial voice, "I'd still like to read one of your stories."

"Damn, she asked again!" he thought and nodded to her. "I'll bring you something." The best he'd be able to do was *Grand Canyon Suite*, a short story where the uncle falls in love with his nephew, but the focus was more on the dysfunctional family. Red knew he would be risking his job with this, or at best arousing her suspicions, but she'd asked twice, so he had to deliver.

It had not been his intention to lead a double life. It just turned out that way in a hostile society, where he was forever condemned to be a stranger. Even gays had achieved some measure of acceptance and could be "out" in their professional lives. Not so for boy lovers, the sacrificial lambs for gay acceptance.

Behind her, a faded marquis-sized poster announced *Bundle of Joy*, a major motion picture starring Terry Thomas and introducing Faye Collins, "fresh and fun." Designed in the bright yellow, bouncy, bubbly cartoon style of the mid-sixties, it hovered over middle-aged Faye like the ghost of childhood past, as did the yellowing framed stills from the film that lined the walls showing fourteen-year-old Faye making faces at Thomas. The movie was a Technicolor comedy about a stuffy British professor and a little American brat, a sexless, through-the-looking-glass knock-off of Kubrik's *Lolita*. *Lolita* made Sue Lyon famous. *Bundle of Joy* marked the early demise of Faye's once budding film career.

Maybe it was the movie that arrested her emotional development. She was condemned to be a fourteen-year-old screen brat forever. Red could relate.

Red to Malcolm:

"Theo once called me 'an arrested adolescent,' and maybe he was right. But I'd rather be an arrested adolescent than arrested with an adolescent."

"Same thing, sooner or later."

Red had seen Faye's movie when it first came out thirty-three years ago. He remembered it not so much because it was memorable, it wasn't, but rather the circumstance of his seeing it. He had missed a train connection in Cincinnati, on the way to his summer gig as an acting apprentice at the Cherryland Playhouse in northern Michigan. He had four hours to kill and took in *Bundle of Joy* before catching the next train.

So Faye had played a minor role at an important moment in his life, his summer of unrequited love, when his girl, a pretty fellow apprentice from California, was stolen by a rich college boy, the son of the producer.

The Moralist

In retreat, seventeen-year-old Red wrapped himself in reading. He discovered a strange book, selected almost at random from the shelves of the local bookstore, that told of Aldous Huxley's experiences with psychedelic drugs. This single volume contained two novella-length essays titled *The Doors of Perception* and *Heaven and Hell* that were later to become icons of an age. But during the summer of '65, they were simply a matter of curiosity to Red. He'd heard of a drug called LSD that gave you the power "to see ourselves as others see us" and wanted to learn more.

But Huxley's vision was not at all what he'd expected. It described a unity that made sense of much that had eluded Red in his study of poetry at school. All that talk about Truth and Beauty and "Do I wake or sleep?" had seemed mere poetic gush, until Huxley's visions articulated the link between I and It. Unrequited in love, Red discovered a love beyond romantic attachment, the love that connected him with the world.

Upon his return home, he immediately phoned his former high school English teacher to share his discovery. She was one of those great, grand English teachers beloved by parents and students alike for her enthusiasm and skill. Red admired her and had been one of her best students, but that day, was stunned at her reaction. As soon as he heard her wan voice on the phone, the excited young student erupted with his new vision, interpreting its meaning to literature, explicating its relevance to the perception of beauty and experience of love, certain that she too would see the totality of it. Her distant, condescending, and confused response might have been delivered to a telemarketer. Red put down the phone, disillusioned yet again. She had not understood a word he'd said.

He later discovered that it was a truth few understood and fewer still wanted to hear. It called into question all of our assumptions about how things are, and most people don't like that. "You can thump their totems to see if they're hollow," Theo once said, "but don't kick their totems. That pisses 'em off." Theo failed to understand what Red came to learn: Calling a totem into question *was* kicking it.

Red rarely exchanged political views with Faye. This allowed them to work together, a la the marriage between James Carvelle, the Democratic attack dog, and Mary Madeline, his Republican pundit wife, politics raised to the level of performance, which, with their respective theatrical backgrounds, both Faye and Red understood all too well. Red stuck to the business accounts and let Faye do the politics. Thus, his surprise and discomfort when she made her announcement at the staff meeting.

"I have two exciting pieces of news," she began. "First, we have a new client, Tommy DeKalb, the former governor of Kentucky."

"*Republican* governor," Red thought.

"He's been named chairman of the Coalition on Charity in America, and he wants us to handle the publicity. They're studying new ways to help the poor and homeless."

To help them out of their last safety net. First, the Republicans threw everybody off welfare. Now, they were going after the charities!

"You ought to like this project, Richard." Faye addressed him directly, meaning that he would be involved. Knowing that he had refused to do political work in the past, she transparently positioned the matter in terms of what she believed to be his liberal sentiments. "They're going to be giving a lot of money to the charities they identify as models of effectiveness."

"Models of their right-wing agenda is more like it," Red said to himself, having none of it. But he knew he was being presented with a *fait accompli*. "No" was not an option, but this thing stunk on ice. Tommy DeKalb had his sights on the White House, and even though he technically wasn't running for office, the Coalition was obviously a position from which he intended to build a base.

This was what came from sleeping with the enemy. Faye was too shrewd to demand that he work on accounts that were personally repugnant to him, less out of consideration for his point of view than her realpolitik understanding that he would instinctively give it less than his best, if not deliberately sabotage it. He wouldn't do it anyway, but this time he was stuck, and he knew it. "But why me?" Red asked himself. It didn't make sense. The Coalition was based in D.C. Why not let Deborah in the D.C. office handle it? She was a good Republican.

As if reading his thoughts, Faye continued, "Deborah, of course, will be handling most of the day-to-day stuff in Washington, but, Richard, you know the philanthropic community and the philanthropic press from your work on that planned giving lawsuit last year."

"Enough to know what's really going on," he thought. Conservatives were no friends to the philanthropic community, who howled when the Republicans suggested that private charities pick up the welfare slack. The right-wingers shot back with attacks on the "liberal agenda" and "social engineering" of the large foundations. Red saw very clearly where this so-called Coalition was headed. He didn't even have to ask where the money was coming from, some big conservative foundation no doubt.

"I need somebody here in Dallas to be on top of it while I'm out of the country—and that brings me to my second bit of news: Worldwide Express is opening up China, and I'm going to Hong Kong."

That explained it. Faye would dearly love to have been the publicity star for Tommy DeKalb, possibly the next President. She must have thought it would be like Ronny all over again, but when Worldwide cried "froggy," she jumped. And Hong Kong would be fun. Tommy DeKalb and his Coalition would have to take the second string.

"So it looks like we will all be getting big bonuses!" she declared to sweeten the kitty. "Now," Faye paused to get their attention with her ever-precise sense for the dramatic moment, "I'm taking orders for the bazaar!"

The women were instantly atwitter over silks and rugs and jewelry. No opportunity for protest, but he was not happy. Faye knew she was making him bend over for this assignment and could see from his cool, pale expression that he wasn't buying her spin, just as he understood that, in terms of available resources, with her out of the country, he had no choice. LuAnne was swamped with Happy the Hippo's national tour, and the rest of the piranhas were juniors just out of college.

After the meeting, she privately confided, "I think you'll like the Coalition, Richard. They're nice people. Many of the board members run their own charities. They're on the front lines: homeless shelters, drug rehab, battered women. They're doing good work. I need somebody who's good with the press. Deborah's not as aggressive as you are. She lets them walk all over her, and we need ink. Tommy's put a lot of faith in us, and the Withers Foundation has never even heard of us. We need to show them that we can deliver."

"I'll take care of it. Have a good time in Hong Kong," he said, thinking how he could confine his efforts to the press contact, the PR grunt work, and let Deborah handle the rest of it.

Faye handed him two tickets to the symphony, her final ploy. "I think you'll enjoy these. It's a special performance by Izhak Perlman, but I'll be on the plane to Hong Kong. I hope you can find someone to go with you on such short notice."

"I think I might."

She smiled her phony sweet PR smile, satisfied that she had shoved it up his ass as gently as possible, "Great! Have fun!"

FAX MESSAGE: Please Deliver Immediately to Jonathan Frame

Jonathan:

I have two tickets for us to hear the most famous violinist in the world at the Myerson Symphony Center. I understand that classical violin is a far cry from cuttin' heads on bass in Deep Ellum, but it's just another kind of music, and if you've never been to the Myerson, seeing a world-class concert hall alone is worth the trip. We have a private box for Saturday night. Can you join me? You will need your parents' permission. Call and let me know if you can make it. —Red

Red called Darren, his best friend and fellow ped, twenty-five years his junior. They met seven years ago as rivals chasing the same boy, but more of that to come.

"I don't know about this, Red. You're moving into uncharted territory taking him to something outside the school, being alone with him. I hope you're being careful about this," Darren cautioned him.

"Love is always subversive."

"I just don't want you to get yourself into something you can't get out of."

"I'm taking my student, who likes music, who plays the guitar and the recorder, to hear the most famous violinist in the world at one of the finest concert halls in the world."

"Yes, that's what it looks like to them—to his parents and the school authorities."

"That's what it is, a great cultural opportunity for both of us."

"It is also your first date. It's not just teacher and student in the classroom anymore. You'll visit his home and meet his parents. It's a major step, and you know it. Look at it this way: You could have invited Penny. She would have appreciated it a lot more. But you didn't. You chose your boy instead."

"Of course. Wouldn't you have done the same?"

"I'm not sure. It's different when they're that young. Is he even pubescent? Are his tits hard?"

"I've never seen his tits. I'm just taking him to the symphony, I'm not having sex with him."

"But you will. This is just the next step."

"I love him. I want to expand his horizons."

"That's not all you want to expand."

"Very funny."

"It won't be long before he's adolescent, and in the meantime, each step along the way will build the love and trust between you, so that when he's ready, it will be very hard for either of you to say no."

"Why would we want to? That is, assuming I continue to see him after the program's over, assuming that his parents will let me, assuming he wants that. I can't be so certain as you, so I content myself with enjoying the moment."

"That changes nothing. Whether you admit it or not, you are starting down a road of no return."

The invitation to the symphony posed new questions, or rather one big question: Whither goest thou? It was easy enough to love the boy by teaching him and sending him notes and faxes and even calling him on the phone to relate this or that new idea about the story. Darren was right. This was a different ball game, loving him one on one, not just teacher to student but man to boy. Once Red broke that barrier, how far would he go? As Darren pointed out, even without deciding, each step to expand the relationship was in itself a decision to go forward. But what was the alternative? To stop? To draw the line? That was the last thing he wanted. He wanted to go further, further and further. Going forward was the goal of love. He was already on Darren's road of no return. The Crossroads, cutting heads with the devil.

Faye was bustling out the door to the waiting cab when Red handed her a manuscript. "A little something to read on the plane," he smiled. She thanked him and stuffed it into one of the several bags hanging from her shoulders, as she climbed into the cab. "Bon voyage!"

<u>Jonathan's Journal</u>

I wish we lived in a nicer place. My dad had a good business, but his partner got into drugs and ran off with all the money. Now, my dad's outta work, and we live in a run-down little house, only three rooms and a kitchen. I have to sleep on the couch, but it's better than sleeping with my older sister. I told my mom that Mr. Rover (I don't call him "Red" to her) invited me to the symphony. I showed her the fax, and she was overjoyed. She said I would have to get a suit, so we went to MacFrugals where they sell suits for boys. I already had a Disney tie with Goofy all over it. I hate ties, even if it has Goofy on it. I had to get a haircut, too, and I hate haircuts. She combed it all over. I want it to grow out. This better be worth it. Red said it was cool. Izhak Perlman. What's this Izhak? Sounds like a video game. I got a new suit out of it anyway, except it's too big. Mom says I'll grow into it. I can't wait. Then I'll be a teenager, and I can tell her what's cool, but for now, this is it: combed over hair, a baggy suit, and a Goofy tie. Goofy is right!

Snow in November was rare for Texas. The forecasters were warning motorists of slick streets and advising everyone to stay indoors. With a freak storm like this, anything could happen. It could melt on contact, blanket the city, or turn to ice. "Will it get worse?" was Red's only question. Would he be driving the boy home on ice-glazed streets? Would they be forced to get a room in town for the night? Or the most pressing question of all: Would his parents trust their only son to a stranger on a snowy night? His phone didn't ring, and Red dared not call and raise the issue. He was determined to follow through. The decision was made, no matter what. If he were going to be denied, they would have to tell him to his face at the door. He wrapped himself in his cashmere coat, silk scarf, and suede gloves, tickets to Perlman safely tucked in his pocket.

The trusty Mustang crawled through the heavy snowfall, big wet flakes that melted instantly on the windshield, so far so good, to a scruffy neighborhood behind the Sony Multiplex, a little green dollhouse on a blasted patch of ground, landscaped with a single scrawny hibiscus sprouting out of nowhere.

The door was partly open, even in the cold weather. Red stood before the Christian amulet, a wooden cross with a scroll at the base: "Bless ye all who enter here." It reminded him of Dante's entrance to hell, "Abandon all hope, ye who enter here," or the entrance to the Enchanted Forest in *The Wizard of Oz*, "I'd turn back if I were you." He felt embarrassed to knock on an open door, and before he could, a voice called from within, "Come in."

He stepped into the bright little doll living room with a little doll half sofa and child's armchair and dollhouse fireplace, a space the size of a small bedroom. Red felt like Gulliver in Lilliput. The invitation was from Melanie, Jonathan's mom, appearing from a back room, heavy and sluggish. Following his wife was a tall, thin man with front teeth missing and red hair trailing past his shoulders. This must be Jon Sr., the cliché of the working class couple, fat and skinny. He offered Red a limp hand and introduced himself.

Another female voice called from the back. Jonathan had mentioned a sister. "Jonathan! Mr. Rover is here!"

He was meeting the family. Darren was right; it was their first date.

"I've been reading the faxes you've sent him," Melanie called him back to reality. "You're teaching him some very advanced ideas about writing."

"He's very talented!" Red effused truthfully, but thought it sounded phony. "I can go fast with him. It's graduate level stuff, but his mind soaks it up like a sponge."

Mom's eyes sparkled. She was a part-time teacher herself. She, too, saw her son's rare beauty, as moms usually do.

As if on cue, the boy entered in his baggy suit and Goofy tie, with a shy smile. Blushing, he lowered his head wishing he could disappear.

But had he looked, he would have seen that Red was enthralled to see the kid dressed up without his tattered flannel. "You're lookin' pretty hip there, buddy," he smiled at the sight of the boy's embarrassment. "That baggy look is hot in Deep Ellum. Cartoon ties, too. You could walk into any club on the strip in that outfit!"

Jonathan looked up proudly and beamed, "It's new. I just got it today!"

He stepped into the little living room, where his parents and sister were now gathered to admire him Norman Rockwell style and wish them off. What would be the title of this tableau? *A Boy's First Man*?

"Be careful driving in this weather," was all that Melanie had to say on the subject of the snow, to Red's astonishment after his hours of agonizing.

Jonathan was prepared for the drive with his favorite tape. "Check this out," he insisted, popping in a collection of vintage rock'n'roll: Chuck Berry, Buddy Holly, Bo Diddley, songs that echoed deep in Red's memory. Thirty-eight years ago, he had jammed to this very same music at Jonathan's very same age.

In college, Red discovered an antique junk shop with racks of arcane hard-plastic records bearing the old original Victor label from the twenties. He brought a few back to the frat house and played them for his drunk brothers, who laughed at the quaint, tinny songs from a long-past era.

This experience did not exist for Jonathan and Red. With rock'n'roll, the cultural divide in music had narrowed. Instead of a generation gap, the man and boy shared a timeless connection, and even more to Red's pleasure, Jonathan understood that.

Red glanced away from the snowy street for a visual snapshot of his young protégé. He could almost see himself, jamming to the music. Alter-ego, lost boy. If Red were Jonathan's window on the world, Jonathan was Red's window on the past.

At the concert in their private box, Red furtively observed the boy perched on the edge of the red velvet Queen Anne chair too big for his skinny boy legs, his feet not even touching the floor. It seemed almost impossible that he sat with his beloved rapt in Perlman's silver web of sound that stretched across the elegant cavern of inlaid wood, brass, and tiffany glass.

Jonathan beamed with wonder at the place. How different it was from the gritty Deep Ellum coffee bars where Tarzan's Boy ground out its late-night sets. Classical violin, rock'n'roll, all the same like automatic writing, whatever comes to mind, just different kinds of music, like Red said.

After the performance, exiting their private box through deco double doors, Red asked the boy how he liked the performance. Jonathan responded with a grin, "Hot licks!"

Red laughed, perhaps too heartily, transforming a sob and wiping the tears from his eyes.

"The invasion has begun. Outer defenses breached. First hymen broken," Malcolm raised his glass.

"A girl has only one. A boy has dozens."

"So what's the next scene in your saga of seduction?"

"Christmas. It was our last meeting before the Holiday break. After that, I wouldn't see him until January. But the rules said I could give him a gift—two, since his birthday's on Christmas Eve. One, I had already chosen, some safety gear for his elbows and knees before the little daredevil smashed them up for good on that bike of his. The other: I wanted to see my Christmas boy during his holiday, so I took him to the movie *Titanic*, as promised."

"Did he like it?"

"He fidgeted for the first hour. After it was over, he gave me his one-sentence review: 'It sure took 'em a long time to get to the iceberg!'"

"The eleven-year-old perspective."

"Twelve. He's twelve now."

5

Faye returned from Hong Kong. Silks and jewelry were spread over the conference table like a booth in a bazaar, gifts for all. She distributed Asian munchies among the staff, fried prawns like pork rinds and hard yellow ginseng candies. After the party, she asked Red to meet with her privately in her office.

"How was the concert?" she inquired, bending over to fish in her bag of tricks as she talked, forcing him to reply to her ass.

"It was fun! I invited my young student from the Authors of Tomorrow. He plays in the school orchestra. He loved it."

"How sweet! And you?" she continued from between her legs.

"Very much. It was a wonderful evening." Surely, she was aware how this looked, presenting her ass to him like a baboon. Was it a test to elicit some comment? Red could only imagine what he might say: "What, ya got bad knees? Ya can't squat down? Lemme tell ya, neither man nor woman, I don't care who it is, they don't look very graceful bending over like that, not to mention what it must be doing to your back. Are you showing off that you can still bend over like that, pushing fifty? (She was a year younger than he.) Why dontcha ask me to do it for you?" Or maybe, like the baboon, she expected something more?

"I have a special gift for you, Richard," she finally explained, and wheeled around presenting a large decorated wooden box containing four small replicas of the famous Chinese terra cotta army, a nicer gift than the others. "This is for picking up on the Coalition for me." He hadn't done a damn thing for them. She continued, "Normally, I would handle it myself, but I have to go right back. This Hong Kong thing is going to require my full attention, at least through the first part of next year. The British are handing the whole colony back to the Communists in six months, and Worldwide Express has to have all its systems in place for the Chinese market. So it looks like the Coalition is going to be in your basket for a while. They're holding conferences on charity all over the country, and I want you to glue yourself to them."

Republican charity! There was an oxymoron! Red arranged the terra cotta soldiers on his mantle in poses of fellatio and bestiality.

"Oh, one more thing," she added, pulling his manuscript from her bag. "I read your story on the plane."

"Oh, yes?" he tried to sound eager for her comment. At least the Coalition assignment ensured she had no plans for showing him the door. "I hope you enjoyed it."

Handing him the manuscript, she observed off-handedly, "You write with a lot of anger."

That was it. Like Melanie and the snowy weather, for all his anxiety, this was the sum total of her commentary. She probably didn't even read it, and that was fine with him.

"But I wouldn't show it around the office, if I were you," she added. "I don't think some of our younger staff would understand."

Incredulous, he agreed, like that was something he would actually do!

Red and Jonathan walked across the parking lot to the car.

"They sure took a long time gettin' to the iceberg," he complained.

Red laughed, "What's the matter? Too much kissyface for ya?"

"Yeah, and not enough urgency, except at the end."

"Good for you! What about setups and payoffs? Can you name one?"

"The necklace."

"Absolutely! A-plus, buddy!"

"But analyzing it like that takes all the fun out of it."

"Why? Just because you understand how it's put together doesn't mean you can't enjoy it. When you appreciate the artistry, you enjoy it more."

They returned to the dollhouse where Melanie was stretched out on the couch. Jonathan played his guitar to Red's delight, the heavy instrument as long as the boy was tall, but he mastered the beast, commanding its deep cries and stinging its "pickups" that made the creature growl and groan. The power to make this noise was masculine adolescence on the hoof, and this ragged little room surrounded by speakers and amps was paradise city for a boy. At its center, young Apollo was grinding out his bass line.

After the private concert, he put the guitar back on the stand and curled up on the couch next to his mom, as Red presented his odd-shaped gift. Jonathan passed his delicate hands over the package like a medium and declared a helmet and pads before even tearing the colorful paper.

"You're too smart sometimes, ya know that?" Red observed.

Melanie agreed with a chuckle, and for the first time, Jonathan smiled proudly instead of fidgeting. He tore into the wrapping and held up his treasures.

"Merry Christmas and Happy Birthday!" Red declared, "And here's a stocking stuffer, too. Hold out your hand." The boy obeyed, and Red placed three yellow ginseng candies in his palm. "Ginseng, from China."

He stared hard at the golden candies in his hand then looked up into Red's golden eyes, just as in his dream. "Are you a sorcerer, Red?" he asked with sly innocence.

Melanie giggled, at once delighted and embarrassed at her son's smart tongue.

"Artists are sorcerers," Red replied. "You're one, too, y'know."

"Jonathan does magic tricks!" Melanie announced on the subject of sorcery.

"So I hear," Red replied.

"Show him your rings," she eagerly encouraged her son.

Shy again, the boy buried his face into his mother's bosom like a little boy—probably for the last time, Red thought. Just like his childish fidgeting, twelve would change all that.

"You do the rings?" Red asked, drawing him out. "Johnny Carson used to do the rings!"

"Who's Johnny Carson?"

The boy's question jolted Red with the cold shock of time. Jonathan was five when Carson went off the air. "He hosted *The Tonight Show* before Jay Leno. He started out in show business doing magic tricks, just like you. Show me your act. I'd love to see it."

"I haven't done it in a while."

"That's okay. I'm easily fooled."

With Melanie's encouragement, he retrieved his rings from the back. Putting on a tape of circus music, he performed a smooth series of passes. What an elegant illusion this was! Magic as ballet, real prestidigitation, the skill of hand and body without the cheesy technology of most other tricks. He missed a pass, and his face reddened.

"Keep going!" Red cried, and the young magician did until the grand finale, as all three rings dropped linked together at once. He bowed, and they applauded.

The following day, Red flew to Atlanta to visit his elderly parents for the holiday weekend at their shaded home on Peachtree Street, a lush and lovely place they enjoyed in good health. Yet, as he sat before the hearth, at one side, his mother reclining on her couch with her puzzles and books and TV remote on the other, his father in his Laz-e-Boy recliner, they quarreled over who said what to whom.

What arrogance to indulge such bickering in paradise! He'd heard it all his life, and still it hurt. His *joie* sank in the oppressive atmosphere of this moribund scene, until he felt the air go out of him.

Red excused himself and wandered the empty house like a ghost. The place was dreamlike. His mother had planted family memorabilia like land mines, so every room and closet opened a window to the past.

An ancient snapshot of Red in a black cat costume at his sixth-year Halloween birthday party. Jonathan was Christmas; Red was Halloween.

Red's mounted portrait of his daughter Cindy taken more than twenty years ago on the beach. The little girl in painted nails and wet T-shirt bent over the green water in wonderment at some discovery beneath the surface. His ex-wife Jan put it on a postcard advertising the Catamaran Motel, the mom-and-pop on Speed Beach, where Cindy grew up. Red and Jan had agreed to run the place for his dad, because she wanted a child. So they left New York, where Red worked in the Off-Off-Broadway theater, and moved to the beach. The child was born, but when Red invited Theo down from the City to collaborate on a play, they became lovers, and everything changed.

After midnight, the Catamaran Motel transformed into "The KozmiK Kat," a satyrnalian riot of men and boys. The play careened out of control finally to become the novel *Seeing Red*. Jan couldn't take it, and inevitably, the mom-and-pop became just mom, when Theo and Red escaped to Theo's alma mater, Harbour U.

Absent of self-awareness, the little girl in the photo expressed her profoundest innocence in the absorption of her discovery. The same was true of her unselfconscious love for living things. As a child, she filled her mother's house with a menagerie of lizards, fish, rabbits, hamsters, turtles, birds (an aviary of parrots, finches, budgies, and love birds!), a dog, a cat.

The Moralist

When she was ten, her mother said she couldn't have a cat, so she found a wounded tom nearly dead from a fight, a scarred and feral beast that had crawled up under the motel building to heal or die. Feeding her "Tiger" every day, she nurtured it back to health. The beast even allowed itself to be carried in her arms. When she introduced her new kitty, it glowered at the human world in stark terror. As soon as he was strong again, Tiger returned to his untamed world. After his departure, Cindy got her cat.

And finally as it often is with girls, horses.

Red opened a closet door. Among long abandoned jackets and sweaters that should have gone to Goodwill twenty years ago hung his original Boy Scout uniform. He pulled the shirt around him and threaded his arms into the sleeves. The heavy, stiff khaki cotton held firm as it stretched across the middle-aged man's body, the shed skin of his twelve-year-old self, Oedipus in reverse, donning the mantle of the boy.

He draped the merit badge sash over his shoulder and checked himself out in the foyer mirror, his muscular frame stuffed into a little clown tunic and adorned with a sash of embroidered circular patches: masks for drama, a telescope for astronomy, a gavel for government, the Golden Arrow he received at the last Boy Scout camp.

Red loved summer camp, the chance to escape his barren suburban life and tormenting older brother, but as they turned fourteen, his gang quit the Scouts, leaving Red with the twelve-and thirteen-year-olds, who loved to hear the older boy's tales of sock hops and making out.

Inspired by their amusement, Red spun out a running yarn about Sally the slut with the giant vagina that sucked him in like Alice down the rabbit hole and all the amazing things he found down there that left the younger boys screaming with laughter.

One night, his tent-mate Jeffrey, a slight shy twelve-year-old, crawled into Red's cot and wrapped his slender arms around his hero. They did not speak but found each other in the dark. Jeffrey followed Red everywhere, signing up for all the same activities, always wanting to be in Red's company and hanging on his every word. Red was flattered by the attention, understanding all too well the love of hero worship. He gladly accepted the role of guide and midnight lover to his admiring protégé, teaching him how to canoe and communicate by semaphore, teaching him right and wrong, and at night, the pleasures of love, but they never spoke of that.

The Scouts were more militaristic then, an outgrowth of the War. As Jeffrey's mentor, Red embodied the qualities of leadership that boys learned in scouting. The Scout leaders noticed and awarded him the Golden Arrow for best camper. At summer's end, the two boys shed tears at their parting. Jeffrey was from Tennessee, hundreds of miles away. They corresponded for almost a year afterward, long after Red retired his uniform to the old-clothes closet, where it remained for more than thirty-five years, until now.

Jeffrey discovered girls, and the letters stopped. Red, too, had a girl by then, and didn't miss this end to their correspondence. He'd grown embarrassed by Jeffrey's letters.

"What an arrogant ass I've been!" Red thought. "Who am I to say what's right and wrong for a kid? Who is anyone? It's some kinda weird 'I'm in charge; I know what's best' kinda thinkin'." It no longer made sense, as it had only a year before.

Merit badge memories. It sounded like the title of a porno flick.

Christmas at the club, Red sat erect at the table with champagne and wine flowing and candlelight twinkling in crystal goblets. Surrounded by his bickering parents, pretentious older brother CJ, scheming sister-in-law, and neurotic neice (his younger brother, mad Norton, rarely attended these gatherings), Red saw them, himself included, as zombies in a mausoleum, trading gifts in a ghoulish ceremony. His father observed that everyone at the table had one thing in common, the name "Rover."

"That's about all!" his mother burst forth in a moment of brilliance to the amusement of Red who was thinking the same thing.

Banality recovered from Truth, as the conversation turned to money, a deal to sell some land. Red wanted to scream, not so much from the shallowness of it all as simply the absence of joy. But, like Emily from *Our Town*, no one hears the screams of the dead. His father was right. He was one of them. The despair this thought inspired was a glimpse into the abyss, "The Big O," as Theo used to call it.

Jonathan's Journal

I love my family. My aunts and uncles and cousins and brothers and sisters and Mom and Dad get together and exchange gifts by the tree. It's a happy time for me. For Christmas, I got a new skateboard and a Gameboy and a CD player. My Dad and Mom are happy. My Dad is working, and Mom is getting certified to be a full-time teacher. Things are going better for us. I wish we lived in a better house, though.

On New Year's Day, the phone rang.

"Hello, Red, this is Jonathan."

Red's heart leapt at the voice of the boy. "Hey, Jonathan! What a pleasant surprise!"

"Happy New Year!" he burst out, as if streamers and confetti were flying around them. "Happy New Year, Red!" he cried again.

Red laughed at his little friend's histrionics. "Well, Happy New Year to you, too!"

Returning to his sweet boy voice tinged with shy irony, he added, "I was calling to wish you a," he burst out again, giggling, "Happy New Year!"

"Your call makes my New Year happier than you can imagine, so your wish is already fulfilled. What did you get for Christmas, for your birthday and Christmas?" Red listened with pleasure and exclamations of delight as Jonathan recited his booty. It was Red's first USIP (unsolicited incoming phone call) from the boy.

That evening, the two men drove into the city. On the second-floor veranda of a popular corner bar overlooking the Castro, Red had a few martinis, big fat fucking kickass delicious martoonis, but there was nothing of interest on the boulevard of queens below. The scene didn't seem to have changed that much, since he'd been there with Michael fifteen years ago. Yes, their numbers had been decimated. Yes, the free sex and 48-hour parties were gone. But the queens survived. The martoonis kicked in, and as Malcolm had predicted, Vampyra rose from her grave.

The following morning, their final day together, was leisurely. Malcolm read the *Sunday Times*, as Red packed. They smoked joints and drank espresso.

"You were right, Vampyra came out last night," Red allowed. "It was those martinis. I'm not good with martinis. In fact, you might say I'm bad with martinis."

"That's what makes them martinis."

"Excellent tautology!" he laughed.

"I knew you were in trouble when you sucked that last one down like lemonade and started talking to that bald black George Kastanza at the bar. I was sure you were headed for some black dick up your ass."

"Hardly. I was just doing the bit Theo taught me. You turn to the person next to you and start talking. It's an especially useful technique, when, well, how can I put this politely?"

"We were boring you."

"No, not you, Malcolm. You're always fun. You are one of the most scintillating people I know. On the other hand, our companions! I told you we shoulda stuck with the profanity gal. She was better company. So I toyed with George Kastanza for a while. I told him he looked like a fireman, and he dropped his jaw. He said he was a mailman, but his lover of seven years had been a fireman. He was killed recently, a hero in the line of duty. I asked George if he was eligible for the death benefit from his lover's pension fund, and he said he had just received the check. Good for San Francisco! It was like I knew everything about him, but all I was really doing was free-associating, 'whatever pops into my pretty little head.' I call it 'instant intimacy.' When I'm really in touch, I'm almost clairvoyant. 'Course a few martinis don't hurt."

"Vampyra unleashed!" Malcolm moistened his eyes from a tiny plastic vial, sinus problems. He'd had his tear ducts surgically removed. Malcolm couldn't cry.

Malcolm sped the Miata along the freeway toward the airport, as Red concluded his story of Jonathan, "Last weekend, right before I came here, was our final meeting. We had to finish the story in time for the publishing deadline, so we met at the school on a Saturday morning."

THE BOY WHO TURNED INTO A DOG
By Jonathan Frame
Conclusion

The Wizard returned to find the old sorcerer stretched out on the floor and pretended to be surprised and called for help. The helpless dog fawned on the Wizard with great anxiety, and he snatched the animal into the air crying, "You are mine now!" But it was not to be. Chan bit him on the nose, as the old sorcerer tangled his legs in a sheet. They ran through the gardens of the

The Moralist

Forbidden City, until they reached the wall. Behind them shouted the guards led by the Wizard holding his bleeding nose. The old man snatched Chan into his arms, and they flew over the wall in an instant. They appeared in the plaza on the other side, standing before the merchants of Peking, who were dumbfounded to see a man and a dog appear from nowhere.

Chan and the old sorcerer ran, not from the guards but from the people, who knew not why they were chasing an old man and his dog. Rumor ran faster than feet and paws, and soon everyone had heard that a magician was loose from The Forbidden City, but the old sorcerer's magic was faster still, and they vanished into the mountains.

They had made their escape, but in the quiet of the alpine dusk, as the old sorcerer slept from exhaustion, Chan understood that his life of luxury was over. As he watched the old man lying on the hard ground wheezing away, he wept and whined at the thought that he would remain a dog forever, for the rest of his life.

At that very moment, the sorcerer sat up, his eyes glowing yellow like the ginseng pills, and reached out for his companion, pulling him close.

"You wanted to become a sorcerer, so you could make yourself rich," he whispered, voice fading, "But I made you rich, so you could become a sorcerer."

In shock at the old man's words, Chan squealed and jumped away landing on both feet. He looked around. The sorcerer had vanished. "Old man, where are you?" he cried, but the sorcerer was nowhere to be seen. Suddenly, he realized he could talk. He was no longer a dog, nor had he transformed back into a boy. Chan had grown into a young man.

Chan came upon the emperor's army, who asked him about an old man and a dog. He knew nothing of this.

No trace of the old sorcerer and his dog was ever found, but to this day, there are stories of a young man, who wanders the mountains doing good deeds.

The End

"A very nice fable. Good work, my friend."

Erastes and his eromenos sat side-by-side at the computer. Jonathan read his story out loud, as Red tapped away at the keyboard, fine-tuning as he went.

Red wanted more description of the dog, so Jonathan retrieved from the stacks an encyclopedia volume that showed a picture of a Chinese crested dog with a hairless body but for a shock of long hair falling down over its eyes like a punk teenager. He pointed to the picture and said this picture was the inspiration for his story, then started to giggle so hard his face glowed scarlet. Red laughed with him, bewildered at what was so funny to his clever twelve-year-old mind.

When the stories were published, a short commentary from each mentor was included. They usually went something like "Jimmy is very talented, and it was a pleasure working with him." Red's described that moment of Jonathan's laughter at the picture of the exotic dog.

The librarian interrupted them. "You will have to finish up soon. There's going to be a dedication ceremony for the school. The mayor will be here, and there will be a buffet with cakes and brownies. You're welcome to stay, but you'll have to turn off the computer."

Volunteer ladies came in with plastic-covered trays of cakes and pizza rolls and miniature quiches. Mentor and protégé scrambled to finish the story. Red hit the "Save" button, just as the suits began filing in, led by the mayor and reporters.

Seeing the pederast and his boy at the computer, the mayor drew his retinue around the table, observing aloud that this was what the new school was all about. Cameras flashed to capture the tableau.

"Will we be in the newspaper?" Jonathan later asked.

"Probably," Red replied, both amused and saddened by the irony of that moment. Had the mayor known the truth of Red's love, his pride would have transformed into horror. Red imagined the day when the irony evaporated, when the mayor praised the boy lover *because* he knew.

Red and Jonathan ate the little quiches and brownies but left soon afterward to wander about the schoolyard, Jonathan leading the way, his stomping grounds, his baseball diamond, his soccer field on a late winter day, the sun dipping in the sky with golden light.

Red drove him to Reverchon Park and showed him another baseball diamond where amateur teams played.

Ten years ago, this quiet park had been a nightly block party for teenagers. The hip youngsters of Dallas who couldn't get into the bars gathered here instead. They lined their cars along the parking lot next to the silent diamond and partied the night away. Inevitably, the scene attracted the chicken hawks cruising the boys, who clustered around their music, climbing in and out of cars. Sometimes the party moved off to some hawk's high-rise condo nearby or backyard pool in north Dallas.

At the back of the lot in the shadows was a large oak demarking where the rich old hawks dutifully backed in their Lexus, Porsche, Beamer, Mercedes, Jaguar, Town Cars, and waited to pounce on the wandering chicken, who strayed too far from the flock. Some wag tacked a cardboard sign to its trunk dubbing it "The Troll Tree."

Red first met Darren there, and Mark. The adventure began with a gay friend from work, Tom, who ran ads for jack-off parties. Red was having none of it, but when Tom received a response to his ad from sixteen-year-old Larry, Tom gave him Red's phone number instead.

Larry and Red hooked up for a motel rendezvous. Red stripped the boy bare as, ironically, Mahler's fifth, the theme from the movie *Death in Venice*, played on the radio. The tall boy with the cherub face luxuriated naked on the bed in the glow of Red's admiration, the thatch of pubic hair and bold erection almost an afterthought to this glabrous, slender beauty.

"You are Tadzio!" Red exclaimed and stroked the kid's smooth young skin, as if admiring a delicate fabric or fine marble sculpture. But as Red's hand slid toward the pulsing stamen of boyhood, coy Larry snatched up the motel door hanger to cover his genitals and smile: "No Moleste."

Despite his disappointment, Red roared at the boy's cleverness. Larry was a whore with the heart of a prude. When he turned 17 and "moleste" was no longer an issue (17 was the age of consent in Texas), he fled his parents' home to live with Red, who held little hope for the future of this relationship.

He decided that Larry needed the company of other queer boys like himself and introduced him to the park scene. The transformation from shy teenager to flaming queen was instantaneous. Red had wondered what eagle might emerge from that shy shell, but he got a flamingo instead.

One night of many at the park that summer, Larry and his newfound queenie friends stopped by Red's townhouse just long enough to drop off a drunk companion. The reeling young man collapsed into a chair like a rag doll, and Red was none too pleased to be Larry's dumping ground, until he took a second look at the eighteen-year-old baby-face with big doe eyes and curly, sandy-blonde hair.

Darren was loquacious in his inebriation, and Red soon discovered he was bright and from a decent family. From his days with the runaways in Speed Beach, Red had learned to appreciate the value of intelligence and socio-eco status in a boy. The slow-witted and ill-educated were a lot more work with often meager return.

Larry went to the park every night, and he frequently returned with Darren in tow. Larry confided that Darren was hot for Red, and Darren always flirted, when Larry brought him over, but Red soon discovered the ploy: Darren was after Larry, but only pretended attraction to the older man as a diversion to break into their circle and make the boy jealous. The older man's predictable lechery provided an easy excuse for the boy to chase after Darren, which is usually what the boy wanted anyway.

Such was the ruthless game of hawks and chickens in the park, a dance of thinly veiled prostitution and betrayal. No doubt, this was why the whore with the heart of a prude enjoyed it so much and exactly why Red disdained it.

Instead of the anticipated lechery, Red confounded Darren's gambit with a surprise proposition: "You want him? Take him! He's yours!" No hawk had ever said that to him before! Darren gladly accepted the offer, and Larry was gone within the week.

Red was more interested in Darren than Larry, but this final turn of events made it clear that Darren was a boy lover like himself. Thus began that rarest of friendships, two boy lovers a generation apart.

A month later, Darren introduced to Red his younger friend, fourteen-year-old Mark, a middle-school footballer already taller than Red, talkative and playful and full of himself with grand ambitions. Mark was the myth of the popular, good-looking jock, and when the boy proposed, Red couldn't resist.

"You and me oughta be lovers," he eagerly declared. "We'll make our own friends with all the gays at the park. Everybody will say, 'That's Red and Mark. They're lovers.'"

"They'll all be after you. They already are."

"Is that a yes?"

"Sounds like fun," Red agreed, as he threw the boy's legs into the air and rimmed his pink athletic ass. So began their surreptitious affair that ended four years later in disaster.

The cops had long since shut down the park scene, but the ghosts of its cheerful vitality lingered, as Red drove by the baseball diamond. Jonathan cranked the radio and tuned it to classic rock'n'roll.

"Is that a station you like?" Red asked.

"Yeah, it's vintage—Zeppelin, Hendrix, Pink Floyd, Black Sabbath, Ozzie, yeah!"

"But last time, it was fifties and sixties."

"Fifties, sixties, seventies, eighties, nineties. If it rocks, I'm there!"

"Hey, I could use some good stuff like that. Why don'tcha program it in?" Red suggested and showed him how to program the radio. The boy reprogrammed every button on the dash.

"You have cool buttons now!" he declared.

"I gotta have cool buttons!" Red smiled and drove them to the other "Crossroads," the queer Crossroads of Oak Lawn, what Larry used to call "fag town."

"I live there." Red pointed out the modest row of townhouses. "Would you like to stop by?"

"Sure," he agreed.

Red turned the wheel sharply right into the bushes between two run-down bungalows. Jonathan gripped the armrest as they seemed to be turning into a bank of shrubbery, but kept his cool and sure enough, the foliage concealed an alleyway to the parking lot next to the red brick building.

Red smiled at the boy's obvious surprise. "I call it 'the bat cave,'" he said, as they climbed from the car, and Red led him along the cracked and broken walkway to his front door. "I've lived here for fifteen years. I like living in a neighborhood where you can walk to the grocery store and the post office. You're welcome to visit anytime. Like the Mexicans say, 'Mi casa, su casa.'" He invited him in.

On the outside, the place was a bit run-down, Jonathan noticed. The gate was broken, and there were cracks in the wall, and everything was growing wild. "I thought he was rich," the boy thought, but inside it was nice and strange. A weird curvy chair sat in the middle of the room next to a coffee table that looked like a sleigh and a futon sofa. The walls were decorated with big photographs Red had taken of all the places he'd been, except for a painting over the fireplace of naked women in a yellow forest. On the mantle were little carved clay soldiers. "One of 'em looks like he's givin' the other one a blowjob!" Jonathan thought and almost laughed out loud, but he was afraid Red would think he was weird.

Red explained they were from China, replicas of an army of life-size clay statues that were buried in the tomb of an emperor. It sounded crazy.

Behind the futon hung a poster for a movie called *Rocky Horror Picture Show,* showing a man in high heels and net stockings.

"So many strange things!" he marveled to himself. Red's whole house was like a work of art. He put up the stuff he liked for everyone to see. "That's what I wanta do," the boy thought, "I wish I had my own room, so I could put stuff up on my wall, just like Red's, crazy and weird, whatever I like."

Red popped a few sodas, and they sat on the futon sofa as Red explicated the naked women in the forest.

"It's a painting by a French artist named Henri Matisse from the early part of this century. The name of the painting is *Bonheur de Vivre,* which means 'the joy of life.' It depicts an array of subjects, mostly feminine or of ambiguous gender except for the boy with the pipes, a traditional figure of pastoral romanticism and classical passion, combined in a modern way, cheerful, energetic, seductive, provocative. This is just a print, of course. The real piece is much bigger, about six times that size.

"The influence of Matisse on twentieth century art has been enormous," he continued. "I could walk through any shopping mall in America today and show you fabrics, wallpaper, T-shirts, posters, advertising all based on his designs. Any questions?"

"What's 'provocative' mean?"

"It provokes a response. It challenges the viewer to examine these images within himself."

"And how do you respond to the challenge?"

"Everything I just said."

"No, how do *you* respond to the challenge within yourself?"

The kid was tough. "I *am* the *Bonheur de Vivre.* That's why it's up there. It expresses my life and my perspective, and thank you for asking, you little fuck!"

He glanced around the room. "That's a funny looking chair."

"It's a piece of art. The artist carved it with a chain saw from a single block of pine. His signature is on the bottom."

"I've never seen anything like that."

"There isn't anything like it. That's what makes it art. You're an artist. Being unusual and unique is what artists do."

"Yeah, a sorcerer, like you said."

"That's right," Red gazed deep into the blue sunrise of the beloved's eyes. "There's something else you should know. I'm on your side, Jonathan. I'm your secret weapon."

"Whatd'ya mean by that?"

"I'm the friend you can tell the things you can't to anyone else. When you're here with me, it's a safe place. It's a pleasure for me to hear your thoughts and feelings, and I will listen without judgment or even advice, unless you ask for it, and anything you say will never be repeated by me, even back to you, unless you give me permission. Another word is 'protégé.' As I am your mentor, you are my protégé"

"Is that like a best friend?"

"You could say that. It means 'protected one.'" Red closed his arm around the boy's narrow bony shoulders, breathing in his fresh-air fragrance. With a casual hug, Red received the vibration of the boy, the slight, immature frame of a child, Jonathan's frame.

Red released him and sprang to his feet. "How about some music?"

"Yeah!" Jonathan grinned, energized and happy. He played his Marilyn Manson CD, as they finished their sodas.

Red drove Jonathan back to the dollhouse, where the sun was setting behind the Sony Multiplex. Along the way, he announced, "I won't be seeing you for several weeks. I'm visiting a friend in California. That's why we had to finish up our story today, to get it in before I leave. My friend teaches at Stanford University. Ever hear of it?" He hadn't. "It's a fancy private university outside of San Francisco. Bill Clinton's daughter goes there. Maybe you will, too, someday. I'll bring you a T-shirt."

"So what's next, now that the program is drawing to a close?" Malcolm queried, as they waited at the gate.

"Good question. There will be a banquet at the end of the year when the magazine is published. After that, my institutional opportunities will be limited. I hope I can teach him again next year, but I have to start creating my own reasons to continue our association."

"Like souvenirs from Stanford?"

"And you call me 'Vampyra'! Hah! You're Vampyra's mother-in-law! Last December, I was asking myself 'Should I pursue this?' Now I'm asking,

'How can I keep it going?'"

"And turn your short story into an epic?"

"You know me too well!"

"You're way ahead of your time, Red. I hope you know that. You're going to blow their shit away."

"Theo taught me well."

"Forget Theo! He was a mess. This is you. It's Dionysian. It's dangerous. It's not just literary; it's revolutionary. It's the kind of writing that scares hell out of people."

"That's the problem. It scares publishers, too. They're afraid to touch it."

"I know it hasn't been easy for you, but I hope you keep at it. You are the most cutting-edge writer in America today. Nothing I've read even comes close to what you're doing, certainly no writer in this country."

"Thank you, Malcolm. You've always been a good friend."

"I also mean it."

The doors to the jetway opened, and the two friends said their farewells.

On the plane back to Dallas, Red sadly confronted in his mind the return to Faye, the office piranha, and the Coalition. Only Jonathan held out hope and promise for the days to come. Red's uncertainty how to proceed fell away like the clouds below. His path shone bright and clear like the deepening dark blue sky above. Boy and book were the same. To pursue the one was to pursue the other.

6

The plane landed late, a pleasant, cool spring night. Arriving home, Red poured a vodka tonic in a red plastic cup and walked the lawn to The Crossroads.

"Walkin' the Lawn, Walkin' the Lawn!" a la Judas Priest and *Beavis 'n' Butthead*, "Breakin' the law! Breakin' the law!" Red's nightly walking tour of the neighborhood. So regular were his evening rounds, he was known among the street people as "the man with the red cup."

"The Crossroads." The throbbing heart of the gay ghetto in Dallas (though some might suggest another organ) got its name when a disco, the Village Station, opened across from a popular "s&m" ("standing and modeling") bar appropriately named "JR's," after the leading man in the popular TV series *Dallas*. It was 1980, and disco was still king along with the lamé fans, poppers, and queens shouting "hoo-hoo-hoo" on the dance floor, the golden age of gay, before the Black Death.

Red met Michael there that year, his lanky seventeen-year-old cowboy, standing so close to the giant disco speakers that his bones vibrated to the beat. In boots and Stetson with a dip in his lip, Michael was taller than Red with the cheerful smile of a big bright Texas boy. This was his first time alone in the gay scene, so no accident that his first contact should be a boy lover.

Red quickly discovered that Michael only dressed like a roper. The Village Station was no kicker bar, after all. Michael loved disco, the louder the better, and for the next four years, they danced the night away, until the young man's graduation from college. Now, eighteen years later, Michael was the age Red had been when they first met, and had traded his Western wear for leather. "Just when you think you know what you have got, it's what they're not." The boy grows up.

Now, the Village Station was relocated down the street, replaced by a coffee shop with big glass windows like a fishbowl full of queens. Red slowed down to check it out. A police patrol car drove by suspiciously eyeing Red's red roadie. Open containers of alcohol were legal on the sidewalks of Oak Lawn. But assuming the cops would be ill-informed of the law, Red had researched the city's ordinance and memorized its borders, in case called upon to recite them. Once, on New Year's Day, a cop told him to pour out a champagne flute—on New Year's Day, for chrissakes! Red complied, knowing the cop was in the wrong. It wasn't the champagne. It was the flute that caught the cop's eye. Ninety percent of what passed for justice in society was appearances. The police state was here and now. Everyone Red knew was either a lawyer, involved in a lawsuit, or under indictment. Half his clients were lawyers. They knew this dirty little secret of justice. That's why they hired PR firms.

Red spied the patrol car from the corner of his eye but continued to scan the boys and queens inside and out of the coffee shop. A young man at one of the tables inside, lean with a few days' growth of beard and shoulder-length blonde hair cascading over the grimy collar of his trench coat Kurt Colbain style, puffed nervously on a fag. At the counter, the old pederast who looked like Frankenstein, a former DJ (a lot of DJ's were boy-lovers; it was the perfect setup), pretended to read a newspaper, while he cruised the chicken who wandered in. Unlike the bars, kids were welcome at the coffee shop, so the place had become like the park used to be, a gathering spot for youngsters and therefore hawks and finally young hustlers like our jittery Kurt Colbain.

At The Crossroads, Red leaned against the wall to watch the people in their cars as they drove by. There were three types: the preoccupied, the cruisers, and the gawkers. The preoccupied had more important things on their minds and paid no attention at all to where they were. The cruisers checked out the scene for present and future friends. The gawkers gawked at fagtown with salacious curiosity or self-righteous disapproval or both, until they discovered someone gawking back at them and quickly looked away, pretending not to notice, pretending they hadn't been caught. The gawkers were Red's prey.

Red was startled from his reverie by the sound of a fist slammed against the fishbowl window of the coffee shop. He turned in time to observe the fiery young stud blow out the coffee shop doors, the flaps of his coat fluttering, as if he might literally become airborne and fly over the rent-a-cops, who were now converging on the corner at a full run. Blondie ran, too, but they were coming from both directions. He didn't stand a chance. They surrounded him, billy clubs drawn, slapped the cuffs on him, and hauled him off to their car.

"Law and ardor, the story of my life," Red said to himself with a smile. Walkin' the Lawn, Walkin' the Lawn.

The following day, Red showed up at the office to find the Coalition waiting. An all-day powwow was being convened downtown at the Adolphus Hotel, where representatives from various charities made their presentations. The PR guy was mandated to attend. Red sat among them at the banquet-size table in the middle of a ballroom, surrounded by floor-to-ceiling mirrors like the fucking palace at Versailles. Liveried attendants served lunch, and at the end of the day, the Coalition members and their PR agent enjoyed an open bar and sit-down dinner. This was how the right-wing discussed the needs of the poor.

It was late before Red finally made his escape. Tired, tipsy, and sick of the day's unctuous egos, he collapsed into his office chair and checked his e-mail.

Dear R^2:

I just read your story *The Moralist* and loved it. It's absolutely wonderful! It will be in our next issue of *Pan*. As we have no distribution in Texas, I will send you several copies by mail. —Hawk

He rocked back in his chair and laughed at the irony of this day. "My life, my love, my art are my contribution to the boy love cause," he thought. "Ya talk about hard work, perseverance, and dedication! I am the living expression of the American ethic! Thank you, Walt! Thank you, Ralph! Thank you, Henry!"

Red pulled the Mustang up to the curb in front of the dollhouse. The place looked deserted, but he had just spoken to Jonathan on the phone only fifteen minutes earlier. When he mentioned souvenirs, the boy wanted to see them right away. As usual, the door was hanging half-open. Red poked his head through the crack and called for Jonathan, who instantly appeared holding a finger to his lips, as Red stepped inside.

"Shhh . . . we have to be quiet. Mom's asleep in the back."

The boy led them to the little living room and eagerly snatched the bag from Red's hands. Red sat on the threadbare sofa and marveled at how the late afternoon sun pouring through the window seemed to set Jonathan's strawberry hair afire. The boy peeled away his stained and torn T-shirt, and for the first time, Red viewed the pale, skinny torso. The answer to Darren's question: His tits were flat and so pale pink they were barely visible. The magic of puberty was not yet upon him. Lit by a beam of golden sunlight, his white form glowed like a marble statue, a little Cupid or Priapus. Red longed to run the sensitive tips of his fingers over the smooth surface of this living sculpture, but even that adoring touch was forbidden.

Melanie appeared at the doorway, rubbing her eyes, surprised to see Red alone with her son stripped to the waist.

Red looked up, "Hi, Melanie! Did you have a nice nap?"

She nodded and lumbered toward an overstuffed chair. Even after napping, she seemed exhausted with dark circles under drooping eyelids.

Wiggling into the bright, red-and-white T-shirt emblazoned with the name "Stanford," Jonathan exclaimed, "Look what Red brought me from California, Mom!"

"That's nice," she wearily acknowledged. "Is that Stanford University?"

"Yes, just south of San Francisco. My friend Malcolm teaches there. Maybe Jonathan will go to Stanford. He's got the intelligence and talent for it, although frankly, now, it's more for the Silicon Valley engineers and technocrats than artists."

"Yes, Jonathan is the artist in the family," she agreed, perking up at the implied praise of her son. "At his birthday party, you said 'artists are sorcerers.' What did you mean by that?" Like her son, she had a knack for the pointed question, probably where he learned it.

"Everyone knows that the artist plays with imagination, but what is not so widely understood is that the world of imagination is also the world of myth and magic, image-making, myth-making. The artist is shaman, because he creates and defines our myths."

"Is that what you do?"

"In my art, yes. I've just started work on a novel."

"A novel!" her eyes widened with interest. "What's it about?"

"It's an autobiographical overview of the main character's moral perspective. I call it *The Moralist*." He didn't say it was based on his relationship with her son. He didn't have to.

"Autobiographical? That means it's your own story."

"Told as fiction, yes."

"Am I in it?" Jonathan popped the million-dollar question.

"Yes, your character plays a very important role."

"What role is that?"

"The student. The story is about a teacher and his creative writing student. Teaching Jonathan to tell his story inspired me to tell my own," he explained, revealing way too much.

"But you don't use his real name?" she asked with a tone of concern.

"No, it's fiction. The characters and events are based on a lot of different people and things I've experienced."

"What's my name in the book?" Jonathan eagerly pressed the issue.

"The character's name is 'David.'"

"David instead of Jonathan. I see," his Bible-readin' momma figured it out. "And what do you call yourself?"

"Red Ryder."

"Like your own name."

"Yes, but based on an old comic book character, a Lone Ranger knock-off with a red mask and a cape. The name is also a pun on the word 'writer.'"

"Is that your pseudonym?"

"No, that I don't change. The name of the author is real."

"Then why change it at all? Why not make it a real autobiography?"

"The names are changed to protect the innocent," he quoted the old TV detective show *Dragnet* and wondered if she got the reference.   She didn't.

"And the guilty?" she added wryly.

Red laughed, "Especially them!"

"We have to write an autobiography for Mind Quest!" Jonathan interrupted her interrogation.

"Really? I studied autobiography at Harbour," Red was relieved to change the subject.

"Harbour University? You went there?" She was impressed.

"My alma mater is Emery in Atlanta, but when I was living in New England, I studied autobiography at Harbour with one of the world's leading scholars of the genre." Harvey Sylvan was a lively olive-skinned Jamaican man, who was fascinated by the excerpts from *Seeing Red* that Red submitted for the class but concluded they didn't qualify as autobiography, because they were written in the third person and the names were changed. "Maybe I can give Jonathan some pointers." How to keep it going.

"Like what?" Jonathan insisted.

"For one thing, you should think of the story as not simply a chronicle of events in your life, but a mirror of who you are. Autobiography is different from a memoir. Autobiography reveals the self of the writer. Every character and everything that happens should be written as a reflection of the author, that is, you. What have you written so far?"

"I haven't started it yet."

"You said you were keeping a journal. You can start with that as the raw material. Start with some core quality about yourself. Empathy, for example. Pick out all the events of your life that illustrate your feelings of empathy and how they have influenced your life and your development. That's autobiography. And as we discussed in our writing sessions, if you want to protect someone's privacy, even your own, you can change the names and fictionalize the story."

Melanie chuckled, "Oh, my, Red! If he takes your advice, there's no telling what he might write!"

"But then it wouldn't be an autobiography," Jonathan corrected.

"Yes, you're right. My professor at Harbour said the very same thing. The action the story describes must have actually taken place. Otherwise it's autobiographical fiction, like my novel, or a kind of poetry."

"I wrote a poem, too!"

"Can I see it?"

"Sure!" He ran into the back leaving Melanie and Red alone together.

"Your novel sounds interesting," she began. "Moral issues are so important these days. What church do you go to?"

The big question. Red marveled at the ingenuousness of this personal and presumptuous inquiry but understood full well the imperative of giving the right answer. How he responded would determine his entire future with her son.

"I don't go to church," he replied. "I'm not a Christian. My spiritual perspective is more along the lines of Yogic mysticism, although I do believe that the teachings of Jesus and the Christian message of love are compatible with that."

"Do you believe in God?"

"Consciousness of being is God to me, so to ask if I believe in God is like asking if I exist, and of all the possible doubt that can be raised, that is the one fact I can be absolutely certain of. I do believe that I exist. Does that answer your question?"

"It sounds like you think you are God," she queried further.

"Whether you worship God or discover yourself as God is a fundamental difference between Western and Eastern thought. Christianity allows for both points of view. The New Testament announces that we are all the *novus homo*. But that can be scary for most people, so instead they opt for worshiping Jesus instead of becoming him. The Yogic perspective is that we are all God. We just forgot. If that's so, the experience of life itself is divine. In the abstract, the choice of how to be sounds too obviously simple: enlightenment over ignorance, self-realization over self-delusion, kindness over meanness. But in a world where ignorance, self-delusion, and meanness rule, it's the hardest choice of all, a choice that can get you nailed to a cross, as Jesus clearly demonstrated."

"Do you believe in reincarnation?"

"Yes, but once again, not like most people think. The Yogis say we go through ten thousand lifetimes before attaining enlightenment, but I don't think that means a case of a single ego playing a series of different roles. It's more recombinant than that. Aspects of this or that self from one life recombine to create new versions, new stories, more like a family tree than an individual career. It's the spiritual version of what happens to us in life, except instead of the individual physical characteristics that each of us is born with or develop—blue eyes, blonde hair, short or tall—the characteristics of our spiritual self are moral, degrees of understanding and empathy determined by the will to become itself. At any given moment, we are each a facet of the whole. We sparkle with the light of consciousness, and then we're dark. We rearrange ourselves. The light hits us again, and we sparkle in different poses. My metaphor for the spiritual life sounds like a disco dance floor!" he exclaimed with laughter, then added seriously, "So which is the Truth? Which is God? The dancer or the spotlight? Or both? The dancer becomes the light. Everyone thinks that if you believe in God, it gives you an instant purpose in life, but what if God were just as aimless as the rest of us, and the whole process of existence were its own meaning? Cosmic pointlessness, divine art." He grinned his Cheshire cat grin.

"It sometimes seems that way," she smiled wanly, or was it ennui, a version of Jonathan's ironic smirk. Again, he saw the connection between the boy and his mother. She was intrigued by Red's mixture of profundity and self-deprecating wit. Her son's mentor had apparently given considerable thought to all this, but at the same time, his touch was light and amusing.

"Is this what you write in your book?" she continued, her tone changing from probing to mild curiosity. Whatever impression he'd made, the inquisition was over.

"Not yet, but I will," he laughed.

"I hope I'll get to read it someday."

"I have to finish it first, and I've only just started."

Jonathan bounded back into the room, handing Red a sheet of blue-ruled paper with a poem neatly printed out on the lines, the title in caps *DO I NEED YOU?* "Here's a poem I wrote for you, Red," he grinned.

"Do I Need You?" Red read the title out loud. "Is the answer yes?"

"Read it first, then decide," he retorted smartly.

"Right now?" Red started to read it aloud.

"No, not out loud!" he protested.

"Why not? Don't you think your mom would like to hear it, too?"

"She's already seen it."

"Jonathan shows me everything he writes," she smiled with all the pride and smugness of a mother.

Darren brought over his latest young thing, also named Jonathan, to show him off and for Red's approval. The boy was tall, blond, and cute at first glance with pretty blue eyes and cherry lips and clear, soft skin like fresh cream, which Darren assured extended to the rest of him as well. On closer examination, his profile was birdlike with a beak nose and weak chin.

Red observed that neither of their boys had given way to "Jack," or "John," or "Johnny," so their conversation would have to reference "my Jonathan" and "your Jonathan." For his part, Red resolved the issue with "Thing."

They walked the Lawn amid the usual array of queers and bars. The night was brisk and fresh. Red loved the cool early spring in Texas. Thing's level of conversation barely climbed above admiring not the people but the cars.

Dallas and its cars! Nobody drove a bad car in Dallas. The poorest Dallasite would suffer eviction from his home before giving up his ride, and

"I told you that last night."

"No, I wouldn't forget that little tidbit. You were holding back."

"How old did you think he was?"

"Seventeen, eighteen. Remember Mark. He looked sixteen at age thirteen. Legal, illegal? It's so fucking arbitrary. I didn't ask, because I didn't want to know."

"Okay, I wanted you to meet him first. He's completely out. His parents know he's gay."

"How could they not know?"

"Exactly."

"Do they know about you?"

"Not yet, but he wants to introduce me."

"Wait till his next birthday."

"He doesn't want to."

"He's trying to rope you in."

"No, his parents accept him. He wants to introduce his boyfriend the same as he'd introduce a girlfriend."

"A courageous sentiment, but you're ten years older than he is, and that makes a difference. When Michael and I were lovers, he once refused to attend Thanksgiving dinner with his family, unless I was invited. So they gave in and invited me, and I shared the holiday dinner with his family. Michael had balls, and I admired him for that, but he was seventeen, legal in Texas, just barely, but barely makes all the difference."

"We've had the talk. He knows the rules."

"And he can use them against you. You warned me about my Jonathan, so now I will warn you about yours. Be aware of the commitment you are making, the commitment you have already made. If you are introduced to his parents as the lover of their teenage son, that very act makes you more married to him than marriage itself."

"I know, and it terrifies me. I'm starting to understand what you went through with Mark."

"I wouldn't be so sure about that money, either. Davy Jones is about to go into chapter eleven. He came to us to handle the publicity angle."

Next stop for the Coalition: Savannah, Georgia. On the plane, Red read a story in *The New Yorker* about a fifteen-year-old rock star from Texas, who reminded him of Jonathan. The youngster was packaged and polished by a big-time New York promoter. The man had lived with the boy and his parents at their home for several months, while they worked on songs for his first CD. In the article, the boy's dad described the relationship as "a platonic love affair with my son."

"Musta never read Plato," Red thought. Ironic "platonic." For most, it meant exactly the opposite of its pederastic origins.

Malcolm had once called Red's love for boys the "lost boy syndrome." "How much of your attraction to boys is a desire to be that age again?" Malcolm had shrewdly asked.

Red had replied that it wasn't so much wanting "to be that age," a psychological regression, as wanting to be the boy himself. That was the terrible frustration of it. He could never actually be the boy, no more than the hero-worshiping youth could become his hero.

His heart deflated at the terrible reality of this absurd notion, and a black wave of despair washed over him. The only solution was to be nothing. Only by being nothing could he escape the prison of ego, see the Truth, and live forever. But without the mask of ego, nothingness became a black hole sucking itself away like a snake eating its tail. The Big O. With a heavy sigh, he dropped the magazine between his legs and sank back into his seat, as the plane began its descent.

Savannah was a living relic of the Old South, spared by Sherman's army in his march to the sea. The locals said it was the city's charm that saved it, but Red imagined Sherman was more practical than that. Why sack the last city standing? Then he'd have to sleep in a tent.

For Red, it was more than the city's charm that stirred him; it was the deep memories of mint juleps on the veranda and drunken sex beneath the Union Jack on the bedroom wall of his college fraternity brother Scot, thirty years ago. Blonde, cool, anglophile Scot had been his first real blushing, can't-sleep-at-night love, eight years before he met Theo, and Red wasn't ready for it. He didn't want to be queer. What a laugh that was now! So they parted ways at graduation.

Red instructed the cabby to drive by the old place nestled among the moss-hung trees, but he didn't go in. The last he'd heard, Scot was teaching English at UGA in Athens. He wondered if Scot's dad were still alive, if Scot had held onto the place, who was behind those walls now. Was that Union Jack still hanging? He wept at the poignant memory of those days irretrievably lost, except in memory.

Savannah, too, had changed. Its mixture of Old South grace and decadence had been made famous by a best-selling novel and movie based on an actual local murder and scandal, transforming the city into the latest Disney-style attraction.

Tourists craned from the windows of tour buses that blared from their tinny PAs: "This is the house where. . . On your left is the famous cemetery. . . We are now in the gay district. Notice the homosexuals nonchalantly holding hands as they gaily stroll the promenade."

Were the gaily-strolling homosexuals hired by the tour guide? They should have been. The bus could only show places, not the colorful grotesques from the movie that the tourists really wanted to see but knew they would not, unless, like Disney, the city fathers hired actors to portray the characters acting out scenes from the movie as the bus drove by.

"I shoulda told the tour guides about this parade," Red smiled to himself as he tagged along the Coalition walking tour of the reclaimed inner city, where once guns and drugs had ruled, but now children played, thanks to the efforts of one 350-pound black preacher. Too obese to walk, Poppa Bacon cruised in his white convertible Caddy, leading his own grotesque procession of captive white conservatives on foot behind him through tree-canopied streets like a Vieux Carré funeral, slavery in reverse.

It was a perfect spring afternoon in the South, the breeze gently wafting the moss hanging from ancient oaks. Withers fellow Professor Frye held forth to his female colleague on the Coalition board, ignoring Red who walked with them. Red was just the PR guy, filling in for Faye and not completely trustworthy, not one of them, as she would have been.

"The moss is beautiful here. You know, the South is the only part of the country where it grows," he pontificated like a prelate from a Fielding novel.

"That's not exactly so," Red interjected. "I just came back from northern California, and there's lots of Spanish moss out there."

"Is that so?" Nose and eyebrows lifted in annoyance, as the pompous professor continued, "The moss looks nice, but it's actually a parasite that kills the tree."

"That's a common misconception," Red corrected him again. "Moss is an air plant. It lives off organic matter in the air, and the trees don't mind it at all.

Like my cab driver from the airport said, 'If the moss killed the trees, there wouldn't be no trees!'"

The lady laughed, but the professor saw his entry. "So your source of information is a cab driver."

"No, a botany professor at Stanford University. A couple of weeks ago, I took a tour of the Stanford botanical preserve. It was really beautiful up there in the hills overlooking the Pacific, moss-hung trees and all. I just asked the local cabby to see if he knew as much about Spanish moss as my Stanford botanist, and I am pleased to report that he did!" The lady twittered again, but Withers fellow Professor Frye was stewing. Red had made an enemy for life, not that he intended it, nor that he cared. He was fed up with this unctuous pedant and wasn't going to let his misinformation go uncorrected just because he was an academic. In short, Red loved every minute of it.

Later, at the hotel cocktail reception, Red chatted up the obese godfather of the ghetto, praising the polished manners of the young black boys who assisted him. (Hmm?) After the obligatory hallelujah choir performance, black faces in angel blue and white robes, Poppa Bacon stood up to thank the Coalition for their support and quoted Red on the value of teaching good manners to boys.

"Thank you, Jesus!" Red silently hosannaed. That little plug just bought him the Coalition. He was outsider no more, not that he gave a damn personally, but it would make Faye happy. His real thought was that the only person in the room doing anything important was the fat old con man himself, and he didn't come cheap. The Coalition welcomed him with polite condescension, elegant slumming, but Poppa Bacon knew where the groceries were and how to squeeze the bucks out of that rich Republican tit. Who's zoomin' whom?

After the reception, Red covered the waterfront, now a shopping mall, despoiled by the tawdry touch of capitalism like the French Quarter in New Orleans, Greenwich Village, The Embarcadero in San Francisco, and just about everywhere else in America that used to be cool. Only a few pockets of authenticity remained, either too rich or too hidden to get noticed.

He climbed ancient stone steps to a magic shop literally built into the wall of the levy, part of the mystique of this odd out-of-the-way place. Its shelves littered with "invisible dog" leashes, voodoo books, and fetishes, the quaint little shop was getting its cut of the book and movie hype. But beyond the tourist kitsch, it still offered real tricks for real magicians. Red purchased a set of cups-and-balls, the old shell game. Now, ya see it; now, ya don't.

7

Returning from Savannah, Red checked his messages:

"Mr. Rover, this is Mr. Moony. Volunteers with the Authors of Tomorrow are having a meeting this coming Tuesday night at 7:00 to discuss the banquet where this year's book will be released. I hope you can join us."

"Red, this is Darren. Call me right away as soon as you get this message. Things are happening. Call me."

"Hello, Richard. I'm back from Paris, still unattached, but I got some great pictures. Let's get together, and I'll tell you all about it."

"Brrt! Redrick-aaayyyy! This is Mark on the road, good buddy, calling you from North Carolina. I guess you're on the road, too. Later, dude."

"Hi, Red. We were lucky we made it to the Post Ranch Inn when we did. There was a travel article in *New York* magazine last week that featured our tree house."

Red returned Darren's call first and got the latest.

"He did it. He told his mother about me. He told her I was his lover." Darren's voice was weary. He was not happy with this.

"Were you present?"

"No, it was just between him and her."

"What did she say?"

"She was cool about it. She loves him."

"Have you met her?"

"No, that's the next step. He wants to bring me over."

"Are you going?"

"What choice do I have? And it's not just her. The whole family lives together, aunts and uncles and grandparents, a whole nest of 'em! I'm the new bride about to meet the family."

Malcolm's call was next.

"Now, the place will be overrun with New York yuppies," Malcolm began, referring to the *New York* magazine article. "They called it 'a hideaway for international wood nymphs in their Calvin Klein jeans.'"

"I was wearing my Calvin Kleins when we were there!"

"When you were wearing anything at all."

"Was I your wood nymph?"

"Oh, baby, you can be my wood nymph anytime!"

"When Darren saw my video tape of you in your terry robe, he said you looked like you were ready for sex."

"You showed it to him?"

"Of course! I sent you a copy. Haven't you looked at it?"

"I don't own a VCR, remember?"

"And I guess you didn't dare play it in the Humanities Center lounge."

"I don't trust you and that video camera of yours. That's a dangerous combination."

"I was doin' it before I met you twenty-five years ago with a Sony Portapack, video taping Theo's mad bits on the streets of Manhattan. In the seventies, if you had a video camera, everybody thought you worked for a television station. They would let you get away with anything. Like the time I taped Theo doing a tampon commercial in the women's room of a hair salon, pretending to stuff a tampon up his cunt with waves of pleasure." He mimicked Theo, "'Tampons! They're so much more fun than feminine napkins!' It was instant art!"

"I know that story. Don't forget, I'm one of the few people who has actually read *Seeing Red*. So how's the sequel coming?"

"The short story version is going to be published in a boy book called *PAN* next month. I'll send you a copy."

"To my home, please, not the school."

"It's not porno. It's a literary magazine. Alan Ginsberg used to write for it before he died. You oughta lay it out on the coffee table at the Humanities Center. No, better yet, sit there and read it! I dare you!"

"You love scandal."

"Honey, the last time we were the topic of scandal, you were the toast of the campus."

"So, what about your current scandal? Did you give him his souvenir yet?"

"Yes. I dropped by his house a couple of nights ago. His mom Melanie was there, and I got the big question."

"What's your interest in my son?"

"No. 'What church do you go to?'"

"Ah, the Bible Belt! And what was your answer? Did you tell her the truth?"

"Did I ever!"

"So now she thinks you're a heathen."

"No, I think I blew her shit away."

"Is that a pass?"

"I'm helping him write his autobiography."

"How? By helping him live it?"

"That, too, but now he has to write it down. It's an assignment for this creative program he's in."

"You certainly know the genre! His mom's not stupid."

"That's right. She knows a positive influence in her son's life when she sees one."

"Did he like the T-shirt?"

"Yes, he put it on immediately."

"You must have loved that."

"Almost as much as the gift he gave me in return, a poem. Hold on, I'll read it to you."

DO I NEED YOU?
By Jonathan Frame

> Do I need you?
> Are you my friend?
> Do you live in my dreams?
> Do you live in my heart?
> Do you wander my mind and make me believe in you?

The Moralist

> Do I need you?
> I wish I knew.
> When you're around, do I feel safe?
> Or is someone watching me? Grabbing me!
> Who's that? Did I hear something?
> Are you with me?
> In my heart, my dreams, my nightmares?
> DO I NEED YOU?
> Do you exist?
> I need an answer.
> So many questions and not enough answers.
> If only someone knew and understood
> Like you.

"Is it written to you?"

"He said it was 'for me.'"

"Close enough. Did you answer his questions?"

"Yes. I said, 'Yes, you do need me; yes, I am your friend; yes, I do live in your heart and dreams.'"

"What was his response?"

"He said that the poem isn't about me. It's about the clash between creative expression and a practical education. I told him that didn't change a thing."

"It's amazing, the nuance of what's going on between you! But he doesn't understand any of it, does he?"

"Who can say? I know he has an incisive emotional understanding. Whether he can put it into words is another story."

"It's hard to imagine what your life must be like. You live in a constant state of irony."

"That's the nature of boy-love. It's evanescent. You never quite know where you stand, one of the things I like most about it!"

"It's more than just the irony of youth and age. Your whole life is ironic: hobnobbing with Republicans, while you're carrying on a love affair with a twelve-year-old boy and writing a book about it. It's an irony of juxtaposition!"

"Boy lovers often lead double lives, usually out of fear. For my part, I'm sure someday those two trains will collide, but for now, I'll take irony over fear. Like you said, it's a constant state. Everything I touch turns to irony. I'm the King Midas of irony!"

E-mail

ALERT to all BLN! The following e-mails are a MUST READ! —BLN editor

To the BLN:

For the past three years, I have been pretending to be a boy lover in order to write a book about the boy love movement, and what I have found is criminal behavior that I cannot be a part of. I'm in touch with the police, and I will report to them what I know. —Billy D.

NOTE TO BLN:

Billy D has been LA's lover for several years and is a past member of the BL Steering Committee. Even then, there were those who questioned his loyalty. —BLN editor

To the BLN:

FUCK YOU, BILLY D!!!!!! You're just another con man. BLN members, I am not a police informant, but Billy D is. I knew nothing of his deception. He should be dropped from the BLN immediately! —LA

To the BLN:

LA has suggested Billy D be dropped from the network. I sympathize with his concerns about protecting children and the idea that we should work together. But I want to hear what others have to say and so am temporarily taking his address off the distribution list, so they can express their opinions. —BLN editor

To the BLN:

I appreciate your respect for democratic discussion, BLN, but this doesn't seem arguable to me. His original promise to go to the police is sufficient reason to take him off the list. Furthermore, I recommend we establish a new address for the list. There is too great a risk that the police will extract everything Billy D knows, including access to this list. We need to start a new network and each of us individually should change our addresses. —R²

To the BLN:

R² is right. We should take the necessary steps to protect ourselves as best we can. —Hawk

To the BLN:

All right. I will take Billy D's name off the distribution list permanently. But I'd like to wait and see what he does, before we change everything. —BLN editor

Reply to BLN editor from R²:

I'm not waiting. Please remove my name as well.

At the meeting of the mentors and sponsors of the Authors of Tomorrow, someone suggested asking a local bookstore to donate a gift of dictionaries to the kids. Red volunteered that the Mr. Shakespeare's chain was a client, this his chance to give Jonathan his own personal award. What mattered if all the other kids got one, too? Jonathan would know that Red had made it possible, and would receive the gift from Red's own hands.

Red had fully expected Penny not to return from France at all and so was surprised at her call inviting him over for cocktails. On a balmy night, they stood once again on Penny's aerie overlooking the city.

"Why did you come back? He didn't propose?"

"I didn't accept," she began proudly. "I know I told you he was romantic," she sighed, "but he wasn't the same as I remembered."

"So often the case."

"He took me to the finest restaurant in town with a beautiful view of the valley. Oh, Richard, it was lovely, not to mention that they treated us like the duke and duchess of Arles, which we practically were, since he employs half the town."

"Duke, duke, duke, duke of Arles," Red sang.

"But instead of expressing his undying love for me, he started outlining the business relationship between us, what he was offering and how it was to be structured."

"Europeans are like that about marriage. You should know that. They can be totally romantic and coldly practical in the same breath. Everyone thinks Americans are so materialistic. Hah! Americans are sentimental saps compared to the continent."

"Then I say 'fuck it!' That ain't the Texas way! That ain't the Penny way! Richard, he wasn't like that before."

"Eight years is a long time. Surely you expected some changes."

"Not that much! It broke my heart. I thought, 'Who is this person? Do I know this man?' He was not the same sweet guy who proposed to me the first time."

"So the moment has passed. Maybe he thought, because you rejected him the first time, the romantic approach was the wrong tack, that the money angle was more to the liking of a Dallas girl, like all the rest of your friends."

"Those friends are all miserable!"

"So you made the right choice. You didn't want to be the sad-eyed Duchess of Arles, Cézanne notwithstanding. "

"I guess not. I'm about to turn forty, Richard. That puts tremendous pressure on a woman."

"The old bio clock."

"And social pressure, too. I'm the only one in my class who isn't gay and hasn't been married. But I'm absolutely not going to marry a man who wants to own me as his property."

"Here! Here!"

"His nose was runny, and he kept excusing himself to go to the restroom. He said he had an allergy, but I think he was snorting coke."

"A drug addict to boot!"

"I don't know."

"Penny, you turn down two proposals a week. I've never seen anything like it. Why should this be any different?"

"I thought this would be the one. That's why I went there. I didn't even try on the ring. I started crying. All I could say was, 'I'm sorry, Alan. I'm sorry for taking up your time.' I took a cab to the chateau for my things and flew back to Paris that night."

Walkin' the Lawn

A frail, skinny man ahead slowly made his way down the sidewalk with a walker. "In his early thirties," Red thought, a living testimony to the devastation of AIDS. From the coffee shops to the restaurants and bookstores, curio shops, and bars, the festive air of greasy fried food, cigarette smoke, and alcohol smelled like a carnival midway. The man with the walker was the skeleton at the banquet. "Look on me and enjoy, for to this end you will come," cried this *memento mori* of The Crossroads.

Red used to donate money and food to the AIDS Center, until their leader joined the witch-hunt and condemned boy lovers in the press, so Red cut off his contributions. How's that for alienation! In its quest to join the tribe, the gay community made a blood sacrifice. The notion that somehow boy lovers were separate and different from gays was a lie invented by their enemies, but the gays embraced it nonetheless. 'Sacrifice your first-born,' the tribe demanded (for indeed boy lovers were the first-born of queer), 'and you can have your place at the table.' The gay community eagerly signed this deal with the devil in blood for their souls.

Desire, the Buddha observed, is the source of all suffering in life. Only the absence of desire could achieve the mystical nihilism of samadhi, the cosmic consciousness of the dead. Where was love in this equation? Could we love without desiring the object of our love? That was the distinction between "agape" and "romantic" love that Malcolm mentioned and Red did not make. The beloved's presence was required for adoration.

Thus, the lover desired the attention of the beloved. When the boy was not present, he reflected on their moments together, their sweet conversations, like precious gems, when wit, perspective, and personality came together, when love, trust, and simple enjoyment came together. Or else, he imagined moments to come with sanguine anticipation. All that we owned was our experience in the ever-present, and what more joyful experience than the presence of the beloved!

If we were the accident that science said we were, just ants on a mound, even the grandest among us inconsequential, then all was indeed vanity and the matter of ethics superfluous, good and evil nothing more than constructs of society to maintain order. Ethics was the hardwired, zillion-year-old evolved need for social organization. Physics had made that clear enough.

But science paled when it held up the mirror to itself and asked what is this, how do I explain this, how do I account for the harder truth that I must be present to experience the world? No one knew anything without including consciousness in the equation, a fundamental of the scientific method itself, the so-called "objective observer." It was a truism so obvious that we overlooked its importance. Our existence had a built-in limit. All that we knew or thought we knew was confined to the consciousness of each one of us individually. But for the certainty of that experience, all else was subject to doubt.

This fundamental truth split our condition in two. We were both absurd and profound at the same time. Absurd because we could never go outside that limit, so that our entire experience of life became an exercise in uncertainty and speculation. Profound because it raised the on-going moment of consciousness to the highest level of importance. We could never know the truth, as the experience of truth unfolded before us. "Even *that* is a kind of truth," Red allowed, which also made it suspect.

When the observer became the object of observation, science pompously pronounced, "Well, we've given it a good hard look and our final answer is: neuron firings. The experience of life is neuron firings."

All that we knew, even our idea that we exist, even science itself were neuron firings, at which point the phrase imploded and became meaningless. Consciousness was not so easily nailed. There was still the epistemological question: How do you know? And the answer was always the same: You don't. You can't. All we really knew without question was that we exist.

Science would forever seek to cast this final net over consciousness without success. Because the episteme depended on consciousness as its source, consciousness would always be larger than knowledge.

The dead had consciousness without love and its natural child desire. Love and desire were the wellspring of life. Consciousness and love were the father and mother of ethics. The moral challenge came from the heart. The moralist was a lover.

The cant of morality defined it as an abstraction imposed by parents and society, the channeled Id, the internalized external, this the 20th century gloss to the 19th century notion of the animal child that had to be tamed by society, deified by Freud in the Id-Ego-Superego trilogy. Hamlet says that conscience makes cowards of us all, but in league with the daemon of self, conscience was the source of our strength. Only ego remained as the socialized mask, the real coward, but, of course, our egos would never admit that.

The Moralist

Conscience made heroes of us all. Conscience was the self beyond the chaos of time and space. It told our passions what to do. Our reasoned choice was a second-generation copy of desire, just as desire in turn was the choice of "conscienceness." We were the agents of choices already made.

We were all moralists, like it or not, and it had nothing to do with what we told ourselves and others but everything to do with our passion that defined good, beauty, and truth for each of us. That on-going choice was our true morality.

To the so-called devout, the moralist was a monster who held up the mirror to their invisibility. His passion withered their righteousness like the sun on a vampire. Say not that you have no moral point of view. You would not be able to get out of bed in the morning.

Red was a soldier, and, like soldiers everywhere, he waited and played cards and cleaned his gun until the call to arms, and he rushed from his indolent routine into deadly battle.

His was a crude and ugly time. It was sad to see how grotesque we had become in our notions of masculinity and love. For example, the schmuck on the TV commercial who was relieved to watch his TV sports instead of taking his wife to the ballet, because she had a headache, until it is miraculously cured by the sponsor's product. The myth of American masculinity, the TV consumer lie to our mythmaking mind. A real man would suffer the ballet, make her feel like a queen, and get the best fuck of his life. "Take me to the ballet" means "Take me to bed." But dummass doesn't get it! How straight was that?

Myth, not truth, drove the herd. When you've got 'em by the myth, their morality will follow. Change the manners, change the man. Change the myth, change mankind.

They will kill you for it. They always do. That's the price for changing myths.

Nonetheless, I love him unequivocally. I love his clear, open mind and generous heart. I want to share in his presence as often as I can. You want to know what wrong is? Wrong would be not doing it.

The literary demonic, like lava, oozed from the core, breaking out of the crust, a roiling froth of amorphous worms that renewed the land. Hiiideeho, Mr. Hanky! Mr. Turd! Come back, Shane! Come back, Little Siva!

Returning from the liquor store with a fresh bottle of vodka, Red passed the AIDS man again, this time face to face. For him to cover barely two blocks, Red had walked ten. It felt good to have strong legs and a strong heart! What good were opinions! When you're dead, you don't have any opinions. Like Kramer on *Seinfeld* says, "Don't argue with the body. It's a losing battle."

Red stepped around a dead mockingbird, smashed and dried on the concrete. Living mockingbirds fluttered in the trees above, springtime nookie goin' on!

Red smiled and wished the AIDS man, "Good evening." Walkin' the Lawn. Walkin' the Lawn.

8

The Coalition was cranking up again. They commissioned a poll to take the temperature of American attitudes toward charities, a.k.a., a "push poll," where the questions are written to elicit a desired response. A bogus poll conducted by a bogus organization to achieve a bogus result, and surprise surprise, the results supported their phony agenda. Only one problem: While they were traveling around the country to resorts and fancy hotels studying homelessness, unemployment, illiteracy, and drugs, the Clinton administration was self-destructing with a sex scandal. It was a dream come true for these rabid conservatives whose hatred for their President was nothing short of venomous but ironically a nightmare for the Coalition. Clinton's bad behavior sucked all the air out of the room. As long as presidential sex was in the headlines, the Coalition couldn't get ink from an octopus.

"I still have Tommy DeKalb," Red thought. "That oughta be worth something."

As soon as the poll results were announced, he worked the phones for an entire day, finally landing a spot on Sunday's *Noon Edition* opposite Jesse Jackson. Alas, in contrast to Jesse's purple poetry, poor Tommy was as vanilla as ever. He was going nowhere. Faye must have known. She just wanted to keep her hand in national politics. That's why she took this gig, that and the money.

At least, Red got *Noon Edition*. No matter what else happened, and little else did, he had that in his pocket. The press was not fooled. They scoffed at the Coalition's "transparent right-wing agenda." Red didn't disagree. They could blame the President's sex life for pushing the Coalition off the front pages, but someone's head was going to roll for the press indifference, probably Deborah. He felt sorry that she would take the bullet. Thank God for *Noon Edition*!

The phone rang. Red picked up.

"Hello, Red?" Jonathan's sweet voice, shy on the phone.

"Hey, buddy!" Red answered jovially, barely concealing his joy at USIP#2.

"I finished my autobiography."

"You want me to look at it?"

"Yeah, if you want to."

"I'd love to! Should I come over right now?"

"You can come over right now!" he declared with a giggle as the shyness vanished.

"You're sure it's okay with your mom and dad?"

"They aren't here. They all went over to Aunt Susan's."

"And left you alone?"

"I didn't wanta go. I wanta see you."

"I'll be right over."

As soon as Red walked through the dollhouse doorway, Jonathan shoved the little book in his hand. The pages were laid out and stapled into a booklet form with the boy's artless drawings pasted in. Red flipped through the almost twenty pages.

"It looks like you've already finished and published it. I thought we were going to work on it together."

"I had to get it done. It was due on Monday." Red handed it back to him. The boy was stunned and hurt. "Don't you want to read it?"

"I want you to read it to me. I brought my tape recorder. We'll make a tape of it." Red produced a mini-recorder from his pocket and set it on the cluttered coffee table. Jonathan sat in the toy red chair beneath a lamp, his orange hair aglow like a halo, and read.

JONATHAN'S AUTOBIOGRAPHY
(decorated with graphic daisies)

My mother started having labor pains at 5:00 a.m. By 10:00 a.m. I slid into the midwife's hands. My dad cut the umbilical cord with a scissors. He said he never knew it was so tough. Then my mother and I took a bath together in a giant tub filled

The Moralist

with floating sticks and leaves. The midwife said they were medicinal herbs. I was a big baby boy, 10 lbs. and 18 inches long with blue eyes and red hair. They named me Jonathan Barber Frame. Barber is my mother's maiden name. That was on December 24, 1985.

My mom says I spoke my first words when I was 3 months old. I heard her calling the cats, and I started saying, "Here, kitty, kitty, kitty."

When I was two, I took apart her vacuum cleaner. My dad could never get it to work again.

Today is April 25, 1998. I am a 12-year-old sixth grader at Martin Luther King Learning Center. I stand 4 ft. 11 inches tall and weigh 84 pounds.

I enjoy riding bikes and doing magic tricks and playing bass guitar in my dad's band. On the weekends, I enjoy adding onto my tree house that I started building 2 years ago. Now it has 3 rooms and 2 stories and an elevator operated by ropes and pulleys.

My mom says everybody should have a boy like me. She says I'm kind, helpful, smart, and empathetic. That means I can see myself in other people's shoes. She also says I wiggle and fidget too much. But mostly she says, "I am happy that you were born, because you are the sweetest experience of my life."

When I was 7, me and my best friend Joey wanted to play baseball but we didn't have a ball, so we took a lime out of the refrigerator and used that. I threw the lime into the air and swung the bat. Suddenly everything seemed to change to slow motion. Then everything sped up. Smack! My bat bounced off Joey's mouth. Everything was silent for a moment. Then Joey started crying his head off. He was catching blood in his hand and a tooth fell from his mouth. I thought it was a chunk of fat at first, but it wasn't. It was a big tooth. I was sad. I felt empathetic, like I was in Joey's shoes.

My dad and I have a very good relationship. One day we were sitting on the porch talking about bands. He plays in a band called *Tarzan's Boy*. He told me he could teach me how to play the bass guitar. I was overjoyed, but I didn't have a bass guitar. That didn't stop us. He taught me on his semi-acoustic guitar. By my next birthday, I had a Fenders 4 string bass with hot precision pickups.

Now I sometimes play with my dad's band in Deep Ellum where they let me in. Maybe, we'll get noticed someday and become major rock stars! We've got a good sound. I would love that.

I have many achievements. In fourth and fifth grade I had "A" honor roll all year, and I was student of the year in fifth grade. Student of the year has the best academic skills. This year, I am in Mind Quest and the Authors of Tomorrow. I have written a short story that will be published in a book soon. My writing mentor Mr. Rover says I have a good chance to win the Top Story prize. I hope I do. I am very, very proud of these achievements and so are my parents and teachers.

There are four people in my family. There is me, my dad, my mom, and my older sister Angie, age 13. My dad is a carpenter and a musician. My mom is a part-time schoolteacher. They both graduated from college and are very smart.

So far, my life has been okay, not so bad and not so great, because we don't live in a very nice house, and my parents' jobs are barely keeping us on our feet. But our family is very close and loving, and I never feel alone or left out.

I am good at biking, doing magic tricks, playing the guitar, and building tree houses. On my bike, I can jump ramps, do the bunny hop, and ride on pegs with one wheel. One of my worst times was when I was riding my bike and ran into a fence and cut my head open. I was dizzy and couldn't walk straight. They had to keep me in the hospital overnight to make sure my brain didn't swell up, but it was okay.

The Moralist

On a scale from 1 to 10 with 1 being the worst and 10 being the best I would rate my home life an 8. It would be a 10, if my dad's band got a gig, and my mom could teach full-time, so we could live in a nicer house. But my dad is working steady now as a carpenter, and he's been looking at houses. He said he's got his eye on one, if he can get a good deal on it.

I rate my success in school a 9. It would be 10 if I could make A's in science instead of B's. I rate my ability to be a good friend a 10. I don't lie to my friends and I don't abandon them. I don't think I could be a better friend.

I do my best thinking when I am practicing my guitar. I just sit down and play some chords and daydream.

I had fun writing my autobiography most of the time, but sometimes it's hard to write about things that are painful, because when you think about them, you feel the pain all over again.

The End

"It's honest and authentic," Red concluded. "I especially like how you use the story about Joey to illustrate your empathy for other people. Like I said before, that's the organizing principle of autobiography. The stories and the characters are all illustrations of the author's self."

"I made some of it up," he confessed.

Red smiled at the boy's reference to their earlier discussion, "Your secret is safe with me. What about the new house? Is that one of the made-up parts?" He knew Jonathan was embarrassed by the dollhouse.

"No, it's true!" he exclaimed. "It's nice, too. It's even got a swimming pool!"

"Sounds great!" Red's smile concealed the cascade of emotions. He was pleased that things were improving for Jonathan and his family, but terrified at what it might mean for himself, if they actually did move away. The end of the program? Another school? "Do you think your dad will get it?"

"He already did!"

Red's heart froze. No, the range of possibilities was too great. What did this boy know of the nuances of real estate and the many obstacles that lay before a struggling family trying to buy a home of their own? Even if Jon Sr.

had signed a contract, it didn't mean a done deal. Red inquired, his voice upbeat, "Where is it?"

"Mesquite. We'll be moving right after school's out."

This was serious. They were already planning the move. Mesquite was a kind of scrub tree that grows where nothing else will, and aptly named, the suburb of Mesquite was a barren wasteland on a prairie of asphalt and concrete worn by the weight of a million pickup trucks. Still, it was a substantial move up from the inner city.

Mesquite was also a solidly middle-class, redneck world that stood both physically and culturally on the opposite side of town from the Lawn, a thirty-minute drive away.

It was a drive Red would be happy to make every weekend, if allowed. He used to drive fifty miles to pick up Mark at the car wash in Cleburn, their prearranged meeting place, and return another fifty miles back to Dallas, sometimes just for a single day. Their love was forbidden, so they carried it off in secret. But in the end, things turned out badly with Mark. The dysfunction was built in.

Their secret affair itself was the social lie forced upon them. This was how society's opprobrium corrupted the boy-love relationship, so that it could then be held up as proof of its own corruption. To counter this cultural tautology, Red held up a love that was real and unyielding.

Was this the end game? Not only another school, but another school district. No chance for another year with the Authors of Tomorrow, and without it, there arose the question of why this older man sought the company of a boy nearly forty years his junior, especially in Mesquite.

"Isn't my love enough?" Red asked himself. Enough to get him hanged from the nearest tree. It all depended on Jon and Melanie. They trusted Red implicitly as their son's writing coach, but would they grow suspicious of Red's continued attention, driving twenty miles across town to see him? Would they accept him simply as mentor, friend, and lover? If they moved to this new house, Red would be truly on his own.

"I hope I get to see your new digs," he stated optimistically.

"Sure, we can go swimming this summer!" was the enthusiastic reply.

"Sounds like fun!" Red feigned delight, understanding that this invitation could also be the boy's farewell. Not that Jonathan wasn't sincere—he was too gollygeewow for guile—only that saying it didn't guarantee it would happen.

Red watched his soft, rosy lips form the words and imagined kissing them. The house was empty and Jonathan was at his most seductive—playful, shy, sincere. This could be their last time alone together, possibly forever.

Red seized the moment. "Let's do something. Let's go somewhere this weekend. Something fun. Rangers game, Six Flags. How about that new water park that just opened, Buccaneer Bay? How about that?"

"Cool!" the boy beamed.

"Bring a friend."

Darren called. "It's official. I met the family."

"You don't sound happy."

"It's a double-edged sword. They like me, but they're hopeless alcoholics. It's like a *Saturday Night Live* skit come to life! A bunch of screaming crazy drunks. You should've seen 'em last night. They don't all live in that one house like I thought. They just hang out there and drink. So when it comes time to go home, Jonathan's mom, who is totally blotto herself, says to her brother," Darren mimicked the slurring voice of a slobbering drunk, "'Now, you're okay to drive, aren'shoo? If you're not, you can shtay here.' And he's so drunk he can barely stand up, but he goes, 'Sure, sure, I'm fine.' And she says, 'Well, okay.' And off he goes into the night. It's this ritual they perform for each other like she's really concerned about his driving, and he's reassuring her. It's a joke, but it's not a joke to them. They really do believe it! That would make it even funnier, if it weren't so grim! It's their boozed-up version of being responsible."

"At least they like you."

"Yeah, they want me to drink with them, but Jonathan won't let me. He hates alcohol."

"Good for him."

"That's fine with me. I do not want to join that club."

"You already have, whether you drink or not."

"I know. That's what scares me."

"Alcoholics do crazy things sometimes, crazy and destructive and dangerous."

"I know too damn well from my own behavior! But, Red, you oughta see him with his clothes off. He has the most beautiful smooth young male body I have ever seen, not a hair on it except where it counts. He loves me to stroke him and love on him and then roll him over and fuck him as hot and hard as I can. He can't get enough of it, and neither can I. It is pure absolute ecstasy! That's what I don't understand about all that hairy macho queer bullshit. It's nasty. If you want the male at the peak of his sexuality, why not the most beautiful and the most perfect? Sixteen to eighteen, that's the best. Who wouldn't want that?"

"Sounds good to me!"

"He'll be legal in six months."

"Those six months are a lifetime."

"For him, yes, I suppose it is."

"I mean for you."

"It doesn't matter. I've already made my choice. Like you taught me: Beauty is the only choice."

9

On a sunny spring afternoon, Buccaneer Bay stripped them bare, the muscular, shaggy-chested man and the pale, skinny boy, tits pink and flat as ever. Jonathan's usual buddy Ernie couldn't make it, so he brought his sister Angie instead. Two years his senior, at fourteen already a full-grown woman, she was none too eager to hang around with her little brother and his teacher. After a few slides, she lay down to sunbathe and left the man and boy to their own devices.

Jonathan raced to the top of a ten-story tower challenging Red to keep up, who to the boy's surprise matched him step for step, until they stopped on a landing to catch their breath.

Before him, the boy stood still and quiet but for his rapid breathing, his young body turned toward the panorama of the park where he gazed, providing Red the opportunity to study him up close and nearly naked as never before. Red admired the sunlight glistening on the boy's smooth, damp, transparent skin speckled with sparkling jewels of water and sweat.

What an evanescent little creature he was, and human as well, with mind and personality! He seemed like one whom magic had transformed from a bright, divine spirit into glistening flesh. His legs were smooth and slender. His ivory thighs were bare almost to his narrow hips, where bright red nylon fabric clung to his brazenly protruding butt. His bony frame was soft and slight like a bird, a fledgling eagle looking out from his aerie, preparing for first flight.

Entranced, Red stood too close behind and scrutinized the blond down feathering the back of the slender neck. As Jonathan turned his head slightly to catch some sight below, Red caught the heart-stopping profile. On the threshold of adolescence, his face was androgynously girlish and at that rare stage of boy beauty celebrated in art and poetry throughout history.

Red's love had chosen this beauty. You can't see and be beauty at the same time. Beauty required the remove of the lover who desired, adored, envied, and wanted to be it, but was not it, the poignant impossible longing of love.

Still gazing out over his domain, Jonathan sensed the presence and adoration of Red's eyes and turned back to him in quiet curiosity. A faint blush glowed on his cheek.

Though the silent meeting of eyes lasted only seconds, it was too long to be the kind of glance friends might exchange a thousand times a day but a glimpse into their respective souls.

Jonathan smiled sweetly and broke the silence, "You like to hang around me, because it makes you feel like a kid again."

Shocked at the precision of the boy's insight, Red was struck dumb and then laughed. "Yeah, that's part of it," he caught his breath and added, "I also happen to think you are a remarkably beautiful person. What made you say that all of a sudden?"

The boy squirmed. Even if he knew, he wouldn't say. He shrugged his shoulders and bounded up the metal stairs again like a springbok. Red's eyes followed for a moment. Something in the boy's movement, the purposeful way he sailed through space, gripped Red with surprising force, something very much like awe. He followed in hot pursuit.

They arrived at the top of the Blue Chute, a fiberglass pipe in transparent Tidibowl blue like a giant flushing toilet. Riding tandem with the boy on a foam mat, Red spread his thighs around the slender young hips and his arms around the soft lean torso. "Comfy?" Red inquired, hoping for the green light that would send them over the edge before his hard-on became apparent.

Green. They pushed off, squealing with glee down the wet blue tube that spat them out like an easy birth. They skimmed across the landing pool thrilled and breathless, laughing and talkative, Red feeling like a kid again.

At the end of the day, changing in the locker room, Red caught another glimpse of slender, naked Jonathan, but daring not dwell on the vision a second time, he quickly looked away. The boy seemed taller than before, stretched out, but still a kid, no "again" about it.

In the realm of totem and taboo, the deck was stacked. There was no discourse. Taboo demanded shame from the good and beautiful. The lovers had to be convinced that they were wrong. But taboo notwithstanding, the quest for love and beauty continued. Red would visit. He would bring gifts. He would court the boy in the ancient way expressing respect and friendship to the parents. Then, after the period of courtship, he would seek their blessing as their son's erastes, his mentor and lover.

Red read the above to Malcolm over the phone.

"I like what the way it sounds. It's like waves of words breaking over you," Malcolm observed.

"Maybe it's just the way I read it."

"It's interesting what he said about your feeling like a kid again. It shows he's thinking about it. He's trying to give meaning to the relationship. Nobody asked him why this older man was taking such an interest in him. He asked himself, and that was his answer."

"There's a lot of truth in what he said. I am the kid again. With him, the impossible becomes possible. I experience first-hand what Wilde called the joy, hope, and glamour of youth."

"First-hand?" Malcolm chuckled at the pun.

Laughing, "I shall say no more."

"So you're Peter Pan. You want to be a boy forever by reliving your adolescence vicariously through him."

"It's more than that. I'm part of it. I'm the best twelve-year-old buddy a boy could have, because I have the experience and knowledge of a fifty-year-old man. There's something different about me, Malcolm. For some unknown reason, some basic cultural structures didn't take. Or rather they took, but not very well and not very deep, so that they operate only on the surface of my personality. It's as if all that I learned about being an adult, about being a man, was a sham and a lie, and it was up to me to throw off that mockery and look deeper inside myself to find my own way. I rediscovered my child, my youth, and my young man, so that now these points of view are ever-present in my consciousness. I'm all of them at once. That's why I don't experience the 'adult amnesia' psychologists speak of, where a man forgets what it was like to be a boy. I remember, because I'm still there. You called it 'Peter Pan,' the arrested adolescent. When I'm with Jonathan, I'm not twelve years old again. I'm a twelve-year-old for the first time."

"But what you call a sham and a lie, most people would call normal."

"And what I call good, most people would call dangerous. Normal is no moral. It never looks directly into the light."

"Why do you call that 'dangerous'?"

"Because it challenges moral authority. Because it doesn't give a damn what anyone thinks in its pursuit of love and beauty. The good is no respecter of authority, nor tradition, nor what others think is proper. It's Dionysian in this way, and sooner or later, it's gonna piss somebody off, because you're having more fun than they are."

"Your young Jonathan has asked himself why you want to be with him. I wonder if he has also asked why he wants to be with you. Or for that matter, have you asked yourself that?"

"I'm afraid to. Except for the banquet, the program is over, and his family is moving to the suburbs, so I won't be able to teach him next year. But he continues to welcome my presence and attention, and his parents approve. That's all I ask."

"What if he decides, 'Well, the program's over. I don't need to be hanging around this creepy old guy anymore'?"

"That's my greatest fear, so I intend to make his experience with me so damn fun and interesting and compelling, it will never cross his mind. I want to be the person he comes to when there's stuff he can't talk about with mom and dad. I'm not there yet, but I'm working on it."

For all his moralizing, Nietzsche was in error on the matter of good and evil. His assertion that good and evil were really abstractions of what we want, either individually or as a group, was correct. We literally made a virtue of necessity. But he based his conclusion that good and evil did not therefore exist in nature on the incorrect assumption that nature itself was an abstraction, an 'out there.' This was the erroneous notion of physics itself, the false objectification of nature. True, in nature, we could not pick apart the laws of matter and energy to ferret out good and evil. But the physical world told only half the story of our experience. In the more comprehensive subjective world of self, being and nature were one. There, the question of good and evil was the defining aspect of experience. Philosophy's true "bitter pill," as Nietzsche called it, was exactly the opposite of what he describes. It was not that to see the truth, the philosopher must accept the absolute neutrality of nature, even in the motives of men (i.e., the cruelest and most monstrous, the most evil, among us were as much an unfolding of nature as the blossoming of a flower). A pill more bitter still was the ineluctable presence of good and evil in our hearts, for exactly the same reasons that Nietzsche cited: not as an abstraction into principle or projection onto the objectified out-there, but as an on-going component of our life experience. It was a much simpler matter to cast an amoral and objective eye on nature than to accept the uncompromising isolation of the heart alone with its moral motive.

Darren called. "We had a fight. I couldn't take it anymore. He bitches constantly. I took him out for a nice dinner, and all he did was complain. The waiter was reciting the specials, and he told him to go away and stop interrupting us. He can never have a good time. He ruins it for both of us."

"That's his way of staying in control. He's afraid to have a good time, because even that is a loss of control."

"Control over what?"

"You, the relationship, the situation, himself, all of the above. To have a good time is to give yourself up to it."

"Well, it's driving me nuts! When we got home, I said to him, 'Why can't you just relax and enjoy yourself? Why do you always have to pick at every little thing?' I wasn't yelling at him. I just wanted him to see what he was doing. He went berserk. He accused me of trying to run his life. Then he started going off on my life and my career, what a loser I was. So I told him to get out of my house. I didn't want to be around him anymore. That's when he played the trump card. That's when he threatened me."

"What'd he say?"

"He threatened to tell his mom."

"But his mom already knows."

"All he has to do is tell her that I'm taking advantage of him or hurting him in some way, and she'll go ballistic."

"Now you know what I went through with Mark."

"Yeah, he's a lot like Mark. He wouldn't go to the cops himself."

"At least, he's not naïve. It's the naïfs who don't think about the consequences. They're the most dangerous."

"But his mom would. With a few drinks under her belt, she's capable of anything. That's what scares me, Red. My life is in the hands of a bunch of crazy drunks."

"Yes, it is. What did you say to him?"

"I calmed him down. I told him I love him and I want him to be happy."

"Good. You're good at that."

"For now, but what if he tells her? I can't stand this, Red. I can't stand the uncertainty of it. It's driving me crazy!"

"That is exactly the kind of crazy that can get you into trouble. I know this sounds almost impossible, but you must relax, put your anxiety aside, and think with a clear head."

"I don't have time to think! I have to fly tomorrow! I have to get some sleep. Sleep? Hah! Like I can sleep right now!"

"Why don't you come over here for the night? Just like you did for me, when Mark was freaking me out. You need to get away from there. Bring your stuff with you. You can leave for the airport from here in the morning. So you'll be gone for a few days while things cool off."

"What if they don't? What if the cops are waiting for me when I get back?"

"Give me a key. I'll keep an eye on the house while you're gone. I'll call and let you know how things stand. Oh, and one more thing: Take your passport. You never know when you might need to get out of Dodge."

"I can't handle this, Red. I can't be in a relationship where there is always this threat hanging over my head."

"Tell me about it. That's how they've poisoned it. It isn't just the fact that you could be punished for breaking the law. The law poisons the relationship itself. The law makes it dysfunctional."

"I know. I'd like to get counseling for him, for both of us. But I can't. Even if he went to a private shrink by himself, what could he say? The minute he mentions me, the shrink reports it. He has to. That's where we are now."

"That's exactly why I don't think he'll do it."

"This is not working out. I'm staying with seventeen from now on. One year. Big deal!"

E-mail

Dear R^2:

I know you have asked to be removed from the BLN, but a recent post from Hawk has appeared that I think you should know about, so I'm forwarding it to you. —BLN editor

Dear BLN:

I have been raided by the Boston police, who have taken away all the computer equipment in my house. Consequently, I request to be removed from the

The Moralist

BLN, until I can be in touch again. *PAN* will be out of action as well. I believe I was on one of Billy D's lists.

This is clearly police harassment to stop our publication. I was not arrested, but some friends have been. DO NOT TRY TO CONTACT ME BY PHONE OR E-MAIL. THE POLICE ARE RECEIVING EVERYTHING! —Hawk

Reply to BLN editor from R^2:

If you have an alternative way of contacting Hawk, please convey this message.

Dear Hawk:

I am a professional communications consultant. You know me from the publication of my short story *The Moralist* in your last issue of *PAN*. I can assist you in your communication with law enforcement and the media. If you are interested, please contact me at the e-mail address above. —R^2

The Authors of Tomorrow magazine was published. Jonathan won Top Story as promised. "By far the best," Mr. Moony confided to Red at the Tex-Mex restaurant where the banquet honoring the students and their mentors was held.

Red's moment came to award his prize to his boy. He called out the name of each student and presented a gift dictionary from Mr. Shakespeare's Books, until he picked up the volume marked with a yellow sticky-note to indicate that it alone contained his message on the flyleaf:

Jonathan:

You shine with a bright light, not only your intelligence and talent, but also the real person you are. I consider myself fortunate to have the pleasure and privilege of knowing you. I hope you will continue to call me 'friend.'

Always, Red

His voice cracked and eyes welled when he called Jonathan's name. Presenting the gift, he wished the boy a hearty "congratulations" and embraced his young protégé, as he had not done with the others.

Moments later, the Top Story award. Returning to the banquet table,

Jonathan beamed in the flickering light of candles and showed off the shiny brass plaque to his admiring parents. He glanced across the table and caught Red's eye. Restraining tears, Red held up his glass in silent toast. The boy dropped his eyes and retreated to his mom's cuddling arms.

"What should he do this summer?" she asked of Red.

"Here's something to get him started," Red produced yet one more gift, wrapped with a silver bow. Jonathan greedily tore it open to reveal the cups and balls and the video on how to do the trick. "It's the old shell game, the most classic magic trick of all. If you can do the cups and balls, you can do anything. Now you see it, now you don't."

"You're still the sorcerer," he observed with his coy ironic smile.

"And you're the sorcerer's apprentice," Red replied.

Mr. Moony was at the podium wrapping up. Addressing Jonathan, he announced, "We have one more honor for our Top Story writer. Mr. Shakespeare's Books has asked if Jonathan will read his story to kids at the bookstore next month! Would you be willing to share your story at a public reading, Jonathan?"

The boy's face went scarlet. He smiled and shrugged. All applauded. Red leaned toward him, "I'll rehearse you."

"We're moving this weekend," Jon reminded him.

"So Jonathan told me," Red answered.

"I invited him to come over, Dad," the boy chimed in.

"I can wait till you're settled in."

"It's pretty far from Martin Luther King. I didn't know if you wanted to be driving all that distance."

"It will be my pleasure."

After the banquet, the Press Club volunteers headed for the bar. The president, middle-aged Stacey, accosted Red and exclaimed, "I saw you working with your student in the library. It was fascinating to watch you two together. You had such a remarkable rapport. I've never seen anything like it!"

Boy lovers always make the best teachers, Red thought, because they love their students. Pedagogy was pederasty, or was it the other way around? "It was easy with him," he answered modestly. "His mind absorbs everything like a sponge. I would give him an exercise, and he would run with it, no questions asked. He just wrote his autobiography. It's delightful!"

"So quickly!" she exclaimed.

"Well, he's twelve years old. It's not that long." Overhearing, the other Press Club members laughed and speculated on the interminable length of their own stories. Red added, "Maybe thirty years from now, he'll seal himself up in a cork-lined room, drink strong coffee all day, and turn those few pages into 300, and that's just describing his mother's kiss! Here's to Jonathan!" Red raised his margarita to the group, who, missing the allusion to Proust, screwed up their faces but raised their glasses anyway.

Stacey smiled knowingly. She understood that he was charming them with the same enticing, seducing, amusing, mystifying style he used with the boy. What she did not see was that he was also mother-doving them away from the truth of his love, while displaying it so openly that no one noticed.

She made her pitch, "Are you planning to volunteer for next year? I hope you do. You're a natural teacher."

E-mail

Dear R[2]:

BLN has forwarded your message to me. Thank you for your offer. As you can imagine, everything is pretty hectic here right now. The good news is that our last issue was already out to our distributors before all this happened. Thank you also for the great story. It's beautiful! —Hawk

Red called Malcolm: "I'm their new champion. I got the dictionaries for the kids. My boy won the Top Story prize. Now, they want me to come back next year. They think I can do the same thing with some other kid."

"Why couldn't you?"

"I didn't do it for the program. I did it for Jonathan. I don't want to be the mentor of some other kid. I want to keep it going with the one I've got."

"Are you afraid you'll fall in love again?"

"That never occurred to me."

"What if you did? What if you're the type of teacher who falls in love with all your students?"

"I don't think that's true."

"But you can't say for sure. Most teachers fall in love with their first student. They think he hung the moon, until they discover that every student is unique."

"No, it's different. Just like I wrote to him. It's not just his intelligence and talent. It's him. He's such a thoroughly genuine person, no pretense, no phony trying to act like a grownup or any of that shit. He's a boy having fun being a boy. He's good-hearted and generous, and he takes life as it comes. The only other person I've felt this way about is my own daughter."

"There you have it! What parent doesn't see their child as exceptional? And like a parent, you have no perspective."

"I know beauty when I see it. When beauty comes into my life, I embrace it. That is the summary of all ethics."

"Perhaps, but I think you should consider staying in the program anyway. If for no other reason, at least you'll have another experience you can compare it to. At least you'll know that Jonathan isn't just some pedagogic infatuation."

"But, Malcolm, pedagogic infatuation is what boy love is all about!"

"If that's true, then you're just acting out. It isn't the individual person you love. It's the situation, the myth. Can you say for sure that's not so for you and Jonathan?"

"Yes, I love the myth, you know I do, but the myth pales when the real boy stands before me." Nonetheless, Malcolm had made his point.

Darren called: "What's going on? Did you go by the house?"

"A couple of times. Everything was quiet. No one's been there but me. I haven't seen any suspicious vehicles, and I don't think my presence attracted anyone's attention. Where are you?"

"I'm in LA. I fly back tonight. I called Jonathan last night. We had a long talk. He said he didn't say anything, but I think we're going to call it a day. I can't take these threats. If he's going to threaten me like that, I can't trust him."

"Been there, done that. As long as Mark held that trump card, I was powerless. They always argue that the man has power over the boy. What a joke!"

"I think he wants out as much as I do."

"He has someone waiting in the wings."

"I've been getting some strange e-mails on the computer lately. I think he's been chatting with other guys while I was out of town."

"Probably more than chatting."

"Yeah, well, great. They can take him off my hands. By the way, I looked up my stepbrother Quentin out here. He used to be a teacher in Fort Worth, until some kid accused him of 'improper touching.'"

"Runs in the family!"

"No, he's just a big fat sissy who doesn't get any sex. They bounced him out of the Texas system, so he moved to LA. He's a director at a community theater in Santa Barbara, but he wants to teach drama at Stanford. Your friend Malcolm teaches at Stanford, doesn't he?"

"He wouldn't have any clout. He's in Asian Studies. The last thing he'd want to do is go to bat for a big fat drama queen."

"God, you oughta see him, Red! He prances around sporting a big handlebar moustache and a silver-handled cane and Italian-cut suit looking like Diaghilev. We toured the town in a rented limo."

"Sounds like Theo, except he wasn't a sissy, he was a madman."

"We went to Rodeo Drive! It was great! The salespeople would just walk away from their customers to attend to His Eminence. They were afraid he might be a big producer or something. Ya gotta give him credit. He knows how to play it off."

"Then why can't he get on at Stanford?"

"He has to put a show together. Colorful geniuses are a dime-a-dozen out here. It might work on Rodeo Drive, as long as ya got the bucks, but academe is different. They won't take you seriously, till ya knock their socks off."

"He should do one of my plays. That'll get their attention."

"Yeah, I thought so, too. I showed him *Boy-o-Boy!*, but he said it was too controversial. We were in a gay bookstore, and he starts going off on you, 'Who is he anyway? What's he done?' I grabbed a copy of *PAN* off the magazine rack and showed him your story. It shocked the shit out of him. He got all haughty and said, 'He'll get arrested for writing stuff like that!'"

"You can't get arrested for writing fiction, not yet anyway. But give 'em time; they're workin' on it."

10

Grabbing his video camera bag and stuffing a Snickers bar in the side pocket (Want some candy, little boy?), Red locked up the house and drove the old Mustang GT out onto the glistening streets in the rainy late-spring afternoon. Within the quiet, dry confine of steel, leather, and colored lights, he switched on the radio to one of the rock'n'roll stations Jonathan had programmed, classic oldies. The Everly Brothers were singing *Wake Up Little Susie*: "Your friends will say 'ooo-la-la!'" Indeed they would at his love for a boy, who was at the age now that Red was when that song was topping the charts.

After a thirty-minute drive, he arrived at the modest tan brick house in a quiet middle-class suburb. Jonathan's wish for a better place to live had come true. Red folded the story into his pocket, tucked the camcorder under his London Fog, and ran through the rain to the porch. He pressed the broken plastic doorbell, then knocked. The door was not open, as it had been at the dollhouse, where neighbors, musicians, and kids came and went. The new house seemed deserted until he saw movement through the window. Jonathan opened the door and invited him in.

The place was quiet, still a shamble of boxes and misplaced furniture from the move. The family, the boy explained, had gone to his cousin's birthday party. Only he had stayed behind for their rehearsal. Red apologized for keeping him from the festivities. "I didn't wanta go," he elfin grinned. "We have work to do."

"Then let's get started." Red handed him a copy of the story and a pen and instructed him to make margin notes on Red's direction. "Think of yourself as an actor," he explained. "A reading is the same as a play, except you have a copy of the script in your hand.

"They'll probably have a podium," he continued. "Don't use it. After Mr. Moony introduces you, step down in front of it, as soon as you can. You want to play your story in front of the audience. Read directly to the kids. They'll love it. I'm going to teach you how to act out your story, how to move around and play the voices of the characters, and when you become a dog, you will be a dog. You're gonna knock their socks off! Okay?"

"Okay," the boy agreed mildly with that same smile of both sweetness and irony.

"So, rule number one: Louder!" Red shouted. "You might give the greatest performance in the world, but it's no good unless they can hear it at the back of the room. That's the biggest problem young performers have. They don't know how to project their voices. So shout it out! There's a musical play called *Gypsy*, about the famous stripper Gypsy Rose Lee. She was a shy girl from a theatrical family, and in the play, her crazy stage mother is always yelling, 'Sing out, Louise!' to get her to project her voice. So that's my first lesson to you: 'Sing out, Louise!'" The boy shouted his words in defiant mockery. "Yes! Yes! That's it! Do it like that! You think you're making fun of it, but that's exactly how loud it has to be. Not only with your voice but with your body. Make it big and loud and wild and crazy! Do the voices for each character! Do the movement! Use the space! Act it out! Play to the audience! Pick out a kid, and play to that kid. Then pick another one. That's what I want. It's much easier to tone an actor down than build one up. Now, pick it up from where you left off." Red switched on the camera and started taping the boy's performance.

Two hours later, the phone rang. It was Jon Sr. Teacher and student had only barely noticed that the rain was now a full-blown thunderstorm. Some streets were flooded, the father explained, so the family was going to stay at the birthday party. Jon Sr. asked if Red would stay with Jonathan until the storm let up. He was happy to oblige and continued taping.

At the transformation from the boy into the dog, he directed the boy, "Think of yourself as a dog now. How would the dog behave? How would his voice sound? What would he do?" Jonathan lifted his leg and giggled. "Good, that's funny. Chan does that in the story. It'll get a laugh. How about barking and growling?" The boy lowered the range of his voice and growled out the words of the boy-dog. "Excellent! Now, give me some more movement."

Jonathan acted out by falling to all fours and panting eagerly at Red's knee. He lay his golden head in the man's lap looking up with cocker spaniel eyes. "Rowf, rowf," he barked, panting like the doggie boy.

"Yeah, that's great! Roll over, doggie. Can you roll over?" The boy barked again and rolled over, then sat up begging. "What do you want? A doggie treat? Let's see, how about a Snickers bar?" Red produced the chocolate bar from the camera bag. Want some candy little boy?

Jonathan's eyes lit up, and he snatched away the candy, not like a dog but a boy with his hands and devoured the treat.

"That was good stuff," Red put down the camera. "Be a dog now and then. That's a good way to learn it."

"I feel like I'm your dog," he said petulantly biting the candy bar, "the way you've been tellin' me what to do all day."

"I'm directing you. The relationship between an actor and a director is different from the collaboration we did on your story. As your director, I see you as an actor. You still see yourself as yourself. It's important that you understand the difference, and oh, by the way, 'Sing out, Louise!'"

"And stop callin' me Louise," he complained with a coy smile, casually inquiring with a mouthful of candy, "You gonna keep drivin' out here?"

"I was planning a final run-through Saturday morning, before we go to the bookstore."

"What about after? Will you still come over?"

"Sure, if you want me to." Red's heart leapt at Jonathan's simple invitation.

"Yeah, I do."

He continued taping. Jonathan played all the voices: the howling, growling dog, the piping old sorcerer, and finally the sadder-but-wiser young man, giving one last howl, as his dog self faded away.

His voice gave out, and the howl was cut short. Jonathan laughed, cleared his throat, and sipped lemonade from an aluminum pouch. He tried the high hollow howl once more, but again, his voice cracked at the crescendo.

Sipping more lemonade, he declared, "Doin' all those voices is hard on the throat."

"Your voice is changing." Red turned off the camera and slipped the tape into the VCR for review.

"Really? Ya think so?"

"That's what it sounds like."

"I hope so. I can't wait to be a teenager!"

"That was the last howl of your childhood. Just like your story, Chan wants to change back into a boy he once was, but he doesn't. He comes back as a young man."

The Moralist

"So my story is really about me."
"It always is."

The reading was a smash. Even Mr. Moony was surprised, when, after his introduction, Jonathan stepped down from the podium and began to perform his story before the children, who squealed with glee. Fed by his audience, his heroes and villains became larger and louder. He moved boldly about the space, playing first to one eager little boy and then a giggly little girl.

The audience roared with applause at the end. Jonathan's parents were enthralled and Mr. Moony aglow with pleasure and gratitude to Red for making the event a success. The PR guy for Mr. Shakespeare's Books invited Jonathan back to read more of his work.

As Jonathan signed autographs for the kids, Red came up to him like a fan. "Can I have your autograph, Mr. Frame?"

He lowered his head and blushed, as he signed Red's book, then looked up brightly, "Hey, Red, you got a bike?"

"Yeah, uh, sure I do," Red stammered.

"Great! There's a park near our new house with bike trails. It's called Goose Creek. You drive right past it on your way to my house. There's a big picnic shelter next to the parking lot. Come over next Saturday with your bike. I'll meet you there."

"I'm there, dude."

The following Saturday morning, Red stopped by Sears to purchase a bike and headed for Goose Creek Park. As he pulled into the parking lot, he spotted his young friend seated on a picnic table next to his bike beneath a large steel shelter.

After a late spring rain, the sun came out on a steamy afternoon. On their bikes, man and boy cut through the paths of pink petals and pollen. Arriving at a giant oak with outstretched branches, Jonathan ditched his bike and scampered up the tree like Tarzan's Boy. Red grabbed his camera for a few snaps.

Looking down from the tree limb like a young leopard, the boy grinned, "You always gotta do your Hollywood routine."

"Yeah, and I'm damn good at it, too. You'll see. Maybe I'll give your mommy a portrait of you for Christmas."

They hopped on their bikes again and went off-road along a narrow trail. The boy sped up, whizzing through the trees, as Red struggled to follow. "The little daredevil," Red thought. "He wants to show me his stuff."

They came to the edge where a steep bank led down to the creek. The trick was to take the bank, then cut sharp before hitting the water. There was just enough trail along the edge of the creek to do it. Jonathan didn't hesitate.

"Come on, Red!" he called and wheeled over the edge, bouncing down the gravelly embankment.

Red had been challenged like this by every boy he'd ever loved. Steering with his knees, seventeen-year-old Michael caught air with his truck sailing over turtle-top crossroads, as Red sat calmly next to him restraining stark terror. Fourteen-year-old Mark dared him to dive into the lake from a hundred-foot cliff, which he did (this the man who had been afraid of heights as a kid). One of these days, he was going to break something, maybe this day.

Over the edge, he followed, allowing the bike to careen down the bank. You couldn't brake on the loose rocks and dirt. You just had to hold on and then brake hard and spin out for the turn to avoid landing in the creek.

Jonathan hit bottom and skidded into the turn, his back wheel splashing into the water. He kept peddling and pulled the bike clear along the little path. Red followed but caught a patch of mud on the turn and slid sideways into the cold creek. Jonathan laughed, as Red pulled himself and his new Sears bike from the water and mud.

The boy led them to a secluded recess beneath the cliff shaded with low trees. They leaned their bikes against the bank, laughing at their adventure and catching their breath.

"You can really hide down here. No one can see you," Jonathan confided. "This is the boy's private place," Red thought, remembering a grassy berm in a field next to a creek.

Their laughter subsided, and they were silent, listening to the water splashing over smooth stones. Red removed his shirt and busied himself with washing the mud from his face and arms.

"You aren't my teacher anymore," Jonathan observed staring at the dancing water.

"No, I just like to hang out with you," Red smiled.

Jonathan stepped toward Red and wrapped his slender arms around the man's waist. "Thank you, Red. I liked winning the award and reading my story."

"This is only the beginning, my friend. The best is yet to come." Red held the boy and inhaled his fresh golden hair like a drug.

The Moralist

The Coalition's final report was released. Faye dispatched Red to D.C. to pump the media for their National Press Club luncheon and press conference. Already the scapegoat, poor Deborah was taken off the press to manage the luncheon and printing details.

Their earlier press effort with the survey was a bellwether for the media's indifference to the final report. It was DOA. Frank Rich's column in the *Times* called Tommy and his Coalition "hypocrites," and he was right. What he failed to understand was that this crowd would take that as a compliment, what Red called "the Roy Cohn ethic." They preferred a facile hypocrisy to a difficult truth, hypocrisy elevated to a virtue.

Frank Rich certainly didn't dampen the self-congratulatory dinner at the Mayflower in a setting of huge crystal chandeliers and ballroom-size Persian carpets. Even America's moral leader, Bull Barnett, put in an appearance.

Red avoided him like the plague for fear he might actually have to shake the hand of his archenemy, the very incarnation of authoritarian self-righteousness. Such was the ignominy of this nasty assignment that he might have to meet the devil himself. At least, this was the end of it.

At their table, he sat next to a pretty Swedish girl who said she'd worked with Barnett.

Red inquired confidentially, "Is he the same pompous ass in person that he is on television?"

She laughed and exclaimed, "Yes!", wonderfully amused that someone at this pretentious affair had the guts to declare that the emperor had no clothes.

Beside the Swedish girl sat lanky Mickey, Tommy DeKalb's advance man, who had handled the failed presidential campaign, so now missed the D.C. power circles. This dinner was old times and also a swan song for him. He'd hitched his wagon to a falling star, and the next two years with Tommy looked like some pretty dismal politics.

Across from Red sat the balding four-eyed Bible scholar, part of the "faith-based" focus of the Coalition. Red posed a question he'd heard on one of the TV morning shows: "At what age do most American men have their first child?" Twenty-six, twenty-seven, twenty-eight, thirty, they each guessed. The answer was twenty-seven, and Red allowed that he was that very age when his own daughter was born. "A foolish time in my life and a big mistake," he continued to their shock at this unexpected personal revelation. "But if men were wise about such things," he quipped, "the human race wouldn't last a generation." They laughed. "Now, my daughter is studying to be a vet, and I am very proud of her. My greatest folly at age twenty-seven has become my greatest joy at age fifty! So there you are, Molly Bloom!" he declared with a cackle, but this time the laughter barely rose to a confused twitter. They didn't get the reference to Joyce and were too busy doing the math.

Mickey stared incredulously but dared not betray that the man he thought five years his junior was ten years his senior. In his world, one brought oneself to the age of others' expectations. They aged themselves and so were indeed older than Red, though not in years. In a ballroom filled with politicians and academics, who thought they knew what was best for everyone else, he threw the lie back in their faces with the implied question, "But would you trade it all to be fifteen years younger than you are?" They might say yes in their hearts, but their egos would never allow it.

The Swedish girl raised her glass admiringly with a smile, "How lucky you are!" Was she referring to his youth or his daughter? But she revealed no more than that, fearing to inquire further lest she explore the uncanny or sociopathic or both.

Her toast gave Mickey permission, "I can't believe you're fifty years old."

"My fiftieth birthday was last Halloween," Red stated proudly. "I'm a Halloween baby. My parties were always costume parties."

"Some good witch must have put a spell on you, Peter Pan!" the girl declared. They all laughed and drained their glasses.

The Bible scholar was more skeptical and changed the subject to expound on his latest thesis. "The Bible's great leaders are all shepherds and goatherds, not farmers. David was a goat boy. Moses was a shepherd in the desert. Jesus called himself a shepherd. What does that tell us about modern culture that God has always preferred shepherds to farmers? Farmers carve out the land and section it off. They create ownership and fences. You see it in the movie *Shane*. The herders against the sodbusters. When he arrives, Shane is surprised to see the new fences. What a fine film! When I mention it in my classes these days, almost none of my students have heard of it!" Pointedly, he turned to Red, "Do you know that movie?"

"Yes, I saw it when it first came out with Alan Ladd and young Brandon deWilde. It's the story of a boy's love for a man. As is often the case, the boy's perspective is the moral center of the film. Of course, I was just a boy myself at the time, but I think I understood it all the better for that reason, its honesty and emotional authenticity. But it doesn't seem to fit your argument. The sodbusters, the ones with the fences, are the good guys. The open-range herders are the bad guys."

Taken aback, the scholar allowed, "True, but that's society's point of view, not the Bible's."

"I'm more interested in hearing about the shepherds," the Swedish girl interjected.

With a smug smile, he continued, "Shepherds lie around and play music on their pipes. The Christian message is that the world is man's garden, not for toil, but like the shepherds who pluck the fruit from the earth. They enjoy creation, but they don't create for themselves."

"From that perspective, human creativity might be seen as a source of evil," Red concluded.

"In a sense, yes," he agreed.

"But your goat boy goes back before the Bible, y'know. On my wall at home, I have a print of the Matisse *Bonheur de Vivre*. There's a goat boy in it. He embodies the pastoral myth of human natural innocence, exactly what you're talking about. The whole painting is a garden of earthly delights, very much a representation of your vision, and very sensual as well. Pastoral innocence is the Christian version of an ancient myth and ritual that was originally a drunken frenzy of music, dance, and sex that celebrated creativity as the engine of life itself. The pastoral shepherd's ancestor is the half-goat satyr with a foot-long phallus, drunk and mad and telling dirty jokes. They do have one thing in common: no boundaries, as you said, but from exactly the opposite perspective. Creativity begins with no boundaries. The lilies of the field may not toil, but their existence is divine creation at work. And who are history's greatest poets but the pastorals with time on their hands? You make some very good points, but the Bible cannot expand beyond its own mythology, unless viewed in its historical and cultural contexts."

"You make some very good points yourself," he grudgingly acknowledged, as the meal arrived and conversation turned to what else but the Lewinsky affair.

E-mail

Dear Deborah:

I enjoyed working with you on the Coalition. This experience has taught me that the core of conservatism is endemic unhappiness that engenders meanness towards others. Misery loves company, even if it has to go out and spread some around. I'm sorry they've taken it out on you. —Red

11

Since biking in the park, Red had not seen Jonathan in more than a month. He called to keep it going.

"What are you doing tonight? Maybe we can go to a movie or something."
"My dad's takin' me to a free concert. You can meet us there, if ya want."
"Who's playin'?"
"Mortis."
"As in *rigor mortis*?"
"I guess so. What does that mean?"
"It's Latin for the rigidity of death. It's when a dead body goes stiff. That's why they call 'em 'stiffs.'"
"Yeah, that sounds right. They're a local punk band, but they've gotten some radio play."
"Thanks, but I don't wanta butt in on your dad's thing. I'll call ya tomorrow."
"Come on, Red. He won't feel like that. He likes you."
"I'll think about it, but don't look for me. If I go, I'll find you."
Disappointed, "Okay, I know that means no."
He hung up, but two hours later, the phone rang.
"You still wanta go to the concert?"
"Apparently you do."
"Dad can't make it. You'd have to pick me up."
"I'll be there in thirty minutes."
Red shut down the computer (working on the book), slipped on his Cole Haans, and was out the door in minutes. He later wished he'd taken the time to tie on his Timberlands, the adolescent order of the night. He was overdressed!
They arrived late. Apparently, the concert had been going on all afternoon.

The Moralist

Fresh and happy on a hot summer night, Red and Jonathan walked in the opposite direction of the wasted youths going home early, even before the headliners came on, so there was plenty of room on the open patch of ground where the stage had been erected in the Arts District park, surrounded by the Meyerson and the Museum of Fine Arts.

Jonathan had trouble seeing over the older, taller crowd. Red offered to hoist him onto his shoulders, but the boy was too old for that. He didn't want to look like a little kid on his daddy's shoulders in this crowd of teenagers.

Jonathan climbed instead onto a spotlight platform and watched the concert from there. The operator glanced at the boy and older man together and didn't object. As they listened to the bands, Red cruised the audience of young studs with their chicks.

Such was the remove of the homosexual vision, he thought, to view the mating ritual from a perspective that saw the male as beauty, which changed the equation. Just in front of them, a shirtless young blonde, eighteen or so, leaned on the platform not four feet away, allowing Red to study in detail his broad smooth shoulders, damp and glistening in the steamy air, tapering to the narrow dimpled hips at the base of the back, lean young muscle disappearing into loose-fit jeans.

He turned almost at Red's behest to display a handsome profile, both soft and masculine at the same time, like a Michelangelo sculpture.

A circle of younger boys gathered nearby to share cigarettes and joints. Jonathan smelled the telltale aroma and flashed a knowing smile at Red. The tallest among them, a slender blonde boy, had to bend down to the level of his less mature buddies, the cruel comedy of early adolescence. Red imagined the lean, long frame beneath the baggy clothes. He loved the slender look of a boy more than the young stud and imagined the soft young stamen beneath the denim.

Jonathan tapped Red on the shoulder and awoke him from his fantasy. The boy shouted in his ear, the only way to converse in the din of heavy-metal punk, that the lead guitar was doing distortions with a waffle bar.

The acoustic pyrotechnics drew shouts of approval from the audience. The young stud cried out 'Fuckan-A!' and turned to see who'd heard him, immediately embarrassed at the man and boy behind him. He turned and apologized to Red that he didn't see him there with his son.

Red thanked him for his consideration but reassured him, "Did you hear the lyrics to that last song? 'Don't fuck with me don't fuck with me don't fuck with me!' I could hardly be upset with your language after that. Besides, I teach my friend Jonathan here that there are no bad words. I'm not his dad, I'm his creative writing coach, right, Jonathan?"

"Fuckan-A!" Jonathan high-fived.

Red laughed. "There, you see?"

A look of shock and confusion played across the young stud's face. "Well, fuckan-A!" he managed with less conviction, not at all certain if he approved of this.

Red put him at ease by taking his hand amiably, "My name's Red. This is Jonathan. He's a rock musician. He's heard plenty of lyrics. Hell, he writes 'em. He plays bass in his Dad's band. Jonathan, I want you to meet. . ?"

"Dwayne. Name's Dwayne. You play in a band?" he asked with a tone of admiration for the younger kid. Jonathan nodded demurely. "What's it called?"

"Tarzan's Boy."

"It's you and your dad and a couple of sisters right?" Red prompted.

"Yeah, but not *my* sisters," Jonathan explained. "They're twin sisters who play together, one on keyboard and the other sings. You oughta come hear us. We got a gig at the Bluewater Cafe in Deep Ellum next Saturday."

"Yeah, I know the Bluewater. That's a cool spot. You play there?"

"Yeah, come on over and jam with us."

"I don't play myself. Air guitar, that's about it."

"You don't have to play to jam. The question is: Do you boogie?" Jonathan smiled his ironic smile.

Dwayne grinned again. "Fuckan-A!" they cried in unison with more high-fives. Dwayne turned to Red, "That kid is cool!"

"Yeah, I know."

Aesthetics, assexthics, assethics. Aesthetics was ethics with an ass. Beauty was our sense of the good mingled with desire, also known as love. Call it utilitarian, call it genetic, call it what you will, that feeling was a universal human experience. It was our true self in action, going on all the time, whether we admitted it or not. Our capacity to love drove our moral sense. Moral principle was a shadow of this individual moral vision that was our destiny, identity, dentistry. Beauty's only flaw: He needed braces.

The telephone rang, shattering Red's reverie.

"Hello?"

"Red, this is Darren. Well, he did it. He went to the cops."

"Where are you now?"

"I'm at home. I made bail. My mom helped me out, but I'm in the system now."

"Did they wreck your house?"

"Not too bad. They weren't looking for porn, but they took my computer. It's going to be bad, Red. I don't know if I can take it."

"Ya wanta come over?"

"I can't. I can't leave the county."

"I'll come there."

Red drove to Fort Worth, and they sat outside in Darren's backyard in the light of the setting summer sun. Red remembered the time he'd sat in that same spot, alone and shell-shocked, the summer he fled his home when his own boy, Mark, suddenly self-destructed, got kicked out of school, and became a thief.

"We had another fight, and I threw him out," Darren began.

"But I thought you said he was ready to go. He was already seeing someone else behind your back."

"He was. He is. I came home unexpectedly and caught them in my bed. I'm afraid I wasn't exactly nice about it. I threw all his stuff out in the yard."

"But still, why would he go to the cops? He knows the hell he's let himself in for."

"I don't think it was him. It was his mother. He ran crying to her, and she was drunk and got pissed off."

"You say you think, but you don't know."

"Last night, the day after I threw him out, I get this weird call from him. He says he wants to make up and say goodbye. I said it was probably for the best, but what was he thinking to invite the guy into my house? He said he was lonely for me, that what he really wanted was to have me next to him."

"Yeah, that's what they all say."

"He said, 'I was so horny. I couldn't stop thinking about the last time you fucked me. Remember that?' I said, 'Yeah, it was great. I was really in love with you. I'm sorry it hasn't worked out.' Then he started sobbing, so he could hardly speak. 'I'm sorry, too! They made me do it!' he cried and hung up. As soon as he did, there was a knock at the door. It was a setup. I knew it was over. I was so weak in the knees, I barely made it to the door. They handcuffed me, and I almost collapsed. I sat on the sofa, while they went through the house. All they wanted was the computer."

"Any pictures on it?"

"No, thank God! Some e-mails. You're probably on it."

"I'm on a lot of lists. Do you have a lawyer?"

"Mom is working on that. Do you know anybody?"

"Let me make a few calls. What did you tell the cops?"

"I said I had to talk to my lawyer first."

"Good. How did they treat you?"

"It was hell. They did a strip search just to humiliate me. Then, they grilled me, but I didn't say anything, so they checked me into jail. I wasn't there for an hour before Mom showed up."

"Good for Mom."

"You're not a person anymore. Once you're in the system, you're a child molester, and that's that. As soon as you're arrested, you're guilty. And they make no distinction between violent rape and two lovers making love. It's a witch-hunt. It's crazy!"

"Yeah, it is. I'm sorry you got sucked into it."

E-mail

Dear BLN:

I want to share this story with the list. A friend of mine recently got arrested because of something he said on the phone. He had a sixteen-year-old lover. Their relationship was totally consensual. The boy had even introduced him to his parents as his lover. But then my friend caught the boy in his bed with someone else, and they had a fight and broke up. The boy told his alcoholic mother how my friend threw him out. She got angry and went to the cops. To get the evidence they needed, the cops coerced the kid with threats and intimidation to entrap my friend by calling him on the phone and referring to a recent sexual encounter. Being concerned about their relationship, my friend carelessly acknowledged it, and that was all it took. In the next minute, the cops were banging on his door. They arrested him, strip-searched him, ransacked his house, and took his computer. It will cost him thousands of dollars to defend himself. He could be sentenced to ten years in prison. And he'll be branded a sex offender for life. All that for making love to his lover. Be careful what you say on the phone. Big Brother is listening. —R^2

The Moralist

To R²:

Welcome back! We missed you. I'm sorry to hear about your friend. His story is a lesson for all of us. —BLN editor

Dear BLN:

Arrested for consensual sex with a sixteen-year-old? Does anybody besides me think that's crazy? Not merely unjust and unreasonable, but absolutely hysterically insane! —Plato

Dear BLN:

I guess we all do, but we have to understand that we are dealing with a real live modern-day witch-hunt, and they really do want to burn us at the stake. All this talk about castration and incarceration for life, even after serving a draconian sentence, circumventing the entire judicial process altogether. Do not think that that is reserved for violent rapists. They will apply it wherever they can. They will use it as a threat to coerce us to give them the names of others. I heard one of these child-protection nuts on television the other day. He said it outright: "We're not on a witch-hunt, but we know there are witches out there, and we're going to find them." What a fool! —Ganymede

Note from BLN editor:

Ganymede makes an important point. We can only hope at this point that the public will start to see how these laws are undermining our freedoms and turning America and the free world into a police state, if it isn't too late already.

Dear BLN:

It *is* already too late. That's why we need to start sending out that message now, not that boy love is okay—that has not worked—but that this is another McCarthy witch-hunt that's shredding individual freedoms and creating a totalitarian society. —RB

Dear BLN:

This is one of our problems. We are not clear exactly what our messages are. I volunteer my expertise as a communications consultant to assist with clarifying our messages and developing strategies for communicating them. —R²

Rod Downey

R2:

This is a private e-mail, not broadcast to the BLN list. A weekend meeting is being planned for mid-August at a retreat in Vermont owned by SF. He's on the BLN. He's read your e-mails about communications and wants to know if you would be able to join us. It's a long way to travel, I know, but if you can get to Boston by Friday night, someone will meet you at the airport. A bunch of us are driving up together. It's just a small gathering of about a dozen people. I will be there, as will Hawk, who published your short story. SF's compound is in a secluded location in the woods by a lake, with several private cabins, so there's plenty of room. It's the perfect setting to share ideas, discuss strategies, and develop messages. If you can make it, this would be an excellent time to instruct us in your communications techniques. I think we need it. —BLN editor

By the time he reached Deep Ellum, Red had already put away a few double vodka tonics, understanding the Bluewater Cafe was a coffee house (no booze), and for Red, coffee was a morning drink. The v&t's would have to do for the long night ahead.

At dusk, Red arrived early and sat in the wild ivy and tree-bowered cobblestone courtyard in the back, where the stage was set for rock'n'roll. Jonathan hadn't arrived yet, so Red sat at one of the wrought iron tables and quietly observed the skinny bearded men in denim taking sound checks.

It was instantly obvious how Jon Sr. with his shoulder-length hair would fit in here, as would his son, whose hair had also grown shoulder-length like his dad, very different from the close-cropped style of his eleven-year-old self almost a year ago.

Change was taking place. He was no child, who walked through the door with a guitar as big as himself draped over his shoulder in a canvas sling, but a youth with bright blue eyes and a slender soft Modigliani face and frame. He glanced around the courtyard, and catching Red's eye, his eyes lit up.

"Red!" he called and started toward him. Red met him halfway.

"Hey, buddy! You're lookin' cool with your guitar and all! I can't wait to hear you play."

"I probably won't come on till the second set. Uncle Ira's gonna start, but he has to take off at eleven. I hope you can stay that long."

The Moralist

"I wouldn't miss it." He would've waited all night if he had to.

The crowd began streaming in, a mix of relatives and musician friends, spiritualist women, rock musicians, young children, and aging hippies. It felt like a family reunion.

The air was moist and balmy. Waiters brought out complimentary orange spray cans of insect repellent to ward off the mosquitoes. The crowd jammed, as the band began blasting out its heavy-metal sound, an evening of Hendricks, Clapton, Morrison, and some original pieces.

Jonathan's little cousin Adam, age five with curly blonde locks, attached himself to Red immediately, as kids and dogs always did. Little girls in gypsy dresses handed out tambourines and cowbells for the audience to add their percussion, as if the music needed it.

The v&t's had worn off by the time Jonathan came on. Red was sipping his second espresso, as he watched his lovely boy, colored light flickering across his orange hair and face, delicate fingers dancing over the frets, eyes cast down in concentration. Like a young Apollo, Jonathan plucked his lyre, and eyes overflowing, Red was free to gaze on this vision as long as he pleased.

12

The theme of this year's Niederman Summerfest was Northern Africa: Casablanca, Morocco, the Sahara. At Penny's direction, seats were removed and a floor of sawdust laid, turning the Fairmount Hotel auditorium into an arena for the event, but *Dallas Daily News* society writer George Tildale gave her not a dot of advance ink. No doubt he found this tacky affair sponsored by a local department store not up to his cosmopolitan standards. Never mind that it was a Dallas tradition, and every socialite in town would be there, which forced his grudging appearance two boxes down from Red and Penny.

Her seat was empty most of the night. She was off schmoozing, stage managing, and dealing with the live camel that was to be the grand finale. Red tried to keep up at first but knew none of these people and nothing about camels, except they were more unruly than horses and smelled worse, so took his solitary seat in their box instead.

Sultans paraded the ring in sedan chairs, followed by belly dancers and fashion models exhibiting "the Moroccan look" for fall. Penny made it back to their box in time for the camel's parade, the beast draped in silk and brocade, with golden reins and tassels, led by its trainer dressed in black sateen slacks and a blue satin vest with gold brocade and a matching blue velvet pillbox fez topped with a golden tassel. The mounted model rode side-saddle in a red silk dress, her torso and face wrapped in layers of gossamer blue, white, salmon, and pink veils. The *Dance of the Seven Veils* swelled to a crescendo amid colored spotlights, as the trainer paraded the damsel and her mount slowly by the cheering audience, until the animal paused precisely before Tildale's box to dump a load of camel turds in his lap for all of Dallas society to see.

Gasps, murmurs, and twitters of nervous laughter echoed through the arena. Mr. Tildale stood and bowed politely before beating a quick retreat. They applauded his aplomb and laughed up their sleeves at his humiliation.

Red leaned to Penny's ear, "Did you plan that?"

Convulsing with laughter, she could barely shake her head and gasp, "No, I swear!"

"You might as well take credit for it. You've fulfilled the secret wish of everyone in this room. He's dumped on them often enough! You won't have to worry about ink now. He'll have to write about it!"

Write he did, an entire column of praise for the event. He congratulated Penny by name and took clever pokes at himself. How else could he frame being defiled by a shit-filled camel without sounding like the humorless prig he was?

The following night, Penny invited Red to celebrate over mango margaritas, her latest specialty concocted from her witch's cauldron Cuisinart and poured into plastic nightglow blue twisted stemware. They retired to the wicker chairs on her balcony, where she showed him the abandoned nest in her table-top topiary. Only two weeks before, it had been alive with screeching sparrow nestlings that looked like little mice. In barely ten days, she recounted, they'd become fuzzy fledglings, who hopped from the nest onto the ledge of the balcony and, the hardwired universal animal fear of falling confounded, leapt twenty stories to their future or their doom. Yet one remained, eyes closed but still breathing after the parents, duty done, had flown the nest.

She called her ornithologist friend for advice. The doctor said the parents knew best, but if she wanted to do something, she could put a dab of honey on a toothpick next to its beak and see if it would take the food. Penny stayed up all night getting sloshed on red wine and feeding the baby bird, until she crashed at dawn. At noon, she awoke, and the nest was empty.

"I'd like to believe the little fellow felt strong enough to make the leap. Maybe he's flying around out there somewhere right now."

"Or else splattered all over the sidewalk," Red replied, unable to resist mortifying her treacle.

"You're terrible!" she cried.

"You know my heart's in the right place," he smiled.

"So your sardonic perspective is just a pose."

"All perspective is a pose. There's no such thing as sincerity. Sincerity is a pose."

"If you believe that, then you can never know who you truly are."

"Just the opposite. You can't know who you truly are without it. My pose tells me who I am."

"Then you *are* as heartless as you seem."

"How can you say that after fifteen years of friendship? You know me more by my actions than my words."

"Sometimes words are actions."

"More often press releases. We believe that if our words can convince others who we are, maybe they can convince us, too. Only one problem: Our real self oozes from every pore. So, if it's a press release you want, how about this? I'm like the actor who worked as a longshoreman to research his role in a play. When the show closed, he couldn't find another acting job, so he became a longshoreman. I'm the shaman who wears a mask to become a god."

"Did your theater training teach you that?"

"Yes, and Theo, and psychedelic drugs, and an excellent formal education, and because that's what I wanted to learn. Socrates says the only thing we can learn are the forms we have forgotten. Christ says, 'Seek and ye shall find.' I haven't found anything I wasn't looking for."

"Who's Theo?"

"He was my mentor and lover, but that was 25 years ago."

"Where did you meet him?"

"In New York, when I was managing the Greenwich Church Theater and writing my first plays. He was a graduate of the Harbour Drama School and offered to teach me playwriting, but of course, he also wanted to get into my pants."

"Apparently he succeeded."

"After three years of dedicated persistence, yes. At age twenty-seven, married with a child, I divorced my wife and became his 'boy.'"

"Theo was a boy-lover, too?"

"Absolutely. It was a glorious regression, my second adolescence, to be adored by him. But at the same time, I was discovering that I, too, was a boy lover. We used to pick up boys together."

"Sounds like you learned a lot more than playwriting."

"Yes, I learned how to be myself and how to be a lover."

"How did he teach you those things?"

"Theo was a manic-depressive genius. His mania gave him a preternatural insight into people, including me. He showed me who I was, not by telling me, but by challenging me. It was awfully intense. How does the song go? 'Too hot not to cool down.' We lived together for three years, but I couldn't take it anymore. Besides, the 'boy' was growing up. Again. And inevitably the time came for him to leave his teacher. That's when I moved to Dallas to finish my theatrical education at the Dallas Theater Center. After I graduated, they hired me in the public relations department, which is ironic, because I once told Theo he taught me more PR than playwriting. He could perform miracles on the telephone. One spring, when we were living in New Harbour and working for the university, Henry Fonda was playing Clarence Darrow in a one-man show at Mannie's, the famous Broadway tryout theater, three blocks from our little red brick townhouse apartment on the edge of the campus. Theo got Henry Fonda on the phone. I listened as Theo harangued the great film legend into a meeting with the students and professors from the Drama School." He mimicked Theo, "'You're three blocks from the finest drama school in the world! This is your opportunity to speak to these students and share your ideas and experience. It's your duty as an icon of American film!' on and on like that."

"Was Theo speaking for the Drama School?"

"No, he didn't speak for anyone! That was his magic, that he could do this on the sheer force of his personality."

"What did Henry Fonda say?"

"He gave in, of course. They always did."

"What about the students and professors at the Drama School?"

"Well, when you've got Henry Fonda in your pocket, you're gonna get some attention. He started calling around, and next thing I knew, we had a guest list of about a dozen people."

"They believed him?"

"I wasn't sure I did."

"But you heard the phone call."

"I only heard Theo's side of it. He was the ultimate drama queen. For all I knew, he could've been talking to a busy signal. But after knowing him for six years, I'd learned to restrain my fear and suspicion and play it out. Thus, I became a conspirator in his madness. I had to believe in him, no matter what."

"Whether it was real or not?"

"Yes."

"There aren't many people who could do that."

"No, there aren't. It's a hard line to cross, suspending your own disbelief not to art or fiction but real life. It's a dangerous discipline, and it wasn't easy for me either, but being Theo's lover for two years, following him around with my video camera to record his insane and funny bits, I'd learned a lot. Three days later, the professors and students gathered for their meeting with Henry Fonda. Theo had made arrangements at the hotel rooftop restaurant where Fonda was staying, but he invited everyone to meet at our place first, so I would have to walk them over. Cozy as it was, our bohemian pad was hardly the best place to receive the cream of the Harbour Drama School, Mary Street included."

"The movie star?"

"She was a student then. She was right to go to Hollywood. Her voice was too weak for the theater. She had to scream to emote. My reviews in the *Harbour Daily* called her 'Mary Screech.' She didn't like me for that, but she still wanted to meet Henry Fonda."

"Did she?"

"When our guests showed up at our apartment, they were already rolling their eyes and wondering what kind of scam they'd let themselves in for. Theo was nowhere in sight, which left me to chat them up. When he still didn't show, what else could I do but lead them over to the hotel as planned and hope like hell this thing was going to come off. By this time, some in our entourage were openly voicing their skepticism. I reassured them. What choice did they have? Did they dare back out now and risk looking like fools? No, they had to play it out, same as me."

"So what happened?"

"When we arrived at the rooftop restaurant, the waiters had prepared a banquet-sized table and hoped for a lucrative luncheon. We were seated and ordered water and wine. I kept the conversation upbeat and confident, all the while wondering, 'Fuck Fonda, where's Theo?' Then a few minutes later, he showed up in his Brooks Brothers suit, bearing an elaborate cut-flower centerpiece. Theo knew the value of cut flowers. You can make a dump look good with a nice bouquet."

"The hotel could've taken care of that for him."

"You don't understand. The centerpiece was just his excuse to absent himself and throw me into it. That's how he challenged me, like he was saying, 'Dance your way through this one, Red.'"

The Moralist

"So what happened?"

"As everyone nervously sipped their wines and waters, a trim bright man in his mid-sixties stepped through the archway entrance and sat at the center of the table like Jesus at The Last Supper. For the next two hours, he told us how his training and experience as an actor was for the stage, and he had no intention of working in the movies, but ironically his first big success on Broadway led to his first starring role on film, because Gary Cooper was busy and couldn't do it. Then, he talked a lot about the difference between stage and film acting. He said he liked the stage better, and he thought his stage training helped him become a better film actor, because he always worked on developing the whole character, just as you would on stage, even though the movies break it up into a thousand little pieces. He said some movie actors get sloppy. It's too easy just to prepare for that day's shoot, instead of working on the script as a whole. And he said a lot of it was luck, that he just happened to have the kind of gollygeewow personality they were looking for. 'I really was like that, too,' he said, 'a real innocent. I still am.' Then, somebody asked him about Jane's trip to Hanoi, and we were off onto politics."

"What did he say about that?"

"He said he sympathized with what she was trying to do but thought it was a mistake. He was right. She will never live that down."

"So Theo pulled the rabbit out of the hat!"

"The talented and sophisticated people from the Harbour Drama School, who had the guts to show up for this scam, hung on every word. But Theo didn't do it for them. He did it for me."

Mark called: "Hey, dude!"
"Who's this?"
"It's me, Mark. How ya doin'?"
"Okay. Where are you?"
"I'm in Orlando, dude! Oh, man, I picked up these chicks in North Carolina. We went to a motel, and I banged the shit out of both of 'em. Dude, it was hot with two of 'em. Best sex I ever had in my life! I mean, no offense, but. . ."

"None taken," Red laughed at his ex-boy's simplicity. When they'd met, he was experienced beyond his fourteen years, but experience wasn't maturity. Now, it was the just the opposite. As a grown man, he was still a sweet, dumb kid.

"They wanted me to take 'em to Florida with me. We were gonna fuck all the way. But then I woke up the next morning, and they were gone."

"Did they steal anything?"

"No, dude! Why would they do that? I was their ride to Florida. I went back to the truck stop to try to find 'em. The waiter told me I was lucky. The cops were there lookin' for 'em. They were fifteen-year-old runaways, dude! If I'd been with 'em, they woulda nailed me for a child molester!"

"You're playing with fire taking a chance like that."

"It was worth it, dude. You know what I'm sayin'. Just like for you with me. How about that time when I was fourteen, and you licked my little pink ass? You loved it!"

"I don't remember that."

"Okay, I get it. Ya don't wanta talk about it. Hey, dude, I got a layover here for a coupla days. . . "

"Don't ask me for anything."

"I know, I just thought I might head over to Speed Beach."

"Don't ask me for anything. I told you, if you call, I won't hang up. I'll talk to you, but don't ask me for anything. I thought I made that clear."

"That was three years ago."

"Life is long."

"I'm not the same person I was then."

"I hope not."

"Then, why won't you be my friend again?"

"I take your calls, unlike a lot of the people who used to be your friends. I told you that trust does not restore easily. You didn't understand me then, either. Your words alone are not enough."

"You think I'm lying?"

"No, I mean there is nothing you *can* say. It's what you do that counts."

"But I can't do anything. You won't even let me visit you."

"Send me $500."

"So I have to buy your friendship?"

"No, it's a gesture of restitution for the $500 check you forged in my name. It does not begin to replace the thousands you begged, borrowed, and stole from me, but that's ancient history. What is still very real and very present is the fact that I don't trust you. You have done a lot to convince me that you are a liar and a thief and very little to convince me otherwise. Time and words alone are not going to change that."

"No Speed Beach then?"

"You can go to Speed Beach, if you wish. You'll probably have a lot of fun."

"But I can't stay at the KozmiK Kat?"

"You can stay wherever you want. Just don't ask me for anything."

"Okay, I get it. I think I'll party down here. Orlando's got a better scene anyway. You oughta see me at the bars, dude. The chicks flock around me. I get more pussy than I can handle."

"You've never had any problem in that department."

They said their goodbye's, and Red sadly put down the phone.

Red called the lawyer Penny recommended.

"They got him on tape? That's not a good sign."

"Yes, I think we're all in agreement on that. What I want to know is would you take a case like this?"

"I'd have to talk to him."

"Sure, I'm just making a few calls to see who's available. So you would be willing to consider it?"

"Yes. As you know, I've had quite a few of these kinds of cases."

"That's why I called you. How many have you won?"

"Six out of nineteen and the rest probated sentences. Nobody ever went to prison with me. But you should understand the climate right now. This is a very sensitive issue, sex between adults and minors, especially between a man and a boy. It's a real witch-hunt mentality."

"That's the third time I've heard that word."

"It won't be the last. Public attitudes have a much stronger influence on our justice system than most people realize."

"I understand. I'm in public relations."

"Then you know how much pressure that puts on the defense. You're guilty until proven innocent in a case like this, and it won't be easy or cheap. He can expect my fee to be around ten thousand, depending on how far it goes, and that tape is a big problem."

"What about his character? He's never been arrested. He owns his own home, has a good job, and the boy was a willing participant, six months from his seventeenth birthday. They were lovers. The boy introduced him to his parents. If it weren't for his loony-toons drunk of a mother, this relationship would never have come to the attention of the police."

"That will probably keep him out of prison. All the more reason he might want to consider a quick deal and call it a day."

"Probation is no picnic. It's almost like prison without walls."

"True, but that wall thing makes a big difference."

"I'll pass it along. What's the statute of limitations on a case like this?"

"Ten years, but that's about to change. The legislature is considering a bill to extend it to ten years from the child's eighteenth birthday."

"That couldn't be made retroactive, could it?"

"Possibly. That depends on whether it's viewed as substantive or procedural. Of course, that's just a way of getting around the constitutional protection against *ex post facto*. In this atmosphere, the Bill of Rights doesn't stand a chance. But that won't make any difference in your friend's case. The boy is sixteen. Ten years, twelve years, it's not relevant. So how did I get on your Palm Pilot?"

"My friend Penny Franklin. She said you grew up together."

"Penny! Yes, I saw her at the Neiderman's Summerfest, but she was so busy, we didn't get a chance to speak."

"You saw the camel!"

"Who didn't?"

Red told Darren about Mark's call.

"You didn't say anything did you?"

"Yes, I said I didn't remember anything like that."

"Good. What did he say?"

"He goes, 'Uh, okay, dude, I get it.'"

"You did the right thing."

"I learned from you, but what bothers me is that he'd say something like that on the phone in the first place. It has the sound of a setup."

"More likely the dumb jock truck-driver not knowing any better, but that doesn't matter. The rule stands. They could still be waiting outside your door."

"You ever hear of a singer called Marilyn Manson?"

"Yeah, he's a drag freak glam queen."

"Jonathan says his church thinks he's Satan."

"Yeah, that's him. He's on the cover of *Rolling Stone*. The article says a lot of that hype isn't true."

"It's showbiz. Where can I get that article? I want to give it to Jonathan."

"It's on the stands now, but won't that cause trouble with his parents?"

"No, they're not like you think. They're old hippies. I went to hear him play in his dad's band at a coffee house in Deep Ellum. It was Woodstock revisited! They're rare people. I love 'em."

"You love their son."

"Yes, and that means you have to take the whole package. You more than anyone should understand that."

"Too damn well!"

"By the way, I think I've found your lawyer."

Mark called again.

"Yeah, I had some good times with my Rrrredrick! 'Member that guy Randy, who had that briefcase full of drugs? We did all that cocaine with him?"

"No, I remember you had a friend named Randy, but I only met him once. He invited us to his New Year's Eve party."

Mark laughed, "And I got jealous, 'cause you ran off with that queen."

"I didn't 'run off.' We went outside for a smoke. I was back in time to wish you a Happy New Year."

"You were always there for me, Red."

"Yes, more than I should have been," Red leaned back in his office chair and sighed heavily.

Only a few weeks left before he started at his new school, Jonathan called and asked Red for a ride to the mall. He'd earned some money from babysitting and was eager to spend it as quickly as possible. Red was more than happy to oblige.

Over the summer, the boy had traded his bike for a skateboard, the emblem of his emerging adolescence and so made a beeline for Fast Forward, the skateboard shop, to get an XXL T-shirt imprinted with a giant mushroom. Both drug and phallus, 'shrooms were big with the freaks and thrashers. Jonathan peeled off his Stanford tee, revealing for the third time the smooth pale boy torso with nascent muscles and tits now darker than before, before covering it again with his new 'shroom shirt.

They stopped by the music store to pick up some CD's for Darren's birthday. Red asked Jonathan to make the selections, so Darren would know they had the Jonathan seal of approval.

After the music store, they took in a movie about an evil school that programmed its students like robots, *Stepford Wives* for teens, perfect timing since Jonathan had just that day received a copy of his new school's dress code in the mail. Red railed against the narrow minds of suburban Mesquite that stifled personal growth and creativity in the name of their bourgeois ideals, or worse, just keeping order.

"Yeah, they're trying to turn us into robots, just like in the movie!" Jonathan joined in, Red's words making him bold. He liked it when Red went off like it was okay to be a freak. The dress code was his first clue that things would be different at this new school. His new neighborhood was nice and not so run-down as when they lived at the dollhouse, but MLK didn't have no dumb dress code. He was in middle-school now, soon to be a teenager himself, so they had to have a dress code to make everybody conform.

Last stop, the head shop. Jonathan spent his last five bucks on cans of Day-Glo green hairspray and a pewter 'shroom ear stud. The dress code: No unnatural hair colors, no earrings for boys. Sexist, too.

"Well, I guess we've shot our wad," Red declared as Jonathan paid for his purchases.

"I like to shoot my wad," the boy smiled.

Red laughed, "Yeah, so do I."

Back at the house, Angie and her girlfriends were playing with make-up. When they saw the cans of green hairspray, they wanted to do little brother's hair. He agreed but only at his instruction. Red looked on as they cut away the long orange locks around the side and shaved his scalp with his dad's electric razor. The shoulder-length top was left untouched, so that you couldn't tell any difference, unless he head-banged his mane from side to side like a wild stallion, exposing the bare scalp beneath, or pulled it back into a ponytail like a red coon-skin cap.

The girls were atwitter with delight to have a boy's hair to play with, latent safe sex. One chick, not so latent, ran her fingers through the thick red growth and kissed him on the neck. The others giggled when Jonathan pushed her away.

The girls grew bored with the project and escaped back to Angie's room, leaving Red with the hairspray and the boy. This required open air, so Red ordered Jonathan out to the porch, but hung behind a moment to rape a lock of orange hair from the bathroom sink, fold a tissue around it, and slip it into his pocket.

On the porch, Red sprayed the beloved's hair with a green mist. Even shaved, the boy mane was so thick Red had to spray it in sections, spreading shocks at a time across the palm of his hand. How soft and shimmering it was! Like the teenage girl before him, he caressed it, and also like her, longed to kiss the smooth nape of the neck that offered itself to him. Only inches made the difference between coloring the hair and the kiss that would betray his desire. Those few inches made all the difference.

"Your school will send you home with this hair," Red observed.

"I'll tell them the swimming pool did it."

Two cans were not enough, so the result was a blend of green and ruddy gold. Jonathan led his lover into his boy bedroom adorned with posters of aliens, Hendricks, and Morrison. He turned on a black light to display the full effect of his glowing green hair.

"The green goes with your natural red. You hair is color coordinated!" Red applauded.

"Cool!" Jonathan admired his hair in the mirror over his dresser. Red admired the boy's young vanity.

He gave him the issue of *Rolling Stone* with Marilyn Manson on the cover that he'd bought on the way over. Jonathan lay on the bed Maxfield Parrish style reading the article out loud at his lover's request. How clearly he articulated and understood the words, stumbling here and there over "brouhaha" and "hypocrisy." Seated next to him, Red supplied the pronunciations and meanings like a schoolmaster, as he surveyed the bony shoulders and the line of the boy's spine beneath the loose cotton shirt that led to the plump little ass protruding beneath the denim.

Jonathan basked in the warmth of Red's attention and *joie*.

In their rental car, Red and Faye tooled through the agrarian heartland of Missouri, on their way to give a presentation at the Columbia School of Journalism, a two-hour drive from the St. Louis airport along the interstate. They usually had a driver for this kind of trip, as Faye talked on her cell phone while Red slept. But the school was on a tighter budget than their business clients and insisted on a rental car instead. Red drove. He was not looking forward to two awkward hours alone with his boss but considered he might take advantage of the opportunity to nail her for a raise. Where to jump in?

She finished her calls, and Red switched on the radio to fill the silence, catching a promo for *Call Dr. Flo*, a popular TV call-in show.

Faye initiated the conversation. "Have you ever watched that show?" she inquired.

"I've heard about it, but I'm usually at work when it comes on. I've read her newspaper column."

"What do you think?"

"You don't wanta know."

"Yes, I do. Tell me your impressions."

"Not impressions, the truth. She's a right-wing propagandist parading her extremist, bigoted opinions under the guise of psychological advice, but her credentials are phony. She calls herself 'Dr. Flo,' as if she were a doctor of psychology, but her PhD is in English. She's a deceitful hypocrite."

"You don't think she has a right to her opinions?"

"Sure, but I don't think she has the right to pass herself off as an expert in a field where she has no expertise. The First Amendment certainly gives a liar the right to lie, but that doesn't mean I have to believe her. You asked for my impressions. I warned you. How about you?"

"I think she makes some important points."

"Then we disagree, but please, I hope we can avoid a discussion of her ideas."

"Are you afraid they might have some validity?"

"No, I just don't want to lock horns with you over matters where we're obviously far apart."

"So your mind is closed."

"To the opinions of a liar and hypocrite, yes. If you've taught me anything, Faye, it's the importance of credibility. If the speaker isn't credible, it doesn't matter what she says."

"Or is it simply that you don't agree with her?"

"I don't agree with you, but you're not a fraud. I certainly wouldn't be working for you if I thought you were."

"What about that direct mail guy you used to work for? Sol Herod was the biggest fraud going."

"No, he was a crook. There's a difference."

"So you can tolerate crooks, but not frauds?"

"Crooks just want money. We were talking about ideas and social policy. Sol Herod wouldn't know a social policy if it bit him on the butt."

"From what I hear of his personal life, it just might."

"If it hadn't been for him, I would never have met you, a win-win all the way around!"

"He accused me of stealing you."

"What a joke! He wanted to get rid of me. That's why he didn't give me the raise I completely deserved after three years' service, and oh, by the way, I'm comin' up on three years with you."

Faye still couldn't figure this strange man. She dearly wanted to pigeon-hole him, her Yankee habit of control. His conversation was always light, edgy, and slightly off balance, so you never quite knew if he was kidding or not. He was the most unpretentious person she'd ever met, even self-effacing, but beneath that, there was a cocky cleverness. The more she got to know him, the more variety she discovered. His professional persona was only the tip of a very deep iceberg. There seemed no end to it, as if his ingenuousness were a mask for more subtle, even manipulative facets of his personality that he kept hidden, allowing only a glimpse or a wink. More than a mask, a dance. As long as the dancer was dancing, you couldn't pin him down. In this regard, he was more Oriental than Occidental, or more precisely, Oriental with a plain-spoken Texas twist. His charming mystery both intrigued and disturbed her, but he was smart and got the job done, and he worked for cheap. Obviously, he didn't just want money, another disturbing feature. She gave him the raise.

A knock at the door.

"Whadaya want!" Red growled from within like an angry hermit, his habit with unannounced callers. Ninety-nine percent of the time they were unwelcome as well, so he let them know in advance. This was no exception.

"It's me, dude. Mark."

"Go away!"

"Aw, come on, man. I wanta see my Rrredrick!"

"I told you not to come here."

"I won't come in. Can't ya just come out and say hi?"

Relenting, Red opened the door and stepped out onto the cobblestone landing. Standing before him was Mark, three years later, a full-grown man in jeans, gimme cap, and tank top, a pack of Marlboros rolled into the shoulder strap, with long brown hair, tattoos on both arms, and an ugly little goatee.

Red's heart sank at the sight of his once lovely boy so full of dreams of being a gynecologist and lineman for Penn State, even a fireman, a boy's dreams. Mark knew that Red remembered that. He also knew, in his own dim way, that things had changed forever, and those dreams were no more. Driving the big rigs was certainly a better calling than liar and thief.

Red could still see the boy in the man. Mark's skin was smooth and taut despite the tats, and, except for a nasty knot on his cheek, he was still good-looking with his eagle eyes, now more like snake eyes, and eagle beak. Red felt like Humbert Humbert meeting Lolita again, married and pregnant.

"Hi, Mark." His awkward greeting barely concealed these unhappy impressions.

"Aren'tcha gonna give me a hug?" Mark grinned sheepishly, afraid of rejection.

Red stepped forward and embraced him. "It's good to see you again. You look like you're doing well."

"I'm havin' the time of my life, dude! I'm a man now."

"So I see. What happened to your face?"

"Oh, that. It's just a lump. Guy hit me with a beer mug."

Mark had had a few beers himself. "Are you sure it's not a fracture?"

"Naw, it didn't even turn purple. It'll go away. I'm livin' the life of a trucker, dude. I walk into a bar now, and guys are scared of me." He was a jock and a bully in high school. Things hadn't changed that much.

He asked about Darren, but Red was circumspect. Darren was not his friend anymore, but Mark did not, would not, could not grasp that, this both his denial and sad innocence.

Red spoke plainly. "You have estranged a lot of people, Mark. Many of those who once loved you most, your closest friends, don't want to see you anymore, and I don't think you will ever be able to get them back. I'm the only one sentimental enough or foolish enough to keep this line of communication open."

He wept. "I know. I'm sorry for what I did to everybody. I'm really sorry!"

"So am I. It broke my heart. I loved you. I did everything I could to get you on your feet, and all you did was fuck me over. It still hurts to think about it."

"It hurts me, too, Red."

"It's good to see that you've grown up and created a life for yourself, instead of ending up in jail or prison, which was where you were headed."

"I did go to jail, dude! Three months for stealing that chick's stereo! That's what woke my ass up!"

"Then, good for jail. It succeeded where I failed. But this Kodak moment doesn't change a thing."

After a silence, he said, "I see. Well, I guess I better go then."

It took all of Red's resolve not to invite him in as the big boy-man hugged him one more time in parting. Mark turned and walked away along the cobblestone path back to his rig. Watching his departure with the eyes of a lover, Red saw the boy of fourteen dancing.

Straightening up

The following morning, a Saturday, Red brewed his coffee and retired to his office. He took from the closet shelf a box labeled "Mark." Setting it in the middle of his office floor, he sifted through the contents: notes and cards of love, some on blue ruled ring-binder paper written in class by a bored teenager and decorated with drawings of hoots and babes, ticket stubs to concerts and sporting events, some where Mark was on the field, and hundreds of photographs. The big, skinny teenager in black shirt and loose-fit jeans dancing his full-of-himself dance proud of his good looks, adult size, and agility. The happy birthday boy deliberately flashing his balls beneath loose fitting shorts as he held up his sixteenth birthday gift, a classic-style "New York Yankees" jersey. The golden-tanned smart-ass mooning the camera by the sea. The shirtless youth holding up live lobsters just before dropping them into the boiling pot. The boy standing on a cliff with the profile of an eagle overlooking the river below. The clown dolled up as the ugly black slut character Wanda from the TV show *In Living Color* for Halloween. Three Halloweens, three Christmases, six birthdays. Red had completely redecorated the house after he closed the door on Mark. These photos were the last record of the old look with Mark's personal touches: Beatles White Album and Ton Loc posters, a net fastened to the ceiling decorated with sports medals and stolen hood ornaments. Red gazed sadly on these icons of their love and stuffed them one by one into a lawn-size trash bag, two full days and bags of nostalgia and tears.

On Monday, dressing for work, he listened for the grinding, squealing machine outside. He ran to the curb with the black plastic bags like body bags and handed them into the canvas-gloved hands of the trash man, who heaved them carelessly into the grinding jaws of the truck.

13

Penny returned from D.C. with her latest suitor, a successful stockbroker she'd met at some Republican dinner and brought home like a souvenir.
 She gathered her closest friends for an introductory soiree, asking Red to tend bar. He wondered if this expressed condescension or confidence in their friendship. If it was the former, he got his revenge. He played Big Daddy, offering her gentleman caller a drink and sizing him up. They got into a lively discussion about developing a profile in Dallas for him as a stock expert, until interrupted by the next refill, Jennifer, Penny's old school chum from the first grade, now married with a toddler.

Red asked how was her day, and she confided her angst at dealing with a Neiderman's dresser who was not her regular gal. He tried to express sympathy for her stressful day, but she must have taken it as irony, when she giggled at herself, "I know I sound like some shallow character in a movie." What could he do but agree, laughing amiably, "At least you know who you are."

Darren called, "My mom found a lawyer who's half the price of your guy."

"What's the price for going to prison?"

"He said that wouldn't happen. He's done lotsa cases like mine. He's been a lawyer for forty years."

"How old is he?"

"I dunno, late sixties. He's the senior guy at the firm."

"Maybe a little too senior."

"Whadaya mean? He knows what he's doin'."

"I'm sure he does, but you have to be careful with an old guy like that. He's been around the block too many times. Your case is just routine for him. He works more for the court than he does for you, but you pay the bill."

"You don't know that."

"I hope I'm wrong. What does he recommend?"

"He said I should cop a plea."

"Yeah, the old fart just wants to cut a deal and collect his fee."

"Your guy said the same thing."

"Yeah, but my guy will go to bat for you, no matter what you decide. He's a trial lawyer. He likes the fight."

"You think I should fight it."

"I think you have a case. Jonathan is gay. He was your lover. He has another boyfriend now. He didn't even file the complaint. His mother did, and she's a hopeless drunk. This should never have happened to you."

"But it has happened, and I just want to get it over with."

"I know that, and so do they. That's what they're counting on. That's what your lawyer is counting on."

"So you think I should go with your guy?"

"I just don't want you to be railroaded by the system. Even if you do cut a deal, you need a tough lawyer to negotiate for you. I'm afraid this old fart will sell you out and tell you that's the best you're gonna get."

Red called Penny to thank her for the evening and walked into a buzz-saw.

"I do not appreciate your pitching my clients," she declared in her nicest voice. Penny did not do anger well. She always became overly proper and articulate, but it just came off as phony.

Red recognized the tone. It was like fingernails scratching a blackboard. If it was intended to put him on the defensive, it didn't work. "I didn't know your boyfriend was a client. What does that make you?" he retorted sarcastically.

"What are you saying?"

"From my experience, a woman who calls her boyfriends 'clients' is a whore!"

"I beg your pardon!" To Red's relief, nice and proper were giving way to real rage.

"Look, I was just schmoozing him. You more than anyone ought to know a schmooze when you see one, and I am deeply hurt that you don't."

"You called me a whore!"

"Yeah, and you know what they say in Texas: The hit dog barks." He slammed down the phone. If you want to piss off a drama queen, bring down the curtain. They will spontaneously combust with frustration. Maybe she was picking a fight to push Red back a bit while boyfriend was in the picture.

Or maybe it was her "Daddy" thing. Boyfriend meant severing ties with "Daddy." Ten years her senior, Red played surrogate father, a role he particularly disliked. Penny definitely had a "Daddy" thing. Her real father was in poor health. An alcoholic, diabetic, bed-bound invalid with a full-time nurse, he'd been dying for twenty years. He was dying when Red met her. Estranged from his ex-wife and two other daughters, Goneral and Regan, Penny was his Cordelia. He took shameless advantage of her love for him, scaring away a horde of wealthy suitors, so now she was forty and looking at a life without the husband or family that she dearly wanted and deserved.

Red had never met the man but from her paeans, he sounded smart and charming. He'd probably like the guy. But, Daddy notwithstanding, Red had told her a million times to get the hell out of Dallas and go to Paris where she really wanted to live. But she wanted Red to come with her, *in loco parentis, in loco paternis, in loco penis.* A good time to put Penny on ice.

For Darren's birthday, a hot August night in Dallas, Red invited him for a cookout. Ready to party at the Crossroads, Darren rolled into town with Jimmy, a pretty little queen with blonde hair, a sharp tongue, and a golden voice.

They celebrated with mesquite-grilled steaks and grilled veggies, a Napa Merlot, and for dessert a strawberry cheesecake decorated with candles. They sang "Happy Birthday," and Laura blew out her candles, her world now lit by the lightning of the sex offender laws.

Darren tore into the gifts strewn around the cake like candy, the individually wrapped CD's that Red and Jonathan had selected at Mr. Shakespeare's. Darren immediately put them on the box with speakers that rocked the house like a dance bar.

"I love this!" he cried, "Pan Pipe, Secret Garden, Third Eye Blind! This is fresh stuff!"

"The boy seal of approval! Jonathan picked them out himself."

"It's perfect. Tell Jonathan he has excellent taste."

"He's a musician. He knows this shit, and it was great fun grazing over the CDs with him. He was in his element, and I was with him all the way. Hawg heaven!"

Jammin' on the box, "Third Eye Blind".

Red explicated, "Jonathan said they were queer. The name 'Third Eye Blind' means an asshole. Listen to the lyrics. This song's about drugs and sex. I'm amazed that they play it on the radio."

Little Jimmy jumped up and acted out the lyrics of shooting up and getting fucked with perfect precision. Darren and Red applauded.

"Thank you," Jimmy bowed his head with false modesty and low-class femininity.

Red noticed his glossy display of plastered-down curly blonde hair and glided his fingertips over the crystalline surface. "What do you put on this?"

"Mousse."

"Is that all? When Jonathan spikes his hair, he uses Elmer's glue."

"Who is this Jonathan you keep talking about?" the smart little queen pointedly asked.

"He's my lover, or rather, I'm his lover. He is my beloved."

"And how old is he?"

Before Red could answer, the phone rang. It was the very boy. Red excused himself and took the call upstairs away from his drunken buddies now absorbed in the riotous music, a plus for Red that Jonathan could hear a party in the background with the music he had chosen.

"I want to read my song to you," he began.

"Song? Like song lyrics?"

"Yeah, it's called *I Don't Want To Be Like You.*" He recited:

> I don't want to be like you.
> I want to be weird.
> I want to be different.
> I want to be radical.
> I don't want to be like you.

"Another song addressed to me?"

"No, you're weirder than I am!" he chirped.

"Thank you. I didn't know I was held in such high esteem. Does that mean you *do* want to be like me?"

"Maybe, in a seventh-grade kinda way."

"And so you are, in a seventh-grade kinda way. I take it the 'you' in your song refers to everyone else, because being like everyone else is not being you as an individual. It's a song about conformity and individuality."

"You sound like Frasier!" he howled. "You know who Frasier is? That guy on TV?"

"Yeah, Chelsey Gramer. He plays a radio talk-show shrink."

"That's him! I thought you didn't watch TV."

"I useta like *Cheers*. His show is a spin-off from *Cheers*."

"You talk just like him."

"Thank you, you're just full of compliments tonight! I enjoyed your song."

"It's punk. Ya gotta scream it."

"Like 'Don't fuck with me, don't fuck with me!'?"

"That's it! You got it!"

Red said goodbye to the beloved and returned to his guests.

"Red has a hard on!" Darren teased.

"Where? I don't see it!" Jimmy imagined group sex.

"Red's whole mind has a hard on!" Darren jumped up and ran his hands over Red's aura. "You can feel it!"

Red grinned, "You got that right!"

Returning to the futon, Darren explained to Jimmy, "He's been makin' love to his boy. Just now, while we've been down here, he went upstairs and made love to his boy."

"You mean phone sex?" Jimmy was disappointed.

"Yeah, phone sex," Red replied, taking his seat across from them. "He read his latest song to me. Wanta hear it? You have to understand, he's a punker. It's a punk song." He jumped up and proceeded to scream out the lyrics, "'IdontwanttobelikeyouIdontwanttobelikeyou!' Like that."

"Oh, I see," Jimmy condescended with a defiant turn of the head and roll of the eyes.

Darren cried, "Don't you get it? That's Red's hard-on!"

"Was the song written to you?" he shot back snidely.

Red laughed, "No, it's his adolescent cry for individuality. He wants to be unique. He wants to scream it out."

Darren exclaimed, "He's talented! He's cute!" He showed him Red's framed photo of the panther boy on the limb from their bike trip. "Look at that! He's a rock'n'roller and a poet and a daredevil, right, Red?"

"All that and more."

"He calls his lover to read his poetry to him! Red loves him, and he knows it! He's writing a book about it."

Jimmy curled his lip, "He looks like a little boy! You never did say how old he is."

"He's twelve, almost thirteen."

"I hope you're not having sex with a twelve-year-old."

"Did I say that?"

"Well, do you or not?"

"Would I tell you?"

"Oh, Red! I see what you're doing!" Darren rolled his eyes, turning to Jimmy, "He doesn't. He hasn't."

"How do you know?" Jimmy retorted.

"Red, you haven't. I know you haven't."

"I don't kiss and tell."

To Jimmy, "I'm telling you, this is his trick! He's playing you. He sees that you're trying to judge him, so he's jacking you off!"

"I get it. You're not gonna give me a straight answer," Jimmy confronted Red again.

Red roared, "A little queen like you asking for a *straight* answer! Now, *that's* funny! But I will contain myself long enough to clarify your confusion. I consider your inquiries about my personal life presumptuous beyond imagination, and on that score, I'm free to respond any way I wish. How's that?"

"You opened the door by saying he's your lover," he persisted.

"I love him. What else should I call it?"

"A lover means sex."

"That's a matter of interpretation. What are you, a lawyer?"

"I'm a recruiter."

"So am I!" Red quipped with a sly smile.

"No, it's true. He really is," Darren explained. "He interviews high school seniors for technology scholarships."

"Poison ivy. You can look, but you'd better not touch."

"I'm not into boys. I prefer men."

"You say that now, but wait till some starry-eyed beauty comes on to you."

"All the Chester Molesters I ever knew were creepy old queens," he sneered.

"Then, be careful you don't become one."

Darren dove in to defend his boy from being eviscerated before he knew it, "Jimmy knows all about that, girl! Trolls hit on him all the time, even straight ones!"

"Cute men, too," he pecked Darren on the cheek, "and don't you forget it." He turned to Red, "He's a boy lover, too, isn't he? That's why you two are friends. He likes pretty little boys like me."

"Why ask me?"

"I do, it's true," Darren smiled and kissed his little queen the way he wanted to be kissed, and that was that. Red retreated to the bar.

Serpent-tongued Jimmy slithered into the bathroom. Darren joined Red, as he mixed fresh drinks. "I'm twenty-eight years old, Red! Can you believe it?" he cried. "For the first time, I can look back on my life and have a perspective on Alan and Terry and Brandon I and Brandon II and Steve and Jonathan and all the rest of them, since we met nine years ago. You've known them all. I understand it now. If you're straight or gay, you grow old with your lover, but the boy-lover's beloved will always be a boy."

"And you grow old alone."

"You're as young as who you feel! And your love for every one of them lasts a lifetime. You taught me that."

"They always come back, that's for sure!"

"Yeah, both are true." He nodded toward the bathroom. "So whadaya think? You don't like him, do you?"

"He's a little smart-mouth queen. But at least you have to be smart to have a smart mouth. How old is he?"

"Don't worry. He's twenty-one, but God, Red. . ."

"Yeah, I know: When the clothes come off, he becomes thirteen!" Handing him a cocktail. "I'll drink to that."

Billy Budd's was a crummy karaoke bar. Red and Mark used to play pool there. Then, only the drinks and the magically lit green felt of the pool table mattered, where he competed with his young football stud, who win or lose, would fuck him good that night. Without Mark's magic aura, Red saw the place with clearer eyes: concrete floor and cheesy wooden tables scattered with ugly, dreadful queens nursing their alcohol. The place belonged in a Mexican border town.

They were greeted at the door by Tristan, the diminutive karaoke troll who singled Red out with a leering grin revealing spaces between his teeth. "You look like a plantation owner in your Cancun T-shirt, puffing on a stogie."

"I went scuba diving there with my daughter." Biting the stogie in his teeth as he talked, Red played his assigned role. "It was great fun."

"Enough about the daughter. I want to hear about your adopted son," the troll cut to the bone. Red knew he was in the program. Darren brought him over one night, and Red showed off his photos of the boy.

Tristan represented all that Red despised about society's corruption of boy-love, the coffee shop society of young sissies and old chicken hawks playing mix and match. The gay world of the Crossroads was an adult world of cowboy boots and cashmere, pickup trucks and BMW's. The grown-up queens wanted nothing to do with this youthful sub-subculture. It would grow up, join the life, and compete with them soon enough. Tristan was at the lower end of this food chain.

Red couldn't be too disdainful. When the park was active ten years ago, he, too, had participated, but that part of his life was over now, less a matter of his appearance or age, than refinement of taste. Unlike the paunchy, balding, gray-hairs his same age who desperately worked the boy scene, he could still get away with forty. But after Mark, he'd had his fill of the air-headed chicken and implied prostitution that world offered. Red wanted a real boy and real love, which meant a more dangerous approach. To find that boy, he would have to enter the other world of home and school guarded by the sentinels of law and authority, but he had no notion how to go about it. Those who functioned in that world did so by establishing membership as schoolteachers, coaches, priests, and scoutmasters, so that when they got caught, as they often did, they were condemned as much for betrayal of trust and abuse of office as for messing with the boys.

Intentionally, society failed to acknowledge how neatly the deck was stacked to produce this result. Boy lovers were either degenerate fairies engaged in prostitution or traitors to authority and corruptors of youth. If you were neither of these, there was a third category: predator, kidnapper, and rapist. There was no room in this equation for the man who simply wanted to find a bright loving boy and become his best friend for life. That the myth proclaimed was not possible.

In this context, what Red had accomplished with Jonathan was miraculous beyond belief. His volunteer work had provided him with the entrée he could never have consciously engineered on his own. (If he'd had an ulterior motive, he'd surely have been disappointed, or worse, found out.) That his student would be the perfect boy, a bright young artist, intelligent, talented, and compassionate with no trace of maladjustment, corruption, or effeminacy. That the boy should want to continue the relationship beyond the program.

That his parents would allow it. It had all fallen into place so perfectly, it felt like destiny.

Responding to Tristan's inquiry, he said, "He called tonight to sing me his latest song. He's a musician and song writer."

"Aren't they all!" sneered the troll.

This annoyed Red. "He plays bass in his dad's band. They've got a regular gig at The Bluewater Café. You oughta check it out." That shut him up, but Red instantly regretted his retort. What if troll took him up on it? What if he went there and spoke to Jonathan, saying he was a friend of Red's? These two worlds had to be kept apart.

The birthday celebrants took their seats at a table near the stage, and Jimmy continued their conversation in the repressed judgmental style of Mike Myers' *Saturday Night Live* Church Lady. "So he reads his stuff to you. Do you ever read your stuff to him?"

"He's never asked me to."

"You don't ask him, but he does it anyway."

"I do ask him. I have made it abundantly clear that I want to read everything he writes. I'm his writing coach."

"Not anymore. Darren said the program was over."

"Yes, the program is over, but I'm not over, and my love for him is not over."

"And this book of yours is a monument to that love!" he said sarcastically. Red could almost hear, "Isn't that spe-shul!"

"In some ways, that's true," he replied. "I don't know about monument. I would say more 'paean.' That means song of praise. He writes his songs, I write mine."

"Then why don't you read them to him?"

"I probably will, when the time comes. It's pretty adult stuff for a twelve-year-old."

Jimmy was horrified. "Do you actually write things about a twelve-year-old boy that get you off?"

"Some of it is erotic, yes."

"Hey, haven't you ever read a book that gets you hard?" Darren interjected.

"Sure, but *writing* it is different, especially if it's true."

"Who said anything about truth? You asked if it got me off, and I said yes. If it gets me off, it gets the reader off. If I laugh, they laugh. If I cry, they cry.

If I cum, they cum!"

"Write it, and they will cum!" Darren roared, and held up his high-five.

Red slapped his hand and scribbled Darren's quip on a napkin.

"That's the jism of it!" Darren squealed again in hilarious glee. He was on a roll. Another round of laughs and high-fives.

Tristan's karaoke was cranking up, so Jimmy interrupted the *bon mots* with his own performance. He pointedly chose an old pop song about boy love, Erasure's *Ship of Fools*.

All applauded, and Darren raised his glass, "Boy love forever! Boy love through thick and. . ."

"Thicker," Red added.

Darren grabbed his crotch, "It's gettin' thicker by the minute!"

The tipsy trio returned to Red's place, and sharp little Jimmy passed out. Red breathed a sigh of relief. He'd had enough of the little queen's sniping, though he'd enjoyed the challenge. If the little fuck weren't so insufferably bouge, he mighta been interesting. Darren was nodding. They wound down with a vodka nightcap.

"So have you done it with him or not? Inquiring minds want to know!" Darren slurred.

"I am the ghost of sex future!" Red dramatically declared. "I see what sex will be like for you twenty years from now."

"Yeah, I know. They get younger."

"There's more to it than that. Look, here's a book, a Nobel Prize winning novel called *The Magic Mountain*, written by Thomas Mann, the same guy who wrote *Death in Venice*."

"I don't want to hear about your books. I want an answer!"

"I'm not recommending it. I mention it as an example. This is all I read now, only the best. I made that decision ten years ago after reading some awful airport novel. I thought enough is enough. If I'm going to spend this time of my life reading, I want only the best, and the beauty of it is, when it comes to literature, the best is usually cheaper than the junk! Not so with boys. With boys, the best is more expensive than you can possibly imagine, and I ain't talkin' about buying your Jonathan a Jeep."

"I shoulda done it! It woulda been worth it for the shit I'm havin' to put up with now! A Jeep woulda been cheap!"

the queens were the worst of the lot in their luxury sedans, sleek sports cars, massive SUVs, and shiny new trucks. Not a smoking hooptie in sight. A creature of his milieu, Thing wanted them all.

Back at the house, Thing to Red: "I can't believe you are forty."

Darren howled.

"I'm not," Red replied. "I'm fifty."

His jaw dropped. "Now you're making fun of me!"

Darren cried, "It's true! He has a twenty-five-year-old daughter, nine years older than you!" Pointing at a framed photograph of Cindy with Thunder. "Look, that's her and her horse. Red took that picture. What a babe, huh?"

"That's incredible. How do you do it?"

"Do what? Take pictures? Have a daughter? Ride a horse?"

"No, how do you look so young?"

"Oh, you wanta know how I keep my youth."

"Yes."

"Oh, God, here it comes!" Darren rolled his eyes and squealed with laughter.

"How do I keep my youth?" Red grinned. "I give him anything he wants." Thing didn't get it, but Darren was on the floor.

"Get it?" Red patiently explained. "How do you keep your youth? Give him anything he wants!"

"I want a Jeep," still not getting it, or else getting it all too well.

Red confided to Darren, "He sure picked up on that in a hurry!"

Darren called the next day. "So whadaya think?"

"I think he's a low-class, barely literate, materialistic, effeminate queen, kinda birdlike in the face—he won't age well—with a peaches-and-cream complexion, a lovely boyish body, and a cute little bubble butt, so if you like fuckin' him, what the hell does it matter what I think?"

"I knew you'd like him. And he's not quite as low-class as you think. There's money in his family. His uncle is David Jones. He owns that string of seafood places."

"Davey Jones' Locker? They're one of our clients!" Red exclaimed. "I met with David Jones just two days ago."

"Great! Next time you see him, tell him that your best friend is fucking his sixteen-year-old nephew."

"Sixteen?"

"What price love? So why not the best? Like you once said, the beautiful seventeen-year-old standing naked before you in the flower of his youth. That's the best. Who wouldn't want that? But I want more. I want the mind and personality to go with it. I want the total package, and I'm not going to find that in the gay life. It's fun when you're twenty-eight. You may think that's too old, but that's the best time! Look at you! You piss and moan with your aging-faggot bullshit, while you're getting more boys than you can handle! The boys love you! I would give anything to have that again, but now that I've had the quantity, I want quality. I read the best literature, eat the best food, drink the best wine, so why not love the best boy? When Jonathan wandered into my life, I at least had the presence of mind to know beauty when I saw it. I knew I had to love him *pas question*, no matter what. I hope that after you've had your fun, your taste can become as refined as that. I hope that you, too, will find your primo love."

"But, Red, this beauty of yours is a snaggle-toothed, working-class preadolescent. He's cute, but he's not a god. Plus, he's too young, even for you."

"His voice is changing, and I'm gonna fix his teeth. I'm in no hurry. I'm already having sex with him."

"You are!"

"Yeah, like you said, every time I'm in his presence, every time I hear the sound of his sweet voice tickling my ear and the clean, thin lines of his thought, making love to my brain. You called it my 'hard-on,' and you were absolutely right."

"Yeah, but sex is still sex. You still want him."

"More than ever, day by day."

"When the time comes, you will tell me, won't you?"

"You know the rule."

"Yeah, don't tell anyone."

"That's right, even your best friend."

"Even if it never happens?"

"Even if it already has."

"Don't pull your tricks on me! I know it hasn't!"

"Then, why do you ask?"

14

Sixty-something, potbellied Rupert ("RB" on the BLN) met Red at Logan, but they would not be able to leave for Vermont right away, because Hawk (his name was Dennis, but his nickname really was Hawk) didn't get off from the magazine until six. It would be five more hours on the road after that, close to midnight before they reached their destination. But for now, they had an afternoon to kill.

Red had met Rupert five years ago at the Gay Writers' Conference, also in Boston, where he'd been invited by *The Ganymede Reader* to sit on a panel discussing boy-love in the arts. In his presentation, he advocated an artist spokesman for boy-love who could reference his art instead of himself and thus avoid the first pitfall of boy-love advocacy: talking about your personal life. From the audience, Rupert argued that a true artist would not be able to draw that distinction.

"In his creative life, that may be true," Red allowed, "but in the realm of anecdote and advocacy, it would be very easy. The artistic product provides a focus for the discourse that allows the artist to avoid the details of his personal life altogether."

"The audience wouldn't see it that way," Rupert rebutted. "They would assume the artist was talking about himself."

"True, you cannot separate an artist from his perspective," Red agreed, "but that doesn't mean he has to talk about who he slept with last night. That has been a significant problem with boy-love advocacy. The debate inevitably disintegrates into *ad hominum* attack."

Red could see his audience didn't get it. Mostly teachers and academics, they still saw public communications as an intellectual exercise, instead of the elaborate duel that it was. He still had a lot to learn about communicating complex ideas.

Rupert drove them back to his apartment next to the college campus where he taught. They walked together through the deserted tree-lined quadrangle toward the copy center, where Red wanted to run off some materials for his presentation, part errand, part tour. Red loved academe, especially when it was alive with eager intellectual youth, which on this sunny August afternoon, it was not, like an empty room with bare floors and bare walls.

He thought of Harbour on a fresh autumn morning, when he rode his bike to the quadrangle and wrote *Seeing Red* under a tree or on the steps of a hallowed hall, as the students began to trickle then pour from the dorms on the way to their classes, or in the evening, when he smoked a quick joint and watched them study or throw a football or Frisbee in the warm cottonwood dusk of spring.

With almost uncanny clairvoyance, Rupert interrupted Red's reverie to observe that living on campus seemed to suspend time, because the students were always young. Only you grew older. Red remembered Darren's comment: "My lover will always be seventeen."

Rupert continued describing his recent affair with a nineteen-year-old from Quebec, where he discovered the custom of government-sanctioned meeting places for men and boys: a swimming pool where boys as young as fourteen, the age of consent in Canada, were allowed to socialize with the men in a nearly naked setting. The cops kept an eye on things to keep out drugs, prostitution, and public sex, but aside from that, it was anything goes, including taking boys home.

It sounded like paradise compared to the oppression that existed in America, but "We still have our Reverchon Parks," Red thought, although even that spontaneous pocket of pederasty was corrupted by its own illicit existence and eventually cleaned out by the police, as they all were until another cropped up.

Rupert's claim to fame was a long-term exception. When he was younger, he wrote of his urban experience, where working-class boys and men formed a subculture of pederasty that passed from generation to generation, a phenomenon of such remarkable rarity that his book had attained the status of assigned reading for sociology and gay studies classes. The scene was gone now, but it had lasted for decades. Red wondered if the book didn't contribute to its demise by exposing it.

After their errand, Rupert announced he was off to visit his mother in the nursing home, so Red would be on his own for the afternoon. Rupert suggested his guest amuse himself at a downtown park known for its young skateboarders and cruisy gay boys looking to get picked up. Red wasn't in the market, but it sounded like fun. Across from the park was the Glad Day Bookstore, where you could easily browse away an afternoon among the stacks of boy-love books and radical tracts you couldn't get in Dallas or anywhere else in the world.

As promised, the park was alive with teenage skateboarders and gay boys and men lounging lasciviously on the concrete benches. The crystalline summer afternoon was a perfect time for fun with plenty to choose from. The blockhouse bathroom on the corner was bustling with visitors. Stinking bathroom sex, the risk of cops and disease were not Red's pleasure. Like a latter-day Aschenbach, he sat quietly on a bench, absorbed in one of his Glad Day books, a thousand-year history Classical pederasty.

Boisterous boy voices distracted him. He looked up and studied these antipodal creatures native to this foreign land and far more fascinating than the ubiquitous and predictable fairies whose eyes darted away the moment he looked up from his book.

The adolescent skateboarders were a separate species. They loped along, until suddenly as if on cue, exploding with the energy and daring of their sport, sailing over stairways and grinding the rails, splitting up for the solitude of their boards then joining together as a unit again.

Working-class city boys, he imagined, in their worn canvas Vans, frayed baggy jeans, punk XXL tees, rings, chains, tats, and greasy, shoulder-length hair. Red had learned the thrasher look from Jonathan's latest interest. Sliding across the pavestones on their boards with the rhythmic clatter of a train, they worked their way across the park in Red's direction.

They halted their progress to take on a picnic table, levitating their boards like magic to its benches and tabletop. At closer range, Red noticed the smallest and youngest among them, a skinny, graceful boy of thirteen or so with thick red hair falling into bangs over his eyes. He was lighter on the board and more agile than the older boys, seeming almost to make it dance for him, his skill no doubt earning his membership.

They clattered by before him close enough to touch. At a glimpse of the kid's angelic face, Red caught his breath. It could have been Jonathan!

As if swept up in the wake of young male energy, Red rose from the bench and followed. The graceful boy at the back of the pack, Red observed his slender frame and narrow hips beneath loosely draped fabric that shifted smoothly from side to side for balance, poultry in motion.

He dropped one foot back and shifted his weight to ollie the board from beneath his feet and catch it under his arm. "Wait up. I gotta whiz," he called to his buddies, who turned and razzed him about the risks of using this particular facility. Red barely made out their New England Boston drawls, as they dared him to go it alone which he did, but he had company.

Knowing full well the other boys were watching, Red followed him in. The damp concrete room smelled heavily of disinfectant. It was eerily quiet. The two stalls were occupied with doors closed and securely bolted, but the urinals were free. The boy was just stepping up to one. Red joined him at the other just in time to catch a glimpse of the full-grown circumcised penis cut loose a thick yellow stream.

The kid stared intently ahead to signal the man beside him there was nothing doing here.

Half hard, Red struggled to release his own member, and the piss wouldn't muster. His heart raced with terror at his folly. Rustling sounds resumed from the stalls, as the boy finished his business and shook himself dry. Red had no choice but to continue his charade of needing to go, but his hard-on betrayed him. The boy glanced over and then back at his own. It, too, was growing stiff. After a few strokes, it was full hard.

The whole thing smacked of a setup, but Red wanted to touch that hard boy cock with its baby-soft skin. Stroking his own, he reached for it. The kid just stood there pushing his hips forward slightly to let it happen. Red stroked it a few more times, and that was all it took to pop a fresh boy load over Red's hand and into the porcelain bowl. Grinning sleepily and catching his breath, the boy took over and stuffed his dick back into the baggy jeans that hid it too well. Still hard and wet, Red wiped his hand on his pants. By the time he zipped up, the boy was already out the door, and once again, Red heard the boisterous Yankee jibes and laughter like music.

Rupert showed up for their rendezvous right on time, and they gathered Hawk from the magazine offices. Pale with thick glasses, barely thirty but already showing salt-and-pepper hair, Hawk was the stereotypical intellectual. He had kept his day job as an editor for a popular gay monthly, but the raid on *Pan* had gutted the thing he loved.

Exhausted by a deadline day, Hawk's mood was dark. Red the stranger listened in silence to the two friends' conversation, as the car found its way out of Boston and onto the Interstate. Hawk's only wish now was to get away and do something else. Raised by a lesbian couple, he'd become a boy-love activist at age fifteen and a young leader and spokesman for the movement. He was the one the news media and talk shows always called when they needed a quote or a boy lover to vilify. He'd stopped doing interviews for that reason. What was the point? That's why Red was on this trip, why the retreat itself was taking place, to figure out how to rebuild from the ruins. The atmosphere had grown so much more toxic than anyone had imagined. The cause seemed truly lost. What was it Rhett Butler said? Lost causes were the only ones worth fighting for.

Hawk was starting not to care anymore. Unlike gray-haired Rupert, who was approaching retirement, he was still young enough to go back to school and begin another career in mathematics. Why were there so many mathematic pederasts? It was like gay flight attendants or hairdressers.

They turned off the highway, and soon the road narrowed and narrowed again. Rupert snaked the car through the black pine forest to the lodge. They parked at the end of a dirt drive crunchy with pine needles and were met by their host Eugene ("SF" on the BLN). He was small in stature, only a few years older than Red but looking much older with a coarse gray seaman's beard and wiry build from his life in the jungles of Central America, where he lived most of the time working to improve health care in the native cultures. During his career there, he'd had several native boys as lovers with the full sanction of their villages and the proud approval of their parents. Boy love was part of the cultural fabric of these people. Eugene was a boy lover of the world!

They joined the others at a long table on the veranda. Gilly, his eighty-five-year-old mother, and two brown Guatemalan boys, about eighteen or so, served a late meal. Across from Red sat Harry (BLN himself), gray with twinkling eyes and the soft face of a loving teacher. His political activity in Philadelphia had attracted the attention of the police, of course, and there was an outcry that a pedophile was teaching elementary school children, but he was clean and, though persecuted, never prosecuted for his politics. The cops finally decided he was "one of the good ones," as Harry often quoted them. He was a fan of both Red's writing and his approach to communications, and no doubt the reason Red was invited. They welcomed each other as old friends who had communicated by phone and e-mail for years but never until now met face-to-face.

The boy lovers conversed late into the night. Eugene was intrigued, when Red mentioned he was writing a book, and asked if he'd brought any of it with him, which of course he had. One of the Guatemalan boys, named Jesus, chiseled and handsome like a Hollywood Indian, twisted a blue napkin into a rose and handed it to Red with a bright white smile against his brown skin. He spoke no English, but Red welcomed the gesture with his eyes, connecting with the bright dark innocent eyes of the boy that said 'My gift is for you.' Red raised his glass and smiled. Was he now to play Oberon and have his Indian boy? It wouldn't be nice to jump his host's boy, or was that the protocol, catamites for the guests?

And what about the white boy in the room? Not a boy really, but a boyish young man in his mid-twenties with slightly thinning blonde hair, a baby face, and stocky frame. He was the only one of the group Red had not previously known through the BLN.

Noah looked like an undergrad but was in fact an associate professor of sexology at Philadelphia University. He was there to present the findings of a study on child sexual abuse, another item on the agenda. Harry confided that Noah was just coming out himself and would be Red's bunkmate for the weekend.

The wooded compound consisted of a main house and individual rough-hewn cabins. Eugene led them down the path with a flashlight to a rugged wooden structure with barely room for two cots and an old-fashioned oil lamp that worked just fine. It reminded Red of Boy Scout camp and Jeffrey. He propped open the wooden shutter to let in the sounds and breezes of the warm August night, hoping the screen would keep the mosquitoes out. It didn't.

Noah invited him for a moonlight swim, a sweet proposition, but it was very late and Red politely declined. There was a time he would have done it anyway just for the fun of fucking a sexologist. It's research! But Noah was already too much a man. Red wanted the Indian boy. He crashed on the bunk and fell instantly into an exhausted sleep.

As the sun came up over Mirror Lake, Red and Noah threw on jeans and tees to make their way along the path to the main house, Red clutching his overfull toiletry kit and plastic-draped, freshly dry-cleaned costume, a French blue shirt, red tie, and pin-striped power suit.

The early risers straggled into the main house. There was a full day planned beginning promptly at nine, Red first on the agenda. They nursed steaming mugs of coffee and ate eggs and toast with little conversation.

Toward the end of the meal, Red ducked upstairs to the cold rustic bathroom with its claw-legged tub and intermittent hot water. He took an army shower and did the full toilette, including makeup and pin-striped armor.

At nine, as planned, the group gathered at a cabin on stilts (Los Innocentes), four times the size of Red and Noah's little bunkhouse, with wraparound screened windows that filled the room with fresh mountain air and a fantastic view of the sparkling lake below. All but Red were dressed in casual shorts, sandals, and tank-tops befitting the setting. Costumed for his performance, Red looked like a banker who had lost his way.

He put on his dog-and-pony show of video examples and interactive exercises, demonstrating how they could communicate the message of boy love, even in the most hostile environment. It was all new to this group of teachers, professors, and intellectuals, which was no doubt why the media had been putting them through the wringer for the past twenty years.

Red concluded his mini-seminar: "Many of my clients feel they can circle the wagons and hunker down in defense against a media attack, and I tell them they're missing the point. The media gives us an opportunity to have our say, but we have to know how to take advantage of it. Our public communications should have one purpose and one purpose only: to deliver our messages to our audiences. You are not there to answer the reporter's questions. You are not there to have a chat with the reporter. You are not there to engage in academic debate. If that's what you think you're doing, they will eat you for lunch, and many of you already know what that feels like. But if you go in with your messages clearly in mind and with the idea that your sole purpose is to say those messages, no matter what, you will at least have a fighting chance. I've had my say. Thank you."

They took a break before Noah's presentation, and Red seized the opportunity to change back to his north woods drag, a pair of stone-washed Calvins, black Mortis tee, and Timberlands.

By the time he returned, Noah's scholarly presentation was already under way, a case study in everything Red had just taught them not to do. After a torturous hour and a half of academic explanation, his audience was literally begging for the conclusion of his statistical study of child sexual abuse: that all the science on boy love of the past thirty years was flawed, that in every case the data did not match the conclusions drawn by the researchers, and in some cases, the data showed exactly the opposite of the researchers' conclusions.

In short, Noah's study found that the entire scientific foundation of the child abuse industry was a lie. The study was scheduled for publication next spring in the *Journal of the American Society of Psychiatrics*, the most prestigious publication in the field.

The gathering was agog. If PR had taught Red anything, it was that you had to have an expert opinion. Now, at long last, the boy lovers had one, backed by the *JASP* no less!

Adult-Child Sexual Contact: A Re-Examination of the Science or "The Cobb-Orlofsky Report" (later shortened to "The Cobb Report" in a stroke of journalistic perversity) was the talk of the dinner table. Red's communications revolution had been upstaged, and he couldn't have been more pleased. He was asked for his take on the study.

"I know I'm probably talking myself into a job," he began, "but the minute the *Journal* hits the streets, we should be cranking out news releases to every major media outlet in the country. I'm willing to take that on. Noah, you let me do the publicity on this thing, and I can get you on every top talk in the country, radio and television."

"No, we don't want a lot of publicity," he replied with astonishing ingenuousness.

Red was incredulous. "What? What have we been talking about for the past six hours? You guys publish a study in the most prestigious journal in psychiatric medicine that says all of the child abuse science of the past thirty years is bunk, and you don't want a lot of publicity? For one thing, what makes you think you're in control of that? This stuff is dynamite! You've got to be ready for it to explode, whether you want it to or not, and the best way to do that is to make the first move. Don't wait for them to call you."

"It's not my decision," he shrugged helplessly. "I can pass your ideas along to Russell, but I can tell you now that he will never go for it."

"'Russell' is Dr. Cobb?" He nodded shyly. Noah was the "Orlofsky," the junior who did all the work. "Then, tell Russell he's living in a fool's paradise if he thinks he can duck the media on this thing. Our enemies will gin it up. It's absolutely predictable. When they get wind of your study, they will do everything in their power to discredit you."

"Then why do you want to announce it?"

"Because if you announce it first, you're in control of the game. This thing's an atomic bomb, and I want to drop it right in their laps!"

Harry the peacemaker interceded, "We all sympathize, Richard, but Noah's right. I know Russell personally. He's a scientist and a statistician. He doesn't have a media bone in his body."

"Fine, then let Noah do it." Noah blanched. If his presentation was any indication, he didn't have any more instinct or stomach for public communication than his boss, but you had to start somewhere. "I'll teach you," Red volunteered.

Shrewdly perceiving Noah's reluctance, Rupert declared, "The important thing is that we have a new weapon in our arsenal. The Organization of Lesbian-Gay Alliances is holding their international conference at The Hague this fall. Would Russell be willing to present the study there?"

Red lit up, "That's a great idea! Can you do that, Rupert?"

Taken aback by Red's enthusiasm, he nodded unctuously, "I'll set it up."

Noah breathed a sigh of relief, "That's more the kind of forum Russell prefers."

"The media will be there," Red reminded him.

After dinner, the boy lovers donned their bathing suits and gathered at the dock for a swim in the silky, azure water, so placid and mirror-like (hence, the name), it seemed you could dive into the magical fluid, and it would simply swallow you up without a ripple. Arrayed about the dock and in the water, the men might have been subjects for a Thomas Eakins painting or a Stephen Spielberg patrol of newly arrived aliens silhouetted against the setting sun.

Noah extended his second invitation for a swim, and Red eagerly accepted. They swam naked away from the others out into the open water. Noah was an athletic swimmer, but Red easily followed, and they paused treading the smooth cool water.

"You're a good swimmer," Red observed.

"So are you," Noah answered with some amazement.

"I love it, pure pleasure. The water is so calm and clear, like a healing bath. I feel reborn!"

"I liked your presentation. I learned a lot."

"It takes more than just a two-hour training to get good at this. I hope I wasn't too hard on you back there."

"No, I agree with you. I would love to publicize the study, but Russell is terrified of the press."

"Why? Does he have something to hide?"

"I think he might. I don't know the details. I don't want to."

"If that's so, then he's right. You should lock him in a closet and don't let him near a reporter. But why didn't he think of these things before doing a study like this? Surely, he must have imagined it would have an impact."

"We did and decided not to pursue it."

"What if it pursues you?"

"When it does, I'll call you."

"By then, it will be too late. Let me teach you now. To begin with, your presentation this afternoon was a study in how not to do it. I understand, you're an academic, and that's what academics do. But the public debate doesn't work that way. You don't have time to build your case. You have to be quick and concise."

"Sound bites."

"Exactly. It's not that hard to learn, but it does take practice."

"Okay. I'll be your guinea pig. It might be fun."

Red swam back to shore, the young man following.

Drying off in the oil-lamp light of their cabin, Red enjoyed his take of the young man's body, thick but still athletic. For an academic, he kept himself in shape. Red mixed a vodka-and-seven from his flask and a can of soda and bowl of ice raided from the main house fridge, giving Noah ample opportunity to draw his judgments about his own physique. They put on their jeans and T-shirts and sprayed themselves with bug repellent to share a joint outside in the piney, starless, moonlit night.

Red continued, "Tell Russell what we're doing, that I'm going to train you as spokesman for the study. We can do most of it by e-mail, but when you have a big interview coming up, I'll fly in and rehearse you on video tape."

Was it the pot or the pedagogy that suddenly transformed Dr. Orlofsky into a boy before Red's eyes? The young man flashed a shy smile and boyish furtive glance. "Oh, yeah, I forgot—the coming-out kid," Red thought.

He put his arm around the young man's shoulder and kissed him on the lips. Noah was immediately passionate and horny, but suddenly to his surprise, Red pulled away. "You're a cute guy, Noah, but you know I'm a boy lover."

"I'm too old for you," Noah pouted.

"You look ten years younger than your age, but yeah, my boy in Dallas is twelve. He'll be thirteen in December."

His academic curiosity took over. "Does he think of you as his lover?"

"I think more as his friend and mentor and fan."

"But none of those necessarily involve sex."

"Where have you been, Doctor? They all do!"

"But not as a lover."

"Twelve-year-old boys don't have lovers. They have fun. I love him, and he knows it. Does that make me his lover?"

"If there's a sexual relationship, the answer would be yes, even if he doesn't look at it that way."

"What if there isn't, and he does?"

"You mean, could you be lovers, if there were no sex?"

"No physical expression. Your professional opinion, doctor?"

"That's more problematic. I would say not. It would be just as you said. You're his friend but not his lover."

"Then sex is the defining characteristic."

"It always is. Where have *you* been?"

"I guess I should expect that from a sexologist."

"You don't need me to tell you that. Ask any teenager."

"Fair enough. We learn it pretty early, don't we?"

"As soon as your voice cracks. So am I to assume then that your relationship with this boy is not sexual?"

"Assume what you wish. I just don't want to be reading about it in the next issue of the *JASP*."

"How did you meet him?" he inquired with a mechanical voice holding in a hit.

"I was his writing coach in a volunteer program at his school, but that program ended three months ago. Now it's just him and me."

"What do his parents think of that?" his question exploding in a cloud of smoke.

"They approve. I'm welcome in their home."

"But you must be at least thirty years older than he is."

"Almost forty."

"Do they know you're a boy lover? Do they know you're in love with their son?"

"We haven't talked about it. On the one hand, it's never come up. On the other, I think they respect my love for their son without question. Frankly, I look forward to the day when we can talk about it."

"Why don't you bring it up?"

"No, I can't do that."

"Why not?"

"They accept me as it is. Why rock the boat?"

"If they questioned you, what would you say?"

"I would say that my commitment to Jonathan is unequivocal and life-long."

"Are you building the relationship now in hopes that you will have a sexual relationship when he's older?"

"You are not the first to have asked me that. If it happens, it happens. I won't push it on him, but I won't try to stop it either."

"So you're grooming him, the classic strategy of a predator."

"Or a lover, depending on your perspective."

"True. It's sometimes hard to put aside cultural bias, even for me. Objectively speaking, the final test is the positive or negative effect on the people involved."

"Just like your study, which shows it's more likely to be positive."

"We never encountered a case where the older man took such a long-term perspective."

"I'm also writing a book about it."

"How long have you known him?"

"A year this fall."

"This would make an interesting article. I would love to interview you."

"I think you just did."

"I wouldn't use your real name, of course."

"I won't use yours either." Red smiled and rolled the tiny butt of the roach in his fingers and flipped it into the dark.

They went inside. Red snuffed the lamp, allowing clear white moonlight to flood through the rustic cabin's open window.

Noah's disembodied voice continued, "You guys are a remarkable lot, from all walks of life, intelligent, socially aware, from all over the world, and with such different points of view."

"You speak as if you are not one of us."

"I'm not sure what I am. It's all so new to me. I'll tell you honestly, I haven't had that much experience."

"Yeah, I was a late bloomer myself, so I can relate. But a funny thing happened when I came out. I hooked up with a boy lover. I was his boy, even though I was your age. Maybe you're like that, too, an arrested adolescent still waiting for his mentor, an older man to teach you how. We boy lovers are very good at that."

"I had an older lover in high school."

"A teacher?"

"No, I was a freshman. He was a senior. It was great. I loved doing it with him! But I thought I'd left all that behind, when I went off to State."

"Yeah, I have a similar story, and I can tell you from experience that you never leave it behind. Like the hippies used to say, 'No matter where you go, there you are.'"

"You're not like the others."

"The first time I heard that, I was flattered. Since then, I'm not so sure."

"It's like you're from another world."

"Oh, you mean the media thing. Yeah, you're right, it is another world, but I can teach you how to compete in that arena."

"That's not what I mean. It's you. You're so incredibly young, it's almost uncanny!"

"The boys keep me young. You know how to keep your youth, don't you?"

"No."

"Give him anything he wants." Silence. That joke needed a rim shot. "We're all Peter Pan," he continued, "and I don't mean some het Disney version. I mean the real Peter Pan, who surrounded himself with the Lost Boys, who defeated Captain Hook by becoming him. The creator of Peter Pan, James Barrie, was a great boy lover. Only a boy lover could have written that story."

Noah didn't reply, snoring softly among the sounds of the forest at night and the "ssst-ssst" at the tiny square window at the foot of Red's cot. He softly made his way to the cabin door in the pale moonlight to greet his silent dark visitor, motioning him to enter. But instead, the visitor took Red's hand and led him out along the piney path to the edge of Mirror Lake, where a blanket lay spread beneath a bower of trees. The visitor pulled Red down onto it, and they kissed passionately, Red's hands gliding along the smooth, firm muscles of the young man's back. The Indian boy rolled over and luxuriated in the older man's attention to his hairless thighs and muscular ass. They bathed in the moonlit lake and parted silently into the night.

Sunday morning, the guests and their host gathered at the main house for a buffet breakfast at the big oak table with a wooden bowl the size of a birdbath filled with wild blueberries gathered the day before by the Indian boys. Assisted by the shirtless boys, Gilly was efficiently in charge of preparing blueberry pancakes with thick greasy bacon and real maple syrup and lots of coffee. Jesus with his big bright smile caught Red's eye and winked.

"Looks like you've made a friend," Eugene observed.

"Did you send him to me?"

"No, that was his idea."

"I love Jesus!"

"He loves you, too. But the 'friend' I spoke of was myself. I've been reading those chapters from your book. I'm impressed. I've never read anything like that."

"Thanks for the vote of confidence. I'll send you a copy of the manuscript when it's done. And if you know any publishers, I'm in the market."

"I do know a man in Paris who has published some boy love books. I'll get you his name."

After clean up, they retired again to Los Innocentes to discuss the issues.

"I think we should advise boys and boy lovers not to engage in sexual activity because of the severe penalties involved."

"No, that's giving in. The greater wrong is holding back the love the boy wants."

"Assuming he does!" General laughter.

"The law assumes he can't."

"Which we all know is not true. That's the point, isn't it? The sex is going to happen. That's natural. That's the way it is. That's why we're here, is it not?"

"But how do you know he wants it? How do you know you're not forcing it on him by virtue of your power as an adult?"

"The old power argument. You know who always makes the power argument? The people in power. Because that's the only way they can understand love. It reminds me of an old poster from the sixties that read, 'The power of love is greater than the love of power.'"

"I can tell you how I know when a boy wants sex. He says so."

"Boy love does not have to involve sex."

"It doesn't have to. It wants to. Sex is a natural extension—excuse the metaphor." More laughter.

The bright sun turned salmon and lowered behind the dark tangle of tree limbs and then the distant banks of the lake. They went for their last evening swim, and gathered again at the main house. Red volunteered to cook the evening meal of chicken, rice, and mushroom sauce, salad, sautéed vegetables and blueberry cobbler with ice cream for dessert. Everyone pitched in at the great table, large enough to butcher a deer.

They sat down for their meal on the screened porch overlooking the now dark woods, soon illuminated by the silver light of the rising full moon, and finished the jugs of wine with conversation.

Red was on a roll. "It's not a matter of law or justice or philosophy or any of that. It's a matter of public perception, cultural mythology, and politics, and if you want to have an influence, that's where you have to compete, because the truth is—and we've seen it over and over again—if they want to get you, they'll come up with some argument to justify it, and if they can't find a law, they'll make a law, but one way or another, they'll invent some proper ritual for praisin' the Lord and hangin' your ass from the nearest tree. That goes for every one of us."

"We are all aware of this, Red," Rupert responded wearily.

"Then why do we cling to the idea that we can change perceptions and attitudes with academic explanations, as if the search for truth will set us free? It will not. We must stop seeing ourselves as intellectuals. We are advocates. We are warriors, who carry a clear and simple message into the arena of public discourse. Only then, only when we change our own minds first, can we begin to change the minds of others."

"But doesn't the truth get lost in all of this?" asked soft-spoken Paul, a lean, bearded man in his early forties.

"Do you think the truth is getting out now?" Red replied.

"No, because the other side has been spewing out lies for the past twenty years," Rupert jumped in.

"And they've done a damn good job of getting people to believe their lies. Their propaganda has been more effective than ours. That's what I want to change."

"But what you're advising is manipulative, sociopathic," Rupert objected.

"Haven't we been manipulated? Hasn't the entire boy love movement has been manipulated? We are at war, Rupert. We are fighting for our lives. With your political experience, you more than anyone should know this."

"If it's a war, it's a fight between lies and truth, not competing messages."

"It's a fight for the hearts and minds of parents, educators, legislators, the police, jurists, boys, and boy lovers—the culture itself. And I agree with you, the witch-hunters have created a web of lies to support their hate-filled bigotry, but they've managed to sell it a lot better than we have. Fear is an easier sell than love."

"Have you ever heard of 'The Big Lie'?" Red continued. "Goebbels said it. If you repeat The Big Lie loud enough and long enough, people will start to believe it. That's what our opponents have done, very successfully, I might add. So we have to combat that in exactly the same way. We have to get our message out clearly and concisely, whenever and wherever we can."

"I don't want any part of it," Rupert declared.

"We don't have a choice. When the invading horde is coming over the hill, the villagers must fight or be slaughtered. That's where we are now."

"Why are you doing this?" Paul inquired of Red with gentle simplicity. "Why do you care about this?"

"It's my contribution. I don't have a lot of money, so I contribute my time and expertise. If I can improve our communications, I think we can start to have a positive impact, instead of digging ourselves deeper into a hole. The lives of good and decent people who make important contributions to society are being ruined in the name of this insane witch-hunt. Their Big Lie is driving an emotional wedge between men and boys—teachers and their students, coaches and their athletes, mentors and their protégés, fathers and sons—and shredding the civil rights of everyone."

"That's true. I'm a public school teacher in Maine," Paul explained. "Now they require that a teacher cannot be alone with a student. Another teacher or administrator must always be present. There's no opportunity for a personal, private bond to develop between teacher and student anymore. Big Brother is always watching, and that transforms teaching into a cold, institutionalized process. There's nothing human left in it."

"That's exactly what I'm talking about. That fear is poisoning our culture, our future, and our souls."

"You are very passionate for a fifty-year-old man," Paul observed thoughtfully.

"I bet you were a cute boy yourself once," Harry grinned, eyes twinkling.

"Like Elizabeth Taylor with eyelashes out to here, even at age thirty," Red blushed at the flattery. "I was twenty-nine the last time I was seriously carded at a bar."

The Moralist

"When you talk to boy lovers, you should share your passion," Paul continued. "Don't just focus on communications. Tell them why it's important. Tell them why you're doing this."

"Doing what? Teaching them how to manipulate what people think." Rupert's cheap shot.

Red laughed good-naturedly, "Rupert understands me better than anyone in this room!"

Rupert and Hawk had to drive back that night, but Red's plane didn't leave until the following afternoon, so Harry invited Red to ride with him and Noah, so he could stay. After Rupert and Hawk said their goodbyes, Harry opened up.

"Thank you for coming, Red. A lot of us welcome your fresh perspective. Rupert has been at this for such a long time."

"I don't expect everyone to accept what I say at face value. I hope he doesn't think of me as a threat."

"I think there is some of that."

"Then I want to make one thing clear. We each have our role to play. I'm your communications consultant, not your leader."

Eugene spoke for the group, "We appreciate that. We need new ideas."

"Even more than ideas, we need consistency," Red added. "Effective communications is so much more complex than I can cover in two hours, or even two days. Our spokesmen not only have to be skilled in using these techniques, their messages have to be consistent. We all have to be saying the same thing. What we really need is a briefing book."

"What's that?"

"It's a ring binder that helps you prepare for an interview or presentation. It has sample questions in it and a collection of background on boy love: statistics like Noah's study, famous quotes, historical references, and anecdotes, stuff you can memorize for your interview. But more importantly, it has our messages in it, so everybody is saying the same thing. The briefing book is our communications bible." They nodded with curious interest and enthusiasm for the idea. "I guess I've just volunteered myself for a project. So okay, if you won't let me promote the study, then I'll write the boy lovers' briefing book instead. But I can't do it without participation from all of you and the BLN. I'll put it together, but everyone has to participate, so we can be agreed on the messages. I warn you, the briefing book is a process that excites debate on just exactly what the messages are. Even this afternoon, we never agreed on anything." They laughed. On that they did agree. "And one more thing: it takes time to pull it all together, a couple of months minimum. But with everyone's cooperation, I think I can have something to you by the first of the year."

The idea excited their imaginations, and as the wine flowed until the jugs were empty, the conversation was lively.

"Everyone in this room is a social and sexual revolutionary," Red expounded. "That's our role. We are expanding people's understanding of what love is, and that is revolution on the hoof."

"But love is not the issue. The issue is sex."

"That's our first mistake. We've bought the line of the witch-hunt. We're fighting on their turf. Just like our discussion this afternoon—sex, sex, sex. As long as the issue is sex, we lose. The real war is on the issue of love, and it's time for us to start making that point. It isn't the sex, it's the love. That's what they want to destroy."

"You can't honestly believe that."

"I do believe it, and furthermore, I believe this goes to the heart of why our enemies are winning this battle."

"Love is not the crime that will put you in prison for twenty years."

"Yes, it is. Don't let them fool you. Sex is a smokescreen. In today's witch-hunt environment, *boy love* is the crime. Boy love is the metaphor for the eternal struggle between love and authority. Our brutal, authoritarian culture has chosen boy love as the scapegoat for controlling love itself. If it allows even the possibility that the love between a boy and man could exist, the whole paternalistic structure crumbles. Only then can we introduce a more human ethic that will become the foundation for the next configuration of our culture. As Nietzsche wrote, 'The evil of today is often the good of an earlier age.' Conversely, today's evil can become tomorrow's good. That's how revolutionary we really are, and we should understand that. It's not just a matter of changing a few laws. We are in the business of changing myths and totems, and our opponents know that. That's why they want to kill us. Our very existence is a threat to their lies."

"You speak so eloquently," Noah beamed with admiration. "I wish you could be our spokesman."

"A few bottles of wine don't hurt," Red grinned.

Breakfast on Monday morning was a perfunctory affair. Everyone was packing bags and cars and downing coffee. Red found a moment with Eugene.

"I finished those chapters from your book. I'm amazed at your honesty," he began.

"It's all fiction, which like every mask gives me the freedom to speak the truth."

"Which is to say that you're telling your own story in disguise. It's affirming. It's important. I was very moved."

"It's unfolding as I write it. I don't know what's going to happen. Or maybe I'll just make it up. Thank you for your generous hospitality this weekend. It was perfect—the relaxation, the conversation, Jesus."

He grinned with a glint in his eye, writing out his address and personal e-mail. "Please stay in touch. In one of your chapters, you write about Dionysus and art. I know a boy in Honduras named Dionys. I would like to tell him about the meaning of his name."

"Originally a Titan in Greek mythology, Dionysus was a god of the gods, the god of the grape and drunkenness and madness and creativity, god of the theater. The German philosopher Nietzsche contrasts the convulsive Dionysian spirit with the measured balance of Apollo as the two competing energies of art. That dialectic has been the most influential aesthetic idea in the twentieth century, though Nietzsche expressed it in the middle of the nineteenth. It's in an essay called *The Birth of Tragedy*. I'll send you a copy."

"I would very much appreciate that. I'll read it to Dionys."

"It will open his mind, I assure you."

"I've been thinking of writing my own story."

"A competitor already!"

"No, it's totally different."

"It always is. I hope you're ready for the firestorm of controversy you will have to endure."

"I've always been controversial. The AMA opposes my work, because I teach people how to be their own doctor. Your work is controversial, too. Are *you* ready?"

"No, but I think I can handle it. I've been writing about boy love for twenty-five years. It's a tough sell."

"Why not write about love without the boy. Disguise it, like Proust did. Make Albert into Albertine."

"That would miss the point. Everybody agrees with sentimental love. Like the Beatles say, 'Love love love, love is all you need.' Who's going to argue with that? But if you talk about love in a different light, people get all bent out of shape, because you're not just talking about love anymore. You're talking about myths and totems, which is where love really resides, not on the surface with the hallelujah crowd, but in the catacombs among the pillars that hold everything up. Like Marilyn Manson says, 'If ya wanta get people's attention, ya gotta rattle their cage.'"

"Is that what you're doing? Rattling everyone's cage?"

"If that's what it takes to expose the myth of moral principle for the lie that it is. Love is the mortal enemy of authority and control. Dionysus the mad god breaks down the boundaries, the antithesis of moral principle, which is a boundary by definition. Art looks into the unmediated heart of love and discovers the true source of power, and it has nothing to do with what they think is power, which is really culture. Love is larger than culture. Love blows through culture like a Texas tornado. History and literature tell this story again and again. The innocent motive of boy love wants nothing more than to adore the beloved—his sweet smile, his cherry lips, his bright young eyes that absorb the world. How simple, pure, and beautiful is that! Love is condemned by those who fear it, because they cannot control it. Humphrey Bogart notwithstanding, the world does not always welcome lovers. Sometimes, it nails them to the nearest cross. Ask Jesus!" He turned to the grinning Indian boy who had just joined them. Understanding not a word of Red's rant but his name, he threw his arms around the man for a goodbye hug and kiss.

On the drive back to Boston with Harry and Noah, the sky had clouded into a summer shower. They congratulated their luck for a sunny weekend as the gloomy weather closed in.

"I have a motel in Florida, Speed Beach, the spring break capital of the world. Maybe we can hold our next gathering there," Red volunteered.

"Spring break? We wouldn't get anything done!" They all roared.

"Honey, some 'thang' would get done, that's for sure!"

"More than one!" They roared again.

Recovering, Red continued, "I meant more like this time of year, late

August. The motel empties out then. The families have to get their kids back in school."

Someone raised an alternate objection. "That in itself could be a problem. We would stand out."

"What about the community? How would they react?" someone else asked.

Red sensed their provincial apprehension, the primal Yankee fear of The Deep South. "There won't be any torches and pitchforks, if that's what you mean. Speed Beach is a transient community. People are coming and going all the time. No one would even notice."

They were academic denizens of the urban Northeast, not beach people. A secluded retreat with a private lake was more their style for not only political reasons. Creatures of their milieus, they feared the eyes of others, a public motel and public beach, where all were stripped bare. It wasn't going to happen. Too bad.

"What an amazing weekend! So many different people in one small group!" Noah signified his reticence by changing the subject. "It was like a mirror of the entire boy love movement!"

"Yes, a mirror like the lake," Harry added thoughtfully.

"It was certainly 'through the looking glass,' that's for sure!" Red quipped.

"That's it! 'Through the Looking Glass.' TLG." Harry cried. "That's the code for this weekend. Refer to TLG in all e-mails."

15

In sixteenth-century medieval Japan, the Kabuki was an advertisement for prostitutes. It was immediately popular, but then the samurai started killing each other over the prostitutes. So they substituted boys, until the samurai started killing each other over the boys. So now in modern Japan, men play all the roles, and nobody fights over them except journalists.

Imagine yourself as a samurai. A willing boy was as good as a woman, in some ways better. He didn't get pregnant, could follow you on a campaign, and hungered with passion like you.

E-mail

Dear BLN:

Last August, a small group of boy lovers met to discuss the issues confronting us today. Part of that discussion focused on what we wanted to communicate to our various audiences: the gay community, legislators, parents, boys, academics, moral and religious leaders, to name a few.

Out of that discussion comes this appeal for your thoughts on the subject. I would like to receive a short message from each of you. Please send me, via the BLN, your one-sentence statements that you would like these audiences to remember and repeat about boy love, boy lovers, the boys they love, beauty, love, sex, the witch-hunt, the totalitarian repression of unjust laws, or any other issue that you think is important.

Please construct your statements as short, simple sentences that claim a positive idea. Examples:

"Boy love relationships are loving and supportive."

"Many boy love relationships last for a lifetime."

The Moralist

"The boy learns how to become a man."

"The unjust laws created in the name of protecting children are destroying our rights of free expression, privacy, and due process."

Think of yourself saying these words. Such statements are empowering. You want your listener to remember them and repeat them to others.

Be careful that your statements do not include strongly negative words like "molest" or "abuse." Examples:

"We are not child molesters."

"We do not abuse children."

The goal of this exercise is to develop a list of messages we want to communicate when talking to our audiences, either in groups or face-to-face, or letters to the editor or on the Jerry Springer television show.

Once your statements have been received, they will be compiled with others and distributed for your comment. Through this dialog, a list of messages will be included into a handy guide I'm creating to assist you in your communications on the subject of boy love.

Also for this guide, I'm collecting scientific, statistical, historical, cross-cultural, literary, and anecdotal references we can use to illustrate our positive messages. I welcome any you may have to contribute.

I look forward to hearing from you. —R[2]

P.S.: BLN wants me to add that anyone who has read my stories in *The Ganymede Reader* or *PAN* will know that I care about our cause and believe in what we're doing. —R[2]

As Red logged off, the phone rang. After two months, it was Penny.

"The Kabuki is at the Majestic!" she announced.

He was happy to hear her voice. "Are you going? You'll love it. It has the production values of grand opera. The performance I saw in Tokyo had a sea battle on stage with a full-size ship and rushes and smog and moving rowboats filled with warriors attacking with swords and arrows and cannon and guns. I've never seen anything like that on a stage before in my life! You'll love it!"

"I want you to go with me, my treat."
"Thank you! I'd love to!"
"I'm sorry for getting mad at you."
"Forget it."
"This will be our bury-the-hatchet celebration."
"Perfect! Speaking of making up, how's the new boyfriend coming along?"
"Another dud! I dumped him after a week. What a load! He certainly wasn't worth wrecking our friendship. What's wrong with me, Richard? Why do I always get the duds?"
"You're too good for them. They don't have any idea what they've got."
"Maybe I'm too picky."
"You know what you want, and you don't want some boring, self-absorbed, pompous ass who thinks it's your privilege to be in his presence."
"Amen, brother! How'd you know that? You only met him once!"
"I've been hanging around pompous Republicans for the past eight months."
"Then why were you pitching him?"
"I wasn't! I was stroking his ego to make him feel welcome. I told you that, but you wouldn't listen. I thought you were picking a fight because you wanted me out of the way for a while."
"I don't pull tricks like that."
"Yes, you do, and it worked. It gave you time to find out what a bore he is. So now he's gone, and we're going to the Kabuki!"
"I'll meet you at Will Call, Friday at eight."

Red called his boy. "How was your first day at the new school?"
"Dr. Borders showed us how to play Bingo."
"Who's Dr. Borders?"
"She's my homeroom teacher."
"She's a doctor?"
"That means she's studied stuff a lot."
"She has an advanced degree. What subject does she teach?"
"Bingo."
"Wow, they've really lowered the standards in Mesquite."

The Moralist

"I forgot the rules, so she sat down beside me and showed me how."

"Did you shout 'Bingo!' with your teacher?"

"Only when I scored."

Red laughed, "You're a trip! What subjects does she teach besides Bingo?"

"She also teaches U.S. History."

"Where does U.S. History begin?"

"With a buncha guys who said, 'This is stupid! I've had enough a this shit!'"

"Were they wearing wigs and ruffles and high heels?"

"Yeah, a buncha fags."

"Or were they wearing animal skins and feathers and beads?"

"Did you ever see a fag without her furs and jewelry?"

"You certainly know your U.S. History."

"I also get to choose my own books in English."

"You want some suggestions? Write these down."

"Just a minute." Red waited, listening to the noisy household, as the boy searched for a pen. "Okay."

Catcher in the Rye by J.D. Salinger, *A Separate Peace* by John Knowles, *Heart of Darkness* by Joseph Conrad, *Lord of the Flies* by William Golding, *Brave New World* by Aldous Huxley. Are you allowed to read translations from other languages? Check on that. From the French, *Strait is the Gate* by André Gide. From the German, *Steppenwolf* by Herman Hesse. Most are short and easy to read and tell a boy's story, except *Steppenwolf*. It's longer, and the boy is a young man, but it's pretty wild. He discovers The Magic Theater. It's your taste."

"Is it radical?"

"Very much so. They all are in one way or another. *A Separate Peace* is the least radical, and even it describes an experience many boys have but rarely talk about."

"What? Being gay?"

"Sorta, but not really gay, more like subliminal homoeroticism in the context of hero worship and jealousy. Read the book and decide for yourself. We can work on your book reports together. I'll clue you in on all the good bullshit. Your teachers will think you're a genius."

"I've got my own good bullshit."

"One of the qualities I love most about you, as you know."

"Did I know that?"

"Would we be having this conversation now if it weren't so? The Authors of Tomorrow is over, but I'm still here, 'cause I like your bullshit."

"Sucka."

"That too."

They laughed together.

"I'm doing a dick sculpture for Art class."

"Bingo and Art! Sounds like a fun semester!"

"We have to make a sculpture out of decorated tubes of paper. I'm makin' a dick."

"That makes sense. What's a dick but a decorated tube? Since pre-history and even in some parts of the world today, they worship images of the phallus—that's another word for dick—as symbols of fertility and creativity. The Greeks and Romans put sculpted phalluses in their gardens and at the entrances to their homes as good luck charms. There's some good bullshit for you. If your teacher asks any questions, tell her that."

"I'll prob'ly get beat up for it."

"Really? Seriously?"

"Maybe."

"Such is the plight of the artist, but I don't want you to get hurt."

After they said goodbye, Red reflected on this conversation with pleasure. The sexual banter between them was new. Most adolescent boys talk like that when they speak freely among themselves but rarely with adults. That Jonathan did so with Red indicated his acceptance of Red into his inner circle. Such conversations violated the adult role of authority, which was why the witch-hunters sought to forbid them. In some states, it was illegal for an older person to discuss sexual matters with a twelve-year-old, unless they were a parent or teacher or priest (and even the priests!). As Red had observed in Vermont, sex was a smokescreen. The true goal of the witch-hunt was to pollute every opportunity for love and trust between a man and a boy.

Red picked up their tickets at the box office and waited on the sidewalk outside the Majestic in the late afternoon heat of downtown Dallas. He eavesdropped the drawling commentary of the Texas elite, as they arrived in their

The Moralist

Friday night finery, most with barely a clue what they were in for. "Awl the women's parts are played by men." "My husband's brother was killed at Okinawa." "We saw it in Tokyo. It's hard to follow the story even with a translation." At least they were there, which reminded Red of who wasn't.

He cell-phoned Penny. No answer. He checked his messages at home. No messages. He heard the koizumi drums within announce the beginning of the performance but still no Penny.

"Bitch! Was this her trick to get back at me?" he thought. That wasn't her style. She might be a drama queen, but those tickets were seventy-five bucks a pop. The theatergoers evaporated from the street and lobby, as the play began. He turned in the tickets and headed for home.

On his answering machine was a recent message in a wan voice that sounded drunk, "Richard, I'm sorry I missed the Kabuki tonight. I tried to call your cell phone, but I don't know if I have the right number. I hope you enjoy the play." He called back to say he was on his way.

She answered the gilt door in a rumpled silk robe with fright-wig hair and a wine-stained smile. After a clumsy, lavish hug, she broke into sloppy, drunken tears. "I was mugged, Richard! I was mugged last night outside Star Canyon!"

"Are you okay?"

"Of course," she waved her hand and staggered about the living room. "Can you believe that? Star Canyon! If there was anywhere in the world you wouldn't get mugged—"

"Yeah, with all those valet parking guys running around."

"I wasn't getting my car. I was taking some air. It was girls' night out, so we went to the Star Canyon. But all they talked about were babysitters and shopping. I couldn't take it anymore. It was driving me crazy! I needed some air, so I walked one block—one block!—and these two Hispanic men attacked me from the bushes. I didn't have anything. My purse was back at the restaurant. They pushed me down and took my jewelry. My head hit the sidewalk! I was unconscious!" She swooned and fell onto the oriental brocade sofa.

"How does your head feel now?"

"It still hurts. There's a bump, right there." He examined the nasty purple swelling on her scalp, the skin unbroken. "Don't touch it! It still hurts!" she cried.

"Are you taking a pain killer?"

She raised her glass and grinned her purple grin. "I went back to the restaurant to ask Shelly and Jennifer for help, and they said I was drunk and acting crazy. I asked them to call me a cab, and they wouldn't even do that! I walked home, Richard. I walked home by myself for five miles."

"The valets would've gotten you a cab."

"No, I wanted to walk. I wanted to think. I wanted to think about all this. These people are not my friends, Richard. I grew up with them, and they are not my friends!" she bawled.

"No, they aren't."

"I don't have any friends!"

"Yes, you do. You have me and Edouard and a few others. You just need to sort 'em out. Did you call the police?"

"No, what could they do? They can't do anything."

"They might get your jewelry back."

"I don't care about that."

"So you've been holed up here for the past twenty-four hours?"

"I cancelled everything."

"Except the Kabuki."

"I was planning to go. I didn't want to miss you. Tonight's our bury-the-hatchet night! But my head still hurts!" she wailed.

Red held her face in his hands and looked her squarely in the eyes, "Penny, I want you to go to the hospital with me right now."

"Why? Do you think I'm crazy, too?"

"No, I think you have a concussion, and you're lucky to be alive. Which hospital do you want to go to? You name it, and we're there. Bring your wine. I'll drive."

"You are not going to commit me, Richard!"

"Commit you? I just want to make sure you don't wake up dead in the morning. Listen, a lot of times people with concussions don't realize there's anything wrong. You think you're okay, but you're not okay."

"I missed the Kabuki!" she cried and pulled away. "Do you know how much those tickets cost?!"

"Yes, and I regret we are not sitting in the theater right now."

"Let's go. It's four hours long. We can still make the second act!"

"I already turned in the tickets. There's only one show we need to see. It's called ER!"

"You're not going to do this to me, Richard! I won't do it."

"I can't force you."

"My mother had me committed!"

"I am not trying to—"

"I was a *cum laude* graduate in music from Trinity, and she had me committed! It lasted less than a week. It was very clear to them that I didn't belong there."

"Your mother's the one who should be committed."

"Yes! That's what I told them, and they believed me! Because of that experience, my uncle who was a state legislator changed the law. He changed the law! You can't commit people like that anymore, all because of me! Me, goddammit! Me!"

Red took out his cell phone. "I want you to call your father."

"My Daddy? What the fuck does he have to do with it?"

"You won't listen to me. Maybe you'll listen to him."

"All right, I will call him." She took the phone from his hands and punched in the numbers. "This is a very good idea. I've always wanted you to meet him." A gravelly voice answered. "Hi, Daddy?"

"Don't go into any long explanations. Just introduce me, and tell him I need to talk to him right away. It's urgent." She followed his instructions and handed the phone back to Red. "Mr. Franklin?"

"Hey there, Richard Rover! Penny talks a lot about you," said the hearty Texan voice at the other end.

"Same here. I feel like I've known you for years, so I'll get right to the point. Penny was mugged last night, and she's suffered a head injury. We were supposed to go to the Kabuki tonight, but she couldn't make it, because she's still disoriented. I think she needs immediate medical attention, and I want you to convince her that I should take her to the hospital right now."

His voice lowered, "That sounds serious. Thank you for calling me. Put her on."

Red handed her the phone. She launched into her tearful tirade. "It was a revealing moment for me, Daddy. I know where I stand now with my so-called friends. No, I feel fine! I'm not going anywhere! I'm doing what I want to do, and I'll go where I want to go, and I'm staying right here." She handed the phone back to Red.

"You see what I mean? She doesn't see it. She thinks she's okay, but you hear how she talks."

"I'm not crazy!" she screamed angrily.

"He wants to talk to you again." Red offered the phone back to her.

She turned away and grandly paced the room like a queen. "I'm through talking. Tell him good-bye."

Red spoke into the phone, "I don't know what else to do, short of calling an ambulance. I can't force her to go."

"You are not calling an ambulance on me!" she screamed. Red thanked Daddy, folded the phone, and put it away. She turned and hissed, "Get out of my house!"

"Penny, listen to me!"

"You are conspiring with my father against me!"

"Listen to yourself. You're not making sense."

"Go ahead and call an ambulance. A lot of good it will do you. I'll call the doorman. He won't even let them in."

"I'm not calling an ambulance. Do you see a phone in my hand? I'm not calling anybody."

"Good," she declared, triumphant and regal. "Now, please go."

When Penny got drunk, she threw everybody out of the house. "All right, come with me. You need some fresh air anyway."

"I'm in pain!"

"I understand. That's what concerns me." He took her hand with a reassuring pat. She liked a man to protect her. "That bump on your noggin looks pretty nasty."

"It's feeling better."

"Good. That's good, but it's still a dangerous injury, more than you know."

"Doctors wouldn't either! What do they know!"

"At least they could be there if something went wrong."

"I don't want to be alone in some cold hospital bed. I want to sleep here in my own bed. Stay with me tonight. If something goes wrong, you'd be here."

"I'm not a doctor."

"I'd rather be with you." She guided his arms around her waist pressing her big tits against him, her wet cheek against his shoulder with a sigh of release. "Oh, Richard, it feels so good. Thank you for keeping me company. I'm sorry about the Kabuki." He tightened his arms and pulled her close stroking her frazzled hair. "Yes, hold me. Hold me. I love you, Richard. You're the only one who came to see me."

The Moralist

"No one knows. You haven't been answering the phone."

"Shelly and Jennifer know. They didn't call!"

"They're not your friends. Maybe that hurts more than your head."

"I'll still see them. I see them everywhere. They wouldn't even get me a cab!"

"I'm sure you'll handle it with your usual grace and style."

"You're damn right! I'll tear their hearts out!"

"They owe you an apology, which you will graciously accept and then put them on ice forever."

"Like you did with me?"

"For barely a month, and you accused me, don't forget."

"I do forget. Tonight, we bury the hatchet, remember?"

"That or Penny's revenge."

"What are you saying?"

"True or not, it's wonderfully clever. I waited in the heat for an hour at the theater, and now you get me up here for this emotional wringer. I love it!"

"You don't believe me? You think I planned all this? Well, I'll tell you one thing, I would never blow a hundred and fifty bucks to get revenge on you! I'm not that crazy!"

"I see. I'm not worth the hundred-and-fifty-buck revenge. I get the bargain-bin revenge."

She whooped with laughter. "The bargain-bin revenge! You are so funny!" Her robe fell open.

"You're pretty funny yourself," he grinned not looking away.

She cupped her tits in her hands and grinned playfully. "Do you like my boobies?"

"Yes, I always have." He sang out loud with a raunchy gravelly burlesque sell, "Pretty legs and great big knockers, a pair of real show-stoppers, that's what keeps 'em comin' back for more."

She danced around the room in a mad reverie, the robe now more a cape for her capers. She arched her back and rolled her breasts from side to side in a saturnine frenzy, then grew dizzy and almost collapsed.

He jumped up to catch her. Lolling in his arms, she pressed her face against him. "I'm going to bed now. Will you come with me?"

"I will in a minute. You go on in."

She staggered toward the bedroom pausing at the door like a silent-film siren. "Will you hold me? Will you put your arms around me?"

"You know I will," he grinned and raised his glass.

"I love you, Richard. You are my only friend." She blew him a kiss and, turning to exit, dropped her robe like a stripper. His eyes followed her ample, feminine ass. She looked back with a provocative grin. "And no clothes either."

She disappeared into the dark. Revenge or seduction? He finished his drink and stripped according to her instructions. In the dark, he climbed into her soft bed embracing her from behind, his cock already hard and pressing against her backside. She turned and kissed him. "You feel so warm. Thank you."

Lying on his back, he pulled her to him. She rested her head on his chest and ran her hands over his shoulders and arms. "Such muscles! You have such wonderful muscles! I love a man's muscles and the hair on his chest, a nice little mat where I can lay my head and all the pain goes away."

He spoke to the ceiling, "If this mugging thing was a ploy to get me in the sack, I'm going to be really pissed."

She raised her head. "Hah! If I wouldn't do it for revenge, I certainly wouldn't do it for sex. And you've got a pretty high opinion of yourself, Mr. Big Stuff." She reached down and squeezed his hard-on. "You *are* Mr. Big Stuff!"

He rolled over onto her to let her feel it. She wanted it now, but he backed away. "You're a hot babe, Penny, and it's pretty obvious you turn me on, but I think I'll pull over here."

"Because you like boys. You're in love with a boy."

"Yes, that and about a dozen other reasons, all of which I'm almost ready to overlook. But there is one reason I can't ignore. You're not in your right mind, and you haven't been since you were mugged."

"That doesn't mean we can't have some fun!"

"Yes, it does. Believe it or not, I'm not going to take advantage of you."

She sat up and addressed him with tight-lipped sarcasm, "You are such a gentleman! You're just using that as an excuse."

"If you insist."

"Then maybe you should go."

He pulled her close to him once again. "Let me hold you and caress you and make you feel protected, until you forget your pain and sleep." She yielded, and he held her once more, stroking her hair. "Tomorrow, you should go

The Moralist

to your doctor and get an EEG or a scan or something that will take a look at your brain to make sure you're okay. Will you promise to do that?"

She answered in her little girl's voice, "Yes, Daddy."

"So if I won't fuck you, I'm your daddy, is that it?"

"Yes, Daddy."

"You're not the only one with a concussion. I've got one listening to you for the past two hours."

She barely raised her frazzled head for one last blast. "If that's how you feel, then get out of my house!" But she could barely finish before collapsing again into his arms. "I love you, Richard. You are such a man!"

He considered again her desire for a ready cock, but all this rapture over chest hair and manly muscles was strange to him for whom rapture was the hairless nascent musculature of a boy. She was right. He was in love with a boy. Sex with a woman was a long distant and irrelevant memory.

Her breathing became quiet and regular. He gently laid her aside and slipped from the bed.

In the lobby, the Negro gatekeeper wished a leering "good-night" to the gentleman caller leaving the lady's rooms at this late hour, the ironic contrast between appearance and truth.

Red called his boy. "How did your art teacher like the dick?"

"She thought it was a Greek column."

"Close enough."

"I got attacked by a buncha bullies on the way home."

"Are you okay?"

"Yeah. One of 'em socked me in the stomach."

"I hope it wasn't because of your dick sculpture."

"Kinda. They're a buncha redneck ropers, always beatin' up on the freaks."

"What does that have to do with art class?"

"They called me a fag. They said only a fag would make a giant dick. It was just an excuse to pick on me."

"Where did it happen?"

"I was ridin' my board home from school, and they surrounded me in the alley behind my house. They were gonna beat me up, but one of 'em knew my sister and told 'em to chill. They were about to let me go. Then one of 'em hit me in the stomach, and they ran away."

"Did you tell anybody?"

"I told Angie, and she told my mom. I asked her not to, but she did it anyway. Now, the kid who hit me is gonna get in trouble, and I'm gonna pay for it. I don't feel good, and I gotta go to school tomorrow."

"If that kid threatens you again, hit him when he's least expecting it. It's called a 'sucker punch.' If he tries to talk trash with you, smack him while he's talking. Don't wait till he's got his posse with him. I have a friend who was threatened by a bully once. The asshole cornered him in an empty classroom and said, 'I'm gonna see you after school.' But my friend didn't wait for after school. He picked up a chair and knocked that piece of shit across the room. My friend got suspended, but he kicked that bully's ass, and everybody knew it. Don't wait for after school. If you have to fight him, take him on the spot, when he's not expecting it."

"You're a trip, Red! You think I'm a trip? You're the trip! You aren't like any other grown-up I ever met. You always take the kids' side."

"I always take your side. One of these days, you'll understand that."

"I do now."

E-mail

Hi, Red:

I enjoyed meeting you at our retreat. Your presentation was an eye-opener. You requested anecdotes. The following may be useful:

When I returned from our retreat, I received a telephone call from a student I taught in the mid-seventies. He told me that he had been arrested for sitting in a playground unaccompanied by a child. Apparently, signs there warned against unaccompanied adults sitting in that area. He is heterosexual and has no sexual attraction to children. Though the charge is only a misdemeanor, he is outraged at this encroachment on personal liberty and is looking for ways to fight it.

There is a debate among teachers of young children in England about a rule that prohibits them from applying sunblock lotion on their students. Sun damage is a substantial danger for young children.

Another anecdote concerns a colleague who once gave me a lift to a computer fair. On the way, he noticed a group of kids being led by an adult. He remarked that he no longer took students on outings. I asked, "Is it because it's too much work?" He said no, he enjoyed them, but now he was afraid of possible charges of molestation years down the road. At more than one professional conference, I have heard fears expressed by teachers about showing their students any kind of affection whatsoever.

In this vein, some key messages might be:

Teachers are afraid of showing affection to their students.

Adults are increasingly afraid to come to the aid of children in distress? (It is now illegal in Massachusetts for adults to address children unknown to them.) —Paul

Re: R²'s call for one or two sentences:

Henry S. Lukas (in *The Renaissance and the Reformation*, 1934) showed that the hysteria against marginalized groups, like witches, was really nothing more than a method to distract growing discontent and to maintain the reigning power's authority and privileges. Similarly, starting in the 1970s, the hysteria against marginalized groups, like boy lovers, have been nothing more than yet another method both to distract discontent and to maintain proper subordination to authority and privilege.

On the issue of power, contrary to the conventional thinking, the man uses his power to lift the boy towards security, happiness, and thriving amongst his peers.

Liberating sexuality means promoting the variety of ways people may sincerely connect and be valuable to one another. This is a very important aspect to pioneering and promoting more constructive and meaningfully democratic societies. —Barry, New Zeeland

Red:

We will be presenting the study at the OLGA conference at The Hague next week. You were right. Reporters from all over the world will be there, mostly the gay press. A lot of people, especially the lesbians, are upset that we've been invited. A year ago, OLGA wouldn't even talk to the boy lovers, but now we're hearing expressions of support. —Noah

Noah:

> Congratulations! Your study has opened the door! —Red

> Red called his boy. "How'd it go? Did you bust his chops?"
> "No, nobody fucked with me."
> "Great! How'd ya pull that off?"
> "My buddy Austin walked me home."
> "A classmate?"
> "No, he goes to high school. He's fifteen."
> "But that's a different school, isn't it?"
> "His mom dropped him off."
> "To escort you home?"
> "I told him what happened. He's a thrasher, too. He lives down the block."
> "Thrashers stick together."
> "Damn right."

Penny called. "I took your advice and went to my doctor. They did an EEG. I had a concussion, just like you said."
"Your memory is apparently intact."
"Perfectly. I remember everything. We had some fun."
"'Pretty legs and great big knockers!'" he sang, and they laughed.
"Thank you for last night. You were the only one who was there for me. You were right. I didn't know what I was doing. I'm not sure if I do now. My doctor said I should get lots of sleep and take it easy for a couple of weeks."
"Take her advice."
"You could have taken advantage of me, and you didn't."
"I almost did!"
"I had you goin'!"
"Oh, baby!"
"Yee-hah!" she rebel-yelled in her best Dallas style.

<u>E-flyer from Noah</u>

Other Voices, a study conference. The Hague, November 15.

The Organization of Lesbian and Gay Associations (OLGA) presents *Other Voices* on the issue of intergenerational relationships. American psychologist Russell Cobb will talk about the findings of his analysis that will be published in the *Journal of the American Society of Psychiatrics* (JASP). His most spectacular conclusion: Almost all available research shows that, among men who in their youth had sexual experiences with adults, the majority looks back on that without displeasure and show no evidence of long-term negative effects.

In a time when almost every detective, public prosecutor, politician, and therapist is convinced that any sexual experience between an adult and a youth by definition results in severe, lasting damage, it is worthwhile to test this "opinion chic" against the findings of Cobb and his team.

16

    Peter Pan
    Peter, the phallus
    Pan, the satyr
    Peter Pan, the phallic satyr.

Red called his boy.

"How was your day?"
"Another bad one."
"What happened?"
"I got put on reassignment."
"That sounds like punishment."
"It is."
"For what?"
"I told the janitor, 'You make me horny,' and she told the principal."
"What?"
"It's a game I play with my posse. When we see each other in the hall, we yell out each other's names. Whoever says the name first, the other guy has to say, 'You make me horny,' to somebody, so I said it to the janitor. I had to go to Mr. Blackman's office."
"The principal?"
"The vice principal. I was wearin' a Marilyn Manson T-shirt, so he asked me if I liked Marilyn Manson."
"What did you say?"
"I said, 'He's a performer. He puts on a good show.' So he goes, 'But what about all the bad words he uses?' I said, 'There are no bad words.' So he put me on reassignment."

"What does that mean?"

"I get moved out of the advanced classes. Now I'm with all the other kids."

"Because you expressed an opinion he didn't like, he hobbles your education."

"It's only till the holidays. If I don't get in any more trouble, I get moved back."

"If he asks you again about Marilyn Manson, tell him you don't like the bad words he uses."

"But that's a lie."

"Yes. This is how our public schools teach hypocrisy."

"So what about your day?"

"Thank you for asking. The Authors of Tomorrow has started up again. I have a new student, Chuy Martinez, Hispanic kid."

"Yeah, I knew him. We had a class together."

"Really? What was he like?"

"He was into bein' cool, too cool for grammar school."

"That's him! He's more physically mature than the other boys. He looks more like a teenager."

"I didn't know he was a writer." Was that a tone of professional jealousy?

"Yeah, but very different from your stuff. He writes in the language of the streets, about gangs and cars and chicks. He already has a girlfriend."

"I know. I got her for him."

"Yeah? How was that?"

"He told me he liked this girl and asked me to tell her, so I did."

"You were his go-between! How ironic! I had no idea of this connection between you!"

"We are ironic, aren't we?"

"More than you know. Wanta go to a movie this weekend?"

Noah called. "Red, I told you I would call, if I needed your help."

"I'm glad you did. What's up?"

"Russell's not going to OLGA."

"Why not? I hope they're not taking you off the agenda."

"No, it's because of the personal issues I told you about. He wants me to present."

"Great! I'll prep you."

Rod Downey

"Like I told you, we don't want publicity."

"What do you think the gay press is?"

"They're different. At least, they'll give us a fair hearing."

"Yeah, they're all closet boy lovers, but you'd never get one to admit it. It'll be a good venue to cut your teeth on. I've been working on the briefing book. I'll send you the key messages I've got so far. Should I come up there?"

"There isn't time."

"Then we'll have to rehearse by phone before you leave."

E-mail

A useful quote for R^2's communications handbook:

> "Children of the future age
> Reading this indignant page
> Know that in a former time
> Love, Sweet love! Was thought a crime."
>
> —*Little Girl Lost*, a poem by William Blake (English poet, engraver, painter, mystic; 1757-1827) —Hawk

Messages for R^2:

ABOUT MORALITY:

We must either choose the wisdom residing within human nature or contort our natural selves to fit a corrupt moral authority.

The ultimate moralist is a passionate, loving human being.

ABOUT LIBERTY:

The free man follows his passion.

ABOUT LOVE:

Boy love is a love of beauty, an aesthetic experience.

When I held the boy close to me, a soft purring sound came up from down deep in his throat.

The Moralist

ABOUT JUSTICE:

Man/boy love is the model for a new justice. Its core is loving touch and emotional bonding to achieve harmony.

Conventional justice labels and punishes misfits. The new justice welcomes the very behaviors that the old justice disapproves of.

—Fritz, Frankfort

Noah:

I'm attaching a collection of key messages I've received. Memorize a few of these and use them in your interviews at OLGA. Best of luck! Let me know how it goes. —Red

Red pulled up to the curb and spotted Jonathan in the front yard practicing his skateboard. Recognizing his mentor, the boy put his hands to his cheeks in an expression of horror, mimicking Munch's *Scream* or at least Caulkin's *Home Alone*. Red smiled, charmed by the boy's playfulness, Jonathan's ironic alternative to being excited to see him.

He chose some nasty horror flick about a possessed devil doll named Chuckie. Red loved horror and science fiction flicks, even bad ones, since he was Jonathan's age. He still watched videos of Harryhausen's *Earth Versus Flying Saucers* and *It Came from Beneath the Sea* with nostalgic glee, appreciating their retro charm and pre-adolescent magic.

The Chuckie movie was less appealing. Aside from not being scary, it was tasteless and boring as well, this a third or fourth sequel, so all the scary had been bled out of it. That was the problem with horror sequels. You saw the beast once too often. It became commonplace like a neighbor's mean dog that you knew if it ever got free would really hurt you, but it was nowhere near as frightening as the goblin under your bed. The movie-makers must have been aware of this, as the sequels inevitably substituted self-parody and gore for real horror.

After the movie, the two friends stopped at a sandwich place.

"Here's some good bullshit about Chuckie," Red began. "In the catalog of horror stories, Chuckie is a 'devil doll.' There are dozens of these kinds of stories in many different languages and cultures. The cuddly little child's doll is suddenly animated by some demonic force, possessed by a demon or spirit or ghost, and becomes an agent of death. Sigmund Freud, the father of modern psychology, analyzes the devil doll myth—"

191

"Anal-izes?" Jonathan interjected.

Red smiled. "If you knew Freud, you'd know how really funny that is. Freud's essay *On the Uncanny* deals with the devil doll myth. You know what 'uncanny' means? It means weird stuff, stuff that makes you feel creepy. Freud was trying to figure out why certain stories make us feel creepy"

"Chuckie wasn't creepy."

"That was the problem. Chuckie takes the elements of the uncanny and reduces them to banality and violence. But the devil doll myth on which Chuckie is based is very creepy. The doll is portrayed as truly lovable, the child's favorite toy."

"That's in the first Chuckie movie! The little boy is lonely, and Chuckie is his only playmate. He does everything Chuckie tells him to."

"Yes, which is probably why the first movie was a success, but still, having seen the first one, I can tell you that it goes astray when the plot focuses on how the doll came to be possessed by a murderer and misses the whole magical point of the uncanny."

"What's that?"

"The doll is the child's projection of himself into the outside world. Before we are born, when we are still in the womb, there is no distinction between 'I' and 'It.' Our body and the outside world are the same. A good part of our childhood, from which you are just emerging by the way, is devoted to learning the distinction between the individual self and the rest of the world, what in psychology is called 'ego.' In infancy and early childhood, ego barely exists at all. That's why children are so imaginative. They have imaginary playmates. They have favorite toys that they invest with real lives and real personalities that are all versions of themselves. In the child's mind, the doll, the favorite toy, the imaginary playmate are as real and alive as they are."

"You're startin' to sound like Frasier again."

"That's what makes it such good bullshit. Most of your teachers don't know this stuff. Did you have an imaginary playmate as a kid?"

"Yeah, Mr. Hanky." Mr. Hanky, the animated turd from the TV cartoon *South Park*.

Laughing, "Okay, right again. Mr. Hanky is a gross parody of the imaginary playmate. The imaginary playmate, the favorite toy, is the child's expression of his sense of unity with the world, his sense that he and the world are connected. Emotionally, the doll represents to the child his own unified and immortal pre-natal world. Your Mr. Hanky is more appropriate than you know. A turd, literally a product of yourself, is probably the best expression of that." Red took a bite of his sandwich and continued, "As the child's ego develops and he learns to distinguish between himself and the world, the doll loses its power as the proof of infantile unity and immortality, so he casts it aside. You, for example, are entering adolescence, where your ego starts to define itself in very specific ways. You are discovering who you really are."

"I don't wanta talk about me," he squirmed in his old-fashioned childish way.

"As part of this process, something remarkable happens. In order for the ego to establish itself as our idea of who we are in the world, it has to pretend that the time when it didn't exist never existed. That's called repression. It's normal. It pushes the memory of the infant and the little child out of its consciousness and pretends it never happened."

"But it did happen."

"Exactly. That's where the devil doll myth comes from. In these stories, the favorite toy comes to life again, but this time, not as a comforting friend but as an evil demon. Why? Because the truth of its existence is a threat to the ego's idea of itself as a distinct individual. The repressed childhood experience comes to life again, which threatens the ego and inspires fear. When repressed feelings return to consciousness, we experience anxiety. That's why stories like the devil doll make us feel weird and afraid. What was once a source of comfort and assurance of immortality becomes a *memento mori*, a reminder of our mortality and a harbinger of death."

"Am I your devil doll?" As always, the boy cut to the chase.

"Too damn true!" Red roared. "The grown-up version of the imaginary playmate is called 'alter ego.' You once said I like to hang around you, because it makes me feel like a kid again. There is more truth to that than you know. I love you as a projection of myself, as the boy I once was."

"Then why don't I scare you?" he smiled coyly.

"Because for some reason, the repression didn't 'take' with me like it does with most people. So instead of being frightened by you—many adults *are* afraid of young people—I'm attracted to you."

"So you never grew up?" he asked in all sincerity.

"Yes, I did, but still, it's all there before me like a smooth, sparkling lake. I can dive as deep as I want. That's the beauty of it. That's the fun of it." Red changed the subject. "Speaking of scary stuff, a scream park just opened. It's called Blood County Fair. Ya wanna go next week? We have to wear a costume."

"You should go as Peter Pan!"

"I will."

"Gay and innocent and heartless." What was this word "innocent"? We knew one thing. Children supposedly had it, and grownups didn't, so it probably had something to do with sex. And then there was the question, Did it exist at all? Red remembered little that was innocent from his own childhood. Or was innocence our profoundest archetype on which all taboo was based? If so, what in ourselves needed innocence and guilt? The Christians say this need is borne of original sin, but if you were not a Christian and looked at the matter with a more probing eye, the Christian myth of original sin became not the cause but the expression of it.

The psychology of the Jesus myth:

Being born of a virgin, Jesus had no human father, so the natural Oedipal resolution was denied him. In manhood, he retained the sexless "innocence" of a child, "gay and innocent and heartless." Jesus Christ was Peter Pan.

Adam was first ashamed, then proud, the birth of original sin and by extension the law of the Old Testament, until the child-man-god came along with the good news that man was born into grace. Only it was a lot tougher sell than anyone would've imagined, except Jesus himself. Christ on the cross: "I knew this would happen!"

Self-awareness was the mind's own whirligig. Even the word itself was hyphenated. The mirror held up to the mirror, the snake eating its tale, as in fairy tale, for what else could our awareness consume but its own self-story? That's where Plato got it wrong: Our myths were not shadows but mirrors.

Red called Malcolm.

"He'll be thirteen in a coupla months."

"They can be very sexy at that age."

"That is the sexiest age. He tells me dirty jokes. He makes penile references."

"No doubt you are including them in the book. How's it coming, by the way?"

"It's on hold. After the meeting of boy lovers in Vermont, I volunteered to put together a communications briefing book for boy lovers, so I've been researching boy love throughout history and culture."

"Like what?"

"Let's see, the Romans considered it natural that a man would be sexually attracted to a boy. The definition of boy, *puer*, was between the ages of about twelve to seventeen. The beauty of a boy as an object of sexual desire was that he should as closely resemble the physical maturity of a man but without the hairiness. The appearance of hair on the boys legs and around his anus were the beginning of the end of his beauty as *puer*. At the same time, the attraction of a man for another man was regarded as degrading and emasculating—judging from the poetry of derision where if you really wanted to smear your opponent, you talked about him marrying another man and shaving his ass to resemble a boy. The clear idea was that sexual desire of one man for another, the desire to be fucked by another man like a man might fuck a boy, was contemptible and pathetic. The ancient Greeks thought like that, too. Aristotle said that a man would have to be born blind not to see the beauty of a boy. But male homosexuality was unmanly. It's exactly the opposite of the way we view these matters today. Reluctantly, our society has acknowledged as acceptable the desire of one man to be fucked by another, but at the same time, it declares the desire of a man for a boy as psychopathic, sociopathic, and criminal. Our modern ideas of what is normal and right are a total reversal of the classical point of view."

"But that was then; this is now. Why should that matter to anyone today?"

"It undermines the authority of our cultural assumptions. It shows that different points of view are possible, especially when they come from such sophisticated cultures as ancient Rome and Greece, the very foundations of Western society. From a historical perspective, our modern psychiatric establishment is nothing more than a primitive shaman pronouncing its shibboleth in praise of taboo. In 1974, it declared homosexuality was no longer a disease, so sixty years of psychotherapy is turned on its ear overnight. You want to know what a culture whore psychology can be? Ask any lawyer. If the proscription against pederasty comes down to taboo, we can no longer dress it up as science and moral righteousness. Other cultures as sophisticated as we, in some ways more, have held boy love in high regard, not only ancient Greece and Rome, but medieval Persia and seventeenth century Japan. Their vision was more honest, honorable, and humane."

"Righteousness?"

"Nietzsche's observation that the evil of today is often the good of an earlier age implies that good can become evil. How can good become evil without sacrificing the idea of a fixed moral principle? Our contemporary guardians of moral principle condemn such thinking as 'relativism,' but they are the most relativist of all, since their so-called principles are nothing more than current cultural myths. So the question becomes in a free society, 'Where does the moral center lie?' In a free mind, 'Where does the moral center lie?'"

"I hope this is in the book."

"That's why I'm writing the book."

"Your writing is becoming more political."

"I've always written about boy love. The issue has become more politicized."

"But in *Seeing Red*, you were telling a story. Now you're arguing a point."

"It's the same story, twenty-five years later. Red is still learning. He's examining the social and moral implications of his love for a young boy, and that leads him to examine his own moral vision. It's Molly Bloom through the looking glass!"

"Is the love relationship with the boy a sexual one? I mean in the book. I don't want to know your personal answer to that question."

"It's headed in that direction, but I'm not sure it matters that much."

"Of course, it matters. You've been cooped up with that book too long, dear!"

"Writing about it isn't doing it."

"In your case, I'm not so sure. You're conflating your art and your life in a way I've never seen before, and I don't think it's healthy."

"Like Mishima, I'm living out a literary myth."

"More like Don Quixote, with one important difference. Don Quixote is a fictional character, but it was Mishima's own real head that rolled across that floor."

"Then irony has come full circle. I'm not Don Quixote. I'm Don Quixote's revenge!"

"Exactly my point."

The Moralist

Red lifted the two suitcases from the car and carried them up the walk to Jonathan's front door. Melanie invited him in, then retired to her kitchen while they tried on costumes for their excursion to the Blood County Fair, $5.00 discount if you came in costume.

He unzipped the suitcases to reveal an explosion of colorful wigs and garments accumulated over 20 years of theater and Halloween: a werewolf, Japanese Samurai, satyr, Superman, Flash Gordon, and yes, Peter Pan. Jonathan chose Superman's one-size-fits-all blue Lycra unitard with red cape and emblazoned crest, but first the T-shirt and baggy jeans had to go.

The boy stripped down to his Warner Brothers jockey shorts printed with Tasmanian devils and protruding with another Taz beneath. He turned crimson with embarrassment all the way down to his dark, plump tits. "You make me horny," he grinned.

Red snapped the stiff little pole with his finger and laughed. "Yeah, that time of life. I remember."

"I got hair, too," Jonathan grinned proudly. "Take a look." He stretched open the elastic of his shorts to reveal an uncut steel-hard four-incher staring up between faint puffs of pale reddish hair.

"Congratulations. You wanted to be a teenager. You're well on your way."

"Two more months!" he crowed.

With Melanie in the next room, Red did not want to prolong this tableau and handed him the unitard. "Here, put this on."

As Jonathan stretched his limbs into the limp garment, Red pulled on his own woodland green tights fastened about the waist with a leafy loincloth. Over this, a red felt vest with a ragged hem and completing the look, pixie slippers, a green pixie hat with a red feather, and a boy's wooden sword held by a rope around his waist. Peter Pan.

The entrance to Blood County Fair looked like an old cemetery with cracked and fading tombstones, gnarly trees, billows of fog, and ghoulish zombies wandering about. Superman and Peter Pan made their way along the foreboding path.

A zombie jumped out from behind a tree and growled at them. Red turned and erupted with his own diabolical laugh that took the zombie by surprise. He grinned and shook his head, "Damn!"

"You made the zombie grin!" Superman marveled at his strange older friend.

They toured The Dungeon of Dr. Doom littered with grotesque experiments gone horribly awry, were abducted by aliens to their space lab, and rode the haunted hayride in the cool clear autumn night complete with harvest moon and headless horseman. They ran from steel-clawed Freddies, clowns with chainsaws, and a teenager in a trench coat with an automatic rifle. (This last bit was dropped the following week when someone complained. You can only rattle their cages so far.)

Over corny dogs, Superman inquired, "So what do you think about the Columbine school shooting?"

"I think those boys should've been having more sex," Peter Pan replied. "It's psychological displacement. Teenage boys go crazy about sex, and if they ain't gettin' any, that energy has to go somewhere: football, greed, violence, whatever. That's the trouble with all this abstinence bullshit. It's crazy. Telling teenagers not to have sex is like telling the sun not to shine. It ain't gonna happen. And if you succeed in stifling it, it shows up in other ways, sometimes really terrible ways. If those boys were gettin' busy, they wouldn't have time for all that violence." Superman grinned and gave Peter a high-five.

As they waited in line for Superman to dip his hand in hot wax and create a horror hand with long drippy wax claws, this requiring several dips and therefore several waits in line as the wax cooled, the boy who never grew up continued, "Cultures throughout history have dealt with the issue of pre-marital sex in a variety of ways, often encouraging sexual relations between younger and older adolescent boys or between men and boys as a form of birth control and social safety-valve. In ancient Greece, for example, there was a system of institutionalized pederasty, a mentoring and sexual pairing between an older man and an adolescent boy. During this time, the boy learned from his lover and mentor about being a man. Their sexual relationship was regarded as part of that learning process, where the boy learned not only the arts of love but received the nobility and character of his lover in the form of his semen. Once the boy was seventeen or eighteen, a fully-grown adult, he left the bed of his lover and took a wife and started a family, but the relationship between the older lover and his young beloved continued lifelong. The honor or disgrace of the young man was regarded as a reflection on the character and nobility of his older lover. After the young man had himself become a father, he might, if he so desired, seek an adolescent boy of his own and so continue the tradition. Pederasty was an imminently logical institution, especially for these island nations with limited resources. It channeled the sexual energy of the boys and prevented them from fathering children before they were married, and it helped to limit the family size of married men. Sexual energy can also be channeled to violence, just as it was with the Columbine killers, but on a vast social scale, where repressed libidinal energy is channeled into violence by the state. The most violent nations are anti-sex. That's where we are in this country. We're more comfortable with violence than sex. That's the real tragedy."

Superman gave his wax hand the form of a "fuck-you" finger flipping off the world. As they saw it taking shape, amused standers-by asked what he was going to do with it.

"Put it on the dashboard of my car," he replied, "to have it handy when I need it." They laughed and laughed again when he held it to his crotch like an erect penis.

They drove the long expressway drive back to the city exchanging reminiscences of their spooky night, then falling into a mesmerized silence amid the red and white lights of the traffic. Red's moral mind continued its reverie.

There were two fundamental moral energies in the world: self-love and self-hatred. Self-love was characterized by love, compassion, tolerance, understanding, and enlightenment. Self-hatred was characterized by fear, control, oppression, repression, and cruelty. The logic of both points of view was impeccable. Self-hatred assumed by definition that the self was wrong, sinful, diseased, and dirty. Therefore, it made perfect sense that corrective action was necessary to ensure that the self was held in check, which was understood as righteousness, propriety, respect, and principle.

On the other hand, self-love radiated its innate warmth naturally that translated into understanding and compassion. For this reason, self-love was anarchistic. It saw no need for rules, laws, or principles to guide a self whose essence was grace and innocence.

In terms of social interaction, the assumptions of self-hatred translated into political control and oppression. Self-love became an expression of the fundamental rights to life, liberty, and the pursuit of happiness. (Red naturally thought in the language of the Declaration of Independence, because the

American experiment was a living example of self-love in human history that found its roots in a period still known as "The Enlightenment.")

There was an imbalance between self-hatred and self-love. Self-hatred by its very nature could not tolerate any point of view but its own, so in order to validate its perspective, it had to destroy the power that it feared in others. From the self-hating point of view, the organic beauty of self-love was out of control and therefore dangerous. It had to be reigned in under the oppressive hand of authority.

In contrast, self-love by its very nature did not understand the motives of self-hatred. What need was there to control beauty, truth, and love? It didn't make sense. This innocence rendered self-love vulnerable to self-hatred's evangelical spirit. Self-love saw no need to evangelize. Love spread by virtue of its being, not its agenda.

Self-love was confronted with a difficult choice: to defend itself against the onslaught of self-hatred, which sought to imprison or destroy it, or to muster the courage of Christ and Gandhi and offer its neck to the oppressor in the firm belief that self-hatred could crush its bones but not its Truth.

In the real world, few champions of self-love had such courage. Instead, defending themselves against their nature, the self-loving were perceived as weak by the champions of self-hate, who were by far in the greater number. Or they were seduced to combat self-hate with equal vigor, which they mistakenly called justice but was in reality revenge. So they became sadly tainted by their enemies, which transformed the cause and struggle of love into the stuff of drama and tragedy.

Within the self, this struggle was called "moral conflict." In the course of human history, it was called "the fight for truth and justice" or simply "fighting the good fight."

Each perspective mirrored the other, and together, they defined the human condition.

Our inward and outward struggles were the same. The triumph of self-hatred was the love of power. The triumph of self-love was the power of love. Which side are you on?

A drunk roper in a pickup rode Red's bumper from behind and then roared past them. Jonathan donned his wax finger and waved it at the driver as he passed.

Red laughed and asked, "What were you thinking about just now? Before the pickup came along?"

The Moralist

"Whether Dallas County and Dallas the city are the same thing."

"They aren't. Dallas County is a separate government than the city of Dallas, separate services, separate laws, separate taxes, and separate police. The county cops are the sheriff's office, and the city cops are the Dallas Police. And separate courts: municipal court and county court. But the city of Dallas is the county seat of the county of Dallas, so both centers of government for the city and county are located here."

"So what were you thinking about?"

"What a good time we have together."

Later, Red saw the wax finger atop Jonathan's dresser draped with an old bent-up steering wheel. He called it "Road Rage," his first object of found art.

Over Thanksgiving week, Red flew to Gainesville to visit Cindy at the university. The little girl who loved animals and horses was now studying to be a veterinarian and working at the vet school foal clinic. Though she had grown up a thousand miles away, they remained close over the years by phone and mail and jet and car, so that every meeting was as if they had seen each other only yesterday.

She greeted him at her little bungalow nestled among pine trees that she shared with two classmates. It was the weekend of The Big Game, and the girls were planning a party.

The following afternoon, the house was filled with boisterous students cheering the home team. The only dad present, Red loved watching the game with the boys. The room reeked with testosterone. The women tried to get involved. Cindy was actually pretty good at it. Her long-time boyfriend Achi (as in Achilles, "like the heel" as she would put it, an attractive athletic young man) had taught her, just as Mark had taught Red terms like "nickel defense," "out pattern," and "flea-flicker" (sounded like something you did with your tongue). He got pretty good at it, too, predicting the plays and knowing when to groan at some stupid call that cost the possession, often calling penalties and touchdowns before the officials. But football remained a marginal entertainment, more a social focus than an attraction in itself, like his college days when The Big Game was an excuse to get drunk with your buddies. He kept the tradition going with rumrunners and frozen strawberry daiquiris for all. Everyone got buzzed and thought Cindy's dad was really cool.

"You made a big hit," she observed, loading the dishwasher. Women and gay men always cleaned up (except Theo, who never did), one of their most endearing qualities.

"I understand young people. It's my special talent."

"Like you understand me."

"Yes, but that's different. Today, I was having fun with the boys."

"*That's* your special talent!"

He grinned, "To be sure!"

The bungalow restored to its feminine quiet after the masculine roar, they ordered a pizza and surfed the TV channels for a movie.

"I brought one with me," Red volunteered, "if you don't mind something heavy. Remember when we were talking about tragedy?"

"*King Lear*? You brought *King Lear*!"

"The Royal Shakespeare Company. The best. The production is kind of spare, and they have these awful red chairs, but aside from that, it's a stunning piece of work. Still, it's Shakespeare. You have to get into it."

"I'd love to see it."

"It'll certainly be a change of pace from the football game," he added, rummaging through his bags, finding the tape, inserting it into the VCR, talking all the while, "There's something I want to make clear to you about this play. A lot of people like to quote the famous line, 'How sharper than a serpent's tooth it is to have a thankless child.' Those who see the play in those terms are missing the point. True, it's about an old man and his vicious daughters, but *King Lear* goes way beyond family relationships. I mention this specifically in reference to you and me, father and daughter watching a play about a father and his daughters. If you decide there's some connection there, it's okay with me, but I'm sharing this play with you, because it has been a favorite of mine since before I had a daughter."

Preparing for bed, they discussed the play for several hours. He lay beside her and scratched her back, as he had done for twenty years. She loved the loving touch of her father's hand.

Speaking out into the dark, he expounded, "Lear's tragedy is precipitated by the foolish act of giving away his kingdom, but the tragedy itself is psychological not political. By giving away his kingdom, Lear loses his identity. He loses his 'self' and goes mad. His madness gives him a new insight into the human condition. He sees the nihilistic Truth of man as 'a poor, bare, forked animal.' Lear's tragedy is that his loss of identity reveals the Truth at the price of his life."

"But the tragedy is not just Lear's," she added. "Everyone in the play is tragic. No one, not even the evil characters, is to blame. They are all victims of fate. It's a fatalistic play. Lear is no more or less at fault for being a fool than Edmund for being a bastard and a villain, just as he says in the play."

"You should know that the bastard's monologue justifying his evil acts in terms of society's opprobrium is a convention of Elizabethan theater. There are several plays with that sort of speech, but still, you make a good point. The implication is that there is no moral responsibility. This play has some of the most monstrous characters in all of Western literature, but by the end of it, we're moving very close to the idea that the evil is general and not specific to any characters. Yes, we know who the good guys and bad guys are, but Lear sets it all in motion unwittingly."

"That's the compassion part. We're in the same boat. We think we're doing the right thing, but we don't know. We can't, except after the fact, after it's too late to do anything about it," she looked back and smiled her own Cheshire Cat smile that Red knew so well as his own.

"So the identity thing, the moral thing, the family relationship thing are only pieces of the larger tragic puzzle, and when they all come together, it's a portrait of fate."

"Yes, and with that, sadness."

"Sadness, yes, the modern addition to tragic catharsis. Greek tragedy is not sad; it's awful. The fate of Lear and Cordelia is sad. *King Lear* is as close to the fatalism of *Oedipus* as we can come in a Christian culture, or even an existential one."

"What does the audience feel about *Oedipus*?"

"Awe, humility, and beauty. I dislike all this talk you hear about 'the tragic flaw.' Oedipus' tragic flaw is not rashness or hubris any more than Lear's is folly. Those are merely the qualities within them that move the hand of fate along. It's a very Nietzschean perspective. Nietzsche said the hardest pill for the philosopher to swallow was to accept that good and evil don't exist. I don't agree, but I think I understand the concept. The die is cast for Oedipus before his birth, so his rashness and hubris, qualities of character, are nothing more than the working out of fate within him, just as we have been describing Lear and Edmund and all the rest. These qualities of character are neither strengths nor flaws, neither good nor evil. They're part of the larger fatalistic tale. So, getting back to your question: What is the audience supposed to feel?

We experience awe at the perfect complexity of it, humility at the implication of acceptance it imposes on us, and beauty at the wholeness and harmony of the vision. Taken together, these are the elements of catharsis that Aristotle describes and it has very little to do with emotional gushing that most people imagine that word to mean. Yes, no matter how many times I've seen *King Lear*, I always weep at the deaths of Lear and Cordelia, just as I did tonight, but the awesome, humiliating, and beautiful experience of that play is a vision of terrible perfection beyond sadness."

"We've certainly covered a lot of territory tonight," she yawned, her eyes droopy and dark-circled. Even as a child, her eyes grew dark rings just before sleep.

"Yes, we have!" he enthused, "English, German, Greek. How appropriate that your lover is a Greek! I love it! But we've left out the French, and I can do the French: Gide, Genet, Sartre. Sartre is the opposite pole of fatalism. Existentialism is the philosophy of choice in the twentieth century." He laughed at his pun.

"Let's save the French for another time." She patted the hand of her nutty daddy and dozed off.

They'd stayed up way too late, and Red was sucking down a giant Burger King coffee, as Cindy drove her snazzy red 4X4 to the clinic for her morning shift. They had a full day ahead. After her shift ended at noon, she planned to take Salome, a two-year-old Arabian pony, to a "training" show for young riders, where she wanted to exhibit the young mare and maybe sell her. Ah, the stamina of youth!

Red loved the early morning, and the coffee was working its magic. He looked forward to seeing the famous University of Florida vet school but dreaded the long afternoon at a children's horse show, when he would be ready for a nap. He served as Cindy's stable hand and groom at these events, a role he enjoyed, glad to help out, but once the work was done and the show was on, he would be at loose ends for hours. Maybe, while Cindy was in the ring, he could curl up in the truck. It didn't turn out that way.

At the clinic, Cindy gave him the nickel tour, including the chance to see an equine surgery even at this early hour. Cindy explained that was not unusual, because owners would often wait a day when a horse was acting funny and after a rough night, bring the horse in the next morning for emergency treatment.

The bay mare lay on its side on a large solid steel table with a corrugated plastic hose extended from her mouth. The surgeons were just suturing up the abdomen, which was fine with Red. Horse innards might have been too much for eight o'clock Sunday morning, the coffee notwithstanding.

"Probably a twisted intestine," Cindy speculated. "Horses get that a lot."

"How do they get the horse back to the stall?" he asked her.

"Take a look."

Two techs drew four chains suspended on pulleys from a track imbedded in the ceiling toward the operating table. Bands at the end of the chains were wrapped around the animal's hooves, and working in concert, the vets and techs pulled on the chains to lift the legs vertical and guided the hanging creature like a rack of meat along the track toward a padded stall adjacent to the operating room. The anesthesiologist followed with the ventilator cart, holding the hose steady in the horse's throat.

Red and Cindy exited the operating theater and headed for the foal unit for her rounds. As they crossed the sandy campus in the bright November sun, Red was astonished to see a large white horse being hauled by the prongs of a forklift under its belly.

"There's a unique way of moving a horse around," he observed.

"That horse is dead," she replied off-handedly, this the little girl who used to cry at the sight of road kill, such that when Red spotted a mangled blob of fur and blood along the highway, he tried to distract her eager mind with conversation. He admired her compassion for living things, which was why she was there. But in her green scrubs and stethoscope, she now had the professional polish of a doctor in training, compassion tempered by experience and strength.

She loved her sick babies in the foal unit, mostly new-borns with fuzzy coats and the trusting gentleness of a child. Examining the eyes and skin of a little sorrel filly, she cradled its head in her arms, describing its condition as she conducted her examination.

"This little girl is very sick," she explained.

"That's funny. She looks healthy to me. Her eyes are bright. She's standing up."

"You're right. Foals are like that, and it sometimes fools the owners. This baby's mommy died giving birth. Even though she was born healthy, she never got the benefit of her mother's milk, and that's how foals develop their immune systems. There are enzymes in the milk that ward off bacteria, and without it, a healthy foal is a sitting duck for all sorts of infections." She pressed her hand gently on the animal's flank. "See how billowy the skin is here. There's an infection in there, and it's causing the skin to separate. If the skin starts to die and slake off, it's like a burn. The animal has no protection, and the bacteria will invade everything."

"What do you do?"

"We bandage it, pump her full of antibiotics, and hope for the best."

"But even if you succeed, will she ever have a normal immune system?"

"That's the good news. If we can get her through the first six weeks, her body will start manufacturing its own defenses, and she'll probably be a normal little filly. I'd give her about fifty-fifty."

"It must be hard not to get attached to these cute little babies, knowing how fragile they are."

"Yeah, it is. When one dies, you see a lot of tears around here. I hope this one lives. She's such a sweet little girl." The foal pressed its muzzle into Cindy's embrace.

After her rounds, they drove out to the farm where Salome was boarded and loaded her into Cindy's trailer for their drive to Ocala. Unknown to most but those who'd been there, this northwestern corner of the Florida peninsula displayed countryside of rolling hills and swaying trees distinctly atypical of the palm-tree-and-flamingos stereotype of "The Sunshine State." You might think you were in Kentucky or Tennessee, and like those places, it was pure horse country.

Cindy took her number "6" and led Salome to the warm-up ring to put her through her paces. Red busied himself posting flyers of the pony for sale on bulletin boards, trees, and even the restroom door, as a mid-adolescent boy in riding togs swung it open, catching Red almost square in the face.

As both apologized, Red studied the slender fifteen or sixteen-year-old with a long effeminate face, large eyes, and fleshy vermilion lips that wanted to be kissed. This boy was gay, and this encounter no accident. Red handed him a flyer and pitched the sale, "She's easy to handle and good-looking. She's in the advanced class later this afternoon. You can see her for herself."

"I'm in that class." He turned to reveal his number "9" pinned to the back of his shirt.

"So's my daughter. May the best rider win."

The Moralist

"You don't look old enough to have a daughter in the advanced class."

"She's the horsewoman in the family. I just put up the flyers. Come take a look. She's up there in her trailer."

"Your daughter?"

"The filly."

Red shepherded him to the top of the hill where deserted trucks and trailers were scattered in the shade of trees. That was the beauty of gay boys. They didn't fuck around, or rather, they did. As they walked, Red noticed the tan fabric of the boy's breeches stretched across his young thighs and ass. When they arrived at the trailer, there was as planned no pony in sight.

"My daughter must have taken her down to the ring already," Red concluded trying to sound disappointed.

"I guess I'll have to look for her in the ring," turning away in disappointment.

"Wait, come in here a minute," Red opened the trailer's tack-room door and stepped up inside. The boy followed into the metal closet that smelled of leather. Red turned and pressed his mouth against the soft, pillowy lips, pulling the young frame to him with absolute abandon and confidence in the boy's response.

The kid reached immediately for the man's hard-on, pulling apart his jeans, as Red peeled down the breeches like the skin of an onion whose core was sweet and hard and perfectly ready for Red's mouth and throat that thrilled at the soft hard head pressing against his soft palate, exploding with youthful nectar, while the boy stroked Red's own full cock. Red swallowed and cleaned up with the help of a stall towel. They dressed, and he kissed the boy again.

"You have delicious lips!"

The gay boy reciprocated, "You're pretty hot yourself! I never met anyone like you before."

"I'm one of a kind," Red smiled, as he stepped from the trailer.

The kid followed, "What's your name? Where do you live? I want to see you again!"

"My name is Red, but I live in Dallas, Texas." Red produced a pen and a flyer. "I get to Florida frequently. Write me your number. I'll call when I'm in the neighborhood."

Chad wrote his information as he spoke, "Please do. My name is Chad."

Walking down the hill together on this sweet, sunny afternoon, they were fast friends, but Red and Chad never saw each other again. The young rider competed with Cindy in dressage. 6 took blue; 9 took red. He did indeed!

The following morning, Cindy and Red took the big red truck to Speed Beach. Along the way, she asked about Jonathan.

"It's been more than a year since we met," he said. "He celebrates his thirteenth birthday next month."

"No longer a little boy."

"No, he's adolescent now."

"Does he talk to you about sex?"

"Sort of. Once, he was telling a joke about '69.' I asked him what it meant, and he said, 'Come on, you know what it means,' and I said, 'I know what it means to me, but not what it means to you,' and he says, 'Okay, so figure it out. One head is up, one head is down.' 'Okay, I get it,' I laughed and added, 'We'll have to try it sometime,'"

"What did he say to that?"

"He laughed. It's just banter. Boys his age talk like that all the time, calling each other 'faggot' and 'queer' and saying 'suck my cock' and like that. It doesn't mean he wants to do it, or maybe it does, but talking like that is not necessarily a proposition. I know when the signs are right, and it has very little to do with what is said."

"But your response sounded like a proposition."

"It probably registers like that at some level, but mostly it shows that I let him kid with me like a buddy, and he lets me kid back. That's what I love. It tells him that I am not a figure of authority or his 'moral leader' or any of that bullshit. Ironically, I am, but not like the guardians of conventional morality might imagine. I'm teaching him the true morality of self-discovery, and if in that process, he comes to me, then so be it. Physical intimacy would be a pleasure with someone I care so much about, but I'm already making love to his mind."

"What do you want from him? Do you want him to be your lover for life?"

"Yes, but not like I think you mean to imply. The romantic or physical aspect of boy love relationships usually lasts only about three or four years."

"You go into the relationship knowing that it's going to end?"

"That aspect of it, yes."

The Moralist

"So it's like each of your lovers is The One in his time, with the understanding that there will be others yet to follow."

"You make them sound like a series of one-night-stands."

"Well?"

"It's inevitable. By nature's design, the boy grows up."

"So it always ends, and you know it's going to from the start."

"Like I said, that aspect of it, but the love goes on forever. It's not that different from other love relationships. The passionate love transitions into something more permanent. The only difference with boy love is that you don't stay together as a couple. The boy moves on. He has to. But the love remains. Theo loved me till death. Michael still loves me, and so does Mark, despite the fact that he betrayed me. He still calls. He still considers me an important person in his life. That's the special position the boy lover occupies. It's unique and permanent."

"But the boys remain young, as you grow older."

"As my taste has matured. Darren wants as much boy sex as he can get. I did, too, at his age. Now, I want only the best. I know what the best is, and I'm willing to do what it takes to get it."

"You're a connoisseur of love!"

"Yes!" Red exclaimed. "What shrewd insight you have!"

"I learned it from my Daddy."

"God, she's the bride of Frankenstein!"

Thanksgiving dinner at Nick and Barb's was always an opulent affair, like something out of *Better Homes*. Achi and Cindy had been an item for years, so the joining of the families, including ex-wife Jan and Red's mom and dad, for the holiday was already a family tradition. This year, a new addition: Nick Jr. and his ten-year-old son Scottie. In his mid-thirties, stocky, hyperthyroid Nicholas was the classic black sheep, an off-and-on cocaine addict of questionable enterprise. His bright, skinny boy with the monkey face lived with his mother. The presence of father and son together was a rarity.

Little Scottie attached himself immediately to Red, as boys instinctively did. Red delighted in the little monkey's imitations of the characters from *South Park*, Kartman the fat kid singing the *Cheesy Poof* jingle. He wanted to pitch in for dinner, so Red showed him how to chop vegetables for the salad. Barb, his "Yaya," twittered her concern about giving the boy a knife and objected when Scottie called Red by his nickname, despite Red's protests that it was okay.

Electrified by Red's attention, Scottie chattered on, until Yaya put a stop to this childish intrusion into the adult world and relegated him to the children's table.

After the meal, the parents instinctively retired to the conversation nook, leaving the young people clustered around the rec-room bar toasting shots. "The young people" also included Red, who fit in more with them than the parents, just as Nick and Barb more easily related to Red's own parents than to him. This odd dislocation of the generational protocol was simply assumed with an instinctive understanding of Red's unique position as somehow younger than his age, though no one asked how or why this was so.

After downing a few shooters, Achi surreptitiously took Red aside and asked for his daughter's hand in marriage. The question shocked Red back to the cold reality that he was indeed the father of the girl this young man loved. He smiled and shook his head. "You're making me feel old, buddy! You know I like you, and I know Cindy loves you. I can't imagine anyone who would make her happier."

"Is that a 'yes'?"

"Absolutely. I just wonder what took ya so long!" He laughed, and they toasted another shot.

Back in Dallas, Red checked his e-mail:

Note to Through-the-Looking-Glass:

This is a private post to TLG only (not BLN). Paul Steiner, who was with us last summer, has just been arrested for indecency with one of his students. He has good legal representation, but it does not look good for him. Apparently, the relationship has been going on for some time, but the parents recently discovered some incriminating e-mails he exchanged with the boy. The police are holding him without bail, a completely punitive measure. A lesson to all of us: DO NOT PUT ANYTHING IN WRITING. That has always been true, but it's especially so with e-mail that's too easy to transmit and too hard to erase. —BLN editor

17

Korn was in town, the favorite punk thrasher band. They were there, dude. But the concert wasn't until that night. Red met Jonathan early, camera bag in hand.

"I used to support myself in college as a photographer doing models' resumes," he explained. "It's portrait photography, what you call my 'Hollywood routine.' Well, today, I brought my real camera, and I want to do a shoot with you before we hit the concert. The light is perfect today, especially when the sun gets a little lower in the sky. We'll go to your stomping grounds in Deep Ellum. Lots of good backgrounds there. Bring your skateboard and guitar. We'll use them as props."

Jonathan spiked up his hair with Elmer's glue, and they were off.

Deep Ellum was virtually deserted on a Sunday afternoon. Most of the shops and eateries were closed, perfect for the shoot. No one else muddying up the shot, and the muraled walls were brilliant in the golden light of late afternoon autumn sun. Jonathan played his role as model impeccably, striking rock'n'roll poses with his guitar, punk, pensive, poetic, and doing "ollies" on his skateboard against painted brick cartoon backgrounds.

As the light began to fade, they packed up their equipment and went for sandwiches and chips at the only place open, the Bluewater Café. The courtyard that once were filled with kids and aging hippies was empty now. Autumn leaves swirled about the stage where Jonathan had played. The days were growing shorter and cooler, so the man and his boy sat inside at a dimly lit booth. Red could see little more than a silhouette of Jonathan across the table, munching his chicken salad on a roll and drinking from a brightly painted green and blue bottle of flavored tea. They were the only customers in the place but spoke nonetheless in muted tones in keeping with the mellow coffeehouse ambience.

"Where'd you learn to pose like that? You were modeling like a pro."

"I read a lotta rock'n'roll magazines," he answered innocently gobbling chips. "I was imitating them."

"You never cease to amaze me! I'm afraid I'm quite the fan," he was that close to confessing his love in the quiet, darkened room, but no, that was forbidden. Boys didn't want to talk of love. It scared them and sounded queer. Even after sex, a mutual respectful silence was preferable to emotional gushing. Red continued in another vein, "It must be hard for you living in that conservative, bourgeois suburban environment and growing up with such a bohemian home life. A lot of kids who are smart and artistic and non-conformist like you would have trouble fitting in."

"I adjust," he replied, guzzling tea from the wide-mouthed bottle and adding, "I mean, I don't adjust myself to them. I adjust them to me."

"How do you do that?"

"It takes a while. They all thought I was weird at first, but I found my own posse."

"So the ropers don't gang up on you anymore."

"Thrashers stick together."

"But your school doesn't seem to like it."

"They know I'm smart, so they cut me more slack. The smart kids can get away with stuff the dumb ones can't."

"True. That's why it's important to keep your grades up. If they start to slip, the school will use that as an excuse to come down on you."

"Yeah, they're assholes," he concluded with simple finality and returned to his sandwich.

Reunion Arena was packed with youngsters, mostly male, Jonathan's age and older, up to early twenties, but past that, they were parents with children younger than Jonathan, plus one or two boy lovers with their boys. Just as gays had their "gaydar," boy lovers had their "pedar." Red was easily the oldest person in a room of twenty thousand. He stuffed his ears with spongy plugs and head-banged with his young friend, hooting and screaming at the appropriate moments and raising his arms to display a variety of hand and finger gestures.

During a break, they made their way to the T-shirt concession. Jonathan picked out a Korn tee for himself, then urged Red to get one, too. "That way,

The Moralist

we can trade 'em. It'll be like having two shirts each," he shrewdly computed. There was nothing Red would enjoy more than to wear his beloved's tee, still ripe with boy funk, and know that the boy was wearing his.

The following weekend, Red drove again across town to visit his boy. That's the way it was now. He'd become a fixture, part of the family landscape, not "a friend of the family," the malicious phrase of the witch-hunt that called into suspicion the most common relationships. Their paranoid goal was to poison everything male. It was a radical feminist conspiracy, and the poor schmuck guys didn't have a clue, joining in for fear the finger would be pointed at them. This made Red's position truly unique. He waved at Melanie as he headed for the boy's room. He was friend of the family only insofar as he was their son's friend first.

Today, he'd come to show the results of their Deep Ellum photo shoot. How much Jonathan had changed in the short time since Red had taken those snaps of the little boy on the tree limb last spring. Comparing them side-by-side, he studied the dramatic transformation that had taken place, how, over the summer, the round cherub face of the child had stretched out long like silly putty, how the shoulders were now more angular than round and the bones more gangling. Jonathan bore the stamp of his ectomorphic father.

No sooner had Red pulled the photos from his bag of tricks did Jonathan greedily snatch them away, rifling through the images with glee. They were all good. Red had edited out the crap and held back the best five for last to wow the boy even more.

"That's the okay stuff," he explained, handing over the remaining prints. "Here's the primo." The poet-minstrel with his guitar in a bag thrown over his shoulder, the freak thrasher frozen in an ollie, the demonic rock'n'roller staring at the camera with evil eyes, the thoughtful poet with the far-away gaze, the naughty prankster grabbing the tits of a nude mural painted on the bricks behind him. "I'll have one of these blown up poster-size for your room. Pick the one you like best." Out of all the cute boy shots, he chose the demonic one. Red was not surprised and instantly understood the concept. Taking back the selected print, he said, "You can keep the rest. I have double prints." He had a duplicate of that one, too, but didn't want the boy to see it again, until he returned with the poster for Jonathan's birthday and Christmas number two.

Putting away the photo, Red asked, "So what do you wanta do on a beautiful Saturday afternoon?"

Jonathan suggested a video arcade. They drove to a nearby mall, but the arcade was closed. He said he needed some jeans, so they headed for the department store instead.

Red knew the brand names by now. The canvas shoes with the flat soles were called "Vans." "Grinders" for belts, shirts, beanies, chains, and wallets. And the jeans were called "Gingkos," the super baggy style that hung over their feet so far, they frayed at the hem.

Instinctively, Red led them to the men's department, but Jonathan corrected him that Gingkos could only be found in "Boys," across from "Women" and separated from "Men" by two floors.

The Gingko poster on display featured a young man catching air on a skateboard but way older than any kid who could actually wear these jeans that were sized for no one over fourteen.

Red served as gentleman's gentleman for the boy's old clothes, as he tried on the new. Standing with his Korn tee draping him like a nightshirt over his thin, smooth legs, Jonathan pulled on the new Gingkos, then exchanged the Korn for a bright blue and gold Grinders tee and matching stocking beanie.

"The colors match your eyes and hair!" Red observed.

Jonathan looked again into the mirror with surprise that he had coordinated himself so nicely. "You always say that! This matches this. This color goes with that."

"I'm teaching you a sense of color. We are artists, aren't we?"

Jonathan gave a smart nod and grinned. Red had only to pay the bill and put the old clothes into a bag, as his boy sported his new Gingkos and Grinders through the mall.

They stopped at the food court for a fast-food lunch of burgers and fries amid the brightly colored swirl of shoppers, children, and teenagers. Red preferred to see the throng as a kinetic collage of reds and blues and yellows, rather than imagine their tawdry lives, primitive spirituality, and tortured minds corrupted by the myths of materialism. Ah, the shopping mall!

"Can you keep a secret?" Red began. Abusers always demand that their victims keep secrets, the witch-hunters cried.

Sipping his chocolate Smoothie, Jonathan paused and looked up with deep blue eyes enhanced by his new outfit. "That all depends on what the secret is."

"So I have to trust you," Red concluded. "I think when I tell you, you will understand why I would prefer that you not share this with anyone, especially not your mom and dad, but also your sister, because she will tell them, if you do."

"Then you will have to trust me."

"Okay," he continued, "I told you that I edited out a lot of the pictures from our photo shoot. They were all the shots that showed your teeth, because your teeth need work."

He blushed but kept his pride with a smile pointing to his crooked incisors coming in high on his gums. "My vampire teeth!" he crowed.

"Yes, your vampire teeth. I want to take you to an orthodontist and get you fitted for braces. Now is the time, while you're teeth are still developing. I'll pay for it, but I need your parents' cooperation, so I want to tell them myself. That's why I want you to keep it a secret, until I do. If you tell them in advance, it might not happen. They might not let me do it. I only tell you now, because I need your cooperation, too. Would you go through with it? Would you let me do this for you?"

"Maybe."

"You've grown so cautious in your old age."

"Now I've got something on you. Maybe I'll blackmail you with this little secret of yours," he said with his sly smile, concealing his sensitivity about his appearance with adolescent cool.

"Blackmail? You little fuck!" Red exclaimed facetiously. "You don't know how important a great smile is. And what do I get for my trouble? A little enthusiasm? A simple 'thank you'? No, I get blackmail! Why do I put up with this abuse?"

"I think my mom has a dental plan," he grinned his vampire grin.

Red drove the forty miles along the turnpike to Fort Worth to visit Darren. Traffic was backed-up, an accident. He hated stop-and-go traffic. That's why he lived in town, so he wouldn't have to commute. How could anyone put up with this every day? No wonder everyone in America was crazy! It was the traffic!

Darren was eager to help. He filed through the shots of Jonathan in Deep Ellum and exclaimed, "These are fantastic! He's not a little kid anymore."

"No, he isn't," Red replied. "Last weekend, we went shopping together for a new outfit—baggy jeans, T-shirt, beanie, the whole thrasher look. He picked it out himself."

"You're dressing him!"

"With great pleasure. It's almost as good as sex."

"Almost."

They retired to the computer room and scanned in the demon shot, as Red explained, "He wants this one blown up poster-size. You get the idea—Marilyn Manson."

"I'm way ahead of you." From Red's description on the phone, Darren had dug out the Manson cover of *Rolling Stone* they could use for reference to make up the face, streak the hair, and tint the pupils of the demonic eyes red and green like Christmas in hell. For the finishing touch, Darren replaced the brick wall background with a curtain of fire.

Red took the disk to Kinko's and had it poster-sized and mounted.

E-mail

Red:

Good news and bad news from OLGA.

Good news:

Our study was received with great enthusiasm from many quarters, many expressions of support, and the gay press ranged from positive to balanced, reporting both sides of the controversy. I think I did okay with them. I managed to say several of my talking points like you taught me.

Bad news:

Many members of the gay community, especially the lesbians, are not at all happy with us. I'm afraid we have opened an old wound. The advanced billing brought out much more press than expected, mostly European but some American, looking for the sensational story. I was overwhelmed. After two days of non-stop interviews, I felt like a babbling idiot. You were right. I had no idea how hard it is.

One moment does stand out:

A right-wing talk radio guy from Philly asked me about our "agenda." I said, "Our agenda is to establish a healthier bond between adults and children than the current hysteria allows." Then he asked, "Does that include a sexual bond?" And I said, "It can in some cases." Then he zinged me, "So your agenda is sex between adults and children." I protested, but I'm sure they'll edit that.

What are your thoughts about this? —Noah

Reply to Noah:

Congratulations on your single-handed effort. You've showed great courage and stamina. That was just a taste of what you can expect once the study is published. (When will that be?) I hope this trial by fire gives you the confidence you will need to carry it off successfully, when the real dook hits the fan.

It's good news that there was so much press there. Your study should be publicized. People need to know what lies they have been told dressed up as scientific fact.

Regarding the radio interview, the reporter laid a trap for you, and alas, you walked right into it. The trick is the word "agenda." Scientists should have only one agenda, discovering the truth. Any other agenda will color your conclusion, just as your own study reveals. At least, we've learned to be careful about using that word. I'll ad it to our list of negative words. —Red

Reply to Red:

Now it's "agenda." What about "sex"? Even "sex" is a negative word! Pretty soon we won't be able to say the word "boy" without implying some dastardly innuendo! That's how impossible it is to talk to these people! They own the language!

I apologize for my outburst, but I can tell you frankly, Red, I don't think I want to go through anything like that again. —Noah

The Frame house and outside walkways were awash with Jonathan's posse, an all-male cast, playing computer games inside, grinding the curb out. Red moved among them with ease, cheering Jonathan's skateboard tricks, taking pictures with his pocket Nikon, speaking to those boys who knew him from past visits. One scruffy, dog-faced kid, older than Jonathan with dull eyes and a fuzzy chin, pointedly inquired, "You're the guy who takes Jonathan to all the cool concerts, aren't you?"

"Yes, I am," Red answered proudly. He liked that the kid seemed to envy Jonathan's special older friend.

"There's some concerts I'd like to go to sometime."

Was that a knowing leer in this clumsy hint? Dog-face thought he had it figured out, so why shouldn't he get in on the action, free concert with probably a good blow-job in the bargain? How crude! His little peon brain didn't have a clue that it was exactly such an equation that Red had had his fill of ten years ago. If all he wanted was a boy whore, he didn't have to drive twenty miles across town for a goat dog. There was plenty of that at The Crossroads, and cuter, too! "Great! Maybe Jonathan and I will see you there!" Red gave him a hearty slap on the back and walked off.

The sky grew dark early on the short days of December, but this was Texas, and the air was warm and moist, more like spring than the first day of winter. The thrashers came inside for the buffet-style spaghetti dinner Melanie had prepared. The meal was a chaos of kids and grown-ups perched on whatever broken-down furniture they could find throughout the house and bent over their paper plates piled with pasta and sauce. Even the gathering for the cake and presents was helter-skelter with half the party-goers not in attendance to sing the birthday song or cheer the opening of gifts.

The rock-star poster was a hit, rating a "Bad-ass!" in the boy lexicon of plaudits and immediately mounted on his bedroom wall amid the pantheon of Clapton, Plant, and a day-glo Hendrix. A flash of lightning lit the room with impeccable timing.

A winter thunderstorm was threatening, and the crowd began to disperse. Red found Melanie ensconced on a velvet recliner in the living room, chatting with a fiftyish woman with fiery red hair whom she introduced as "Aunt Ariel." He collapsed wearily onto the sofa next to her.

"Have you grown tired of the boys, Richard?" Melanie asked with the same sly irony he knew so well in her son.

"They're all taking off to beat the storm," he explained.

"So you decided to spend some time with the grown-ups for a change."

"It's been a fun birthday party. Thank you for inviting me."

"I didn't. Jonathan did. It's his party. Do you still teach in that program for young writers?"

For the first time, Red realized how important it was that he be able to say "yes" to that question. "Yes, but my new student is nothing like Jonathan. He's more of a street kid. He and Jonathan used to know each other."

The Moralist

"After he finishes his story, do you think you will stay in touch with him as you have with Jonathan?"

"No, Jonathan's special."

"Do you love him?"

"Very much. He's a bright, compassionate person, and I consider myself fortunate to have met him."

"I'm sure his teachers at school love him, too. But they don't bring him gifts and take him to movies and amusement parks and concerts."

"They haven't had your permission as I have," Red replied diplomatically.

"He likes you. We let Jonathan choose his own friends."

"You trust his judgment. So do I. We have that in common, which brings me to something I want to talk to you about—my Christmas gift to him."

"You've given him so much already."

"This is a little different. I need your permission and cooperation."

"You sound so serious. What is this gift?"

"I want to get his teeth fixed."

"Fixed? His teeth are fine. What's wrong with his teeth?"

"I mean straightened. I want to correct what he calls his 'vampire teeth.'"

"Oh, you mean braces."

"Yes."

She nodded thoughtfully to herself, "I have a dental plan."

"Great! We can split the cost!"

She instantly produced pencil and paper to write down the pertinent information: the name of the plan, her full correct name, Social Security number, and the name and address of an orthodontist whom she knew took her plan. It was almost as if she were expecting it. Did Jonathan tell her after all? He hoped not. This was foolish paranoia. But her instant, unquestioning acceptance surprised him, like her acceptance of him from the very beginning. He had agonized for weeks over this moment. How would they take it? Presumptuous? Intrusive of a private family matter? An implied judgment against them? Or simply the embarrassment of accepting charity? Which this was not. But none of that happened, or if it had, Red was not privy to it. Maybe, she just accepted it, impassively, like she accepted the chaos of kids that poured through her house every day. She wasn't a Christian, she was a big female Buddha.

The storm hit just as Red was leaving. He had to run for the car and plow through a flooded street. He had barely driven two blocks before the old

Mustang started to sputter and choke, and then it died altogether. Restarting the engine was hopeless, so he ran back to Jonathan's house. By the time he arrived at the front door, he was soaked like a wet dog.

Melanie gave him a towel and a robe and threw his wet clothes in the dryer. He thanked her and asked for a phone book to call a tow truck, but Jon Sr. advised against it.

"Did you drive through any big puddles?" he inquired.

"Puddles? The whole street was a river!"

"You probably splashed some water up into the carburetor. Why don't you wait here until the storm passes and let the car dry out a little? I bet she'll start right up."

Red took Jon's advice and looked for his young friend. Jonathan had also removed his shirt that had gotten wet in the rain. He sat in the middle of the living room laying out cards on the carpet to the amusement of Angie and her girlfriends, happy to have a half-naked, teenage boy tell their fortunes.

Red stood in the foyer and watched, studying the nascent back muscles and frame stretched beneath the boy's pale skin. The cards were oversized and featured only a single letter, his latest magic trick: the cards always spelled out some word or words in response to their questions. Jonathan felt the gaze of his lover and turned around, inviting him in to have his fortune told.

The girls dispersed, and Red sat cross-legged on the carpet facing the boy, examining, his lean rippled tummy, slightly cut chest, and long hairless arms foreshadowing the tall man to come. Slender delicate fingers held all the cards.

"I will tell you what you will be doing five years from now," he announced, handing the cards to Red. "Cut the deck three times."

Red obeyed, and taking them back, the boy laid out card by card to spell out the words "PORN WRITER" to Red's amusement and amazement at this clever trick that he truly could not figure out, and at the astonishing accuracy of the prediction, more than the boy himself could possibly have known, though obviously he did know in some deep instinctive way.

"Now, I will predict how it will end," he pronounced with mental theatrics, touching each card to his forehead like Johnny Carson's Karnak before laying it out to spell "SUICIDE."

"I guess there are lots of ways to commit suicide!" Red exclaimed. "You are the Delphic Oracle. How do you do that?"

"The cards know all," he proclaimed with impish eyes and vampire smile and continued. "Now, I will tell my own fortune. What will I be five years from now?" He laid out the cards with more performance to tell his own story with flourish: "CROSS DRESSER."

Red laughed, "That's funny! Is that what you want?"

"The cards never lie," he pronounced with solemnity.

Recovering, Red inquired, "Who were all the girls?"

"Angie's friends, Dana and Lacie. I went to Dana's birthday party last month."

"She likes you."

"How do you know?"

"I was watching her."

"She's always hangin' around."

"That counts." A long silence ensued, as the boy processed this information. "Hello? Anyone home? What's the matter? I thought you liked becoming a teenager."

"Not really."

"Why not? Just last spring, you said you couldn't wait."

"I'm not so sure now."

"You seem to be doing all right. Look how quickly you've made friends at your new school. Look at all the kids who came to your birthday party! I'm impressed!"

"But I liked being a kid."

"And becoming a teenager means leaving childhood behind."

"Yeah, I miss it."

"You're not alone in that. Everybody goes through it. The psychologists describe it as a kind of mourning. You weep for the loss of the little boy you once were. You want to do some good writing? Write about your feelings of excitement and anxiety about becoming a teenager and your sadness at saying goodbye to childhood. In some cultures, the transition from childhood to adolescence is regarded as your coming of age into manhood. They don't have a 'teenager' period. As soon as you're physically mature, you're a man, and that's it."

"But I'm not physically mature, not even close." He made a joke of smelling his smooth, pale armpits.

"That doesn't mean adult. It means adolescent—sexual maturity. It varies from boy to boy, but by age thirteen, you know what I mean. That's why boys are so sexy and horny at your age. Nature intends for them to produce children right away. The whole teenage 'waiting period' is a cultural myth. It's not nature's way. Have you masturbated yet?"

He blushed, "I have a Christmas present for you!" He bolted away and returned in an instant with a small sculpture made of three floppy disks fastened at the edges to create a half-box like the corner of a room. Sprawled on its floor with wire legs spread, a little wooden figure with pennies for eyes displayed an erect Q-Tip penis dripping with metallic blue cum, and the whole corner was splattered with the stuff. Scrawled on the "wall" were the letters, "ME.ORG." Presenting it to his lover with a coy smile, "Merry Christmas, Red."

Red took the rare sculpture into his hands like a fragile bird and laughed, "Well, I guess this answers my question!"

"It's a found-art construction," Jonathan explained, using his latest art class lingo.

"So I see. What did your teacher have to say? There's no mistaking this for a Greek column."

"I didn't make it for school. I made it for you."

Red took a pen from his pocket and handed it to him. "Here, sign it. You should sign and date all of your work." As the boy was making his mark on the back of the piece, Red continued, "It's good we're having our Christmas now. I'll be making my annual visit to Atlanta, and we probably won't see each other for a while. So I have my Christmas gift for you, too. I spoke with your mom about your teeth. You were right. She has a dental plan. When I get back from Atlanta, we're going to get those vampire teeth straightened out."

Music suddenly filled the house, but not the recorded kind. They joined Jon Sr. in the music room where he was cranking up a jam. Jonathan hoisted his big guitar over his shoulder and picked up the bass line.

The storm moved on. Melanie took Red's warm clothes from the dryer. Dressed and dry, Red waved goodbye to Jonathan and his dad jamming to James Brown's *I Feel Good*, rockin' with the rhythm of his music. He wished them all a Merry Christmas and walked out into the cloudless night. Jon Sr. was right. The old Mustang started right up.

When he reached home, there was a message from Darren on his machine to meet him at Billy Budd's, which he did. What a remarkable contrast between the rare and beautiful world of the boy and this tawdry drag bar! How much more creative was our CROSS DRESSER than the floor-slapping drag queens? PORN WRITER was such a fine joke and how remarkably close to the truth! What entertainment could the funny drag clowns offer to match that? The thirteenth birthday of a darling boy, an artist and musician who gave him a jack-off art construction for Christmas! It was worth any price in the hardest currency there is—his time, future, and freedom.

Meanwhile, Darren was paying that price.

"It's like you said. My lawyer's just going through the motions. He wants to plea me and get it over with."

"What's the deal?"

"Ten years' probation. No time."

"Is that it?"

"I have to go to some kind of behavior modification school."

"Can he keep you off the list?"

"The sex offender registry? No, that comes with the plea."

"Probation isn't like being a free citizen, y'know. You will be a convicted felon. You can't own a gun. You can't vote. They control your travel. For what? For making love to your lover. It's not fair. A decent person like you shouldn't have to suffer that in our so-called free society."

"It still beats prison."

"He's selling you out, and I promise you, if you don't take his deal, he'll drop you as a client. That's what a tired old fuck he is!"

"I know, and Richard," this, a rarity that Darren called him by his given name, "even if I fought it and lost, I think I could handle the time. I could even handle getting raped by 'Tyrone,' if it came to that. But I don't want to get AIDS in prison. I'm gonna take the deal."

Red flew to Atlanta for the annual Christmas ritual. Why did he keep coming back to this experience of depression and death? Alone with Mom and Dad, he was okay. He could navigate them, but the family portrait was another matter. His older brother CJ, this time sans wife and daughter, and his younger brother mad Norton, skinny, balding with a salt-and-pepper beard and thick cracker accent. (Where did he pick that up? Red could not fathom; his parents' spoke genteel Southern.) He looked like the crazy hermit stereotype he was, not merely eccentric, but really nuts, normal most of the time, unless you accidentally stepped on one of his delusional land mines, and then he exploded in your face.

It was the first time in a decade Norton had shown up for Christmas dinner. As we have seen, the holiday table was often the occasion to discuss money, and this discussion was particularly important. The land deal had gone through, and the topic was the disbursement of funds. Norton didn't feel he was getting his fair share. He might be crazy, but he wasn't stupid. The atmosphere was ripe for the argument that predictably ensued.

Red sighed with weary sadness, as once again, the Holiday abyss opened up and swallowed him. Money wasn't the issue between CJ and Norton. It was a personality conflict. CJ condemned Norton as a bum because he couldn't keep a job. How can you have a personality conflict with a crazy person? Wouldn't that mean that you were as crazy as he was? At best, it was an exercise in futility. Why couldn't CJ just say, "Well, he's nuts," and leave it at that?

Back home, the family dispersed as quickly as possible. Red found himself alone with his father in the TV room watching the ball game, he seated on the sofa with a cocktail, the old man reclining in his Laz-e-Boy. Red hated those damn chairs and vowed he would never own one. They reminded him of coffins.

His former next-door neighbors, a mousy little gay couple who both had AIDS, had once invited him over to show off their new purchase, a matching pair of Laz-e-Boy recliners. Red smiled grimly at the sight of the two large billowy chairs covered in deep-blue velvet with reclining backs and pop-up foot rests. He felt like he was in the viewing room of a funeral parlor with the corpses standing at his side. Six months later, one of them did die in his Laz-e-Boy. They could have hauled him out of the house and right down to the cemetery without even taking him out of his chair.

His father abruptly interrupted Red's reverie. "So what are you going to do with your money?"

"I'll think about that when I have it in hand. I know how these deals go."

"Oh, it's a done deal, all right. That's why CJ and Norton are at each other's throats. They know it's real."

"Then I'll quit my job and finish my book."

"What book?"

"Something I've been working on over the past year."

"I'm not sure that's such a good idea."

"Why am I not surprised to hear you say that? You've never approved of my writing."

"I wasn't talking about your writing. I was talking about your job."

"I don't think you were. I think talking about my job is you're your indirect way of expressing your disapproval of my creative work without actually coming out and saying it."

"That's not true. I've never opposed anything you wanted to do."
"Yes, you have."
"When?"
"What about those career talks we used to have when I was thirteen?"
"Thirteen?"
"Yes. We used to have these father-son chats about my career, as you drove me to the theater for my play rehearsals. I used to lie awake at night preparing my arguments for those talks, because I knew full well that your unstated purpose was to dissuade me from wanting to become an actor, and it worked. Only one problem, I became a writer instead, which is worse."
"I'm amazed that you even remember that!"
"It's the book. It brings back all this stuff with astonishing clarity, like one of those dreams where you swear it's real, like it never went away. I guess it never does. The child never forgets. Remember that bet we made when I was six?"
"What bet?"
"That spiders weren't insects. I won that bet, and you welched on me, because you wouldn't admit you were wrong."
"That I do remember. You've never forgiven me for that one."
"The child never forgives either. Do you remember how much the bet was?"
"Ten cents."
"One damn dime. That was the price of your son's faith and trust in your integrity. Isn't it strange how these seemingly innocuous childhood experiences become icons of one's life. If only parents understood the enormity of the damage they cause when they betray a child's trust, not so much damage to the child as to themselves for what they lose in the process."
"So this book is about your childhood?"
"Do I detect a spark of interest?"
"Shouldn't I be?"
"You never have before. Take tonight, for example. I tell you I'm going to take some time off to finish my book, and you didn't say, 'You might enjoy that,' or even, 'What is your book about?' No, instead, you say, 'I disapprove of that.'"
"That's not what I meant. How could I disapprove? I've never read anything you've written."
"And there we have it!"

"All right, show me some of this book."

"Don't let me twist your arm."

"I mean it. I want to read it."

"No, you don't, or you would have asked before now."

"I'm asking now."

"All right, I'll send you a few chapters, but I should also warn you: This book is from the other side of the boat. You should know that going in. If you read a page or two and decide it's not for you, I'll understand. At least, you will have made the effort. And by the way, for the record, I wasn't planning on this conversation, and I don't expect a big hug at the end."

Struggling from his Laz-e-Boy, the old man said, "Good-night." Red hugged him anyway.

What surprised him most about this sudden and unexpected confrontation was how uncomplicated it was. All was said and done in less than ten minutes. He was lucid. He spoke with simplicity and clarity, without anger, shame, or fear. The words had fallen from his tongue without a thought, as if he had written it all out before, which come to think of it, he had.

Returning to Dallas, Red tried to call Malcolm. No answer. He left a message on his voice mail.

18

After their long separation, Red was eager to see his boy again. It was not unusual for two or three weeks to pass between their meetings, so every one was special. He longed to see the boy's bright trusting eyes and hear the happy young voice, no longer shrill and birdlike, as it had been only a year ago, now taut and smooth like the string of a violin.

Driving up to the curb, Red's heart leapt at the sight of the kid practicing his skateboard on the sidewalk. He sported his blue and gold tee, Gingko jeans, and now blue spiked hair, but his concentration on grinding the concrete curb was complete and un-self-conscious. In that sunny moment, Red understood how purely mythological this vision was. He desired only to be close to this living myth, to feel its warmth, embrace it, and be one with it.

Seeing Red, Jonathan tucked his board under his arm and greeted him at the car window.

"Ready to go?" Red began. "Where's Ernie?"

"Inside, callin' his mom."

"Is she gonna let him come?"

"I don't know. She's pretty strict."

At that moment, Ernie burst out the front door running toward them. The news was "go," so the boys piled into the Mustang, and they were off to Planet Game. Red had promised on the phone, "I'm gonna take you to the mother of all video arcades. We couldn't find one last month, so we're gonna make up for it today, but I want you to bring a friend. I'm no good at video games." The last time Red had played a video game was Pac Man. Video games had passed him by.

Red first met snaggle-toothed Ernie at MLK, when Jonathan was still his student in the Authors of Tomorrow. They encouraged having lunch with your student in the school cafeteria, and Ernie had joined them. He was a bright little boy with lively eyes behind a shock of dark brown hair. Now that Jonathan was hangin' with his new posse, late-bloomer Ernie seemed a blast from the past, a last link to Jonathan's fading childhood. Perhaps that was why Jonathan held onto the friendship, even though Ernie now lived across town. In the cafeteria barely more than a year ago, they were two little boys, but together now, Jonathan was a lanky youth next to his stubby childhood friend.

They entered the two-story high-tech emporium of flashing lights and beeping, crashing, screaming sounds, a phantasmagoria of virtual adventures: hockey, soccer, bikes, bowling, surfing, auto racing, basketball, snowboarding, wave-running, even skateboarding, the obvious favorite. Red fed $20 bills to an electronic panel that returned two plastic credit cards that he distributed to his young guests with the instructions, "Knock yourself out."

They did, moving from game to game. Ernie won the motorbike and Indie 500 races, Jonathan shrugging with a diffident smile, a gracious loser. He made up for it on the skateboard track where they remained for the rest of the afternoon.

Red hovered, observing them from a distance, or at times, catching sight of some other pretty boy lost in concentration on his game, so that Red was free to examine him unaware, his face aglow in dancing colored light, the smooth small muscles of the long lean arms rippling beneath the skin as thumbs worked to make the next big score.

Finally, Red abandoned his guests altogether for a beer at the pizza pavilion. It wasn't like last spring, when he felt the adult responsibility to stay at the side of little-boy Jonathan every moment. Now, the youth was almost as tall as Red himself. The magic, delight, and tragedy of boy love—the boy grows up.

Returning from his beer, Red found the boys still enthralled with the skateboard game. As he scanned the room, he spotted Darren across the way competing with Jimmy at an air hockey table. Darren looked up instinctively, taking his eyes off the game just long enough for Jimmy to score before turning to see what had caught Darren's eye. Jimmy waved and started to come over, but Darren held him back. They smiled and nodded in silence.

Jonathan interrupted the wordless communication, "Come on, Red. What do you want to play?" The skateboard game had grown stale, and the boy was thoughtfully including his older friend.

Red had been content not to display his woeful inadequacy at video games to boys who were hard-wired for this stuff, but one game had caught his eye.

It was part video game, part ride, a two-story vertical tower with seats that rose and fell according to your accuracy at shooting virtual terrorists in a virtual building.

"That one," Red replied. Not only did it look like fun, but it was one the boys hadn't played before. At least he had a fighting chance and scored highest as his chair jostled him up and down like a madcap elevator. Jonathan congratulated Red's victory, proud that his lover was still cool for an old guy.

Ernie envied Jonathan for having this grown-up friend, who called him "buddy" and treated him like an equal, who took him to the coolest video arcade in the world and gave him twenty bucks and said, "Knock yourself out." He tried to compete for Red's attention with clever comments and sharp observations.

At the photo booth, the boys giggled and mugged for the camera. From the choice of frames, Ernie selected a phony twenty-dollar bill with his own face in the cameo, and over Cokes and pizza, he handed the bill to Red, as if to pay him back for lunch.

Touched by the boy's sweet gesture, Red refused. "Thank you, Ernie, but you keep it as a souvenir." Ernie's parents were divorced, and he lived with his mom. His need for love was greater than Jonathan's, and he would be easier to love for that reason, but that was beside the point.

Jonathan had positioned his mug shot on the body of an angel, an unusual choice for a boy, but Red understood it was designed to complement the "Marilyn Manson" poster on his wall at home.

"Is Jonathan your little angel, Red?" Ernie boldly inquired in Jonathan's presence.

"I prefer his demon," Red replied, more for Jonathan's benefit than Ernie's.

"I'd like to have a friend who takes me to fun places like this," Ernie continued.

"You do. Jonathan invited you today, and he probably will again."

"No, I mean somebody like you. I know I'm not as cute as Jonathan—" Jonathan shoved him, but Ernie persisted, "I know my teeth are kinda crooked."

Anxious to defuse this conversation that was now embarrassing them both, Red replied, "What about Jonathan's vampire teeth? They're more crooked than yours!"

"He said you're going to have braces put on."

"That's true. We have an appointment with the dentist in a couple of weeks."

"That's what I mean. I'll never have a friend who would do that for me," Ernie despaired.

"If you want braces, I'm sure your mom would get them for you," Red encouraged him, but this wasn't about braces. Ernie was right. It was harder than ever for boys in America to find someone to love them. As desperately lonely as they were, their culture murdered and imprisoned the love for a boy and left the boys themselves to wander alone and forlorn like truthful Ernie, who would probably get his braces but never find the male love he knew he needed.

They had to get Ernie back early, but Jonathan was free for the rest of the afternoon. Remembering their fun picking out CD's for Darren, Red suggested they go to a music store. As before, Red encouraged Jonathan to make the selections, this time for his own collection. He chose not a CD but a video biography of a punk band called Limp Bizkit. The music store was close to Red's place, so they went there to watch the video on his entertainment system that had the digital surround speakers required by boys everywhere.

Red pulled the Mustang into the bat cave, and they climbed from the car. He paused and pointed out to Jonathan a chattering squirrel to ensure that anyone looking on would get an eyeful. This wasn't the nosey suburbs. It was Oak Lawn, where everybody minded their own business, but Red wanted to make it clear he had nothing to hide. He defied the madness that required that a man *never* find himself alone with a boy. As Paul from Maine had said, most public schools had already implemented that insane policy. Of course, he was in jail now.

Nonetheless, once Jonathan was inside, Red closed the blinds. For only the second time since they'd met more than a year ago, the boy was actually present in Red's home, now as Jonathan the youth, not the little boy.

"Would you like something to drink?" the proper host inquired.

"Got any rum?" the youth grinned.

"Yes. I didn't know you drank alcohol."

"Sometimes," he replied, following Red into the kitchen.

"How do you like it?"

"With Dr. Pepper."

The Moralist

"Sounds good. Two rum-and-Dr. Peppers coming up." As he mixed the drinks, Red remembered sixteen-year-old Michael twenty years ago. "I used to have a friend not much older than you who drank this very same drink. He called it a daktari. Daktari is Swahili for doctor."

"All the kids drink it. I didn't know it had a name."

"Now ya know. Do you get drunk?"

"I can handle it," he answered proudly. "Austin gets messed up. One time, he got smashed and crawled up on the roof of the A-frame and started howlin' like a dog. It was a riot! Then, he got scared of the height and was afraid to come back down. We had to climb up and get him."

"What's the A-frame?"

"It's that picnic shelter in the park where we went biking, with the big metal roof."

Red vaguely remembered the structure overlooking the boy's secret place down by the creek. "Oh, yeah!"

"We party there on the weekends. Some guys bring their girlfriends and go make out in the woods."

Violating Jonathan's secret place, no doubt. Some things never change. He handed the boy his drink, and they returned to the sofa to watch the punk rock video and sip their cocktails like grown-ups.

With this shared moment, Red broke the barrier of age between them. He was also breaking the law, moving from admired mentor to corruptor of youth. Such was the price of Jonathan's inner sanctum. What other barriers might be broken on this sunny winter afternoon?

By the end of the video, the sun was gone, and the room grew darker with the fading light.

Jonathan drained his glass.

"How was your drink?" Setting it down, the boy nodded but declined Red's offer for another. "Probably just as well. I don't want to take you home drunk." He excused himself to the kitchen. "How about a lemonade?"

"Yeah, that sounds good."

Red returned with an aluminum foil pouch pierced with protruding straw. "These little foil pouch lemonades are my favorite. I discovered them last summer when I saw you drinking one."

"Yeah, they're my favorite, too." He sipped from the pouch, then cradled it in his lap with both hands like a cup of tea.

Red sat beside him. "Did you have fun today?"

"Yeah, it was great."

"What did you think of our conversation with Ernie?"

"He thinks you're cool. He told me."

"What do you think?"

"I think you're cool, too."

"That's not what I meant. Remember the last time you were here? It was almost exactly a year ago. I told you I was your secret weapon?"

"You said I was your. . ." he searched for the word, ". . .'protégé'—yeah, that's it. I'm your protégé. It means 'protected one.'"

"That's right, and I said you were safe here. You can talk about anything you want. What would you like to talk about?"

"I don't know."

"Then, ask me a question. I'm lucid. I'll tell you anything you want to know."

"You ask me a question."

"All right. Who am I to you?"

"You're my secret weapon."

"That's my description. I want to hear yours."

"You're my best friend. You don't treat me like a little kid. You listen to what I have to say."

"Have you ever wondered why I chose you?"

"I guess 'cause you like me, and we have fun together."

Red stretched his arm around the boy's broad shoulder and pulled him close. "I chose you, because I love you."

The boy's hands squeezed the pouch between his legs, and a squirt of lemonade erupted from the straw. Brushing the liquid from his pants, Jonathan stood and walked across the room. He perched on the big sculpture chair, high up like a totem or an idol.

Pretending he had not seen the ironic accident, Red changed the subject. "I'm not your only admirer, y'know," he continued. "My new student Chuy told me that you were his hero."

"Me?"

"That's what he said."

"Why'd he say that?" he inquired with bashful pride.

"It had nothing to do with your being his go-between. I never even mentioned that. He said it was because you always made good grades, and you were a writer. He said you inspired him to write his story. Love comes in many forms, some of which you may not even be aware." Red tossed down the dregs of the cloying daktari. "I gotta get you home now."

In the car on the drive back, Red spoke to the boy, both their eyes fixed on the highway, "I enjoyed our afternoon together, but I want to remind you about our cocktails. Some people would not approve of that, and we could both get in a lot of trouble if they found out."

"I ain't tellin' nobody."

"That includes your friends, especially them. That's the hardest part, because you might be tempted to. But if you do, then they'll all want to come over, and I don't want that. Like I said, this private time is just between you and me and nobody else."

"That's what I like about it."

"Yeah, me too. Just you and me, buddy. Just you and me."

When he returned home, Red called Darren. "So you finally got a glimpse of Jonathan. What'd ya think?"

"Was he the one with the blue hair?"

"Of course."

"He looked like a skinny little kid."

"Maybe that's because he was with Ernie. Ernie hasn't hit puberty yet."

"No, they both looked like little kids to me. We walked by them earlier. You musta been off somewhere. I noticed the blue hair, but they were just a couple of kids to me. I didn't even give 'em a second look."

"Good, I hope you remember to keep it that way."

"Don't worry. I found what I want! It's called Clearwater Beach, outside of Tampa. Wait till you see it, Red. Beautiful boys everywhere, just like you said Speed Beach was in the seventies. They've moved to Clearwater! I met a fifteen-year-old boy, blonde hair, smooth and perfect!"

"Only two years older than Jonathan."

"What a difference two years make! He was smart, too. We talked for a long time on the beach. Then I invited him back to my room, and we talked there, too. I pulled out some straight porn I got off the Internet. I said I was gonna jack off and invited him to join me. He said he couldn't get hard with me in the room. I thought he might be embarrassed by his little cock, so I went into the bathroom, but I could still see him in the mirror through a crack in the door. He pulls out this enormous shlong! Man, he was huge! I waited till he was hot and came back in, but I didn't go for it. He was really shy. I just jacked off with him, but right when I was about to cum, I told him to stand up in front of me, so I could look at his big dick. I shot all over the place! It was hot! He was fucking beautiful!"

"Did he shoot on you?"

"No, he never did cum. I don't think he really wanted to."

"Darren, don't you realize how dangerous that is? What if he freaked out and went to the cops?"

"I can't stop being who I am. Besides, it's Florida, not Texas. So did you have fun with Jonathan and Ernie?"

"Ernie had to go home early, so Jonathan and I went to my place to watch a video."

"Oh?"

"Not that kind—a music video, a punk band."

"So how'd it go? Anything you want to tell me?"

"No, but I'm close. We're in the red zone now, twenty yards from the goal line."

"But no score."

"I'm getting mixed signals. On some levels, we are incredibly intimate. He's basic and thoughtful, and he speaks from his heart. But I have to pry it out of him. Sometimes I feel like we communicate in code. I only wish I had the key."

"It's not what he says. It's the boy himself. *He* is the code, and you are the code master."

"The lover wants to strip the beloved bare."

"You still have to accept him for who he is. At thirteen, he's goin' on instinct. He doesn't have the key anymore than you do."

"It depends on the boy. Remember Mark at that age? He was easy to read with all his bluster about becoming a gynecologists and living in a mansion in L.A.!"

"Yeah. Now, he's a truck driver."

"At Jonathan's birthday party, I was talking to a boy his same age who in a matter of minutes was telling me all about himself and his plans for the future. It was thrilling! In those few minutes, he revealed more about himself than Jonathan ever has."

"You've answered your own question. It depends on the boy. Consider yourself lucky for the intimacy you do have. I've never had that with a boy."

"I want his confidence. I want him to open up to me."

The Moralist

"Open up indeed!" Darren laughed.

"I was referring to verbal intercourse."

"You sound like a woman. That's what women always say: 'He won't talk to me! We don't communicate!'"

"Yeah, well, I'm a boy lover, okay? I ain't John Wayne."

"Maybe, he's waiting for you to open up to him."

"I told him I love him."

"Oh, God, you didn't! No wonder you're striking out. You just violated the cardinal rule: Do not talk about love."

"I wanted to kiss him."

"Rule number two: Don't kiss him. They don't want to kiss. Suck him off and never mention it again. That's what they want. *You* taught *me* that."

"I guess I blew it."

"You *didn't* blow it. That's the problem." Red laughed half-heartedly as Darren continued, "There's more to the red zone than gaining his confidence. It's all about the moves."

"Yeah, he moved away from me. We were talking close. I almost made a move on him then, but he stood up and took another seat across the room."

"Maybe he knows what's goin' on, and he's telling you no."

"He's not ready."

"That's what every lover says, but are you prepared to be rejected? Have you considered that?"

"You're right, I missed my shot. I should've just jumped his bones and let the sparks fly. Sex breaks down the barriers."

"Sometimes it creates barriers. When my beach boy was pulling his jeans over his big fat dick, he said, 'Now, I can't talk to you.' Sex was the end of it for us, and I felt bad about that. We'd had such a good afternoon together, and I think he really wanted to get to know me as a friend, but after the sex, I was just another faggot."

"Jonathan and I have a little more history than one afternoon."

"All the more reason to take it easy. Maybe you read him right and exercised appropriate caution. You sure as hell don't want to end up like me."

"One can be too cautious. Faint heart ne'er won fair boy."

"It'll be spring soon. Take him canoeing on the Guadalupe, like you've done with all your other boys. Pitch your tent by the river, then take your pick—a long late talk by the campfire, or a night under the covers."

"I want both."
"The love train is leaving the station."
"All aboard!"

During a moment of imaginative ecstasy, the phone rang and shocked Red out of his pleasure. He considered not answering, but the damage was done. He picked up the phone and, trying not to sound annoyed, sounded stupefied instead, "Hello?"

"Richard? Did I wake you?" Penny's voice was tearful and crazy. She was sloshed again.

"No, I was writing." That is, he had been, until the passion of his prose got the better of him. He often sounded dazed when the phone interrupted his work. It was like being awakened from a dream. You don't know you're dreaming until the alarm goes off.

"Richard, Daddy is dead."

"I'm sorry, Penny." It's about time, he thought. She was free at last from this burden that had wasted her youth. Surely she must be thinking the same thing. Maybe she was just waiting for the money. "I know how much you loved him, how much you still do."

Bursting into tears, "I do love him! But I can't anymore! He's gone, Richard! He's gone forever! I thought I was prepared. I thought I was ready for it, but now that it's really true, he's really gone. . ." She fell into heavy sobs.

"We're never prepared. How can we know what it feels like, till it happens?"

"You understand! You're always so understanding. I still don't believe it. I have to make myself realize that it's true."

"Don't rush it. Just let the grief happen. Are you by yourself?"

"Edouard said he was coming over."

"Good, so am I."

"I'm not dressed for company, and I've had a few drinks."

"Have a few more. Get as drunk as you want. It takes the pain away. I'll bring dinner."

On the way out the door, he filled a plastic bag with the meal he'd planned for himself and a bottle of vodka. Penny would have plenty of wine.

When Red arrived at her high-rise crib, Edouard and two others were already there: another new boyfriend, stocky, bald, and no doubt rich, another emotionally frozen load attracted to her combination of Dallas glitz and bohemian style, everything he lacked (Nothing more clearly displayed this truth than his present ungraceful discomfort), and a swarthy Brazilian named Luis, a lithe and lovely friend of Edouard.

Edouard and Penny had been an item ten years ago. Red was certain then that Edouard would finally be the one to land her with his Castilian accent and continental manners, but it didn't happen. She said she thought he was gay, and it looked like she was right.

Poor Penny, that she moved in these tony circles of gay men and emotional cripples! At least Edouard was a caring friend, more than could be said for the fat and forty boyfriend already eying the door.

In her wild blonde hair, blue satin housecoat, and wine-soaked grief, she was not exactly putting on her best show—or, depending on your point of view, maybe she was. She performed long reminiscent monologues about Daddy that erupted into bawling outbursts, as she collapsed into the arms of the nearest guest. After several of these tragic tableaux, she fled into the bedroom, and the curtain of sleep finally fell.

The boyfriend seized the moment and made his escape.

"That's the end of him," Red confided to Edouard, who smiled and agreed.

The room grew dark, and lights went on. Red retired to the kitchen to work his magic from the plastic bag of goodies. The tasty aroma from the grill aroused her for an encore of wine and tears as Red emerged with a steaming platter of crab cakes ringed with sautéed vegetables and a side of béarnaise sauce.

By candlelight, the quartet gobbled greedily, toasting Daddy along the way. Red was grateful for the opportunity to do more than offer a soggy shoulder. Luckily, he was scheduled out of town on client business the day of the funeral. He'd never met her father (except that one time by phone) and didn't know her family and friends. From her descriptions of them, he didn't want to. This modest meal was his contribution to her father's memory, so he restrained expressing his true thoughts for a later date.

E-mail

To the BLN:

Last fall, Paul Steiner, a teacher in the public school system in Maine, was arrested for indecency with a student with whom he had been having a relationship for more than a year. His trial was last week. He was found guilty and sentenced to eight years in prison. He will have to serve at least three years of that before he's eligible for parole.

Rod Downey

I am personally very upset at this news, as I have known Paul since we met at a BL gathering ten years ago. He is a very thoughtful and sensitive person who I fear will not adjust well to prison life. His entire career has been devoted to teaching, and perhaps the saddest part of all this is that the state of Maine does not appreciate the loss it has suffered by denying Paul's contribution to the education of its children. None of his twenty years of service as a teacher was recognized by the judge who handed down this cruelly unjust sentence. It was just the opposite. It was because Paul is a teacher that the judge was so harsh.

I urge each of you to write Paul a short letter of support. Even if you've never met him, he was a frequent contributor to the BLN, so you have all read his posts. Your letters will help him get through this difficult time. Address your letters to him at the Charleston Correctional Facility in Charleston, Maine 04422, USA. A note of caution: Remember that all correspondence with inmates may be opened and read by prison officials. Keep your comments positive and general. —BLN editor

19

Mark called. "Rrrrreeedddreekay!"

"Mark?"

"You know it's me, dude! Who else calls you 'Rrreeedddreekay!'?"

"Ya got me there."

"Waassuuup?"

"Not much—workin', playin', writin'."

"Ya writin' about me?"

"Sometimes."

"I never seen anybody like you, Red! The way you were always grabbin' your little note cards and writin' down somethin' I said."

"You gave me good material. It was funny."

"Well, here's somethin' for ya—I'm gettin' married, dude!"

"No shit? F'real?"

"Yeah, f'r real! Her name's Tammy, and she's got a kid, a little boy. We been datin' for a coupla months, and I asked her to marry me."

"I assume she said yes."

"Damn straight she said yes!"

"Straight indeed."

Effeminately, "I don't show her my gay side, girl!"

"Smart move. I doubt if she'd understand."

"No, trust me, dude, she wouldn't."

"So when's the big day?"

"Sometime this spring. We haven't set an exact date yet, but you're on the invitation list. Can you come?"

"Thank you for thinking of me, but are you sure that's such a good idea?"

"I've told her about you."

"I doubt if you've told her everything."

"Not about *that*!"

"Who am I to her?"

"I told her you're my friend who helped me out when I ran away."

"What about your dad? Is he on the invitation list, too?"

"Course he is. Whadja expect?"

"What if he shows up? You gonna introduce us?"

"He's never met you. He won't know nothin'. I'll say you're just an old buddy from work or somethin'."

"Never met me? How about that time you brought him over to help move that sofa I gave you? You told him I was your friend's dad."

"Oh, yeah, I forgot about that."

"You're a lousy liar, Mark. You never could keep your stories straight."

"That was five years ago. He won't remember you."

"What if he does?"

"Does that mean you won't come?"

"Send me an invitation. I'll think about it."

They said "good-bye," and Red hung up. Not in a zillion years would he attend that wedding.

Red drove into the school parking lot and took a space next to a Mesquite Police patrol car. He entered the spacious modern foyer of the building that couldn't have been more than a few years old. Jonathan lived in one of the newer developments of the sprawling suburban town. The blue concrete block walls were decorated with angry stinging insects and cut-out paper banners demanding "Go Yellow Jackets!" Signs directed visitors to a reception window for sign-in. Red told the clerk that he was there to pick up Jonathan Frame for his dental appointment. She checked the computer but no record was on file.

"He should have given you a note from his mother this morning," Red explained, containing his frustration. He had given Jonathan explicit instructions: "Schools today are absolutely rigorous about this. If you don't have a note, they won't let me take you." The receptionist studied the computer screen, then thumbed through a file of odd and crumpled sheets of paper, shaking her head. No note. He was a bright boy, but still a boy with the carelessness of a child. Red was on the verge of being furious but continued calmly,

"Do you have his mother's work phone in your database? She teaches in the Dallas school system."

The receptionist did a search of her computer and made a phone call. What luck! They found her, and after a short wait, Red smiled to see the happy boy with his backpack, oversize T-shirt and baggy Gingko jeans loping down the hall. This vision of beauty was so pleasing, Red instantly forgot his anger about the note and didn't even mention it.

They hopped in the Mustang and headed out of the school parking lot, leaving the patrol car behind. Spiriting the boy away from school under the watchful eye of the law was itself a secret pleasure.

Out on the expressway, Jonathan pushed buttons on the radio tuning in a morning rock DJ who was quizzing a caller: "At what age does a boy's penis reach its full length? Fourteen? Sixteen? Or eighteen?" The caller guessed eighteen, and the DJ hit the raspberry buzzer. The correct answer: fourteen years, nine months.

Red observed, "Well, ya got about a year and half to go. It won't be long now."

Jonathan smiled, "But it will be long then."

Red laughed at the boy's quip. "You are so clever." Noticing his T-shirt, Red asked, "Can I touch your monkey?" Jonathan's face went crimson. Red let him off the hook, explaining, "Your T-shirt says 'Touch My Monkey.'" Jonathan looked down at it and laughed. "What does it say on the back, 'With Your Lips'?" Red continued. The boy howled.

Another Mustang pulled alongside in the next lane, white instead of red, with a pretty blonde at the wheel. Jonathan noticed. "Looks like a lady Mustang is after you."

"That's a standard six. This is a 5.0," Red explained. "Watch this." He punched it and they took off like a rocket. The old Mustang still had it in her.

Jonathan looked back to see the white car trying to catch up, "She wants you, 'cause you're well-endowed."

So the banter went, until they arrived at the dentist's office on the other side of town. The waiting room was decorated in Southwestern hacienda style with adobe-looking plaster walls and a big heavy door with black wrought iron hardware. The ped and his boy sat in rough-hewn straight-back chairs filling out forms on a clipboard. Jonathan's dad had accompanied him on his first perfunctory visit, when they took a mold of his mouth. This second appointment meant business and required Red's presence to arrange for payment.

They joked about the patient questions: "Are you taking any drugs? What are the effects?" Jonathan whispered to Red, "Smoking blunts. Getting buzzed!"

Jonathan's name was called, and they were led into a conference room, where they sat at a round table of polished pine in Santa Fe-style with chairs of welded steel depicting stylized snakes and howling dogs wearing kerchiefs around their necks. A baby blue and beige woven rug with geometric native American designs was spread over a shiny dark-red ceramic tile floor. It looked expensive. "Good," Red thought, proud that his boy was getting quality care.

A pretty young dental assistant, neat and poised with sculpted brunette hair like a lawyer in white, joined them and set on the table a dingy yellow plaster mold of Jonathan's upper palate.

"The good news is that we won't have to pull any teeth," she announced heartily. "We just need to make room for those incisors to drop down." She spoke directly to Jonathan, who listened intently. "The problem is that your palate is too narrow, so we're going to widen it just a little with this device that fastens to the roof of your mouth."

She produced a tiny chrome screw and fitted it crossways into the arch of the plaster palate. Then she inserted a metal stylus and gave it a quarter turn. The ends of the screw extended and pushed against the gums on either side.

She turned to Red. "You will have to do this every day or so to keep it tight."

"I'm not his father," Red explained. "I'm just helping out with the finances." He turned to Jonathan. "You'll have to show your mom and dad how to do this."

She nodded, "Fine," and turned again to the boy. "It might cause some slight pain at first, and you might feel some fluid in your sinuses, like when you get water up your nose in the swimming pool, but that should go away in less than thirty minutes. You might want to carry some Tylenol or ibuprofen, in case the pain bothers you."

"Then they'll bust me for bringing drugs to school!" he laughed.

Red took him seriously. "He's right," he said to her. "He should have a note for that."

The Moralist

"Yes," she said and continued sympathetically, "you'll be surprised how quickly you'll get used to it. If it's any consolation, we've all been through it. You're fortunate to have people who care enough to get this done for you while you're teeth are still forming. It may be a lot of trouble for everyone now, but we try to get the whole family involved!" She laughed at her well-worn quip, adding, "But you'll be happy with the results. You're going to have a very attractive smile, Jonathan. I'll get that note."

She left the room. Red and Jonathan stared at the plaster mold lying upside down on the table, still fitted with the tiny device that looked like a thumbscrew in reverse.

"We live in a so-called classless society," Red expounded. "We don't have dukes and earls and shit like that, but there are some basic determinants of class in America. Two of the most important ones are good grammar and good teeth. You've got the grammar. Now we're workin' on the teeth. That will open doors for you that would otherwise be closed, but once you get inside, it's up to you."

The pleasant, poised assistant returned with the note and financial papers to sign. She explained the numbers and gave Red a coupon book. How perfect and efficient it all was, and with Melanie's dental plan, the price was right! He was completely pleased and eagerly signed the papers, glancing up at his boy, "She's right, buddy. You're going to have a very nice smile." The business complete, she ushered Jonathan into an operating room. Red waited, as they inserted the tiny thumbscrew that would ever so gently crack the bone of his hard palate.

On the drive back to school, Red kept the conversation going, "So what are you studying at school this semester? Anything interesting?"

"Yeah, in Sex Ed, we're doing the effects of drugs on the body."

"Sex and drugs! Where's the rock'n'roll?"

"Actually, there is a chapter on the effects of music."

"My kinda class!" Red exclaimed with a laugh as they zipped along the freeway jammin' to a heavy metal CD. Red turned down the volume. "I have another idea for us to do. Have you ever been canoeing?"

"Yeah, once, on Lake Texoma at a family reunion."

"Okay, but I mean on a river with rapids."

"No, is it dangerous?"

"Not this river. Just enough for a few thrills. I've run this stretch a dozen times. Church groups do it."

"What river is it?"

"The Guadalupe, about two hundred and fifty miles south of here. When it gets a little warmer, we could drive down one weekend. Early spring is good, because the water is usually high and the bugs aren't out yet."

"I'd have to ask my mom and dad."

"Tell 'em they're invited, Ernie, too, or maybe one of your posse would like to go."

A knock at the door: Darren had driven forty miles in the rain from Fort Worth.

"I'm violating my probation just coming here," he began.

"Maybe you should have called instead," Red suggested, handing him a towel from the bathroom.

Drying off, he continued, "I'm afraid to call. I think my phone is bugged, but I need to talk to you. I have to tell you what's going on. Two weeks ago, I went to a suite in a big office building. The sign on the door read 'Psychotherapy Services.' It was like a doctor's office. A nurse took me back into a dark room with a reclining chair covered in paper and closed the door. I had to take off my pants and sit on the recliner. There was a wire with a rubber band on it. The nurse in the other room gave me instructions through a speaker. She told me to put the wire around my dick."

"They made you take a 'peter meter'?"

"It's called a plethysmograph. After I got hooked up, they showed me a buncha slides of naked people—men, women, teenage boys, teenage girls, little boys, little girls. Every time a slide comes on, you have to describe out loud what you see. Are they standing, sitting, or lying down? Do they have big boobs or little breast buds? Pubic hair? Big cock or little cock? They want to make sure you're looking at it."

"The description itself is arousing."

"That's the point. You can't control your dick. Every once in a while, they showed a landscape or something—the control, to see what your neutral zone is. The nurse is in the other room reading a printout. Then, they do an audio version. They told me to put on the headphones next to the chair and listen to these scenarios—a guy describing how he seduced and raped a little girl, then a violent rape inflicting pain, the child screaming. God, I hated it! But you have to listen to it. You have to describe what you heard."

"They're abusing you."

"Then, there was a grooming scenario."

"Grooming? Like picking lice?"

"Not exactly."

"Oh, you mean the kind of grooming some people call love."

"Not these people."

"Yeah, it's all about power to them. They can't understand love, except in terms of power."

"Yeah, the classes are like that, too. They're in complete control."

"Classes? You have to take classes?"

"It's sex offender school. It's supposed to cure me of my 'criminal thinking.'"

"Brainwashing school is more like it."

"I have to pay for it, too! It's a scam!" He angrily threw down the towel and began pacing the room.

"It's an industry."

"It gets worse. After the peter meter, you have to fill out a questionnaire. It musta been twenty pages. They want to know the entire history of your sexual experience with very specific questions: Have you ever had sex with an animal? How many times? Were there drugs involved? Are you going to do it again? Some of the questions ask for descriptions of specific events in your life, ten lines with room on the back. I made it all up. I wrote about Buffy and Mary Lou. Not a word about all the boys I seduced when I was a boy myself, including Mark, and I'm sure not going to tell 'em about you. I'm not going to let them store my whole life in a computer somewhere, where anyone can look it up whenever they want."

"Don't they test you on your answers?"

"I had to take a polygraph."

"If they find out you're lying to them, they'll send you to prison."

"Shit, I blew it away!" he declared proudly. "That ain't the first polygraph I've beat. It's easy, and it has nothing to do with your answers. Ya just relax! It's that simple! Only, most people don't know how."

"So what's the class like?"

Calming, Darren sat down and continued, "It's about fifteen people, mostly guys, a coupla women. The first day is the worst, because it's on-going. Some people have been going for years. I was the newbie, and everybody gave me a hard time, especially the teacher. Right off, you have to stand up and tell everyone what you did, in detail, and if you don't give the details, the teacher asks for them. Nothing is too personal. Nothing is too private."

"That, too, is abusive. It's a psychological boot camp."

"That's the point. After just two classes, it's very clear what they're doing. They break you down, so then they can put you back together the way they want to."

"Yeah, classic brainwashing. What goes on in the class?"

"We talk about stuff, but they're in control. Like today, the teacher asked a question: If a man held you at gunpoint and gave you the choice of sucking his dick, taking a bullet, or molesting a child, which would you choose?"

"What did you say?"

"I said I'd suck his dick. Some said they'd take the bullet. Nobody said they'd molest a child. It's a setup. There is no right answer, because no matter what you say, the teacher grills you on it. The only reason why he poses the question is to grill you, so you'll learn not to tell them what you think they want to hear. But speaking honestly isn't the point either. The only reason why they want you to speak honestly is so they can tear you apart. That's what I mean—it's fucked! They want to break down your thinking. What would you say, Red? How would you answer the question?"

"It's a preposterous hypothetical. I think I'd take the bullet, because hypothetically, I could be Superman, and then the hypothetical bullets would hypothetically bounce off. No, I think I'd tell him I'd suck his dick and then offer to hold the gun, while he unzipped his pants. No, I think I'd tell him to wait there, while I go find a child to molest. No, I think I'd take my chances with the gun. After all, only a crazy person would offer such an insane choice. I'd wonder if the gun were even loaded, or if it were even real. Usually, all you have to do with crazy people like that is pretend to go along for about two seconds before you knock the fool on his ass and run away. Any more preposterous hypotheticals?"

Darren shook his head. "You would not do well at sex offender school. They call that 'incompliant.'"

"In other words, any reasonable, thoughtful, realistic response."

"They don't want you to think, and you can't *pretend* to go along, either. The whole purpose is to invade the last refuge of your privacy, your own mind."

"I wish I was there. I'd rip those pigs a new asshole."

"No you wouldn't. The teacher told one guy, 'Look, you either cooperate, or I'll send your ass to prison.'"

"That's their trump card. It's like his hypothetical question—*he's* the one holding the gun to your head. What you're experiencing Darren is historical. It's the American Inquisition. If you're gonna have a witch-hunt, ya gotta have an Inquisition, and it isn't the trial. It's this brainwashing school. The message is 'I am right, you are wrong, and I am holding all the cards, so you will see things my way, including your willing acceptance of the fact that you are wrong, or else.' Was it Henry Kissinger who said, 'When you've got 'em by the balls, their hearts and minds will follow'? It's all about power. Brainwashing another person's thinking is the ultimate power trip. If this psychologist really believes in what he's doing, then he has blinded himself to the gross immorality of it. It's like Adolph Eichmann: He didn't see the horror of shipping people to death camps, because he was too busy juggling train schedules. It's what Hannah Arendt calls 'the banality of evil.' To brainwash others, you must first brainwash yourself."

"He's also making money at it."

"So was Eichmann."

"They have homework, too," Darren continued. "I have to tape record myself jacking off to a fantasy. It's called a 'masturtutorial.' First, you write out a fantasy. They have to approve it. Then, in private, you turn on the tape recorder and read the fantasy to yourself while you're jacking off, until you cum. They have to hear you doing it. They have to hear the sound you make jacking off."

"I don't understand. That sounds like it would encourage your 'criminal thinking.'"

"No, it's supposed to desensitize you. After you cum, you have to repeat a mantra for fifteen minutes."

"What kind of mantra?"

"I have three of 'em. You have to make 'em up yourself, and they have to approve that, too. Mine were: 'stiff young dick,' 'tender hairless balls,' and 'hot boy cum.' After fifteen minutes, you're supposed to get tired of it."

"I'm not sure I'd ever get tired of it. How many times do you have to do this?"

"Once a week for six months, twenty-four tapes."

"That's insane."

"Wait, there's more. I also have to do a 'covert scenario.' It's another sex story that I wrote myself where I'm about to get it on with some cute boy, and then something terrible happens—the kid pulls out a knife and cuts my dick off."

"They have to approve it, of course."

"Yeah, it has to be sufficiently awful to scare you."

"Sadistic, salacious, voyeuristic! Do you have to jack off to that, too?"

"No, you just have to read it on tape—once a week, six months, twenty-four more tapes."

"How long do you have to go through this?"

The air went out of him. He seemed almost in tears. "Three years. It scares the hell out of me, Red. I don't know if I can get through it. There's another part called 'controls.' It's the worst. I'm not going to do it."

He handed Red a sheet of paper. At the top read "Controls for Criminal Thinking" and below was a list of things to do:

- Don't go to a public restroom where there are children present. If you see a child in a restroom, leave and come back later, or if you have to, use a stall with the door locked.

- Avoid the toy section of department stores.

- Avoid going to movies that attract children, like Disney animated films, for example.

- Avoid schoolyards and playgrounds. It is a violation of your probation to be present at these places.

- If you start to think criminal thoughts, yell at yourself: "No! Stop that!"

- Carry an "inhibitor" at all times and use it. Types of inhibitors include:

- Soak a piece of cotton in ammonia and put it in a film canister. If your mind starts to think criminal thoughts, take it out and sniff it.

- Wear a rubber band around your wrist. If your mind starts to think criminal thoughts, pop yourself with it.

As Red looked over the controls, Darren recovered his determination. "I'm not going to let them brainwash me, Red! Like you say, my feelings for boys are a good thing, and they are not going to make me believe it's bad. What they're doing is wrong, and I refuse to say that wrong is right." Then his tone changed again. No wonder he'd driven forty miles in the rain. He was nearly hysterical with helplessness, a rare feeling for Darren, who always took pride in his savoir-faire. "After the three years is up, they do another peter meter and an evaluation. If I don't pass or if they think I haven't made a sincere effort, I go to prison. I don't know if I have the strength to fight it for three years. What if I can't? What if it fucks me up? Either they fuck me up or they lock me up. There's no escape."

"You need a drink." Red headed for the bar and changed the subject. "I invited Jonathan to go canoeing."

"Canoeing or camping out?"

"Both. Drive down on Friday night, come back on Sunday."

"I don't know if that's such a good idea, Red."

"It was your idea!"

"That was before all this shit. You don't want to go down the road I'm on. It is not fun."

"I won't give in to fear. This is just one more outing."

"Outing' for sure!" They laughed. Red was pleased to see his friend's wit return. Darren continued, "Red, even if nothing happened, even if he just said the wrong thing to the wrong person, it could all be taken the wrong way."

"I understand that. I've also invited him to bring his dad and a friend."

"Okay, but what if it was just you and him? Would you do it? Would you go?"

"You're damn right I would! *Pas question*!"

"Would you bust a move?"

"If the moment were right, if that's what he wanted."

"You know it's not that simple. You start talking about girls and sex and next thing you know, you're in the tent showing off your hard-ons."

"I guess we'll see."

"I want a full report."

"I've told you before, there are some secrets I have to keep, even from you."

"You know you can trust me, Red."

"Would you perjure yourself in open court for me?"
"You know I would."
"No, you wouldn't. We all think we would, but we've never been through it."
"I have. I'm going through it right now."
"Which makes you that much more vulnerable. They'd threaten to revoke your probation, unless you gave me up. I wouldn't blame you if you did. I know how they play it, and so do you. It's not a justice system; it's just a system. It's Kafka's *The Trial*. They process you, until they come and put a bullet in your brain."
"Then, will you read me a hot chapter from your book?"
"I can do that now!"
"Only if it's real."
"Now you see it, now you don't."
"Red, it wouldn't matter anyway. If they got into your house and took one look at the stuff you read and the stuff you write, they wouldn't need me."
"No kiddie porn, not one shred, and no journals either. I'm as clean as Clorox, and there's no law against what I read and write."
"They'll make a law just for you."
"I wish they'd try it. I'd love to see the thought police try to use my writing against me. I'd get every writer in America on my side, not to mention the ACLU. They'd make me famous."
Darren slammed his fist against the wall. "I hate it! I hate this world that treats us like this! For what? For loving a boy. This craziness pollutes everything. Listen to us! We sound like a couple of desperados!"
"Or social revolutionaries, which we are, whether we admit it or not."

Jonathan called. "I wrote a new song called *I'm Comin' t'Getcha*."
"I like the title. Sing it for me."
"I haven't got the music yet. I'll read it to you. . ."

> I'm comin' t'getcha.
> A light in the sky,
> Big black eyes and silver robes.
> To beam you away for anal probes.
> I'm comin' t'getcha.
>
> I'm comin' t'getcha.
> Fist on the door at night

The Moralist

Screams of fright
Thugs growl and shadows fight.
I'm comin' t'getcha.

I'm comin' t'getcha.
To steal your soul
To shove my rules
Up your hole.
I'm comin' t'getcha.

I'm comin' t'getcha
To suck your toes
To suck your tits
Touch my monkey
With your lips.
I'm comin' t'getcha.

"Well, come and get it!" Red laughed.
"No, get and cum it," the boy retorted. "Get it?"
"I'm gonna get it, 'cause I'm comin' to getcha."
"You're a good getter."
"You're good to get."

Faye summoned him to her office for a closed-door. Her voice was urgent, "I want you to come with me to Washington next week."

He didn't like the sound of it already. "What's up?"

"Bull Barnett wants me to prep him for his testimony before Congress. I assume you know who Bull Barnett is?"

Even hearing the name twisted Red's gut with anger. He replied coolly, "Yes, speaker, pundit, author of *The Death of Decency*, the very embodiment of unctuous morality. I do read the newspapers, Faye. It's my job."

"Then you must also know that he's been called to testify before Congress on the moral state of our nation."

"A Republican publicity stunt on the taxpayer's nickel."

"Yes, I can't deny it, but the important thing is that he wants me to train him."

"So what do you want me to do?"

"I want you to play the rabid Democrat and roast him with tough questions."

Red was expecting as much, but he wanted to hear her say it. His heart racing, he stared at her in silence, then answered calmly, "You know I can't do that."

"You're not training him. I'm doing all the training. You just play the interviewer."

"The interviews are part of the training."

"I thought you'd enjoy it. You have my permission to chew him up one-on-one. Be the angry liberal. Pull out all the stops."

"Is that why you want me? Authenticity?"

"Yes! You'll tear him apart. He needs that."

"Why don't you get Deborah to do it? She's a good Republican, and she's already in D.C."

"Deborah's not a man. Congress is mostly men. I'm afraid he won't take her seriously."

"Faye, Bull Barnett is anathema to me. He stands for everything I abhor."

"You abhor morality?"

"His brand of it, yes. Y'know, you pushed me pretty close to the edge on that Coalition thing. I went along, because I knew you needed me, but that was nothing compared to this. No, I'm sorry. I can't do it. I won't do it."

"Barnett's not running for office. You said you wouldn't support Republicans running for office."

The dam of anger broke: "Or Republican causes, or the Christian Coalition, or the Family Research Council, the Family Values League, the 700 Club, the Withers Foundation, or Phyllis Schlafly, Rush Limbaugh, Dr. Flo, or any other self-righteous, right-wing hate-monger, and that includes Bull Barnett."

"Some of those people are my friends, Richard."

He could see he had gone too far. "I'm sorry if I've offended you, but that's one more reason I shouldn't do it. This is an area of disagreement between us, Faye. I thought you understood that. How could I in good conscience work for someone who is my mortal enemy?"

"Don't you think that's overstating it just a bit? I hardly think Bull Barnett is your mortal enemy."

"More than you know. Suffice to say I oppose his cause and will not help him in any way. That's my final answer. I'm sorry to disappoint you."

"I didn't know you felt so strongly."

"Now, you do. Let Deborah do it. A woman would be good for him. There are plenty of angry liberal women in Congress, and the media."

"Not as angry as you."

"Thank you. It's nice to be appreciated. Is that all?"

But Faye wasn't giving up so easily, "You'll be living at The Mayflower for a week, crab cakes with grape sauce from room service every night. Do a few interviews in the morning, and you'll have D.C. to yourself."

Smiling, Red admired her perseverance. "Now, you're talking my language! There's just one problem. I want Bull Barnett to make a fool of himself before Congress. I want to see him fail, and I don't think that would make me a good trainer, even as his sparring partner."

"Are you kidding? That would make you the best trainer in the world!"

"You're gonna turn my head, Faye," he grinned.

"You amaze me, Richard. I know so many people who would love an assignment like this."

"Just as I know so many who would cringe at the thought of it, myself among them, but thanks for thinking of me." He rose to go.

"There is one other assignment." He sat back down. "We have a new client, a nursing home in rural Louisiana. Some greedy tort lawyer is trying to gin up plaintiffs with a videotape he planted in one of the residents' rooms. It's already been on *The CBN Morning News*. Now *Newsline* has picked it up. They need a spokesman, and one of your philanthropy buddies recommended us. The home is part of a high-end, for-profit chain. Not exactly the Mayflower, but a nice place."

"Will I be staying at the home?"

"No, I wouldn't do that to you. There's a Country Inn nearby."

"No crab cakes with grape sauce, I imagine."

"Crawfish and Tabasco maybe. I was going to send Deborah, but it's your call."

"Yes, it is."

"Done. I'll miss you in D.C. Bull's testimony will be big-time national news."

Red was making his exit. "All you have to do is transform him from a pompous prig into a real person. You've got your work cut out for you."

She looked up, "So do you, mister."

Faye was right on that score. The CBN piece was an accomplished disaster. The hidden "granny cam" showed a couple of nurse's aides manhandling poor naked Mama Wilkes, a mean and demented old woman, as she screamed obscenities and racial epithets. You couldn't call the aides' behavior abusive, but it wasn't gentle and caring, either, not that Mama Wilkes inspired gentle and caring. She harassed the entire staff with her rant, and the home had suggested daughter Wilkes take her mother elsewhere, but daughter Wilkes refused and installed a hidden camera instead, apparently more interested in a lucrative lawsuit than her mother's welfare—not to mention exhibiting her naked mother on network television.

There was an element of racism, as well. In the Deep South of Louisiana, the Civil Rights Movement had somehow escaped the notice of Mama Wilkes, and the mostly African-American aides were less than eager to step-n-fetchit for the bigoted old crone.

That made no difference to the tort lawyer who knew a deep-pockets defendant when he saw one, nor to *Newsline*. Despite its high-minded pretensions, television news was driven by image, not truth. The network magazine shows followed a strict black-hat, white-hat formula and the videotape was made to order. It was great TV, and that was all that mattered.

Arcadia Manor was Belle Reve on the bayou, a white two-story ante-bellum colonial with wrap-around porch nestled among mossy oaks on a manicured estate-sized campus. It reminded Red of another Southern manse he'd known in Savannah thirty years ago.

Inside, the rooms were lined with cathedral paneling and floor-to-ceiling drapes with fresh cut flowers delivered daily. A string quartet played in the sitting room. Arcadia Manor was a home for the wealthy aged from New Orleans and Baton Rouge. It wasn't The Mayflower, but Red might've preferred it to the Country Inn.

The administration was shell-shocked. Red met with the director, Dan Chung, a frightened little Asian man with a thick Louisiana accent, and his nurse administrator, Sarah Moore, a sweet, soft-spoken woman who knew not at all what to make of this dirty business.

"We're putting ourselves in your hands," Mr. Chung said sincerely.

No sweeter words were spoken to a spin-doctor's ears. The rest of the day was devoted to working with Dan and Sarah to develop messages, then videotaped rehearsal, Red fielding questions as Dan and Sarah played reporter.

The Moralist

During a break in the training, they determined the physical therapy room was the only space large enough to accommodate the equipment. This was no local news reporter with a camera and strobe. Network television sent out an entire crew. Red met with the home's physical therapist to make sure he interrupted and cut short the interview at the appropriate time.

The Country Inn was down the road that ran along the bayou between a gas station and a white clapboard vet clinic with a rusted metal sign out by the curb that read, "GROOMING." Red thought of Darren and the sex offender school, how they twisted love into something ugly and would not be satisfied until you believed it, too. *1984*—they were going to execute Winston Smith anyway, but not before he learned to love Big Brother.

Across the street was a Pizza Hut, the only choice for dinner. Red ordered a large pepperoni by phone, Louisiana room service, and dragged a heavy wooden motel chair from the room down to the edge of the asphalt parking lot to watch the sun set over the bayou. Sipping Sprite and vodka from his ubiquitous flask, he watched the sun's rays stream between moss-hung trees as the frogs began their nightly symphony of grunts, barks, trumpets, chirps, cries, screeches, and howls.

What a pleasure indeed, and one that he would never have known had he succumbed to Faye's enticements. There, he would have been surrounded by people he didn't like, working with a man he detested. Here, he had an early spring sunset in bayou country. He pulled out his Nikon and captured his vision on film.

At 8:00 a.m., the *Newsline* stringer crew arrived from Baton Rouge. Shortly afterward, Red's crew arrived, as well. When dealing with network television, it was standard operating procedure to hire your own crew and make your own tape. There was even a name for it, "the litigation crew." The two crews knew each other and exchanged high fives and war stories, as they worked side-by-side to transform the physical therapy room into a television studio. Lights encased in large black fabric tents stood on tripods. The network crew set up three cameras, one on the spokesperson, one on the correspondent, and a mini-cam for close-ups of the spokesperson. Furniture, vases with flowers, and potted plants were arranged. Monitors, tape recorders, and mixing consoles were installed. At the center of this elaborate array stood a tiny arena, two chairs for the combatants and a small monitor on a table to play the "granny cam" tape.

The show producer, a short New York Jewish woman, and correspondent, a good-looking man in a tan trench coat with tan hair and a tan face, showed up at ten.

Red took his seat opposite Mr. Tan. The make-up gal in a smock powdered Red's face, as a tech clipped on a mike. The cameras started to roll.

"When you discovered Ms. Wilkes had installed a hidden camera in her mother's room, what was the reaction of the nursing home?"

"Y'know, Bob, it's really not appropriate for me to discuss a matter that's before the court, but I can tell you that we encourage family members to come to us with their concerns, so we can resolve them. For example, just last week, the wife of one of our residents told me she didn't think her husband Buddy was taking his medication. Medications are usually given by the nurse's aides, and they're supposed to make sure the residents take them, but sometimes a resident doesn't want to. So we asked one of our head nurses, Ms. Percy, to give Buddy his medication herself, and make sure he took it. Ms. Percy is one of Buddy's best friends here. They play Scrabble together in the game room. So he took his medication from her. That's the way we like to do things here at Arcadia Manor."

"So you'd prefer that the family members come to you?"

"Exactly. Open communication is important to the quality of care we've been providing here for over fifty years."

"But Ms. Wilkes says she did come to you when her mother complained the aides were not responding to her calls."

"As I said, it wouldn't be appropriate for me to discuss specifics of that case, but I can tell you. . ." and he was off on another heart-warming anecdote.

Tan was getting annoyed. "Well, if you can't talk about this case, can you tell me Arcadia Manor's policy about putting cameras in the residents' rooms?"

"There are pros and cons. Arcadia Manor respects the privacy and dignity of its residents. This is their home. . ." Another anecdote. Red was killin' him.

"Does that mean you wouldn't allow it?"

"We would, but no one asked us, and after all, who's going to watch all those tapes? We think there are better ways to preserve the privacy and dignity of our residents." Another anecdote.

Tan fumed, "Well, why don't we watch this, and you can comment on it?"

He played the ugly tape of the naked old crone screaming epithets, as the black woman in white pushed her aside to change the sheets. "Is that the way you usually treat your residents at Arcadia Manor?"

"Of course not, but there were hundreds of hours of tape. I doubt if you've seen them all."

"We've seen enough right here."

Red pulled a videocassette from under his notes. "I have a tape, too. Let's watch this one taken from the same camera."

"We'd have to review it first."

"We're not live. You can edit it as you wish, so why not put it on?" The tape was blank.

"I'm the reporter," Tan icily reminded Red. "I ask the questions."

The interview was interrupted by a knock at the door. As instructed, the physical therapist spoke to the producer. It was time for senior aerobics!

Tan protested, "But we're not done."

"At Arcadia Manor, the residents come first," Red shrugged his shoulders apologetically. "You've got enough for a couple of good sound bites." He turned to the producer. "If you're crew can just move this stuff to one side to make room for the treadmills, then they can take their time packing up. Why don't we get some B-roll for you?"

The crew began moving equipment, as Red and the producer led a cameraman into the hallway. Tan threw on his tan trench coat and made an irritated getaway. "Don't give 'em what they want; just give 'em something they can use." That was the rule, and if they got pissed off, it wasn't Red's job to make 'em happy.

As the van drove away, everyone breathed a sigh of relief. The client was happy, and that's all that mattered.

Bull Barnett was all over the press, and Faye had every reason to be proud of his performance, a clearly articulated argument peppered with pithy sound bites, attacking the arts and the First Amendment freedom of expression. Irony of ironies, Red's interview on *Newsline* appeared opposite the live telecast of Barnett's testimony, another coup for Faye to have two clients on different networks at the same time, and Mr. Chan couldn't have been more pleased to have his story buried by America's moral leader, nor could Faye, nor could Red.

Darren called. "I have to put up a sign."

"What kind of sign?"

"It says, 'A Person on Probation for a Child Sex Offense Lives Here.' It's as big as a Stop sign, and I have to put it out front where you can see it from the street."

"That's outrageous! It's a scarlet letter!"

"It's an invitation to get my ass killed. Somebody already spray-painted 'pervert' on my mailbox, and I've been getting hang-up phone calls. I star-69'd them back, but it's always a pay phone."

"Move."

"It'll just be the same wherever I go. I can't leave the county anyway. My job is fucked, too. The FAA doesn't allow convicted felons to work on commercial aircraft."

"What are you going to do?"

"The union says I can retrain as a ticket agent, but my flying days are over. It's a cut in pay, but I'll manage."

"This is wrong, Darren. This makes me mad."

Two envelopes arrived in the mail, one stark white #10, the other cream-colored and textured.

Dear Red,

Thank you for your kind letter. You cannot know how important contact with people on the outside is to those of us who have been taken prisoner. The system in which I find myself trapped monitors my every thought and feeling as well as my actions. This is what they call "therapy," an excuse to invade every corner of your privacy. When I'm not being abused by the system, I'm being harassed by my fellow prisoners to whom I am a pariah. Murderers have more status here than a child molester. I have requested solitary confinement, because I fear for my safety. In that context, you can see how much I value your correspondence. Please, write again. —Paul

P.S. Be careful what you write. They do read our mail.

Inside the other, a matching card with blind-embossed figures of a bride and groom looking dreamily into each other's eyes, their names printed in black script at the bottom: "Tammy and Mark." Red smiled at the sweet, sappy design in the style of an invitation to the senior prom.

20

Red's life was dynamic, like a star trying to explode and collapse at the same time. A shift in the balance created a nova.

Ernie couldn't make it for the canoe trip. His mom said no to going off with an older man she didn't know, and Jonathan's dad was busy on a job. As Red had hoped beyond hope, that left only two. Jonathan's mom asked him if he felt okay to go on his own, and Jonathan simply said yes, it would be fun.

Now that his fondest fantasy might come to pass, Red was apprehensive. He would be spending the night alone in a tent by the river with his boy. The last six inches, the red zone. It could be a tense and awkward moment where each was afraid to make the first move, or worse, the boy had not a clue, or worse still, Red misread the signals and made a false move with the ensuing fear, embarrassment, anger, and even danger.

He would be risking everything, not only his love for the boy but his life and freedom as well. Wouldn't things be simpler as they were? Another outing with his sweet, bright, funny boy, like those before and the many yet to come, as he watched him grow into a man? No, that would be giving up.

Or would it go the other way and Jonathan give up his hope that Red would make love to him, grow bored, and find someone else to show him how? The boy lover's greatest fear was not a buddy, but another older man.

The truth was none of the above. Jonathan had never camped out, except with his family, had never done anything on his own away from home, except go to school and play with his friends. Red was good for getting him out of the house. He was older than Jonathan's own dad, but he didn't act older. He broke the rules just like any kid, but he was cool about it. He always said the right thing in front of Mom and Dad. They loved him. But when man and boy were together, it was just like Red had told him: He said what others could or would not say, and you could say anything you want to him.

They would share not just an afternoon at the movies and the mall, but a weekend in the woods canoeing on white water. The idea of lying in the arms of his lover never crossed the boy's mind. On the other hand, he was not unwilling to explore. He wanted adventure.

Friday morning before work, Red loaded the car with camping equipment, so he could duck out early and drive directly from the office. When he reached the boy's home, Jonathan was, as always, practicing his skateboard along the walk out front.

"You ready?"

Jonathan led him into the house, and they gathered up his bedroll, duffel, and pillow. Jon and Melanie were nowhere to be seen.

The campers were on the road before sunset, a four-hour drive. Jonathan managed the music from his CD case, playing the newest punk groups Red had never heard. As the boy carefully manipulated the jewel cases, Red took his eyes from the road to capture the contour of his profile, the spiky, black hair, high forehead, button nose, barely perceptible eyebrows, and blue eyes focused on the task at hand. In quick glances, Red took visual snapshots of first the little boy he'd met a year ago and now the teenager, with gangly arms and legs, attractive but not a pretty boy, impressing his peers and the girls more with his musician's cool, creative intelligence, and sweet charm. And finally the grownup man, tall like his dad and northern European pale, hair thinning, nose more prominent, broad-shouldered. The perspective of the pederast: He could watch a boy grow into a man in an instant of imagination.

After they listened to several cuts at ear-splitting volume, Red turned down the music to spark some conversation. "Like I've said, I'm a great resource for you. Sex, drugs, religion. Pick one, and I'll tell you anything you want to know about it."

Religion was boring, and sex was embarrassing, so that left only one choice. Jonathan was interested in drugs anyway. He was a rock'n'roller who wanted to get high.

For the next two hours, Red unloaded the vast expanse of his experience—depressants, stimulants, narcotics, and hallucinogens, and the various names, effects, pleasures, and dangers of each. He warned against the brain-rotting and addictive powers of the more dangerous varieties with medical evidence and personal anecdotes of those whose health and lives he'd seen destroyed by them but not omitting the fact that amphetamines had gotten him through most of college and grad school.

He gave particular emphasis to hallucinogens, extolling the mystical visions of those who had experienced the heavy psychedelics and how they had changed people's lives, even his own. His favorite was the milder marijuana that stimulated the free flow of imagination. That's why artist's liked it so much.

He told of when he managed the Greenwich Church Theater in the Village. The living quarters they provided with the job was attached to a runaway house, also sponsored by the church and run by conscientious objectors to the Vietnam War. One night, all the hippies and runaways pooled their pot—Red, too, contributed a bag—and rolled it up in a sheet of butcher's paper stretched the entire length of the community dining table that sat eight on a side, the biggest blunt in the world. Everyone partied and smoked it down in a single night.

"Bad-ass!" the boy marveled.

Red knew it was only a matter of time before Jonathan got high, so he might as well have as much information as possible.

"I found my dad's stash," he revealed.

The confidence Red had been waiting for. "Did you smoke any of it?"

"No, but I coulda. He has two stashes, one in his bedroom and one in the tool cabinet, but I think he's forgotten about the tool cabinet. It's been there for a while."

"Does he smoke in front of you?"

"I've been to some jams with his friends. I know what it smells like."

"Musicians have been smoking pot since the beginning of time. You're a musician. You'll do it, too, and it's fun as long as you don't let it take over your life. Maybe we'll get high sometime."

"That'd be cool," the boy declared.

Red knew first-hand from his experience with Mark the risk of marijuana abuse to adolescents, destroying their motivation and achievement, interfering with their physical development. "But I should warn you, I had a friend who started smoking pot when he was twelve. He matured early and was big for his age. He played offensive line on his high school football team. But his balls never grew to what I would call a normal size, and his arms and chest to this day are as hairless as when I knew him. Maybe it was genetic, and he woulda been like that anyway. But I've always wondered if maybe smoking pot didn't affect his sexual development. It's not harmful taken in moderation, but you can abuse any drug."

"How did you know what his balls looked like?"
"He used to stay over. I saw him naked lots of times."
"But you were older than him. He was a kid just like me?"
"Yes."
"Is he the one that drank daktaris?"
"No, that was someone else."
"Another kid?"
"Yes, he was seventeen. He's thirty-four now. He's a lifelong friend."
"You've known lotsa boys, haven't you, Red?"
"A few."
"Did you do it with a'em?"
Red looked away from the road with a flash of surprise. "Do what?"
"You know, get it on."
Red's eyes turned back to the road. He smiled, "I don't kiss and tell."
"You said you would tell me whatever I wanted to know."
"Except for that. You're asking me to betray a confidence, and I can't do that, the same as I would never do that to you."
They fell again to sweet, silent thought, as the Mustang sped through rolling fields awash in early spring bluebonnets, the loveliest time of year in Texas. Jonathan ejected the CD and played with the buttons on the radio. *Love Song* by The Cure came on. He started to change the station.
"No, let's hear it," Red protested.
They listened to the bittersweet and plaintive lyrics.
"That's my song to you," Red stated simply, staring straight ahead.
"Will you always love me, Red?" Jonathan smiled his ironic smile.
"As long as you let me."
"Do you wanta do it with me?"
No waiting. The moment of trust was happening now on the open road in the golden light of the setting sun. It wasn't the sex. It was the conversation.
"Maybe, if the time is right."
"What about right now?"
"Kinda hard to drive."
"I mean this trip."
"We'll see."
"Isn't that why you invited me?"
"I invited you, because your company gives me pleasure, whatever form it may take." Ah, the surprises of Jonathan! The boy was coming to him even before they arrived at the campsite.

"We always have a good time!" Jonathan grinned his vampire grin now lined with a thin wire fastened to the teeth like a tiny fence. Stretching, he leaned back in the bucket seat revealing the little tent pole lifting the denim of his Gingkos.

It was almost dark when they reached the campground and pitched their tent by the light of Red's old-fashioned gas lantern. Timidity mingled with excitement, each afraid the other might have been joking in the car, as they had joked so many times before. The first move would still be up to him, Red thought. The boy would look to the man for that. Even the sex was pedagogic.

In the pale light of the moon beaming through the cracks of the tent, Red spread out an old comforter as a mattress that covered the tent floor. Jonathan dutifully unrolled his blanket separate from Red's.

Red instructed, "Do it like this," and spread out both blankets so that they overlapped into a queen-size bed.

They modestly undressed to their underwear, Red in white briefs, the boy in his favorite "Taz" boxers, like phosphorescent ghosts. Ooo-ooo-ooo, what a little moonlight can do to you!

"Is there a Taz in there?" Red joked.

"You'll have to find out," Jonathan smiled peeling back the blanket and crawling under on the far side of their pallet.

At the first gray light of dawn, Red listened for the boy's quiet breathing, then silently slipped into shorts and shoes. He grabbed his towel and kit and padded along the woodsy path to the showers, bathed in the love of his boy. All was changed now, like Darren's beach boy said. Red, who could imagine a thousand possibilities of heaven and hell, had no idea how the change would manifest. He could only play the moment as he always had, but for now, he felt only joyous fulfillment and love.

Love was pleasure spiked with pain, like the song said, like a spicy meal and a deeply satisfying one at that. Boy love was a delicious refinement of thought, feeling, and physical desire, the finest hour for the connoisseur. He caressed himself with the towel that could never wipe away this grand feeling, come what may.

The day was bright and clear. Jonathan reclined on a chaise in shorts, half-naked in the morning that danced on his pale evanescent skin. Red greeted him with a hearty "Hey, buddy" and fed him a man's breakfast of bacon and pancakes with syrup. He gobbled them down, as Red sipped his coffee and wrapped sandwiches for lunch.

"You were right. It was fun," Red's only reference to the night before.

His mouth full, the kid nodded and gave a muffled "mmm" of agreement, as much for the pancakes as the sex. Enough said. To ignore it, as boys do among themselves, would have been weird. To dwell on it suicide. Framing it as fun made it easy and uncluttered.

"The fun has just begun," Red added, referring to the river. "The weather is great, and we're gonna have a good ride. We'll go over some small dams. There's some rocky white water, and at the end, we run The Chute. It's a perfect day trip, but make no mistake, this is a real river, not Six Flags. How we handle our canoe is up to us."

"What's The Chute?"

"You'll see."

The canoeists lowered their fiberglass bark into the swift current and were immediately swept downstream. Grabbing their paddles, Jonathan in front paddled left and right like an eager brave, Red steering from the rear, watching the glistening sun-kissed shoulders he'd kissed the night before. Jonathan preened in the glow of his lover's gaze.

They slid over a small dam into a rocky cascade and snagged against a boulder. Red threw Jonathan a rope, "Hop out and hold on. Wrap it around your arm and don't let go. I'll push it off." Red jumped into the deeper water that pinned the canoe against the rock and him as well. He pushed the boat free, but the crashing current forced him back, and the canoe took off on its own. "Here it comes! Hold on!" Red cried, and the wet boy held the rope fast against the current, the muscles of his back and shoulders straining with all their strength. He would have let the canoe drag him down the river before letting go. Red slipped around the stone and waded through the rushing water to help. They dragged their bruised bark toward a placid eddy.

Dripping wet, they high-fived. "Good work! You held on! It's a lot harder without a canoe, especially with our lunch in it."

"What about the dent?"

"That's nothin'. These fiberglass rental canoes get wrapped around that rock all the time. They just pop back into shape. Hop in. There's more to come."

A bright spring day, the sun pierced the cliffs of the river's Hill Country canyon with pure white light, as they drifted down the quiet river. Jonathan pointed to a rocky hill and said, "Let's go up there for lunch."

They scrambled up the bristly limestone and bramble slope to a cliff overlooking the river. The activity of the morning had fed their appetites, and they gobbled their precious dry sandwiches and chips, washing them down with foil-pouch lemonade from Red's mini-cooler. Sleepily, they gazed down at the other canoes and inner tubes drifting down the river below. The boy lay back against a boulder and loosened his belt and pants from a satisfying meal. Red finished the job, freeing the kid's prominent hard-on and kissing the redolent head. Reclining, elbows propped on the rock and fairly glowing in the crystal sunlight, the boy dropped his head back and gave himself up to the lightning pleasure.

The sun was low in the sky when they reached The Chute, a fifty-yard flume carved by the water from a broad yellow limestone slab, fast and narrow with outcropping obstacles that hurdled the canoe directly toward the rocky bank, unless you made the sharp turn back into open water.

Red and Jonathan paddled frantically to make the turn and hold their course. Whooping and laughing, they cheered their success as The Chute spat them down a waterslide and into a deep green placid pool. They steered for the bank and pulled up the canoe, where waiting hands from the campground loaded it onto the rack of a trailer drawn by a bus.

The man and boy stuffed themselves into the standing crowd. Red held onto a rail and wrapped an arm around the kid's slim waist, to others the gesture of a father holding onto his son, to the lovers an erotic pleasure.

They bantered with their fellow passengers amid the camaraderie of a day's adventure that all had shared, as the bus and their canoes trundled through the rocky, scrubby limestone hills back to camp.

Red grilled steaks and corn-on-the-cob for dinner beside the swift water. Night in the camp was young and raucous, a patchwork of private parties with kegs and coolers of beer, college kids from UT. The church groups had their own field away from the water up the bank where they circled around large campfires and sang hymns. The families were up farther still to escape their noisy neighbors.

Jonathan liked being with the college crowd. They played their music, too, and the smoky smell of grilling filled the air.

Red directed the boy to shuck the corn and set the table, while he minded the steaks. Jonathan admired the efficiency of the man who in T-shirt and denim shorts moved from step to step seasoning the meat, preparing the fire, and tending the grill with such ease that he would mostly just sit and relax with his glass of wine, as the meal seemed to cook itself.

Their appetites were sharp from the day's adventure, and they relished their cookout under the stars surrounded by the party sound of the college kids. It was the best steak he'd ever eaten.

Red finished first and sipped his wine. Jonathan helped himself to seconds with the bottomless appetite of adolescence.

"I've told you I'm writing a book about you and me," Red began.

"Can I read it?"

"That's the first time you've ever asked me that."

"Things are different now."

"I brought a short story with me that's taken from the book." Red produced a copy of *PAN*, as if he had planned this conversation in advance, which he had. "It's in this magazine. Would you like to hear it? I'll read it to you."

"What magazine is that?"

Red showed him the cover. "It's a literary magazine, essays and short stories. A lot of famous writers have been contributors—Allen Ginsberg, William Burroughs, Michel Foucault. I know you're not familiar with those people, but if you're interested, I'll give you some copies of their work. It's pretty wild stuff."

"Wild as your book?"

"Judge for yourself." Red handed him the magazine.

He greedily flipped through the pages. "It's all pictures of boys," he observed.

"And essays, and my story based on you." Red directed him to the title page. "There. It's called *The Moralist*, the same title as the book."

"It's not a bunch of church stuff, is it?"

"Hardly. It'll blow your shit away. I'm not kidding . . . well, maybe a little," he smiled to himself at his pun.

"Let's hear it!" He handed it back to Red.

As the boy hungrily gobbled corn-on-the-cob and bites of steak that he wrapped in bread, Red read aloud about Red Ryder and his student David, their first meeting, their lessons, the Perlman concert, the boy's 12th birthday, and New Year's day, Red Ryder falling in love.

As they cleared the table, Jonathan was silent. Red did not intrude.

He relaxed beside the boy as they stretched out side-by-side on their chaises by the river on a balmy night, loud music, the voices and laughter of youth echoing across the water.

"So what's going on in that brilliant mind of yours?" Red began.

"That's not the way it was," Jonathan concluded, a glacier of thought moving beneath the calm surface.

"Yeah, I changed it. What I just read to you is fiction, a work of literary art. I changed it to fit the concept of the story, to protect the people I love, and to protect myself from the police. Those are three very important reasons: aesthetic, ethical, and existential."

"It's crazy!"

"Did it blow your shit away?"

"Yeah, it did."

"How?"

"It's like you're making a story out of me."

"Like I taught you, tell your own story."

"What about last night? Ya gonna put that in the book, too?"

"Probably, but not like it really happened."

"Red, are you gay?"

What a pleasure this question! How sweet! "Not like most people think of that word," he replied. "I love you."

"What's the difference?"

"I prefer boys, that is, a boy, that is, you. I have loved you from the moment we met. Remember when I asked if your teachers knew how bright you were? You blushed and squirmed, because you knew it was true. You are bright, and I see it, too. In your autobiography, you quote your mother that she wished every mother could have a boy like you. I see what she sees, and it's not just intelligence. It's compassion, joie, pluck, wit, fascination, and endless curiosity, not to mention your incisive conversation. Those are wonderful qualities and rare in a boy as young as you. I'm lucky to know you and will do everything in my power to help you grow into a truly formidable man."

"You say those things 'cause you want my ass."

"I want your ass because those things are true. Most gay men don't share this perspective. Many would condemn me. A hundred years ago, that wasn't the case. 'Gay' and 'boy lover' were practically the same thing, but that's not true now. Oscar Wilde once called the love between a man and a boy the noblest form of affection, where the man has intellect and the boy has all the joy, hope, and glamour of life before him."

"Who's Oscar Wilde?"

"A nineteenth-century Irish playwright, poet, novelist, and critic. You'll probably read some of his stuff in high school. Most schools still teach his plays and even perform them. They were radical for his day and still damn funny. *The Importance of Being Earnest* is the most well-known. But his radical point of view as a critic and moralist was an even greater contribution. He was Nietzsche with a corsage."

"Did he like boys, too?"

"Yes, but your teachers won't tell you that. He was imprisoned for it, which destroyed his reputation, and finally his health. He died two years after his release. It's even worse today. The penalty for loving you would make Oscar Wilde's imprisonment look like a day at the beach. For you, too."

"Whadaya mean?"

"If there were ever any suspicion about us, they would come down on you with every subterfuge in their power to get you to betray me because only with your cooperation can they condemn me. Only then could they say to themselves, 'There you see, Jonathan turned him in. Jonathan knew he was being abused.' You might think you could say to them, 'Red is good to me. He loves me, and I know it,' which would be noble indeed, but it's not that easy. They have ways of coercing you, threatening you, harassing you and your family. That's how corrupt and abusive the social environment is right now, and it's serious business. They're trying to make something beautiful into something ugly, and I'm sorry for that. It's deluded, cruel, unjust, and morally wrong, but that's how it is. That's why it's so important for both of us not to talk about our personal relationship to anyone, and if anyone asks—your mom and dad, your sister, teachers, school counselors, best friends, the cops, anyone—there is only one answer: 'No, we don't. No, we haven't. No, we never have.'"

"What about your book?"

"The book is fiction. You said so yourself. Fiction is a made-up story, and they can't use that against us. Not yet anyway."

"People will think it's me. People will think I'm a fag."

"Not your people. Most of them will never even hear of this book, and if they do, just say, 'It's fiction. Red is an artist. He made it up.'"

"They won't believe me."

"Stick to your story. They'll believe you. It's the truth. Has anyone ever asked you about me?"

"Austin did once."

"What'd he say?"

"He asked if you ever came on to me."

"And what did you tell him?"

"I said 'Hell, no, Red ain't no Chester Molester. He's my mentor.' Then he asked, 'What if he did? Wouldja do it?' I said I might, if you were cool about it."

Red sat up, "Have I been cool?"

"Cool enough," he grinned his metal-mouth grin.

Red leaned over to kiss his soft blushing cheek, but the chaise dumped him over and he rolled onto the ground.

Jonathan laughed, "Not that cool!"

Red collected himself and sat beside him. "When did this conversation with Austin take place?"

"Back last fall, but I never thought it would really happen."

"When did you change your mind?"

"That day at your house." He confronted Red with his cold blue eyes. "You didn't do nothin', but you wanted to, didn't you?"

Red looked deeply into them, "Very much, but I didn't think you did. I wasn't getting the right signals. I thought I scared you."

"You did. I kept thinkin' 'Austin was right! Red wants to get it on with me.' It freaked me out. I had to think about it for a long time."

"What did you think?"

"I thought it might be fun, but I don't want nobody sayin' I'm a fag."

"You aren't. Straight boys have lovers, too. Like I told you, my last lover is about to get married. Besides, who's gonna find out, unless you tell them?"

"I ain't sayin' nothin' to nobody."

"That's a good policy."

"Cept one thing."

"What's that?"

"I wanta tell Austin about yo' fatty-bo-batty blunt."

Red smiled. "Fair enough."

"Now, go in the tent and take off your clothes. I'm in charge tonight." Charmed by the boy's imperial command, Red gladly obeyed.

The sperm of the boy gives youth to the man. The sperm of the man gives wisdom and character to the boy.

The late morning sun shone bright, another brilliant spring day. They packed their gear into the car mechanically, as if waking from a dream. What were our lovers thinking on the long drive back to town? Wild abandon in the wilderness was one thing, their respective milieus another.

Jonathan relished the memory, how cool it was that Red really loved him and was writing a book about him. How cool was that for an artist and musician? What an adventure his life had become! He was a real bohemian!

Red broke the silence with almost clairvoyant insight, "That's one of the great things about camping out. You really get to know each other."

"You said you chose me because you love me," the boy said thoughtfully, working out an idea.

"Yes, that's true," Red smiled. "All the true lover wants is the presence of the beloved."

"But what if I chose you?" he slyly grinned.

"That's the beauty of it. We chose each other." Red swerved to miss a Saab and caught his breath.

21

Red called Malcolm and left a message on his machine. Then, he called Darren, whose line was disconnected, so Red called his cell.

"Hello?"

"Darren, where are you? I tried to call your house, and the phone was disconnected."

"I'm in Elysian Fields."

"Is that like Heaven?"

"Hardly. It's 'a gated community.' Have you ever been to one of these places, Red? It's surrounded by bars. The security guards have their own patrol cars. I shit you not!"

"You're not in jail, are you?"

"More like jail with amenities. It ain't cheap, either! My little one-bedroom apartment is almost a thousand a month, and it's not even in town. I'm out in the middle of farm country!"

"What are you doing there? Why aren't you at home?"

"This is my home."

"Are you on the run? Don't answer that. Just tell me if you can why you've left your house."

"I don't have a house. They burned it down. They killed Rusty!" He broke into tears.

"Darren, I'm sorry to hear this. Are you okay?"

"I wasn't home. I was visiting my mom. They made sure of that. It was someone in the neighborhood, who knew when my car was gone. But they forgot about Rusty, or maybe they didn't. Maybe they knew he was there. He tried to break the window, but it was too high up. They found him on my bed. He wasn't burned. The smoke got him. They killed him, Red! I buried his body in the back yard two days ago. I'm sure the killers were watching. It's a very nosy neighborhood. They knew what they were doing. They were sending me a message: Don't come back, or this will be you."

"How do you know any of this? How do you know it wasn't an accident?"

"The fire detectives showed me. Molotov cocktails through the kitchen window. They'll never catch 'em."

"They won't even try. Have the media been involved?"

"They reported it as an arson fire, but they missed the sex offender angle. I ditched the sign. The detectives didn't know shit, and I wasn't gonna tell 'em."

"Too bad. People oughta know about the effects of their laws."

"Yeah, with my picture plastered all over the six o'clock news? No thanks! Everyone would sympathize with the arsonists!"

"You don't have to post that sign now, I hope."

"No, my probation officer gave me a pass. There's lots of other stuff. Come over, and I'll fill you in."

"I'll bring some steaks. Do they let you grill out?"

"We have to go to a special picnic area."

"'The Yard.' Rib eyes at eight. Pass it on."

Darren gave Red the grand tour. Elysian Fields was a hilltop fortress surrounded by an esplanade. Invading hordes would be visible for miles. The elevation provided a perfect vantage for watching the Western sunset over a grassy plain, if you didn't mind the grid of steel bars blocking your view. They were sprayed black and textured to look like wrought iron, but it didn't cover up the impression of a prison. The only thing missing was the razor wire.

It was a warm and lovely dusk. Red fired up the grill and tended the steaks as Darren told his story.

"The insurance company wanted to build it back, but I said fuck that, show me the money. I'm not going back there. So, okay, the killers win. I know where I'm not wanted."

"How much is the offer?"

"Seventy-five."

"Do you get to keep the property?"

"Yeah, and I can sell that, too. It could be worth as much as the house, maybe more."

The Moralist

"Sounds like the arsonists did you a favor."

"Maybe so. I just wish they hadn't killed Rusty."

"So where ya gonna live?"

"I'm thinkin' about it. That's why I'm here. I'm running out my living allowance while I sort things out."

"What are your options?"

"My probation officer says this whole business puts me in a different category."

"Yeah, it's called vigilantism."

"He said I might be able to move out of state if I want to."

"They want to get rid of you. You're the dirty little secret they want to cover up. Where to?"

"Clearwater Beach!" he grinned. "I wouldn't have to post a sign, no brainwashing school, either. The union has put me in touch with a budget airline in Tampa that needs a ticket agent."

Red cheered, "Go, Darren! They're not going to beat you down!"

Over mesquite-grilled rib eyes and corn-on-the-cob with a hearty merlot, the conversation continued.

"What were you calling about?"

Red grinned, "The canoe trip."

"You did it!"

"It was perfect."

"Perfect perfect?"

"All aboard!"

High fives. "All right, Red! I want details!"

"No details, but I can tell you it was the most perfect experience of boy love I've ever known in my life, and it scares the hell out of me."

"He didn't freak, did he?"

"No, he loved it."

"So what are you afraid of?"

"I'm afraid of the power it has over me. I've been in love with him for more than a year. I thought I understood how I felt. But it's totally different now. I'm swept away. Before, I was cautious. Now, I'll do anything to be with him."

"Don't get careless."

"I read him the boy lovers' riot act, just like we all do."

"Yeah, and look what good that did me!"

"He knows how to keep his mouth shut."

"It won't come from him. Something else will happen you can't control. Like you once said to me, you are more married to him now than you've ever been married to anyone."

"I hope that's true. I want it to be true."

They went inside and cranked up a Metallica CD, until a neighbor's complaint prompted a visit from security.

"Ten o'clock on Saturday night, and that little prick from upstairs calls fucking security! I can't believe it!" Darren railed after the guard left. "Why didn't he just come down and knock on the door himself?"

"That's what they're paying for, the right to be an asshole at any time. Ah, the joys of gated living! Twenty percent of our population is already in jail, why not the rest of us voluntarily? I'm really angry about what they've done to you, Darren."

"I'm doin' okay."

"Yeah, you're lucky they didn't make sure you were in that house. And it's not just you. It's thousands like you, decent people—professors, priests, school teachers—who have a valuable contribution to make, but their lives are being destroyed by an ugly, vicious, ignorant lie! It's wrong, and all the uniforms and robes and pinstripes pronouncing their hallowed words of law and science don't make it right. They might as well be wearing voodoo masks and shaking rattles over a sacrificial lamb."

"I'm not sure I like that analogy."

"It's time that people knew about this insanity. They pass all these laws, but they have no idea the injustice they are creating."

"Maybe they do. Maybe that's what they want."

"Yeah, as long as it happens to someone else. I'm not going to wait till they come for me."

"It scares me when you talk like that."

"Don't worry, it won't involve you. That's a promise."

"I'm not worried about me. I'm worried about you, what you might do to yourself."

"I'm mad as hell, and I'm not going take it anymore!"

"What are you going to do?"

"That's the problem. I don't have a clue."

"You've given me this advice often enough, so now I'll give it to you: Don't do anything stupid."

Jonathan called. A rock concert was coming to town, the Gingko Punkfest. "We're there, dude!" Red declared in his best Beavis-and-Butthead.

Standing in the supermarket customer service line, he waited for the poor Hispanic girl alone at the counter with a queue of nervous tobacco addicts.

"Two tickets for the Gingko Punkfest, please," he requested to her helpless blank stare. "G-i-n-g-k-o-P-u-n-k-f-e-s-t. It's a rock concert. They told me on the phone that I could get the tickets here."

As she fussed with the computer, the bored, lanky, red-haired queen behind him queried, "I can't stand it. What is the Gingko Punkfest?"

"It's not a band, it's a brand," Red explained, as the harried girl handed him a pen and scrap of paper to write it out. The sissy screwed up his face as Red block-printed the letters and handed the paper back along with his credit card. "Gingko is a brand of baggy blue-jeans that skateboarders wear. They sponsor a rock music tour called 'Punkfest.'"

"I wouldn't take you for a skateboarder," he observed.

How sweet! He's hitting on me, Red thought, and replied, "You got that right! I wouldn't get on a skateboard if my life depended on it. It's for my teenage boy."

"Really? You don't look old enough to have a teenage son."

A double compliment! He thinks I'm straight and young. Not a moment too soon, the girl produced the tickets and tab for Red to sign. "Not my son, my boy," he corrected with a smile and a wink at the young man, whose mouth gaped wide.

The Punkfest was more like a street fair than a concert, with booths selling and promoting boy stuff to the mostly boy crowd—computer games, radio stations, record labels, thrasher brands of clothing and jewelry. Skateboard competitions played out on a giant half-pipe, as several small stages and the giant main stage ground out punk music through the sunny spring afternoon.

Red and Jonathan moved through the sea of boys. Red felt their eyes on the boy with the spiked purple hair sprinkled with glitter and the older man in cargo shorts and a loose rayon shirt printed with colorful comic book pictures of Superman. A few of the grown-ups manning the booths inquired, "Is he your father?" "Are you his father?", with implied approval of the cool dad and his far-out son. But when the answer came, "No, we're just buddies," the approval turned to curiosity and suspicion, as the unspoken question hung in the air: Is he one of *them*? One boozed middle-aged babe attending with her fellow moms and kids gushed, "I think that is so cool you guys can be friends like that!" until her friends dragged her away, glancing back with different opinions.

The kids made similar assumptions. Red overheard some older boys snicker derisively, mimicking a whining kid, "I wanta go to the concert, Dad!'" Like Malcolm said, "a constant state of irony." But most simply approved, "Cool hair!"

"Your hair's a big hit!" Red declared.

"It's more than just my hair. It's you," he replied. "They see me, and then they see you. They think you're my dad, but they're not quite sure. That's why they ask. You oughta say, 'No, I'm his lover,' and see what they do."

"Yeah, and you would be furious."

"No, I wouldn't. I'd like to see the look on their faces."

"No, you wouldn't. They'd prob'ly call a cop."

"It pisses me off! Everybody thinks it's queer, and it ain't queer. We just have fun together. What's wrong with that? Why should we have to pretend?"

"You know why."

"That doesn't make it right."

"No, but that's the way it is, and I don't think it's gonna change any time soon."

"You could change it, Red. Maybe your book will change it."

"Maybe. I hope you don't mind being in my book."

"No, it's cool. It's fiction, remember? It isn't me."

A clown handed them sticks of sidewalk chalk. Jonathan wrote "Freaks Rule" in a multi-colored freaky style with 'shroom accents. Red started scrawling in giant pink letters, "The degree and kind of a man's sexuality. . ."

As he wrote, a teenage audience gathered. He could hear them reading aloud and wondering what was to come. "'. . .reach to the highest peaks of his intellect.'—Nietzsche" The kids twittered, murmured, and speculated among themselves. It wasn't the naughty bathroom wit they expected, but provocative to their curious young minds. Red and Jonathan walked on.

"We drew a crowd," Red observed to his friend.

"Yeah, it had 'sex' in it. Sex gets everybody's attention. Who's Nazi or whatever?"

"You're not far off. Hitler loved Nietzsche. Friedrich Wilhelm Nietzsche, nineteenth century German philosopher, who many believe set the tone and ethos of twentieth century art, letters, and politics. You might enjoy reading him sometime. It's pretty wild stuff and much more interesting and relevant than most philosophy. Nietzsche was the freak philosopher. He went mad in later life, but there's a lot of disagreement about that. It's easy to imagine this raving mad philosopher, and his writing sounds like that sometimes, but those who knew him said he was good-looking, articulate, and brilliant."

They continued their tour of the grounds, pausing to listen to a band and watch a stunt biker on a half-pipe.

"Red, do you do it with anybody else?"

"No, I've been virtually celibate since I met you."

"Virtually?"

"Well, I've had my moments, but you have been the sole focus of my attention."

"So you had it planned all along, you and me."

"The only thing I planned was to be with you. That's all I wanted. Whatever else might happen was out of my hands. I understood that. I still do."

"But you made it happen. You made me look up to you."

"I look up to you. Did you make that happen?"

"What about our canoe trip? You set that up."

"Yeah, with your father and Ernie. We woulda had a great time, but they couldn't make it, so we had a great time on our own."

"You're not gonna do it with anybody else now, right?"

"I wouldn't think of it! You're The One. I love you exclusively, unequivocally, and without question. I don't expect the same from you, by the way."

"You don't? Why not?" He was hurt.

"I mean that as your mentor and lover, I occupy a unique position that is safe and private between you and me. Yes, I would be hurt if you found some other older lover to take my place, but aside from that, you are free to experiment and explore with other boys or girls or whatever you need to find out who you are and what you want. I want you to."

"I told you, I'm not that way!" Now he was annoyed.

"I'm not making any assumptions. All I know is that you're a fuckin' wild-ass, compassionate loving person who gets pissed off 'cause he can't just be his own real self and have some fun without everybody getting all bent outta shape. I love your anger and authenticity. That's the real you, not some phony worried-about-what-everyone-else-thinks you. Hold onto that. Hold onto that for dear life, and don't let anyone take it away."

They stopped for hot dogs at a concession booth.

"I heard a concession joke recently," Red continued. "What did Buddha say to the hot dog vendor?" The boy shrugged. "Make me one with everything." He didn't get it. "Okay, Buddha is this big fat guy with the earlobes, right? He was an Indian ascetic who founded the religion called Buddhism, which seeks unification of the self with the cosmos. So what did Buddha say to the hot dog vendor? 'Make me one with everything.' Get it?" Jonathan chuckled, patronizing him. "That's another book you might enjoy— *Siddharta*. It's the story of Buddha, but it ain't boring or religious like you might think. It's a novel by the same German writer who wrote *Steppenwolf*. It's about a young prince and his journey through life. It's a short read."

"You sure know a lot of German writers."

"German, French, Russian, English, whatever. I read what I like."

"Do you read all those languages?"

"No, in English translation, and so can you. I'll give you some."

They paused at a radio booth handing out watercolor tatts of the station logo. Removing his shirt on the hot afternoon, Jonathan took two and pressed them onto his swollen young nipples, posing for Red's camera.

Snapping off a few shots, "I'd like to lick those off with the tip of my tongue."

"Then, do it."

"Not here."

Back at Red's, he'd barely closed the door when the horny boy wrestled off his clothes and landed them both onto the futon, kissing his lover like a madman. Red did indeed lick the watercolor tatts from the hard young nipples.

Jonathan whispered breathlessly, "You said one time you wanted to '69'."

"You remembered!" Red smiled.

"Yeah, let's do it! I wanta do everything!"

"We can't. Too much machinery." Red pointed to the boy's teeth. He never liked '69' anyway. He found it distracting, and boys were notoriously bad cocksuckers. "How about a backrub?"

Jonathan rolled over onto his tummy as Red straddled his waist, running his palms along the soft pale skin up to the boy's neck and shoulders.

"That feels good," Jonathan sighed.

"You're muscles are tight. Try this: Relax your shoulders." It worked every time. When the boy relaxed his shoulders, his whole body went limp. Red enclosed the young frame in his arms, and they lay still as if suspended in time.

Jonathan's fist clenched tight around Red's erection, exploring the stiffness of it. He climbed on top and held both together, the younger smaller smoother member pressed against the thick veined shaft of his lover, examining the two together.

"I want one big as yours."

"Fourteen years, nine months."

Noah called. "I thought you'd like to know, the spring issue of the *Journal* is out, and our study is in it. No word on the radio interview yet."

"Do you think you're ready? Do you need my help?"

"I'm no good at this, Red. I learned that at OLGA. I already screwed it up once."

"Don't be so hard on yourself. You don't have to be glib to be articulate. All you need is a few key messages, and don't repeat the reporter's negative words."

"That's easier said than done. I know that now. I wish you could do it."

"I'd love to, but I don't have the standing. Who am I? I'm nobody! It's your study. You're the point man."

"Not anymore. We're going to issue a statement and let it go at that."

"That's not enough. People will think you can't even speak for your own study."

"The study speaks for itself."

"Not in today's world. Today, it's the person. It's post-Gutenberg. We're back to the oral culture. The man has to stand up for himself. Do this one thing for me: When the phone starts ringing, and it will, don't say 'no comment.'"

"What should I say?"

"Write this down, so you can read it over the phone."

"Okay, shoot."

"Say, 'Thank you for your interest in our work. I prefer not to take questions over the phone, but I'll be happy to provide you with a written statement.' Then, send the statement to them right away by fax or e-mail. You and Russell should start working on that statement now."

"We already are."

Rod Downey

"Good. I'd like to take a look at it, when you've got something."
"I'll send it to you."

E-mail

To the BLN:

I have some sad and troubling news. Last weekend, Paul Steiner was found hanged in his prison cell. The authorities are calling it a suicide, but there were bruises on his body that indicate he was beaten before his death, which is doubly strange, since he was supposed to be in solitary confinement. I'm afraid we will never know what really happened. Condolences can be sent to his wife, Marla, at the address below. —BLN editor

"While I was making love to my boy, gentle Paul was being beaten and murdered," Red thought.

He tried to call Malcolm but the line was disconnected.

22

The following weekend, Noah's interview aired on *The Don Giovanni Show*. As described, Giovanni skewered him on the "agenda" issue, but that was only the beginning, folks. Dr. Flo picked it up. Red was pleased. You couldn't buy that kind of publicity, but you had to know how to handle it without getting slaughtered. Alas, Noah was right. He and Russell did not.

Dr. Flo was on in the late afternoon going head-to-head with Oprah and not doing too bad, fifteen minutes per topic with call-ins and a final comment. But for this show, she changed the format. She had found herself a *cause célèbre*, and this show had one topic and one topic only. Red tuned in.

Theme music, applause, old-fashioned microphone logo, Dr. Flo's disembodied voice, "This is Dr. Flo. You're on the air." As the logo faded, the camera zoomed to Dr. Flo, seated on a chrome and leather barstool in a mock radio studio a la *Larry King* with microphones clearly visible on the high table, and a place for the next guest. It was talk radio come to television with a studio audience.

Close up, Dr. Flo had that strained look of the sexual hysteric, the skin pulled tight and dry like a mummy beneath the make-up, exposing the tense sinews of her neck, her skull-like face all eyes and mouth. That was one thing all the anti-sex crusaders had in common: Who'd wanta fuck 'em anyway?

She spoke to the camera, "Today's show has a title. It's called 'The Evil Within Us,' because today we are going to talk about a new pseudo-scientific study that threatens our children, our families, and our society.

"It has the unwieldy title *Adult-Child Sexual Contact: A Re-Examination of the Science*. In it, the researchers claim that sexual abuse of a child by an adult is not necessarily a bad thing and that when there is a 'willing' sexual encounter between an adult and a child, it can be a positive experience!"

She continued almost in tears, "When I learned about this study, it made me sick to my stomach. I wanted to disbelieve it. But I've done my research, and I cannot stress strongly enough how deadly serious this is.

"This study is the first step on the road toward normalizing pedophilia, just as homosexuality has been mainstreamed to the point where tolerance is no longer sufficient. We now have to embrace it.

"I want to recap for you my own journey of discovery in this horrifying story." Taking out a piece of paper. "I received this fax from Bob, a concerned father, who had just heard Don Giovanni's morning talk show in Philadelphia, WBJ-AM, where he interviewed one of the authors of this study. This pseudo-scientist claims that not all children who engage in sexual contact willingly with an adult show any lasting damage. He further stated that to call this sexual contact 'abuse' is a mistake, because it's consensual.

"Bob's letter goes on to say," reading, "'These researchers have an agenda that should scare all decent people. The next time some pervert gets caught with a child, I'm sure this is the first study his scum lawyer will drag out to defend his actions.'

"I immediately thought this can't be happening, but Bob was right. This study will now be used to normalize pedophilia. It is part of an ongoing plot against the family." Holding up a copy of the *JASP*, "And to make matters worse, it is published in the very respectable *Journal of the American Society of Psychiatrics*! While this may not be a statement of the ASP's official position, I hold them accountable for what I have been told by numerous professionals is garbage research. After this break, we will meet one of those professionals, Dr. Günter Horst of Germany, who is here with us today."

Theme music and applause dissolved to commercials for drugs, diet shakes, and a laundry detergent where a lively young boy peeled off his favorite shirt at mom's insistence. When the show returned, a small, balding gray-haired man with a goatee and a frumpy tweed suit had mounted his barstool.

As if no consumer myth of boyhood and motherhood had interrupted her, Dr. Flo continued right where she left off, "Dr. Horst has a Ph.D. in psychology and has written several books and articles on homosexuality, pedophilia, neuroses and family issues. Please, welcome Dr. Horst." As the audience applauded politely, the little man managed a pompous nod.

"Dr. Horst, thank you for joining us today."

His accent was thickly Germanic, "Sank you for inviting me, Dr. Flo."

"Tell us, Doctor, what is your assessment of this so-called study."

"It is seriously flawed science. To begin mit, dis study does no original research. It is zimply a re-analysis of other people's data. It is all based on statistics."

"You mean it's like Mark Twain said: 'There are lies, damn lies, and statistics.'" Laughter from the audience.

"Exactly, Dr. Flo. Die study says dere vas no harm done to de boys who vere interviewed. But dat is only based on questionnaires and short interviews. At best, dey can only give a very rough indication of subjectively perceived discomfort. But in very many cases, dey do not even do dat. Harm is much more than 'I do or do not feel okay,' or 'I didn't like dat experience.' Harm after child sexual abuse is often an increased distress mit respect to adults, a distorted and unhealsy view of sexuality, a distorted view of der own or die opposite sex. It can be subsequent sexual abnormalities. It can be marriage and udder relational problems later in life, problems functioning as a parent, sometimes later promiscuity, and in many cases, inferiority complexes, because children who have been misused often feel verseless. In short, vhat dese psychologists offer us here is an insult to true scientific dinking."

Perched on her barstool like a gargoyle, holding her chin in rapt interest, Dr. Flo prompted, "And what about their motives, Doctor?"

Horst continued, "I sink die sexual reform movements of da Vestern vorld vant to liberate sexuality in all its forms. Und zo dere is a zilent, not so zilent in die European community, cooperation of die sexual reform organizations mit die cause of die militant pedophiles. Fur example, die European Association for Sexual Reform has special meetings for pedophiles every week in many cities."

"And such groups gain power and authority by attacking the opposition as phobic, intolerant of diversity, bigoted and mean," she added.

"Exactly. You vill do a vonderful ding to make people aware of dis, and zay to people, 'Don't let yourself be intimidated. Don't doubt your own common-sense judgment of dese tings.' Because people are overwhelmed mit all kinds of pseudo-science. Dey dink, 'Who am I? Perhaps I'm wrong, I'm old-fashioned, I'm a victim of my Vestern culture.' Dey have to be supported as to der own convictions."

"So you're saying that the point of liberating the sexual mores in general is, ultimately, to have access to kids."

"Ya, dat's vat it's for: getting kids sexually active and den getting sexually active mit kids. Pedophiles have a patological obsession. It's not a normal kind of sexual drive. It is the nucleus of der whole life. Like many disturbed people, der attitude is not dat 'I have to change,' but dat 'the vorld has to change.' Und zo, dey are die ones to crusade to change the vorld, and really dink dat dey can eventually get normal fathers and mothers to give der children to pedophiles for educational or enlightenment motivations. In Die Nederlands, one of the advocates for pedophilia received a royal distinction some years ago for his work to 'liberate' homosexuality, as dey say. He vas in die Dutch senate as a very esteemed and respected senator."

"This his horrific!" To the camera, "Everyone watching this show should know what is happening. The pedophile network is worldwide! Our lines are open: 1-800-CALLDRFLO. We'll be right back."

Red picked up the phone.

A naked teenage boy dropped his shampoo bottle in the shower as the voice-over extolled the virtue of plastics. A lovely hazel-eyed boy smiled proudly solving the math problem with the help of a professional tutoring service.

Dr. Horst had vanished. Alone again, Dr. Flo announced, "The calls are pouring in. We'll be hearing from some of you in a few minutes, but first, I'd like to welcome retired FBI agent Grant Byrne."

Applause as the stiff fiftyish man ("Probably my same age," Red thought), paunchy with an ill-fitted blue suit, marched out and took his seat at the mike, "Thank you for inviting me on your show, Dr. Flo."

"Grant—can I call you Grant?" He nodded. "You have twenty-five years of law-enforcement experience and have investigated numerous cases of child sexual molestation and child rape by pedophiles."

"That's right, Dr. Flo, and for over a year, I worked in a semi-covert capacity in the homosexual community gathering information on pedophiles who were actively recruiting young boys and luring them into sexual relations. I have personally investigated so many pedophilia cases that I was granted expert-witness status in court. NAMBLA lives by the creed 'Sex before eight, or it's too late.'"

"NAMBLA, we should note," she interrupted, "is the North American Man-Boy Love Association, an organization of pedophiles. They are part of this worldwide network."

The Moralist

"NAMBLA wants to lower the age of sexual consent to eight years old. Imagine for a moment a fifty-year-old male being given the legal right to have sexual relations with an eight-year-old child, and a parent being able to do nothing to stop it! These males—I can't call them men—who engage in this type of activity with children are vile and deviant criminals. Instead of calling this 'adult-child sexual contact,' it should be labeled as what it is: child rape and child molestation. I resent that somehow this is being distorted into a 'lifestyle choice.' For the eight-year-old, there is no choice."

"How do you think this study fits into that?"

"It goes back to the homosexual rights movement. The term 'gay'—I don't use it myself—was a carefully thought-out marketing plan to make that lifestyle acceptable, or, as you say, 'normalized.' Homosexuals found words like 'faggot' and 'queer' offensive, so they came up with a name for themselves that was happy and neutral, and it pretty much has worked. I believe that child molesters are taking a page from the book of the homosexuals, and this study is part of a campaign to 'normalize' their behavior."

"But it has the stamp of approval of the American Society of Psychiatrics."

"When the American Society of Psychiatrics redefines a deviant behavior as a lifestyle choice, it's usually prompted by their inability to devise an adequate treatment program to 'cure' the problem. In other words, if it's no longer deviant, it's no longer a problem. It's a form of denial. This is due, in part, to the fact that there is no current treatment plan or medication that will stop a pedophile from offending again. A pedophile will be a pedophile as long as he lives, and the ASP should be viewed with nothing but contempt for their concessions to molesters and deviants. What they should be doing is lending their support for lifetime incarceration of pedophiles, so that they won't offend again. To deny the basic truths of pedophilia is to do all of society a grave injustice."

"Very well said," she approved. "We have a caller."

Lisping voice-over, "Dr. Flo, I was sexually abused as a child by a heterosexual married man, and I can testify to the lasting effects and damage. As a gay male, I am disgusted and offended by any organization that even suggests that children enjoy or somehow benefit from sexual contact with adults. In fact, the majority of the gay community, and every gay person I know, is appalled by NAMBLA. Children are incapable of making such decisions, and I know first-hand that this behavior is destructive and long-lasting."

"Do you have a question?"

"Well, I want to ask your guest—"

"Grant Byrne."

"Mr. Byrne, you seem to be suggesting that you don't like gay people, either. Is that true? Yes or no?"

"I think homosexuality is also deviant behavior. Your friends may be appalled by pedophiles, but from my experience in the homosexual community, you're not that far from it. Many homosexuals prefer younger males, so why not sixteen, fifteen, fourteen? Why not a child?"

"So you're just a bigot, is that it?"

"And you're just a faggot, is that it?" Byrne shot back.

Gasps from the audience. The phone went dead.

"We seem to have gotten off the subject here," Dr. Flo recovered.

"I'd like to point out something our caller said. He said he was abused as a child, and now he is homosexual. He hates pedophiles, because he was permanently scarred by one who turned him into a homosexual. That's what happens. That's the dirty little secret of the homosexual rights movement—that homosexual pedophiles do recruit young people into their lifestyle, and that homosexual abuse of young boys turns them into homosexuals. I've seen it dozens of times, but you'll never get any homosexual to admit it."

"We have another caller. Go ahead."

"Yes, Dr. Flo, I'm an attorney, and I agree with you about this phony study. I'm disgusted by child molesters and their shrinks claiming that the molester's acts were a product of a mental disorder. This has entitled them to reduced sentences, in some cases, no jail time at all, and state-financed therapy programs, among other perks. Even worse, it has perpetuated the false concept that these people are ill rather than evil. The same is true of this study. It will be one more weapon in their arsenal to keep child molesters on the street and free to molest again. That's why programs like yours are so important. Thank you, Dr. Flo, for bringing this outrage to light."

"And thank you, caller. We have time for one more. Go ahead please."

"Good afternoon, Ms. Lipschitz. You said earlier that you were alerted to this study by a concerned father you called Bob. I, too, am a concerned father. My name is Richard. I'm concerned about the lies that are being perpetrated by the child-abuse industry."

"Do you have a question or comment about the Cobb-Orlofsky study?"

The Moralist

"Have you read it?"

"I have read the portions I quoted earlier."

"If you read the entire study, you will find an intelligent, objective analysis by credible statisticians. Your doctor from Germany earlier made the point that the study relies on data from other studies. That is significant, because these other studies are the very ones used by the child-abuse industry to validate their opinions. The Cobb-Orlofsky study says that science is flawed. It knocks the entire scientific foundation out from under you, and that's why you're attacking it."

Groans and boos from the audience.

"I would like to ask this so-called concerned father a question," the fiery Mr. Byrne interrupted.

"Please, go ahead," Dr. Flo managed a smile.

"Sir, are you a member of NAMBLA?"

"No, I'm a reasonable person who knows a witch-hunt when he sees one. The lawyer who called earlier said we should consider people who have such relationships as evil. Why? Because once you label them as evil, then you can burn 'em at the stake with a clear conscience, and that's what's happening now. Where, for example, are the authors of the study or someone from the ASP? Why aren't they on your show?"

"We invited them, and they wouldn't return our phone calls!" she announced triumphantly.

"Given the hostile environment, I'm not surprised."

"*You* seem to be doing pretty well. We'll be doing other shows on this topic, and you are invited to join me as a guest. What do you say, audience?" Boos and jeers. "They don't sound too happy about it, Richard, but you have my personal invitation to speak on behalf of this study yourself, since you seem to know so much about it."

"Thank you. I will."

"Please, give your information to our producer, so we can contact you. We're about out of time. I'm so disgusted by this most disturbing effort to de-stigmatize pedophilia, I've decided to form my own organization against it. It's called 'Go with Dr. Flo,' and if you want to get involved, you can get more information at my website, CallDrFlo.com. We must all uphold the strong values of morality and ethics that are our only hope as a society and a civilization. This is Dr. Flo; you're on the air."

Theme music as the camera pulled back panning the audience with logo and credits before dissolving to commercial. Red hung up the phone and turned off the television. The phone rang.

"That was you! That was your voice on Dr. Flo!" Noah exclaimed.

"You saw it?"

"It was you, wasn't it?"

"Yeah. How'd I do?" Red asked modestly.

"You were great!"

"Thanks. Somebody had to stick up for you guys. The ASP obviously won't. She was killing you! That's what happens when you don't speak up. And she'll do it again and again, until she destroys your reputation. This will affect everything you do from now on—support from the academic community, grant money, the ASP. She'll be going after them, too, just like she did today. Then they'll be pissed off at you for hanging them out to dry."

"I know, I know. We're still working on the statement."

"Good. Get it done. You need it now."

"So, are you going to do it? Are you going to go on her show?"

"They know how to reach me. But you should understand, these on-air invitations have a way of not panning out. We'll see."

Are gays out to normalize pedophilia?
TV advice maven Dr. Flo accuses the 'homosexual movement' of conspiring with the ASP to destigmatize child sexual abuse.

(Crown Press)—There is no connection between pedophilia and homosexuality in the minds of most lesbians and gay men. But nationally syndicated TV talk show host Flo Lipschitz has devoted a substantial amount of airtime talking about a movement to "normalize" adult-child sex, and she has laid blame for that effort on the "homosexual movement."

In a recent on-air attack, "Dr. Flo" (as she is known to her viewers, although she is not a psychologist as many believe; her doctorate is in English) has criticized a study published in the prestigious *Journal of the American Society of Psychiatrics* (JASP). The study finds that young males under the age of eighteen who had had homosexual contact with older men were no less well-adjusted than the general population.

She said the study was an attempt by the ASP to normalize pedophilia in the same way it normalized homosexuality by removing it from the association's list of mental disorders.

The study, titled *Adult-Child Sexual Contact: A Re-Examination of the Science* and published in the JASP, contains no new research but instead uses a technique of recompiling data gathered in other studies over the past twenty years.

It was authored by two Philadelphia University professors, Russell Cobb and Noah Orlofsky. They did not return calls for comment.

A summary at the beginning of the study states that many people believe that adult-child sexual contact "causes intense harm pervasively in the general population." But using the same scientific data on which that belief is based, the study refutes the conclusions of the original researchers.

Citing a "perhaps unconscious predisposition as to the outcomes of their research," the study concludes that the original researchers "misinterpreted their own data." The new study demonstrates exactly the opposite conclusion from those drawn by the original researchers. "The commonly held beliefs as to the negative effects of adult-child sexual contact are not supported by the science in this field," the study reports. The study examines only homosexual male contact.

In a written statement, the ASP says that the findings of the Cobb report are accurate. "The statistical analysis of the existing research is sound," the statement said. But seeming to contradict itself, the ASP also backs away from the study's conclusion that adult-child sexual contact is not harmful by referring to its 1990 resolution that declares "the sexual abuse of children results in long-lasting harm to its victims."

The gay response

Representatives of the gay rights organization tasked with tracking treatment of gay issues in the media said it was already planning to take action to counteract Lipschitz' attacks, even before this latest round involving pedophilia.

"We recognize that she is a menace to our community," said Mariah Champion, spokesperson for Gay-Lesbian Media Watch (GLMW). "She has several million viewers, and she misrepresents facts."

GLMW intends to mount a major initiative in the coming weeks to counteract Lipschitz' influence, Champion said. "We want to expose her for the fraud that she is and to expose her lies. She's completely gone off the deep end with her anti-gay diatribes. It's all a bunch of nonsense, and I'm sure it's politically motivated." —###

Rod Downey

Pedophilia Study Triggers Conservative Outrage

(Beltway News Service)—A national furor has erupted over a study published in the *Journal of the American Society of Psychiatrics* that claims that sexual relations between adult men and boys are not always psychologically damaging and in some cases are a "positive experience for willing youngsters."

Now conservative lobbying groups, politicians, and some psychologists have gone on the warpath, sharply criticizing the study as advocating pedophilia, challenging its findings, and wondering whether it will be used by criminal defense attorneys to get child molesters off the hook in court.

A group of congressmen want the report "condemned" by both Congress and President Clinton. Several states have passed resolutions urging the President and Congress to reject the conclusions of the study.

The conservative Family Values League has scheduled a press conference and demanded that the authors step up to defend their study and a representative from the ASP explain its decision to publish it. —###

E-mail

Red:

Obviously, we do not intend to stand up there and let the Family Values League attack us. Attached is our statement that we will send to them and the press, including Dr. Flo. Please send me your comments. —Noah

Adult-Child Sexual Contact: A Re-Examination of the Science
Authors' Statement

Critics have attacked the study for its conclusions that adult-child sexual contact among males is less harmful than has been widely believed. These critics have implied that these conclusions condone sexual abuse. In fact, in our article, we clearly state that our review of the research literature does not condone abuse of any kind, and our study changes nothing with regard to moral or legal views on abuse. We wrote, "The moral and legal codes of society are rarely based on scientific fact but on cultural attitudes," and that "the findings of this study do not imply that moral or legal definitions of or views on behavior should be changed."

The Moralist

The value of our review lies in its thorough and careful integration of research on the effects of adult-child sexual contact in non-clinical populations, and its examination of how the context of the experience and background variables—such as physical abuse and emotional neglect—may contribute to the reactions and effects reported among the respondents. The methods of the review, including the meta-analytic approach, are sound and appropriate. If there is disagreement with the findings and conclusions, the appropriate response is to conduct a review of the research that demonstrates where errors were made, or, better yet, to conduct further research that can either confirm or refute the conclusions.

Recently, psychologist Joseph Winston wrote in the *Baltimore Banner*: "To criticize the ASP for publishing the study is a bit like scolding the American Heart Association for reporting that the long-term effects of a high-fat diet were less dangerous than had previously been thought and blaming the authors for promoting heart disease."

If adverse childhood events are found to be less psychologically harmful than previously thought, or in some cases not measurably harmful at all, researchers have an ethical duty to report this. Our findings have strong positive implications: Victims do not have to believe that they are "damaged goods," and clinicians may have solid grounds for providing reassurance and hope to those who have had such experiences. Ignoring such data may bring harm to those who have had such experiences by creating negative feelings where there were none previously.

Professor of Psychology Russell Cobb, PhD
Associate Professor of Sexology Noah Orlofsky, PhD
Philadelphia University

Red's reply

Noah:

Overall, you present a good argument, but it's naïve to claim that the study doesn't have social implications. Of course, it does. That's why they're so pissed off. You have some strong key messages, but they are buried and cluttered with too many negative words like "abuse," "neglect," "errors," "harm," etc. My strongest recommendation is that you rephrase these statements with more positive words like "healthy," "beneficial," "positive feelings," since those are actually your findings. The statement that your methods are "sound an appropriate" should come at the *beginning* of the paragraph.

Excellent quote from the *Banner*. Compelling positive conclusion. I especially like the word 'ethical.' —Red

They didn't change any of it. He was not surprised.

Op-ed in *The Boston Star*:

Suppressing Science—a Dangerous Trend
By Bella Hansberry

The Inquisition forced Galileo to recant what we all know today is established fact: The earth revolves around the sun. I thought our civilization had outgrown the notion that we could legislate scientific fact. But not so. On June 12, the U.S. Congress voted unanimously to denounce a study that the resolution's sponsor, Rep. Buddy Hines (R-Texas), called "the emancipation proclamation of pedophiles." In a stunning display of scientific illiteracy and moral posturing, Congress misunderstood the message, so it condemned the messenger.

What got Congress riled was an article in the *Journal of the American Society of Psychiatrics*, which is to behavioral science what the *Journal of the American Medical Association* is to medicine. Articles must pass rigorous peer review, during which they are scrutinized for their methods, statistics and conclusions. The authors of the article, Russell Cobb and Noah Orlofsky, statistically analyzed the major studies on the topic of adult-child sexual contact over the past twenty-five years, involving more than 37,000 men and boys.

The findings, reported with meticulous detail and caution, are astonishing. The researchers found no overall link between adult-child sexual contact and later emotional disorders or unusual psychological problems in adulthood. Of course, some experiences, such as rape by a father, are more devastating than others, such as a loving relationship between a teacher and a student. But the children most harmed are those from terrible family environments, where abuse is one of many awful things they have to endure.

Perhaps the researchers' most inflammatory finding, however, was that not all experiences of adult-child sexual contact have equally emotional consequences, nor can they be lumped together as "abuse." Being molested at the age of five is not comparable to choosing to have sex at fifteen. The researchers found that two-thirds of males who, as children or teenagers, had had sexual experiences with adults did not react negatively. Many reacted positively.

Shouldn't this be good news? Shouldn't we be glad to know which experiences are in fact traumatic for children, and which are not upsetting to them, and which are even fulfilling and nurturing?

The Cobb report, however, has upset two powerful constituencies: religious fundamentalists and other conservatives who think this research endorses pedophilia, and psychotherapists, who have a vested interest in believing that all adult-child sexual experiences in childhood inevitably cause lifelong psychological harm unless they receive expensive therapy from these professionals.

The conservatives have found support from clinicians who still maintain that adult-childhood sexual contact causes "multiple personality disorder" and "repressed memories." These ideas have been discredited by research, just as the belief that homosexuality is a mental illness or a chosen "lifestyle."

But some conservative clinicians cannot let them go. They want to kill the Cobb study, because they fear that it will be used to support malpractice claims against their fellow therapists. And, like their right-wing allies, they claim the article will be used to protect pedophiles in court.

All scientific research on any subject can be used wisely or stupidly. For clinicians to use the "exoneration of pedophiles" argument to try to suppress this article's important findings and to smear the article's authors by impugning their scholarship and motives is particularly reprehensible. They should know better.

The American Society of Psychiatrics (ASP) has been under constant attack by the Christian Coalition, the Family Values League, Republican members of Congress, panicked citizens, radio and television talk-show hosts, and a consortium of clinicians that reads like a *Who's Who* of the child-abuse and sex-offender industry.

At a recent press conference sponsored by the Family Values League, Dr. Joel Grossman, speaking for the ASP, stated that future articles on sensitive subjects will be more carefully considered for their "public policy implications" and that the Cobb study would be re-reviewed by independent scholars. He reiterated the ASP's public position that "the sexual abuse of children is a criminal act that is reprehensible in any context."

These placatory gestures are understandable given the ferocity of the attacks. But the ASP has missed its chance to educate the public and Congress about the scientific method, the purpose of peer review, and the absolute necessity of protecting the right of its scientists to publish unpopular findings.

Researchers cannot function if they have to censor themselves according to potential public outcry or are silenced by social pressure, harassment, or political posturing from those who disapprove of their results.

On emotionally sensitive topics such as sex, children and trauma, we need all the clear-headed information we can get. We need to understand what makes most people resilient, and how to help those who are not. We need to understand a lot more about sexuality, including children's sexuality. The right wing may feel a spasm of righteousness by condemning scientific findings they dislike. But their actions will do no more to reduce the actual abuse of children than posting the Ten Commandments in schools will improve children's morality. —###

[Bella Hansberry is a social psychologist who writes frequently on behavioral research issues.]

E-mail

Noah:

So the ASP cratered. This wasn't their fight. Next time, tell Russell he should consider the public communications aspect of your work, especially as controversial as it is. Don't blame yourself. You just didn't have a point man when you needed one. —Red

Red:

I think your idea is a good one, and I will share it with Russell. Amid all the brouhaha, there is a humorous note. The ASP held its annual meeting in San Francisco last week, and many people told me about a sticker they saw plastered around that said:

"If the U.S. CONGRESS says that 'THE SUN REVOLVES AROUND THE EARTH,' then that fact will be given most careful consideration in all articles published by the ASP."

Have you heard anything more from Dr. Flo? —Noah

Noah:

No word. I doubt we've heard the last of her, but that doesn't guarantee she'll want to hear from me. —Red

The Moralist

Dear Mr. Rover:

Would you be available to appear as a guest on next week's *Call Dr. Flo* to discuss the Cobb-Orlofsky report? Please respond as soon as possible, so that we can make the necessary arrangements.

Sincerely,
Karen Beuleau, producer

Noah:

I just got the call from Dr. Flo. I'll be on the show next week talking about your study. I'll keep you posted. —Red

Red:

Congratulations! If you want me to brief you on some of the statistical data, let me know. —Noah

Noah:

Thanks for the offer, but this is not about statistics. Wish me luck. —Red

Red:

You said we didn't have a point man. Now we do! Good luck! —Noah

23

The phone rang.

"Richard?" His father's voice always sounded distant on the phone, as if he were calling from across a chasm. He usually called about money or travel arrangements. This was no exception.

"Dad? What's up?"

"I have some very good news for you."

"Did you read those chapters I sent you?"

"Huh? Oh, yeah, I have them right here. I haven't—"

"That's okay. You can toss 'em in the can, if you want to."

"No, I—"

"What's the good news?"

"I just opened an account here in your name at Jefferson Savings."

"That does sound like good news! Does it have any money in it?"

"Fifty thousand dollars."

"Thank you very much! I guess the deal went through."

"Yes. You'll be receiving some checks to draw on it however you want. I just put it in the bank, so you'll be earning interest while you decide what to do with it. I hope you don't quit your job."

"That may not be an option."

"Good, I'm glad to hear you say that."

The phone rang.

"I did it, dude! I'm a married man!"

"When?"

"Today! This afternoon! I'm at the reception right now!"

"Congratulations, I'm happy for you." More than Mark realized. Any sign of stability in his life lessened the possibility he would come careening back into Red's own, but the new wife was a double-edged sword. She could relegate Red to Mark's past forever, where he dearly wished to reside, or bring him back into the too terrible present.

"Why didn't you come?"

"Was your dad there?"

"Yeah, okay, I understand, but I wish you'd been here to see me stand up today in my white tie and tails. I've got 'em on right now."

"Did you wear a veil?"

"Oh, girl, I wanted to, but Tammy wouldn't let me! Ser'ous, nigga, I just want you to know I missed you, and I'm thinkin' about you, even if you ain't here. You're an important person in my life, Red. I still love you. I always will."

Red felt the tears well up. "You haven't changed. Underneath all that bluster, you're still the same sweet romantic boy I knew. Thank you for remembering me on your special day."

"I'll never forget you, Red."

"Did you get my gift?"

"Oh, yeah, they're all stacked up there on the table. We haven't opened them yet."

"You'd better get back there. You don't want to leave your new bride alone too long on her wedding day."

"Especially talking to my old lover!" he laughed. "I'll call you after the honeymoon."

The phone rang.

"It's paradise, Red, boys everywhere!" Darren raved. "Real boys, not just hustlers, college students from Southern Florida and kids from town. They all know about it. It's a boy party, like Reverchon Park used to be, except it's the beach and everyone's in bathing suits. It's awesome! They're ready for anything!"

"Please be careful, and I'm not talking about disease."

"I know. You're right. But, Red, these magical places don't last. You have to seize the moment."

"I just don't want the authorities seizing you. If they do, they'll put you away forever. I've had my say."

"Good. Now let me tell you that I just had the best sex I've ever had in my life. There was this one boy, a beautiful blonde teenager."

"Another one?"

"He's eighteen. He's legal. He even had a girlfriend with him, but when I got him alone in the back of his van, he was ready to go. I fucked him, and he fucked me. He was so fucking beautiful, it took my breath away! It still does just thinking about it."

"Stop, you're killing me."

"Red, you've got to come here!"

"It might be sooner than you think."

"What's goin' on? Jonathan?"

"No, Dr. Flo."

"Dr. Flo? The TV bitch?"

"I'll be discussing boy love issues on her show next week."

"With Dr. Flo? On network television?"

"Monday afternoon, CBN, five, eastern. Check it out."

"You have got to be shittin' me! How did you do that?"

"I did it for you."

"Me?"

"I told you it pissed me off how you've been treated. You're a decent, loving person, and it's wrong that they've crucified you like this."

"I would never have come to Clearwater—and I do mean cum."

"You always find the boys, no matter where you are."

"Go, Red! She's not ready for you."

"This is the arena, Darren, at last, my chance to fight the good fight."

"What about Jonathan? What if he sees it? Or his mom? Or your boss? This is some serious shit, Red."

"I'm aware of that."

"Are you sure you want to take this ride?"

"I'm already on it. There's no getting off now."

"I've got one for your boss, if she gives you any shit."

"What's that?"

"That boy I met on the beach, the one I told you about. His name is Billy, young and smooth and gay as a goose."

"I thought you said he had a girl friend."

"You know *that* story. His last name is Barnett. His uncle is Bull Barnett."

"*The* Bull Barnett?"

"The very same. After our tryst in the van, nephew Billy's been over to the house a couple of times. He started tellin' me stories about Uncle Bull, like how he used to sing him to sleep with *The Star-Spangled Banner*. Can you believe that?"

Red laughed, "That's good! So Big Bull has a queer nephew. Ronald Reagan has a queer son. So what?"

"Wait, there's more."

"Don't tell me Uncle Bull got some DNA on little Billy's bunny-rabbits?"

"I think little Billy messed his own bunny rabbits, but Uncle Bull definitely had a hand in it, if you catch my drift."

"That's a hell of a story, if you can prove it."

"I've got it on video tape."

"Bull Barnett?!"

"No, little Billy talking about it. I turned on the camera. He thought it was cool."

"Would he like to get some money for that tape? You, too?"

"How much?"

"Five thousand maybe."

"Split three ways?"

"Each. The networks will pay big bucks for a tape like that."

"You think you could pull it off?"

"There's a chance."

"But how could you prove it?"

"We don't have to prove it happened. The tape speaks for itself. We just have to prove that Billy really is Uncle Bull's nephew."

"How do I do that?"

"Ask him. Maybe he's got proof—a birth certificate, letters, a family photo."

"He might go for it. He's pretty angry with his family for the way they rejected him after he came out. That's why he moved to Florida. I'll see what he says."

"I'll need it by Saturday."

"You're not going on Dr. Flo with that?"

"Ironic, isn't it? Bull Barnett helped create this witch-hunt. Now, he's hoist by his own petard!"

"But how can you sell it, if you give it away on Dr. Flo?"

"Watch the show!"

"It's a promo! Red, you're a genius!"

"Don't give me the Pulitzer just yet. I don't know how any of this is going to play out."

"Yeah, Billy might not want to broadcast his family secrets on the evening news."

"That's what the money's for. Tell him I'll get him five thousand. You, too. But I absolutely must have that proof. Without it, I ain't got dookie."

The phone rang.

It was Penny with important news. She invited him over for cocktails.

In her multi-colored Santa Fe blouse, silver-studded denim vest with matching skirt, and white ropers, she stood on the terrace overlooking the city skyline, clutching her glass of Merlot. Draped with colored stones and more silver, her robust boobs boldly greeted the light of the setting sun. But for the Phrygian cap, she was the Southwest Lady Liberty herself.

"I've settled out my father's estate with my mother, the Evil Queen, and my two wicked step-sisters. I wish they were step-sisters. The thought that I share blood with those gargoyles! Let me tell you, Red, these days, you cannot trust your own lawyer. They just want their piece of me, just like everybody else. I've known Joey since grammar school, and he still screwed me! I took a huge bath, and he was all for it. I'm disappointed and disillusioned! There are nothing but snakes in this town! I've had it!"

"There are snakes everywhere."

"At least, I'm free now, and I got away with a couple of nice properties downtown. I've got the money, and Daddy no longer needs me. There's nothing holding me here. I can go anywhere I want."

"Where is that?"

"Paris."

"What about your high-society lifestyle? Can you leave that behind?"

"I'm taking it with me! We're not going to live like peasants, dear. My society contacts go way beyond Dallas, or haven't you noticed? I'm negotiating right now for a condo in the city. We could be there next month."

"I'm proud of you. You've talked about it for years. Now, you're finally going to do it."

"I said 'we.' I want you to come with me."

"I appreciate the invitation, but I still have a book to finish and a boy to love."

"You can write there just as well as here, and you'll get a much better hearing abroad, especially with me as your agent. I'll make you the toast of Paris! Red Rover will be the poster boy for French sophistication over American philistinism! The new American Gide who had to find his audience in a more refined and tolerant culture. The French will eat it up with a spoon!"

"And the boy?"

"Stay in touch by e-mail. Global relationships are in."

"That's not the kind of touch I had in mind."

"You can invite him over for the holidays, broaden his horizons. I know! The millennium! Invite him to Paris for the millennium!"

"There are other things going on, Penny."

"What could be more important than the millennium in Paris?"

"I'm going on network television next week to talk about boy love. The Dr. Flo show. It has to do with that study I told you about."

"Good work, Richard! This is the perfect credential for your book. Don't forget to mention it. Even if she roasts you—no, *especially* if she roasts you! We can sell it as the book that Dr. Flo hates. When is it on? I'll tape it for you."

The phone rang.

It was Michael, in town for a "leather convention." He invited Red for lunch and suggested they meet at his hotel. Red arrived early and called up to Michael's room. As he waited in the lobby, he eavesdropped the paunchy business Babbitts babbling in their Texas drawl about the leather-clad, tattooed, and body-pierced men who swarmed the hotel. Speaking the word "leather" with leering connotation, the Babbitts congratulated themselves for knowing what was going on, but hadn't a clue.

Red's once bright, smiling boy was teaching a seminar on electricity. His dungeon at home featured an array of clamps and probes with batteries and transformers. The S&M world was a Baskin-Robbins of sexual flavors, beyond the mere "vanilla" (their term) of straight or gay sex.

Tall, lean Michael was now a filled-out man, an HIV survivor in a goatee and leather vest. He showed up followed by his "Boy Tom," but "boy" in this context meant something entirely different from the ped world. Boy Tom was in his mid-forties, slender, quiet, and submissive with a collar around his neck fastened with a chain held in Michael's gloved fist.

At the restaurant, with Michael's permission, Boy Tom described a scene of himself naked, spread-eagle on a wooden table as his scrotum was pinned down needle by needle by the participants surrounding the table. No flinching allowed. Then, they stimulated his anus with electricity. That's when they've really gotcha by the balls.

"Who were these people?" Red inquired.

"About a dozen men in masks and thongs," Michael answered.

"Costuming!"

"Each with his own boy, also in costume."

"A pageant!"

"Was it ever!"

Red turned again to Boy Tom, "Did you like it? Did it feel good?" He shrugged, submitting to Daddy's command to speak only when permitted. "Let me rephrase that. Did it turn you on?" He grinned and nodded.

Michael filled him in, "Red and I were lovers. I was his boy, I mean a real boy. I was sixteen. Red is a boy lover, and I can speak from experience: He is very good at it. His current boyfriend is thirteen, isn't that right?"

"His birthday was just last Christmas. My pageant is listening to his poetry, taking his picture in the golden light of the setting sun, canoeing down a river on a springtime afternoon—all against the backdrop of my friends being spied upon, imprisoned, murdered, their homes torched, their careers ruined, and I'm next. That's my pageant. That's my balls on the table. So at least metaphorically, I can relate, but when it comes to sex, I'm as vanilla as they come."

"Doesn't sound very vanilla to me!" Boy Tom broke the rule, and Michael jerked his chain, literally.

"The fun has just begun." Red told them about Dr. Flo, raising his margarita, "We who are about to die salute you!"

After lunch, they said their goodbyes. Red remembered another goodbye in San Francisco fifteen years ago, when he and Michael stood in the doorway of the Swish Alps apartment, where they were staying and kissed. Their lips parted, and Red took in the glowing beauty of the young man, his eyes and eyebrows artfully shaded and lined like an ancient Egyptian prince by the make-up gal at the after-hours bar called the End-Up, where they ended up after a night of psychedelic dancing in the Castro. It was the last night of their vacation. After a few hours sleep, they would be packing up to return the rental car and hop on a plane back to Dallas. The last night of their love affair—both knew it was winding down. The boy had grown up. He would be graduating college at the end of the year. The last night of the disco era that San Francisco had developed into a nihilistic art form. Already there was talk of a wasting disease that seemed to feed on this lifestyle of unlimited sex and the forty-eight-hour, drug-induced weekend party. So much finality all at once. Red wept as he looked into the smiling Egyptian eyes of his beloved still flushed with the thrill of the night and not seeming to understand any of this.

"This is the end! This is the end of it all!" Red cried without saying specifically what "it" was, because there were too many of them.

Several years after their parting, Michael, too, fell victim to the plague, but survived on the medicines that by then could manage the disease. Red, on the other hand, escaped infection, no doubt in part because he had loved his boy faithfully during those fatal early years.

The phone rang.

Dad again. "I was calling to tell you that I read your book."

"That wasn't the book. That was the first five chapters. The book is almost thirty chapters. So what do you think?"

"It scared hell out of me."

"Good. It had an impact."

"I couldn't sleep after reading it."

"I didn't intend to disturb your sleep—or maybe I did. I want this book to wake people up."

"It's not the book I'm talking about."

"No? I thought that's why you called."

"It's you I'm worried about."

"Dad, you read a work of fiction. That wasn't me."

"No one will believe that. I don't believe that. I know too much of it is true."

"Yeah, my thesis play at theater school took place in Paris, so all my professors thought I used to live in Paris. I've never even been to Paris."

"I just don't want you to go to prison."

"A work of fiction cannot be used as evidence."

"Don't be so sure."

"Yes, that's how far we've come. The thought police are on a roll. It's an evacuation of every legal right we have—free expression, free association, privacy, due process. It's a witch-hunt, and everybody involved knows it, but they don't do anything about it, because they don't want to be next."

"I had a scoutmaster like that once."

"Like what?"

"You know what I mean. When I was twelve, in the Boy Scouts. He had a place on the lake and used to bring the troop out for a weekend of camping and swimming. One night, I was cold, and he invited me up to sleep in his cabin. All the boys laughed, and I didn't know what they were laughing at, so they told me what went on when you got to spend the night with the scoutmaster."

"Did you go?"

"Go? Go where?"

"To spend the night with your scoutmaster?"

"Hell, no! I didn't want my buddies makin' fun of me."

"Somebody went. How else would they know? Do you think you would've gone, if your buddies didn't know?"

"*I* didn't know. You should keep that in mind. Lotta times you might think boys know what's up, because they act like they do, but they really don't know shit."

"Some do, some don't. That whole adult power thing is a myth. The boy has just as much power—more, given the current legal climate—and often as not, he knows exactly what he's doing. It might not have been true for you, but many times the boy seduces the man."

"After a couple of years, our scoutmaster moved us on. No more weekends at the lake house. He was nice about it, very smooth, but we knew what he was doing. He was making room for younger boys, just as he had done the older ones before us. After that, we lost all respect for him."

"Why? Did you want to stay with him forever?"

"No, it was just so obvious. He didn't care about us as individuals. He just wanted young boys."

"That may have been true in the context of taboo, but imagine that he was simply playing a role in the process of your maturity. For example, what if it were allowed as part of your scouting experience that you would sleep with the scoutmaster. If you knew that going in and your parents approved, you would have felt it only natural that he would move you on for younger boys. That was his role."

"But it wasn't that way, and it isn't now, either."

The Moralist

"No, but it has been in other cultures at other times. This taboo is not an absolute. It's a myth and a lie. Your scoutmaster was good to you, but today, he would be put in prison or a nuthouse or both for the rest of his life. Even if he only got put on probation, he would have to post a sign outside his house as a sex offender and risk violence from vigilantes. He'd have to take a peter-meter test and go to brainwashing school to cure him of his 'criminal thinking.' For what? Were you or your buddies permanently scarred by that experience? No. You learned a bit about life and moved on, just like everybody else. This pedophile hysteria is crazy! And it's morally wrong. That's why I wrote that book."

"You're like a bull charging a freight train. I can admire the courage of the bull, but—"

"But he still derails the freight train."

"Do you want to sacrifice yourself for that?"

"I don't intend to."

"You remind me of Don Quixote."

"Funny you should say that. In the book, Red Ryder compares himself to Don Quixote, but not like you mean. You may think I'm being quixotic, but my opponents are real giants, not windmills."

"That's what scares me."

"That freight train might be comin' down the track a lot sooner than you think."

"Why? You're not in trouble already?"

"Worse. I'm gonna be on television."

<u>E-mail</u>

Red:

I got it! He gave me a photo (attached) of him and his uncle in Massachusetts where he grew up. That's Bull Barnett, for sure. I've seen his fat face on TV too damn often! And he signed it on the back: "To my favorite nephew, Billy. Love, Uncle Bull." —Darren

Reply:

That'll work, but electronic images can be altered. I'll have to have the original. Send it along with the tape overnight express. Keep a copy for yourself.

Rod Downey

The video camera mounted on a tripod focused its glassy eye at a single chair in the center of the living room. With tape rolling, Red took his seat in the chair, erect, poised, smiling, and interviewed himself.

A knock at the door interrupted him. A man in a purple jumpsuit handed Red a package and asked for his signature with a stylus on an electronic box.

Closing the door, Red removed a video tape and photograph from the bubble pack. The photo with the inscription on the back was the original of the e-mail version Darren had sent the day before. He popped the video into the VCR.

A willowy young man with long blonde surfer hair and wearing baggies and an open luau shirt seated in a Morris chair spoke to the camera with an effeminate lisp, "Is that thing on?"

Darren's disembodied voice replied, "We're rolling."

"I'm ready for my close-up, Mr. DeMille!"

"What's your name?"

"I hope you haven't forgotten already, Miss Bubble Brain!"

"Just say your name for the camera, Billy."

"Oh, I get it—the 411 on the 911, uh-huh!"

"Your name?"

"Billy Barnett, girl, and don't you forget it."

"You were telling me about your uncle. What's his name?"

"Uncle Bull? Honey, Uncle Bull was my *favorite* uncle!"

"What's his full name?"

"Bull Barnett! Mr. *Death of Decency* hisself. But he wasn't so decent when I came to visit. That was a different story."

"When was that?"

"Six, seven years ago, when I used to live in Massachusetts."

"How old were you?"

"Twelve . . . thirteen."

"So what happened when you came to visit?"

"Well, we were alone in the house one afternoon, and Uncle Bull asked me if I ever, you know, got it off. I said I didn't know how, so he took off my shorts and showed me."

"He masturbated you?"

"My first hand-job, honey, and I loved it! After that, we did it lots of times!"

The Moralist

"Describe another time."

"He used to sing me to sleep with the *Star Spangled Banner*, and my little flagpole was standin' at attention."

"Did he notice?"

"How could he miss it! I was big for my age. Ringling Brothers coulda pitched a circus tent with that pole!"

"What did he do?"

"He just gave me a big squeeze, and next thing I know, he's goin' down on it, hot and heavy."

"With his mouth?"

"Mmmm-hmmm, my first BJ, too!"

"How did you feel about that?"

"It felt great!"

"How long did this relationship continue?"

"A couple of years, till I was fifteen."

"Do you regret that your uncle sexually abused you?"

"Abused? Honey, I wanted it! I was always glad when Uncle Bull came over."

"Why did he stop?"

"I think he was afraid of me, after his book came out. Then, I came out, and that really scared him! He didn't want to have nothin' to do with me after that."

"After he found out you were gay?"

"That's right, him or my parents—right-wing assholes!"

"What did they do?"

"They threw me out of the house. That's when I came down here to live with my sister."

"When was that?"

"Bout a year ago."

"How old are you now?"

"Eighteen. I'm all grown up now, and I got my own life, so fuck those right-wing assholes!" To the camera, "Fuck you, Uncle Bull!"

"You sound bitter about the way he treated you."

"Not about the blow jobs, girl, they were great. I'm bitter about what a liar and a bigot he turned out to be. Right-wing asshole! I want a copy of this tape to send to him. I want him to know how I feel!"

Red dubbed off a few tantalizing sound bites, just enough to suggest there might really be a tape somewhere, and copied the photo on his scanner. Locking the originals in his fireproof safe, he resumed his rehearsal.

Monday morning. The most definitive and irrevocable part of the day was the moment when he stepped into the shower. At dawn, life itself was crepuscular, but when the decision to step into the shower was made, a process was put into motion, and the day began.

Red dressed before the mirror in his Versace suit, French blue shirt and bright red tie. This was how they would see him, youthful and stylish with a big friendly smile. Setting the house alarm, he grabbed his overnight bag and was out the door for a morning flight to New York that would put him in the city just in time for the 4:00 p.m. show.

24

Courts, cops, lawyers, court shows, cop shows, law shows, court-cop-law commercials. The language of the police: "Step away from the taco." "Everything you say can and will be used against you." In our free society, we were obsessed with police and the law. DeToqueville wrote that in America, all culture came down to a matter of law. Ya can do anything ya want, 'long as it ain't illegal. It was the Achilles heel of democracy, because it was possible to pass a law against anything we didn't like, what DeToqueville called "the tyranny of the majority." He didn't take it far enough. Democracy's Final Solution was to put everyone in jail. Like the comic said, "Go back to sleep, America! You're free to do as you're told." For the herd, being real was illegal, being alive was illegal.

> I'm tapin' your show.
> I'm ready to go.
> Are you ready, too?
> I'm comin' to getchoo.

The Big Bang was a consciousness explosion. As dance expressed the harmony of the cosmos, communication was an echo of its original unity, the eternal attempt to knit it all back together again. Communication and love were the same: intercourse.

Red sat quietly in the green room, more rose-colored than green, lined with chairs and sofas and framed photos of TV personalities, including Dr. Flo. The end table between them, strewn with magazines and newspapers, was set with a vase of plastic flowers that only added to the impression of a dentist's waiting room. In one corner, a soda machine and water cooler stood next to a door labeled with male/female icons. Catty-cornered, a TV set was mounted to the wall hospital-style and tuned to Dr. Flo, the sound turned down, and next to it, a clock.

A low murmur of chitchat buzzed among the guests and experts waiting for the show to begin—a handful of concerned parents (of which Red was one), a right-wing pol, an academic, the leader of a "child advocacy" group. Periodically, the make-up gal in a pale green smock led a guest to her chair next door and returned them, tissues emerging from their collars, painted with the seamless pancake mask of television.

No one knew each other. As they informally introduced themselves, each established their place in the show's format and sought to learn where the others fit in. Red was already suspect. In his Versace armor, he looked more like a news anchor than the rest of the "concerned parents" in their baggy suits and frumpy pastel dresses. The pol and the academic, both males, gravitated toward him as one of their own, until they learned he wasn't. When he told them he was concerned about the integrity of science and the undermining of our constitutional freedoms, they coldly drifted away. Now they knew: He was the turd in their punchbowl.

The deck was stacked five-to-one, not to mention the fire-breathing studio audience and the queen dragon herself. But Dr. Flo was not typical free-for-all TV talk, where they put the whole group together to mix it up trailer-trash style. Her format invited call-ins, and so worked best with only one or two guests at a time. How would this group be segmented? Would he be lumped in with the other parents, or set to as contrarian to one or all of the experts, or one-on-one with Dr. Flo?

A producer with a clipboard popped in to explain how things were going to unfold. She looked just like the *Newsline* producer. Why did all TV producers look alike? Always female, always in their little blue or gray suits with their glasses and clipboards. Only their ages varied. She advised them not to leave the green room and to keep an eye on the monitor to see where they were in the show. She reminded them that this was live television. There wasn't time to hunt down a wayward guest. She would come for them here and lead them into the studio and onto the stage where the techs would wire them for sound. She gave no clue as to the order or groupings.

Twenty years ago, Red would have been intimidated by the trappings of network television, but now he was so insouciant it surprised even him. His "second career" was paying off. He'd seen too much of it—the self-absorbed celebrity reporters, the complexity of the technology, the fake-radio stage set with fake skyline background, the boisterous studio audience, the make-up, the lights, the pure theatricality of it with one significant addition: the merciless

The Moralist

camera's eye that projected your being to the attentions of ten million people at once. It heightened the tension of the moment to an excruciating pitch. In an instant, it sucked up the present into its black hole, archiving the past as, the very next moment, the unknowable future awaited its turn. It was easy to see why primitive's feared this distortion of time, when your every movement, facial expression, and tone of voice were captured for replay again and again, where your very soul was stolen and bewitched.

The most frightening discovery was how fast it all went. Live television moved at breakneck speed. You had to know what you were going to say at every moment. Just like the guests on the late-night talk shows had their jokes and anecdotes lined up, you had to have your one-liners ready, but in a not so friendly and funny environment, with a hostile questioner supported by a hostile audience, the lion's den.

Red was well rehearsed, but rehearsal wasn't IT. IT was the river, the current of time. IT was the movement of the moment, unique at every turn. Like canoeing, you can control the canoe but not the river, and Dr. Flo was Class VI white water. He imagined the sunny afternoon with his boy. Ahhh! How refreshing!

The first group was the concerned parents, Red not included. He turned up the volume to hear their sob stories of sexual abuse, themselves, their children. They were professional victims making the rounds. Next came the experts, Red not included. It was clear now. Red was to be the grand finale, mano-a-bitch. The first two segments were tantalizers to whip up the audience, so by the time Red came on, blood was already in the water. Good, he wouldn't have to compete with the other guests for the camera's attention. But he wondered why she was giving him so much air. Her usual M.O. was to give the contrarians a token moment and then ignore them. "She must have something special planned," he thought. So had he, securely patting the cassette snugly tucked into the inner pockets of his jacket and fingering the lucky lock of ruddy blonde hair in the fob of his slacks. He had come to play.

During the commercial break, the producer ushered him through a soundproof door to the wings of the stage. Exiting, the experts glanced ruefully his way. He ignored them, his attention focused on his antagonist in profile bathed in klieg light. She was small and skinny, perched on a tall director's chair like a scrawny little bird of prey with the glassy stare of listening to control-room voices. Beside her, his empty director's chair waited.

The producer led him onto the stage where he took his seat, and techs swarmed around him. The tissues were whisked away, his face touched up, and his body miked with a wireless lavaliere (the mikes on the table were fake). Dr. Flo greeted him with a skeletal grin that wrinkled every inch of her face, like drawing back a curtain. Squatting before them, the head-setted stage manager counted down his fingers and scurried away as ceiling mounted cameras glided in from above like *dei ex machina.*

She spoke to the camera, "Welcome back. We have another concerned father, who has a different perspective on this issue. He says he *supports* the outrageous conclusions of these so-called scientists, so we've decided to let him have his say. Ladies and gentlemen, please welcome Richard Rover." Lackluster applause. "Good afternoon, Richard—may I call you Richard?"

"Certainly," he answered with a big grin. "May I call you Flo?"

"Fair enough. Now, Richard, you are a father, correct?"

"Yes, I have a daughter, Cindy. She's in college now."

"So you don't have any small children."

"She's still my little girl," he smiled warmly.

"I'm sure she is. So what if you discovered your little girl was being molested by some older adult? How would you feel?"

"That's a loaded question, Flo, because the Cobb-Orlofsky study shows that most relationships between adults and young people—men and boys, in this case—are more often positive experiences, and that a loving family environment, a close bond between the parent and child, is crucial to understanding what's going on in the child's life. The real emotional damage comes more often from a dysfunctional home environment than a relationship with an adult outside the home. In fact, such relationships are often a loving sanctuary for the young person whose home life is less than supportive. I know of one young man—he's sixteen, and his lover is twenty-eight. He comes from a family of alcoholics, but he and his lover are clean and sober. His parents are decent people, but his home life suffers from the typical problems associated with alcoholism. In contrast, his life with his lover provides him with the sense of stability he needs to grow into a mature, well-adjusted adult."

"But what about the relationship where the adult seduces the child with gifts and affection or uses the power of adult authority over the child?"

"Examples like that illustrate how hysterical and prejudiced the child-abuse industry is against these kinds of relationships. You can't see the difference between a kidnapper and murderer and a twenty-year-old young man in love with his sixteen-year-old girlfriend, and to me, that just doesn't make any sense at all. I know of a case just like that. A twenty-year-old young man named Adam. He was about to go into the Army. He had a good career planned for himself. But he had sexual relations with his sixteen-year-old girlfriend, and her father found out. The father used the law to get revenge on Adam. He had him prosecuted and put in prison, destroying his career and his life. Adam will never recover from the injustice that was done to him, all because of the hateful, insane, and hysterical attitudes and laws surrounding this issue. That's why I'm here today, to provide an alternative voice to this madness. I am as morally outraged and disgusted at this injustice as you are with the Cobb report."

Stunned by this gently delivered frontal assault, a half-second of shock lit across her face, a shiver of deep mythic disturbance, before she caught her breath and recovered glibly. "Well, it looks like there's plenty of moral outrage to go around, but what concerns me are the hundreds of stories of abuse that I'm hearing from my viewers, and that this phony report is trying to say that's okay."

Cheers.

"So you attack the motives of the authors, because you know the statistical data of this study are sound. In order to be published in the *Journal of the American Society of Psychiatrics,* this study had to go through a ten-month review process. It's the most rigorous peer-review in the entire profession."

"I'm not a statistician, but I know what people are telling me, and they are outraged."

"That's the value of scientific analysis. Drs. Cobb and Orlofsky *are* statisticians. You and I have our anecdotal examples. They have scientific data. This data shows that the commonly held notions about adult-child sexual contact are simply not true."

Jeers.

Dr. Flo addressed the camera. "We're hearing an alternative perspective on pedophilia from concerned father Richard Rover. The lines are open. We'll be right back."

At the commercial break, the techs swarmed in. As his make-up was being touched up, a sound engineer plugged Red's ear with an earpiece, running a wire under his coat to a box fastened to his belt.

"It's for the phone calls," he explained. "So you don't have to rely on the speakers. They're for the audience."

Red kept up his performance, even during the break. He knew the drill: The cameras and mikes were always on. He leaned over to her, not even bothering to cover the mike with his hand. "You are in error about this, Flo, but I appreciate that you allow an opposing point of view."

"It makes good television, and you are awfully articulate on the subject. Have you done this before?"

"No, but as a public relations consultant, I have had some experience with the media."

"You're a writer, too. Isn't that correct?"

"Yes, public relations is a journalistic profession."

"No, I mean creative writing, short stories and the like."

"Some. You've been checking up on me," he smiled.

"I like to do my homework," she smiled back with icy confidence.

So that was it, the ol' Mike Wallace ambush. She had a trump card and was moving in for the kill. Writing. Short stories. Could she have possibly found a copy of *PAN*? He was prepared for that. After all, how was her gambit any different from the tricks he pulled on *Newsline* at the nursing home? But it was a tougher tack. It shifted the focus away from the study to him and his art, a narrow strait in rough water. The Chute!

Returning from the break, the stage manager counted down his fingers again. Red grinned. The warm bright kliegs felt like the sun on a sparkling spring day. Br'er Rabbit was in his briar patch.

"We have a caller, Bernice, from Colorado Springs. Go ahead, please, Bernice."

The disembodied voice emerged from the speakers and through Red's earpiece. "Yes, Dr. Flo, I just wanta say how much I admire what you're doing to expose these child molesters, and it doesn't make sense to me how any real father could be in favor of something like that. They ought to take his child away from a father like that."

"His child is a young adult, Bernice. Do you have a question for our guest?"

"Yes, I just want to ask him if he ain't a child molester hisself, the way he talks."

"Can you take that one, Richard? If I may rephrase, our caller wants to know if you yourself have ever had sexual contact with a child?"

This was it. If he denied it, she would pull out the magazine and throw it in his face. He had to smoke it out of her, piss her off.

"My personal life is not at issue here. I'm more concerned with the real molesters of our civil rights, like Flo Lipschitz and right-wing organizations like the Family Values League, who are conducting a witch-hunt against decent, caring people."

"I wouldn't call child molesters decent, caring people," she shot back. Now, her back was up.

"No, you have to demonize them first to justify burning them at the stake. That's why you have to discredit the authors of the Cobb report and the American Society of Psychiatrics, because you know full well this study corrodes the entire scientific underpinning of your witch-hunt. It exposes that your opinions are based on myth, not fact. The real truth is that by far most love relationships between men and boys are positive, nurturing, and beneficial to the boy's growth to manhood. These kinds of relationships have existed throughout history in cultures around the world, and many of our greatest artists, statesmen, and philosophers from Socrates to Michelangelo to Shakespeare have been boy lovers."

"Are you saying that Shakespeare was a pedophile?"

"His greatest love sonnets were written to a boy. You're a doctor of English literature, Flo. You should know that."

The audience got angry at this—boos, and catcalls.

"He didn't answer my question, Dr. Flo." Bernice interjected.

"I'm not here to discuss my personal life. I'm here to expose the deception that is being perpetrated by Flo and her cronies." He turned to her. "You pass yourself off as a psychologist, but you have no credentials in that field. All you really have to offer are your right-wing political opinions dressed up in scientific mumbo-jumbo that is now proven to be bunk. If anyone has an agenda, it's you."

The audience was growling, and so was she. "And what credentials do you have for your opinions, Mr. Rover?"

"I don't claim any, but the scientists who did this study backed by the American Society of Psychiatrics have plenty."

"Oh, don't sell yourself short! You have more credentials than you let on. You may not want to discuss your personal life—that's fine. But what about your life as a pedophile writer?" There's the wind-up; here's the pitch. She pulled a magazine from under her notes and held it up to the camera's glassy eye. "This should answer our caller's question. I have here a magazine called *PAN*. Can you get a close-up of this? It has the photo of a young boy on the cover. Are you familiar with this publication, Richard?"

"Yes, it's a literary publication. The famous beat poet Allen Ginsberg and the critic-philosopher Michel Foucault have published their writings in that magazine."

"It's a magazine for pedophiles!"

"That's not true. Its editorial focus is on man-boy love relationships."

"That sounds like pedophilia in my book."

"The difference is love."

"You yourself are a contributor to this magazine, isn't that so?" Without waiting for an answer, she thumbed the pages, "In this very issue, there's a short story called *The Moralist* with your name on it. Did you write this story?"

"Yes, it's about the positive love relationship between a boy and his mentor, exactly the kind of relationship we've been talking about."

"It's about a sexual relationship between a thirteen-year-old boy named David and a fifty-year-old pedophile named Red Ryder! That wouldn't be you, would it, Mr. Richard Rover?"

"No, it's fiction. But I would certainly be proud to have the kind of positive, loving relationship the story describes."

She addressed the camera. "I want my viewers to know that this story describes a sexual encounter that is too filthy to read on the air." She turned back to Red. "But there is one passage I can read that I'd like you to respond to, Richard."

Red smiled graciously, "Please do, and I want to thank you, Flo, for sharing my work with your viewers."

"In the story, the fifty-year-old character Red Ryder has a conversation with a friend about his relationship with David: The friend asks, 'What if David came on to you? What would you do?'

"Red Ryder replies, 'I wouldn't think twice. I'd love every minute of it.'

"A thirteen-year-old boy?'

"They are very sexual at that age. I could never reject him, if that's what he wanted."

She put down the magazine. "Is that how you feel about boys, Richard?"

"That's how the character in the story feels, but—" Groans from the audience. Flo rolled her eyes. "Let me finish!" he fairly shouted, and things got quiet. He continued, "Yes, the love relationship in that story is positive and nurturing, and it is typical of the loving relationship described in the Cobb report."

"So you approve of relationships like that?"

"Absolutely! That's why I'm here, and by the way, that story is just the beginning. It's a sketch for my full-length novel, also called *The Moralist*, that takes the whole issue much further. You think that story's a knock-out? Wait till you read the book!"

"I think that story is pornographic filth. Just like the Cobb report, it's a high-minded excuse for having sex with children. So is this story based on your own experience, Richard?"

"The entire book is based on my own experience."

"Then to answer our caller's question, you are a pedophile."

"No, I'm an artist and a concerned father. As I said, the love relationship between Red Ryder and David is typical of the positive, nurturing experience described in the Cobb report."

"Sex between men and boys is not love. It's perversion."

"That's your opinion. That's the point. All you have are opinions, but science has the truth, and you can't change that by shouting it down."

"The phony science! Your bogus science!" She was riled, speaking to the camera. "I want my viewers to understand what's going on here. You see here before you an example of what I've been talking about. Mr. Rover here says he's a concerned father who wants to defend this phony report, but he's really a pedophile advocate. He's a part of the pedophile conspiracy that wants to normalize sex with children!"

Applause, jeers.

"That's preposterous! You're a Jew, Ms. Lipschitz. Does that make you part of the worldwide Zionist conspiracy? There are plenty of hate-mongering bigots who might think so."

"I don't write for their publications, and there's no doubt in my mind that the boy called David in your story is real."

"You're free to think that."

"Then you don't object if I do a little investigating. I'm going to find your young David, or whatever his real name is, and bring him on this show. Maybe, we'll invite the police, too, just in case we need them. Do you think you'd like to join us for that, Richard, or will you be packing your bags to get out of the country?"

"That should be quite a trick, Flo, since David is an invention of my imagination."

"A perverted imagination!"

Taking the video tape from his pocket, "That's a matter of opinion, but I do have a video tape here of a real boy talking about a real relationship with his uncle."

"I think we've heard enough of this."

"You might know his uncle—Bull Barnett."

"What is this?" she hissed.

"Bull Barnett, author of *The Death of Decency*. He testified before Congress last winter." Taking out the photo and holding it up to the camera. "See? This is a photo of Uncle Bull and his little nephew Billy. Billy is twelve in the picture. Of course, he's older on the tape."

"What are you saying?"

"Why not let Billy speak for himself? He's very explicit."

"I will not allow you to smear the reputation of a respected author and moral leader on my show!"

"You can't stop boy love, Flo. It has existed for thousands of years, sometimes where you least expect it."

Commercial break. The audience was stirring, growling, frothing at the mouth, and Dr. Flo didn't have the security of a Jerry or Geraldo. Sensing the threat, she addressed them directly in measured tones that barely concealed her own rage, "Please! The purpose of our show is to address controversial issues, and that includes the airing of all sides. We may not agree with Mr. Rover, but I trust that everyone here will behave like mature adults. This is not Jerry Springer." Her Jewish mother bit, that made her famous, quieted them down. Security appeared, and the studio grew silent.

Red was not relieved. He was alone here, and security was an even greater threat.

She turned to him, covering the mike with her hand. "I'd have to preview that tape before we could air it," she explained in conciliatory tones, skeletal claw extended.

"Maybe another time," he smiled pleasantly, slipping the tape into his jacket.

Her color changed. "I'm gonna nail you, buster!" The red light came on, and she spoke to the camera. "Today we have seen first-hand the smear tactics being employed by the pedophile conspiracy against me and anyone who stands for morality and decency."

Red broke in, "*This* is the smear tactic! What you see here is the smear tactic!"

"Are you going to try to shout me down on my own show?"

"This is the same tactic of personal attack and character assassination that you've used against Cobb and Orlofsky. You can't dispute the science, so you try to shout it down with your right-wing opinions dressed up with an English literature degree and a talk show. Flo Lipschitz, you are the Rush Limbaugh of the behavioral sciences!"

"Now, who's engaging in personal attack?"

"Attack? I thought you'd take that as a compliment!" he smiled good-naturedly.

Even the audience had to laugh at this as the theme stinger cued. She addressed the camera pleasantly, "Well, on that humorous note—and Rush, if you're watching, I hold you in the highest regard—we're out of time for now. But I want to make a solemn promise to my viewers who trust me and my show." The camera sailed in close. "Dr. Flo is going to get to the bottom of this. We will find this boy David that Mr. Rover claims to be an invention of his imagination, and we will investigate the truth of his libelous allegations against Bull Barnett. Richard, I assure you, you have not heard the last of Dr. Flo. This is Dr. Flo; you're on the air."

The cameras instantly withdrew like flying saucers, their big red cop lights blinking off, but Red remained wired to the chair. As the tech disconnected him, he sighed with satisfaction, "Now *that* was good television!"

Flo motioned over security. "Stay with Mr. Rover until he leaves the building. I don't want any trouble."

"Thank you, Flo. That's very kind of you," he smiled and dismounted the stool.

Walking away, he overheard her whispered growl, "I want that tape."

A guard stood in the wings. The other was walking toward him. Red took a sharp left and bolted into the auditorium where the audience was still filing out, unmindful of the sudden drama unfolding behind them. The cameras were off. The show was over. Red melded into the crowd, amazed that no one recognized him from only moments before. For the herd, he only existed in the context of the show, his fifteen minutes. Now, he was nobody once again.

He pushed through the crowd into the front lobby and made his way for the glass doors, but two more guards collared him from behind and escorted him out through a side door with the polite muscle of mob goons, the words "pervert" and "child molester" deliberately audible under their breath. Out on the sidewalk in the warm spring sunshine, he felt for the tape in his pocket. It was gone. He wished he could be a fly on the wall when she reviewed that tape and discovered only a few innocuous sound bites. Mission accomplished, but it hadn't gone at all like he'd rehearsed. It never did.

Rod Downey

His itinerary allowed for a night on Times Square at the Broadway Millennium after the show and a flight back to Dallas the following morning, but it was time to go now. He packed his bag, checked out, and took a cab to LaGuardia. The ticket was full-fare, so he rebooked and was asleep in his own bed by midnight.

25

On the plane home, Red considered the irrevocable impact this day would have. Dr. Flo was only the beginning. He had taken his stand, whatever the consequences, and there would be many.

There were those in his life for whom this new idea of who he was would come as a horrific shock. For himself, it meant at long last becoming the person he had always been but had concealed from all but his closest friends and allies. What lay before him was exhilarating, scary, but more a relief than a concern. The so-called "double life" he had both forged and fallen into, in order to meet the demands of art and career, was over. He never feared being "found out," for he had always lived his life with the full knowledge that eventually this day would come. He had merely been discreet, a very conservative approach of which Faye would certainly approve, ironically, since she would be the most horrified.

For all her vaunted hipness, Faye had the soul of a prude. Once, while searching for an old client file in the office attic, he'd stumbled across a box from the late eighties labeled "President's Commission on Pornography." She had once been a member of the hated "Meese Commission," a key driver of the witch-hunt. And then there was that time last winter when the office thermostat was on the fritz. Her nose actually did turn blue. After he left her employ, Faye would become his enemy.

But she wasn't so much the issue as his entire PR career, which the events of the past twenty-four hours may have already brought to a screeching halt, or more accurately, driven full-speed over a cliff. It was unlikely Faye saw the show. But she would very quickly hear about it, he thought, knowing how much she lived by, for, and on the opinions of others. He needed an exit strategy. He would miss his work at the agency.

Then there were those he loved. They already knew and approved, or at least accepted, him but would nonetheless have to weather this storm by association, and he didn't want to hurt them. Even Penny might turn from him, as her friends condemned her for associating with someone like that. She hated her society world but also clung to it. This would be the acid test. She wanted to chuck it all and escape to Paris. Let's see if she could really live without that world for which she claimed so much contempt.

Cindy, too, could suffer when word got out that her father was a child molester. He would instruct her how to respond with a positive image of a loving father, a committed artist, and a man speaking out against injustice. She could carry it off, but not so for Achi's Orthodox family. It would destroy Red utterly if she should lose her fiancé because of him. He doubted that would happen. Achi was loving, loyal, and understanding, but his parents were another story.

He'd bested Dr. Flo, but she would make good on her threat to sic her dogs on him. That no doubt included law enforcement, but there was no predicting how it would play out. Like chess, all you had to work with was the ever-changing web of the moment.

Dr. Flo had vowed to find "David." Would Jonathan betray him? It was more than possible, but Red would not blame his beloved. He was well aware of the chicanery and abuse the cops were capable of. He knew who the bad guys were.

Even if Dr. Flo didn't find Jonathan, word of Red's performance would surely get back to his family. *Call Dr. Flo* aired in the afternoon. Jon and Melanie both worked, and Jonathan was at school. It was doubtful any of them saw it. Even among those family and friends who may have seen the show, only a handful knew Red well enough to make the connection. But all it took was one afternoon TV junkie to collapse that house of cards.

If the kids at school found out that Jonathan's mentor was a boy lover, the conclusion would be obvious. He would be teased and ostracized. Even though his name had never been mentioned, he might feel with some justification that Red had betrayed him. Not to mention Jon and Melanie, who might come to hate him for disrupting their contented life and bringing unhappiness to their happy son.

Wild cards: the book, the tape. Now that his career in communications was over, his career as an artist had finally begun. Only one thing was certain: There was no turning back. When things went bad with Mark, there were moments of terror. Red was at the mercy of the boy's recklessness, and he knew it. Now, as the fabric of his life was being shredded at his own hands, he was strangely calm. Dr. Flo was only the first battle. The war would continue, and now it really was personal.

Some of what he foresaw actually happened, along with a lot more that he never imagined. When he arrived home, there were messages waiting.

Darren left a message on his answering machine: "You did it, dude! You cooked that bitch's ass! Call me!"

Red called back but got Darren's machine. He left his response: "Thanks for the kudos, but the fun has just begun. I'm shopping the tape. I'll let you know how it goes."

E-mail

Red:

Congratulations on standing up to Dr. Flo. I saw the whole thing! You were awesome! Were you expecting her to read from your story? I thought you were dead meat when she pulled that rabbit out of her hat, but you handled it. You were so amusing and cool. I could never have done that! —Noah

Noah:

She tried to pin the "conspiracy" label on me. But that's the beauty of my position. I'm nobody. I'm not a scientist. I'm not a member of any organization. I only speak as an artist talking about my art. —Red

Red slept well that night. The following morning, he reported to the office just as any other day, but of course, it wasn't. He could tell that the piranha knew what was up from the silence that greeted him as he walked through the door. This was their moment of triumph, but their satisfaction was soured by his handing it to them on a silver platter. One nice thing about being an exhibitionist—you never got caught with your pants down. Chief piranha nose-in-the-air snidely presented the news: Faye wanted to see him right away, a "close the door" meeting.

Sitting behind her desk, Faye was pale and agitated, as if she were the one who wasn't getting any sleep.

"I can't believe what I've been hearing," she began. "Were you on Dr. Flo yesterday defending pedophilia? Do you write kiddie porn stories? Did you accuse Bull Barnett of being a pedophile? Am I going crazy, or is it just you?"

"No, no, no, and, Faye, you're not looking well."

"Do you deny going on that show? Apparently, everybody in the world saw it, except me!"

"I was on the show, but I was there to speak in support of a statistical analysis debunking current myths about child sexual abuse. The study says—"

"I don't give a damn what the study says!" she screamed in near hysteria. "The study is not the issue! Why didn't you tell me about this?"

"It didn't concern you. I know we don't see eye-to-eye on certain issues."

"Don't see eye-to-eye! That is the understatement of the century! And anytime you go on national network television defending kiddie porn, that concerns me!"

"You didn't see it. You know my writing is on the edge. I told you a long time ago, 'In my personal life, I'm discreet; but in my art, I don't pull no punches.'"

"You didn't tell me you wrote kiddie porn!"

"I don't, and I wish you would stop calling it that. You read my short story. If that was such a problem, why didn't you mention it then?"

"All right, I confess, I just read a few scenes. I guess I missed the juicy parts."

"You didn't tell me that. Your only comments were that I write with a lot of anger and don't show it around the office. Like that was something I might actually do!"

"I am flabbergasted! You've been working here for five years, but now it's like you're a completely different person, like I'm meeting you for the first time. I guess we never really know anyone."

"I was only being discreet. Isn't that what all your conservative cronies preach? If you have to be gay, keep it in the closet?"

"Gay? This goes way beyond gay. I figured you were gay! And by the way, discretion ends on network television, or haven't your twenty years working with the media taught you anything?"

"I talked about my perspective and my art, not my personal life."

"You didn't have to!"

"How do you know? You didn't see the show. You didn't read my story. You're making snap judgments based on what other people have told you."

"But that's what counts! You should at least understand that. You talk about it. You write about it. That means you *are* it."

"Yes, I'm a boy lover. Now you know. And I'm not the only one, either."

"Oh, God, the Bull Barnett thing! That really iced it! Did you accuse him of being a pedophile? Yes or no, and don't bullshit me, Red. I invented it."

"I told you no. I didn't have to. His gay nephew speaks very fondly of their relationship when he was twelve. I have that on video tape."

"I can't take any more of this. You have no idea the embarrassment this is causing me. Richard, you have stabbed me in the back!"

"I'm sorry you feel that way. It was not my intent."

"You know you can't continue on here."

"Why not?"

"Why not?" Her voice was in high-decibel. "You know very well why not!"

"No, I don't. I spoke out in support of science over ignorance and bigotry. You're firing me, because you disagree with my opinions?"

The suggestion of wrongful termination knocked her back on her heels. "Well, I wouldn't call it firing. I always maintain relationships, you know that."

"Ya gonna maintain this one?"

She sighed, and was there a smile? "No, I guess not."

"So why are you firing me?"

"For misconduct that reflects badly on the agency. It's right there in the employee manual."

"And what misconduct is that?"

"Writing child pornography."

"You were on the President's Pornography Commission. You know that child pornography refers to images, not words."

"Writing any kind of pornography!"

"You've read my writing. You didn't call it pornography then."

"Are you going to sue me? Is that where this is going?"

"No, I think we can work out an appropriate severance."

"Severance? You want severance? As of yesterday afternoon, you won't be able to work for me or anyone else in public relations. Your career is toast, mister, and that's an argument I can sell in court."

"Faye, that was brilliant! Your Hollywood days are not over."

"Are you taping this? I wouldn't be surprised."

"Calm down. You're getting way too paranoid."

"Are you taping this or not?"

"No, but I'm flattered you would think so."

"Obviously, you have thought this through. What do you want?"

"Full salary and benefits for the next year, and ten thousand dollars right now. You pay for legal to dot the i's and cross the t's. That's a good deal. That's cheap."

"That's blackmail."

"You will never see me again, except maybe on the evening news."

"On your way to prison."

"Tell your friends I did it on my own time. You knew nothing about it, which is true. The next day, I came to the office to get my things, and I disappeared forever, which will also be true."

"Richard, what have you done? You had something good here. Everyone liked you. I don't understand why you've done this."

"I'm an artist first. Is that a yes?"

She gathered herself up and sat down, filling out a form. "I'm authorizing Brenda to cut you a check for ten thousand."

"Can she do it now?"

"It has to go through our accountant."

"No, it has to be right now. You can take care of the paperwork later."

Sighing with frustration, she retrieved a suede checkbook from her purse and wrote it out, "I'm sorry for you, Richard."

"You ought to be proud. Dr. Flo pulled out the guns of Navarrone on me, but I turned 'em back on her, and she knows it. I guess my twenty years' working with the media taught me something, and you've been an important part of that."

"I take no credit. If you think that disaster was a success for you, you're in worse shape than I thought."

"Why not? In one interview, I have accomplished what you've been chasing after for twenty years—instant celebrity."

Handing him the check, "There's a difference between celebrity and notoriety."

"There's no such thing as bad publicity. Hey, I might need your help."

"That's not in the business plan."

"No? You went to bat for the tobacco lawyers. Your right-wing buddies didn't like that, either." He tore up the check. "I've got a better idea. Why don't you represent me? Consider this a first-month's retainer. We'll knock 'em dead!"

She stared, stunned, then shook her head incredulously. "Have you gone completely insane? What do you have against me, Richard? I've always liked you."

"Okay, one more idea: twenty thousand lump sum right now, and I walk out of your life forever. Clean deal, no strings, no hassle, no lawyers."

She saw the wisdom. The check cleared.

Flo was easy. Faye was easy. Jonathan would rip his heart out. That evening, he called.

"You told! You tell me to keep a secret, and then you go and blab it on television!"

"I didn't. Did you see it?"

"No, but I heard about it."

"Your name was never mentioned. We talked about art and science."

"You didn't have to. If everybody thinks you're Chester Molester, what does that make me?"

"Everybody doesn't think that. Most people don't know anything, so let's keep it that way. How did you hear about it?"

"Aunt Ariel told Mom and Dad." Red remembered the fiery-haired woman from Jonathan's birthday party. "She never misses that show."

"What did your parents say?"

"They asked me about you, and I told 'em it was bullshit. Dr. Flo don't like what you're sayin', so she's tryin' to make you look bad. She's narrow-minded."

"Did they ask you about sex?"

"Yeah."

"What did you say?"

"No we don't, no we haven't, no we never have."

"You're great! Bosie was right. It's the love that dare not speak its name."

"They said they want to talk to you."

"Really? That's the best news I've heard all day!"

"Why? You know what they're gonna say."

"I'll give 'em the same answer you did. Talking is good. If they'd already made up their minds, they'd forbid you to see me, and that would be that."

"I wouldn't do it. I'd sneak out."

"You've got guts, you little daredevil, but your mom and dad are not the problem. Dr. Flo said she was going to find you, and she's got the resources to do it."

"No way I'm goin' on television."

"Forget television. She'll get the cops involved, and they'll use you to get to me."

"I ain't tellin' nobody nothin'."

"Good, but we need to be a lot more careful now. If the cops show up, remember this. They can't interrogate you without your mom or dad present, but you have to ask for them. Ask for a lawyer, too. They'll probably come up with some excuse to deny you, but you have to ask. Second is good cop, bad cop. You know the drill—one of 'em's nice, and the other one's a sonofabitch. It's a trick to get you to confess to the nice one. And another thing, no more phone calls. If you contact me again by phone, I will assume the cops put you up to it. No more e-mails, either, except as a warning. Let's see, we need a code word. 'Oberon.' Write this down: 'O-b-e-r-o-n.' If the cops are involved, send me an e-mail with the word 'Oberon' in it, and after it goes through, hit 'Delete.'"

"This is fun. What does 'Oberon' mean?"

"He's a character from Shakespeare. Oberon is king of the fairies."

The boy giggled, "You're crazy, dude!"

A long silence.

"Are you there? Are you okay?"

"Yeah," he whispered with tears in his voice. "I still wish ya hadn't done it."

Red didn't have to shop the tape. The networks were shopping him by e-mail:

Mr. Rover:

Please contact me concerning the videotape you referred to on *Call Dr. Flo*. We are interested.

Sincerely,
Harley Spitz, TBC News

The Moralist

Mr. Rover:

I would like to discuss your Bull Barnett videotape. Please reply.

Yours,
Marilyn Ross-Kendricks, WNN

Mr. Rover:

The producers of *Call Dr. Flo* tell me that your tape of Bull Barnett's nephew is a fake. But they won't say how they know that, since they've never seen it. If you have such a tape as you described on her show and can prove its authenticity, I'd like to talk with you.

Cordially,
Fodor Heinz, National Democratic Committee

There were half a dozen of them. How'd they get his e-mail? Dr. Flo? The cops? This was not a good sign. There was a private mailbox store near the Crossroads. He could mix a drink, "walk the Lawn," and rent a box. He drove across town instead.

<u>E-mail, Red's blanket reply</u>

Please send your bid to Richard Rover, at Box 483456PMB, 289 Lunar Rd., Dallas, Texas 75224, (972)384-2865, overnight express. High bidder will be notified by e-mail on Thursday night. Tape available by Saturday. Authenticity guaranteed. Bidding starts at $15,000.

Jonathan, his parents, and Red gathered in the cluttered living room. The tall, skinny man, his overweight wife, and their son sat side-by-side like a family portrait on the dumpy sofa, Red across from them on a rickety wooden chair. It was the moment he'd been waiting for, just like in the book, where he'd vow his love and ask their blessing. Well, not exactly.

"Is there anything sexual between you and Jonathan?" Jon Sr. asked Red point-blank.

Jonathan jumped up angrily, "I told you no! Don't you believe me?" He stomped across the room and collapsed a fuming heap in an overstuffed chair.

"We want to hear what Red has to say," Melanie said calmly.

"No," Red lied and moved on to the truth, "but I'm committed to his happiness and well-being, and that will not change, as long as he—and you—allow me to be a part of his life."

"But why? What do you want from him?"

"I love him. It's really that simple."

"We thought so, too, until you showed up on television. I don't mind telling you, Richard, we were shocked."

Jonathan burst in, "Shocked at what? Shocked at what?"

She was embarrassed, afraid to tackle the subject head-on. Ignoring her son, she spoke directly to Red. "You have branded yourself, and we can't support you in that."

Red made it easy for her. "You mean that I'm a boy lover?"

"Yes."

"Did you see the show?"

"No."

"It wasn't about me. It was about the witch-hunt hysteria that's poisoning the relationships between parents and their children, teachers and their students, mentors and their protégés, just as it's poisoning my relationship with you and Jonathan right now."

"That may have been what you said, but that's not what people heard."

Jonathan exploded, "What did they hear? Say it! Why can't you say it? Red is a child molester! Isn't that what you mean?"

"I don't think that, but some people do," Jon stated flatly to Red.

"Who? Aunt Aerial?" the boy queried sarcastically.

"And Ernie's mom," Melanie added. "She saw the show. She warned me about you, and she warned Ernie, too. He won't be allowed to go on any more trips to the arcade, that's for sure."

"That is crap!" Jonathan cried.

"Don't talk to your mother like that," his father broke in.

"Ernie thinks Red's cool," the boy explained to her. "He said he wished he had somebody like Red to take him fun places and talk to and stuff. Red's my friend, and friends stand by each other."

"Ernie needs a father, and Dora Fletcher is a smothering neurotic," Jon added.

Melanie continued, "All the same, we have to live here."

"Who cares what Ernie's mom thinks? Does she make the rules?" Jonathan cried, and no one answered. He grew quiet and sullen.

The Moralist

Melanie turned to Red and cut him to the quick, "Are you in love with him?"

To lie about sex was discretion; to lie about love was betrayal. "Yes, I think I've made that clear," Red replied simply and honestly, "but if you want me to make myself scarce, until things calm down, I can do that. If anyone asks, just tell them I was Jonathan's mentor and a positive influence on his education and his character—if that's how you feel, of course."

"I do feel that way. I think we all do," Melanie concluded.

"I might add that you and Jon have been exceptionally open-minded and fair about this. I appreciate that."

"I don't. It's not fair!" Jonathan exploded again. "Why should Red and I suffer because of what other people think? I'm sicka what other people think!"

"It's not just that," Red reminded the boy. "Remember what we talked about?"

"What?" Melanie wanted in on the secret. "Can you share it with us?"

"Dr. Flo threatened to find Jonathan and bring him on her show," Red explained. "She has the resources to do it, even the police, who might contact you."

"We have nothing to hide," Jon declared with confidence.

"The witch-hunt can get pretty nasty," Red cautioned him.

"I've had my share of experience with the cops," the old hippie reassured him with a toothless smile.

No doubt he had, but it was cold comfort. They didn't ask for this. They were the same loving innocents they'd always been, but when the cops started tightening the noose, Jon and Melanie weren't going to fight Red's battles for him. They would take the course of least resistance to protect themselves and their son.

On the way home, Red picked up his mail at the PMB.

Dear Mr. Rover:

CBN News is prepared to pay you $20,000 for the videotape we have discussed with the following conditions:

- That you can verify the identity of the speaker on the tape.

- That you provide us with a signed and notarized release from the speaker to use his name and image (copy enclosed).

Rod Downey

- That CBN News owns the original tape and all copies with unlimited exclusive rights to use it in any manner we see fit. The enclosed licensing agreement must be signed and notarized.

Please reply immediately by e-mail: apons@cbn.com

Sincerely,
Alicia Pons, producer

E-mail

Dear Ms. Pons:

Along with the tape, I can provide you with a family photo of the nephew and his uncle, taken when the boy was twelve (he is eighteen now). Bull Barnett is clearly recognizable. On the back of the photo is a handwritten inscription: "To Billy, my favorite nephew. Love, Uncle Bull."

As soon as I receive payment, the original tape and the photo will be yours with unlimited exclusive rights. I will keep one copy of each for myself.

I assume you will want to send someone to view, approve, and take possession. They should also be prepared to authorize wire transfer of the payment by phone while they are here. Once the transfer is complete, the tape and photo are yours. No cash or checks please. I will make the necessary arrangements to meet your representative at a storefront video facility here in Dallas on Saturday and will hand over the tape, the photograph, and the necessary paperwork at that time. Please provide me with your representative's travel schedule and cell phone number.

Sincerely,
Richard Rover

Darren:

It's a done deal with CBN! Attached is a release for Billy to sign before a notary TODAY. Send it back to me overnight express, early delivery. As soon as I have money in the bank, I will overnight you two cashier's checks for $5000 each, one in your name, one in Billy's. But I MUST have that signed release in hand tomorrow. —Red

American Daily News

Controversial Sex-Abuse Study Won't Be Reviewed.
Review group says science is sound.
By Brock Sterling

The American Society of Psychiatrics (ASP) has abandoned plans to commission an independent review of a controversial child sex-abuse study, sometimes known as the Cobb Report, after the nation's largest scientific organization refused to examine the work, saying it has "grave concerns" over "politicization" of the study's conclusions.

The ASP promised to ask for the review after a resolution condemning the study unanimously passed both houses of Congress. The study, written by researchers from Philadelphia University, has become a *cause célèbre* among conservative groups and nationally syndicated television talk-show host "Dr. Flo" Lipschitz.

In the face of scorching criticism, the ASP took the extraordinary step of publicly distancing itself from the research, saying that it would ask an independent organization, the American Council of Scientific Standards (ACSS), to reexamine the validity of the study, which already had gone through an extensive peer review process.

"No clear evidence"

The ACSS told the ASP that it would not review the study. In his letter to the ASP, Lawrence Birch, a physicist who chairs the ACSS Committee on Scientific Methodology, said his committee saw "no reason to second guess the peer review process." Although it did not do a thorough review of the study and cautioned that its decision not to take on that project should not be seen as an endorsement, the committee also "saw no clear evidence of improper procedures or other questionable practices on the part of the article's authors." Controversy about the study would best be resolved, the letter said, by more research and discussions among scientists in the field.

Harsh words for conservative critics.

"Some of the political statements about this study are clearly self-serving," Birch said in an interview yesterday. "I think some politicians tried to cash in on public sentiment by purposely distorting what the study says."

In a written statement, the authors of the study, Professors Russell Cobb, Ph.D., and Noah Orlofsky, Ph.D., responded to the ACSS decision, saying it was vindication of their work. "The ACSS stamp of approval confirms that our science is solid," the statement said.

But the ACSS decision carried little weight at the office of Rep. Buddy Hines (R., Texas), one of the sponsors of the resolution condemning the study. "Any fool knows that sex with children is wrong, and some pointy-headed research paper is not going to convince me otherwise," he said. —###

E-mail

Red:

Did you see the news? The ACSS has refused to review us! That's our vindication, and I truly believe that you made an important difference. Your appearance on Dr. Flo forced the scientific community to close ranks against the witch-hunt hysterics. —Noah

Noah:

Maybe it helped get them off their butts, but the motives of the ACSS had little to do with me. They don't have a dog in this fight, and they're not stupid. The ASP was trying to pass the buck, and the ACSS was having none of it. But thanks anyway. —Red

> Mark called. "Dude, you were on television!"
> "Yeah, did you see it?"
> "No, but Tammy did. She said you were talkin' about me."
> "What? I never mentioned you."
> "I mean about us, about . . . you know."
> "I talked about boy love as an issue in science and art."
> "But Tammy recognized your name. She started asking me questions."
> "About you and me?"
> "I told her everything, dude!"
> "That wasn't smart. I'm surprised at you, Mark. You more than anyone should know better than that."
> "I had to. I couldn't lie."
> "Why not? You're so good at it," Red rebutted sarcastically.
> He didn't get it. "She's my wife, dude. That's different. I tell her everything."

The Moralist

"You never did before. Why now?"

"You weren't on TV before. She wasn't my wife before. She hears you talking about how you like boys and all that chicken hawk crap, what's she supposed to think?"

"But I didn't."

"That's not what she heard."

"Why didn't you just stick to your story? It's true."

"It's not the whole truth. I didn't want her to think I was queer."

"I'm not sure if telling her the intimate details of our relationship was the best way to accomplish that."

"She says you abused me. She says you're a child molester."

"Great. Let me take the blame. You're off the hook."

"She says I wouldn'ta had all the problems I did. I woulda been okay, if it wasn't for you."

"Then, I guess you didn't tell her how, after we broke up, I continued to support you, how I gave you a car and an apartment of your own, how I gave you my furniture and helped you fix the place up, how I found you a job which you couldn't keep, because all you wanted to do was lie around and watch television and smoke pot all day. And what did I get for my trouble? You lied to me. You broke into my house and stole from me. I guess you didn't tell her any of that."

"No," he lowered his voice with shame at the memory of his past.

"Does she know that before I even met you, your own father had you committed to the Adolescent Care Unit at Heugley for behavior disorder? Did you tell her how you used to get it on with the boys at the ACU?"

"It wouldn't matter! She'd just say that's how you took advantage of me—'cause I was fucked up."

"So I took advantage of you, because you're fucked up, and you're fucked up, because I took advantage of you? That's fucked up."

"Maybe so, but now, she's all freaked out about it! Why did you have to go on fuckin' television and tell the world?"

"I didn't."

"You might as well have, and now it's fuckin' up my life, and it could fuck up yours, too."

"Nothing has changed in your life. Go ahead and live it and forget about me."

"I can't now."

"Why not?"

"She wants me to go to the cops."

"Oh, for crissakes! Do you know how ridiculous that is?"

"I do, but she don't."

"What's she gonna do? Fuck up her whole life, because of something she saw on TV? I hope she's not that stupid."

"She takes this shit ser'ous, dude."

"Tell her to forget about it. That was ten years ago. The statute of limitations has run out. Even if you did go to the cops, they'd tell you the same thing. Go home and forget about it. It's over. I gotta go."

Red hung up the phone. He had broken every rule in the book with that conversation. The social poison at work. What if he taped it? Would he follow through? If so, the cops would be at his door. The phone rang. He listened as the machine picked it up.

"Hi, Dad, sorry I missed you."

He snatched up the receiver, "Cindy?"

"Oh, there you are. Screening your calls again?"

"With good reason."

"You're not in trouble, are you?"

"Worse, I was on television. I guess you didn't see it."

"No, when was it on?"

"Last Monday, I was a guest on *Call Dr. Flo* defending boy love."

"Network! I'm impressed! Why didn't you tell me, so I could watch it?"

"I wasn't sure I wanted you to."

"How'd it go?" she cautiously inquired.

"I kicked butt! Wait'll ya see it!" Red erupted with delight. "I'll send you a copy of the tape. She tried to ambush me, but I turned it into a commercial for my book!"

"Go, Dad! You da man!"

"Wait, there's more. I've gotten hold of some sensational video. Real scandal."

"Not about you, I hope."

"No, I'm sellin' it to the networks. It'll be headline news. I've also quit my job, and I met with Jonathan's parents this afternoon. They're on my side, for now."

"You're on the roller coaster."

"Yes, I am, but you called me."

"It's about Achi."
"He heard something? What'd he say?
"He asked me to marry him."
Red laughed and cried, "My baby!"
"He got on his knees and everything. It was sweet. He's so old-fashioned!"
"I know! He asked me for your hand six months ago. I was wondering when he was going to get around to it."
"You knew?"
"Everyone did, except you."
"He gave me a big, fat rock, too!"
"I'm so happy for you!" Wiping tears from his eyes, he paused to catch his breath. "This is all the more reason I don't want to fuck up your life with my art."
"How do you mean?"
"You and me, it's old hat to us. We've been talking about this stuff for years, and I don't know how much you've told Achi about me, but people are going to start branding me as a child molester, not because of anything I've done, but the things I'm saying publicly, and you'll probably hear about it. If anybody asks, tell them that you're proud of my courage for standing up against the witch-hunt mentality that is polluting our culture and shredding our civil rights."
"That's good. I can do that, but I don't want you to get hurt, Daddy."
"I'm okay. It's your world I'm concerned about. Not Achi so much—he loves you. But Nick and Barbara are very conservative."
"They like you."
"I know, but they won't understand. I don't expect them to agree with me. In some ways, you don't. But it's important that they understand this is a matter of art and politics. It's not personal." He was silent for a moment, then burst into loud laughter. Recovering, "I can't believe I just said that. It's as personal as it gets."
"Don't worry, I'll be okay."
"You're so confident. I admire you for that."
"You've always been my funny Daddy."
"And you are my brilliant and beautiful girl. It's going to be hard to give you away. Have you set a date?"
"Next year, after school is out."

After hanging up, he collapsed into deep sobs. The phone rang yet again, and Red hit "Talk" with careless bravado.

"I've been expecting your call."

"Red? Is that you?"

"Malcolm?" The one call he wasn't expecting. "Where've you been? What's happened to you?"

"It's a long story. I saw you on *Dr. Flo.*"

"So it takes network television to get your attention."

"I'm sorry I've neglected you. I've been going through some pretty tough times. I'm calling you from the nuthouse, as we speak."

"Are you okay?"

"I haven't been, but I'm better now. I've been here for several months."

"What for?"

"Drug addiction, depression. I got hooked on heroin."

"You? Malcolm, I've never seen you do anything more than cocktails and joints. You don't even smoke cigarettes."

"That's when I'm with you. There's a dark side of me, Red, that you've never seen. I've never let you see it."

"So you *do* smoke cigarettes?"

"Worse. You wouldn't understand. You drink and smoke pot for fun. I've seen you walk away from a full cocktail. I could never do that. You're not an addictive personality, Red. You don't understand it."

"A blind spot that has gotten me into trouble more than once, as you know."

"For me, it's depression. I was using the drugs and alcohol to medicate myself."

"Yeah, Theo was like that, too. He used to call it 'The Big O.'"

"So Theo and I have something in common after all."

"Why not? You've both had the same lover. Why do I always get the manic-depressives? I'm the only one who puts up with them, I guess."

"You're the only one who sees the beauty in them."

"I've often wondered if that isn't what killed him. He was drying out when he killed himself. Maybe without the booze, The Big O caught up with him."

"That's what happens. You get off the drugs and the booze, and then you have to face The Big O, and you have no idea what that's like. I couldn't even get out of bed in the morning. So I checked myself into the nuthouse for chronic clinical depression."

"It confounds me, a person of your caliber. I envy your success. You speak several languages. You've lived all over the world. And you've achieved significant stature in your field. You're right, I don't understand it."

"It's a brain chemistry thing. Now I get my drugs from doctors instead of pushers. The doctors' drugs are better."

"So when can we get together?"

"That's why I called. Let's meet in New Harbour."

"Massachusetts?"

"The very same."

"Why there? Is Mother Harbour calling you home?"

"More than you know. I'll be teaching there."

"For how long?"

"Forever. Full tenured professorship, six figures, my own secretary! It's not a loan. I have a chair!"

Laughing, "Malcolm Branson, you are the only person I know who can land the crowning position of your career from the nuthouse! Or was that a resume plus?"

"Probably. Everyone in Asian studies is a mess. We're worse than English departments."

"I studied to be an English professor once."

"Well, there you have it!"

"Bitch! When are you going to be up there?"

"I'll be starting in the fall. How about the holidays? We'll ring in the millennium."

"Sounds good, but I can't promise. Things are changing pretty fast around here. You said you saw the show."

"You were great! Was that tape for real?"

"Too goddam real."

"Bull Barnett and his nephew? That is too much!"

"That's what the nephew says. You'll be seeing it. I just sold it to CBN. I'm surprised you were watching that crap. Is that what the nuthouse does to you?"

"God, they're on the tube 24/7, Jerry, Leeza, Oprah. Shows like that attract the crazies. I just go read a book, but I was walking past the TV room when I saw your face! But how is this going to affect your job? Isn't Bull Barnett one of your boss's buddies?"

"I'm not with the agency anymore. Faye and I cut a deal two days ago. And I'm probably finished in public relations."

"What about your boy?"

"He's on my side. His parents have been surprisingly understanding. The real problem is Dr. Flo. She didn't like what I did on her show, so now she wants to nail me. Things are pretty dicey right now."

"Do you think she'll get the cops involved?"

"She threatened me with that on the show."

"The price of fame."

"The power of television. Because of one single appearance on network television, I'm not the same person I was a week ago. Everybody's all bent outta shape, because it's a ripple in their pond."

"Not everybody. Some of us have known you too long. So you said it on television. It's about time you stepped up. I'm proud of you, Red."

"I'll catch you in New Harbour, if someone else doesn't catch me first."

"You can be my little fugitive and work on the book. How's it going?"

"You once asked me if it was comedy or tragedy. Now I know. It's a comedy. It ends with a wedding."

26

The boy was the emotional and moral center of art and literature in the Western world. From Dostoyevsky to Dickens, from Clemens to Salinger, one had only "cherchez le garcon" to discover the author's point of view. The boy was the voice of genuine feeling, simple honesty, and fair play. By the same token, anyone who harmed, betrayed, or lied to the boy was the villain.

The dapper news anchor with golden silk tie and gray at the temples stared out from the television screen as if confiding the latest gossip, which he was, a head shot of Bull Barnett in mortise over his shoulder:

"In a stunning revelation, Bull Barnett, a leader in the movement to restore the moral fiber of America, has himself become the center of a sex scandal of seismic proportions. In videotape obtained exclusively by CBN News, Barnett's own nephew, now age eighteen, describes numerous sexual encounters with his uncle when the boy was age twelve and living in Massachusetts with his mother. A word of caution: The language in the following clip may not be suitable for some viewers."

The video tape clip played with the boy's face blurred into moving blocks of color and his voice mechanical and distorted:

"We were alone in the house one afternoon, and Uncle Bull asked me if I'd ever, you know, gotten it off. I said I didn't know how, so he took off my shorts and did it for me. After that, we did it lots of times."

Anchor:

"The young man's identity is being protected pending an investigation by the Massachusetts Attorney General's office, which is currently reviewing a copy of the tape. Spokesman for the National Republican Committee Max Nichols commented on the tape."

Nichols (OC with CHRYON):

"This is an outrageous accusation designed to smear the good reputation of a highly respected moral leader. We have a pretty good idea that the source of this tape is himself a pedophile and pornographer. I am confident that it will be proven a fraud, and the perpetrator of this libel will receive the punishment he deserves."

Anchor:

"Mr. Barnett could not be reached for comment."

Red hit the power button before the pundit vultures came on to pick apart the corpse. Revenge was sweet! What a pleasure to see the leader of the witch-hunt tarred with his own brush! He was hiding out now, but the media jackals would find him soon enough, and he would be crushed under the child-abuse juggernaut he himself had created. It was fun to lead the witch-hunt, until they came after you, which they always did. Poetic justice, no doubt, but Red's revenge was soured by the real injustice. Hypocrite he may be, but poor Uncle Bull had done no more harm to that boy than so many other teachers, coaches, priests, scoutmasters, or simply kind and loving men who had already been victimized, no more than Red himself. Barnett's real abuse was rejecting little Billy because he was gay. If he hadn't done that, the boy would never have come forward.

Maybe once he experienced it first-hand, Mr. Moral Conscience of America would at last get a glimpse of the evil he had perpetrated, but probably not. With all his powerful friends, he'd probably find some sanctimonious way to weasel out of it and still feel justified in the bargain. "Stern justice is okay for those nasty child molesters," he would think, "but not for me. I'm not one of them." Such was the nature of righteousness—from its own deluded perspective, it was always right, by definition. This was why hypocrites can never see their own hypocrisy.

How was that for a moral Gordian knot? Because of unjust laws, Darren was prosecuted and persecuted for making love to his lover, which precipitated his move to Florida where he met a gay boy on a beach who implicated the pompous prig who helped create the unjust laws in the first place. In turn, Red used the very injustice he was fighting against to bring down his antagonist.

Now, Red had not only Dr. Flo on his ass but the entire right wing of America. They would have to crucify him to protect their own.

The chaos of the Frame household was in full swing, rowdy with children and adolescents, when the non-descript man and woman in dark rumpled suits stepped up to the half-open door hung with the hand-carved and painted wooden amulet: "Bless ye all who enter here." They knocked, took one step in, and called, "Hello."

They were greeted by Jonathan's little cousin Josh, and asked to see his mommy and daddy. He said they weren't home.

"You're here alone?" appalled, the woman leapt to the easy conclusion, when Jon Sr. appeared in his carpenter's denim overalls, lean and simple like Tom Jode.

"His parents are at work. I'm his uncle. Can I help you?"

The faceless visitors identified themselves as detectives with the Mesquite police, and he invited them into the workshop living room cluttered with current furniture projects.

"We're looking for a young man named Jonathan Frame," the woman asked.

"I'm Jonathan Frame," he responded simply.

She seemed confused, "We had in mind someone younger."

"Your son, perhaps?" the man intervened.

"He's at school. Has he done anything wrong?" the father asked pointedly.

"No, we don't think so, but we would like to talk with him," she continued sweetly, as if talking to a child.

"What about?"

"It concerns a man named Richard Rover. Do you know him?"

"Yes, he said you might be contacting us."

"Oh? Why is that?"

"Something to do with that TV show."

"We don't know anything about a TV show. Our information suggests that Mr. Rover may be a potential sex offender."

"That's what the TV show was about."

"What TV show?" the woman asked.

"That TV doctor. Red was on her show about sex and kids. I didn't see it. My sister did, but she's not here either."

"Red?"

"Richard Rover. He calls himself 'Red.'"

"Red Rover,' like the children's game?"

"What game is that?"

"You know, 'Red Rover, Red Rover, oh, won't you come over.'"

Jon looked puzzled. The man interrupted impatiently, "We are not here to play children's games, Sandra!" Turning to Jon, "Does your son know this man?"

"Yes, he's Jonathan's mentor."

"Mentor? You mean like Big Brothers?"

"No, like a teacher."

"He teaches at your son's school?"

"No, I think he works in advertising or something like that."

The man furrowed his brow suspiciously, "You don't know? How did your son meet this man?"

"Through a school program to teach kids creative writing. Jonathan won Top Prize for his story."

"I thought you said he didn't teach at your son's school."

"He doesn't. We moved since then. Jonathan goes to middle school now."

"So 'Red' is no longer in contact with your son?"

"No, he was here about a week ago."

"You said your son had changed schools."

"That's right."

"Then how can Red still be your son's teacher?"

"Not teacher, mentor. It's like a teacher but also a friend."

"We know what a mentor is."

"Then why all the confusion? It seems pretty simple to me."

"I just don't see how he can be your son's mentor, when he's not connected with any program and your son doesn't even go to the same school anymore!"

"He drives out."

No longer concealing his frustration, "He drives out.' What the hell is that supposed to mean?"

The Moralist

"Red has a car. He doesn't mind driving out to see Jonathan."

"I'm sure he doesn't!" the man exclaimed.

Jon shrugged his shoulders, "I think it's pretty generous of him to drive all the way across town like that."

"And this is what you call being your son's mentor?"

"Yes, he thinks Jonathan is a talented artist, so he's teaching him. What would you call it?"

"I'd call it the textbook behavior of a pedophile."

"I'm not sure what that means."

"Teaching him what?" Sandra queried. "What does Mr. Rover teach your son?"

"Writing, art, photography, how to be creative. He's also a good friend to Jonathan. He takes him to the movies and concerts and stuff."

"You don't find it unusual that a man his age pays so much attention to a young boy?"

"No, should I?"

"You absolutely should," the man broke in again. "A pedophile is an adult who wants to have sex with children."

"You mean Red and Jonathan?" He shook his head, "No."

"How do you know?"

"They said they didn't."

"You asked them?"

"Yes, after Red was on that show. We asked them, and they said no. But Red said there was a witch-hunt going on, and they were out to get him for his writing. I guess that must be you."

The man gathered himself up. For all his simplicity, this fellow was a tougher nut than he expected, "We're just doing our job, Mr. Frame."

"And you believed him?" The woman spoke softly, barely concealing her skepticism.

"Looks like he was right," Jon concluded.

"I mean about the sex."

"I believe my son," he added coldly.

"How is your son doing in school?"

"He's doin' okay. He's smart. He oughta be in the advanced classes, but the school authorities don't understand him. He's too far out for them."

"In what ways?"

345

"He's an individual. He wears spiked hair and earrings, and he plays in a rock'n'roll band."

"These anti-social behaviors don't concern you?"

"It's my band. I taught him how to play bass. I wear a ponytail, too. Ya gonna arrest me?" Now it was Jon who was growing impatient.

"Mr. Frame, we are not here to arrest anyone," the man took over again. "We are here to protect your son from a potential sex offender."

"You said that before. What exactly is 'a potential sex offender'?"

"It means he's a suspect, but we have to be sure."

"Your description of Mr. Rover is classic predator behavior," the woman interrupted, speaking with the smug authority of an expert. "They're extremely patient. They establish a relationship with the boy, in order to become his best friend, in order to seduce him. In your son's case, we might be able to prevent abuse, instead of prosecuting it."

"What if Red just loves him for who he is?"

"That's the worst case. If they're in love with the boy, they become obsessive. They'll do anything."

"My son wouldn't lie to me."

"What if Red threatened him not to tell the truth?"

"Red wouldn't do that. He put braces on his teeth."

"Okay, so it's the other way. He has to protect Red because of everything he's done for him. Jonathan doesn't want to give that up. Mr. Frame, men have been plying boys with gifts for thousands of years."

"So you've got all the bases covered. He's a pedophile, no matter what."

"Aren't you concerned for your son?"

"I know my son, and you don't. He's a happy, loving kid. I'd know if there was something wrong, and there isn't. Everything is right with him and Red."

The man reached into his satchel. "I have a magazine here I'd like to show you."

Just as he produced the copy of *PAN*, little Josh roared into the living room, "Unca Jon, you want some ice cream?" He didn't see the satchel and tripped, spilling the dish into the man's lap. As the little boy burst into tears, the female instinctively tried to comfort him. Jon apologized wiping up with a towel snatched from an unfinished cabinet. He promised the little boy another dish of ice cream and escorted him to the kitchen.

"This place is a madhouse!" the man exclaimed in exasperation.

"You obviously don't have children."

"And you do?" He cut her to the quick.

She shook it off. "I'm just saying you can't walk into someone's house and expect to take over like that. No matter what we may think about their lifestyle, this is still the man's home. We need his cooperation, and you're not going to get that by bullying him."

"I'm in charge of this investigation, Sandra. Don't forget that."

She huffed and sat in silence.

Jon returned, apologizing again, "My hands are pretty full right now. What can I do for you?"

Sandra prompted her partner, "The magazine."

He picked it up, the cover damp and curling, and handed it to Jon, "It's a magazine for pedophiles."

Jon flipped through the pages. "What makes you say that?"

"Turn to the page with the tab on it," the man instructed. Jon did so. "It's a story about a pedophile and his relationship with a fourteen-year-old-boy he meets in a writing program. Much of what you have told us about your son parallels that story, and it was written by Richard Rover."

"Red's a writer."

"It shows what he's thinking."

"Which makes you the thought police."

That was enough! The man erupted, "We are trying to help you, Mr. Frame!"

"Lowell!" she admonished.

This unprepossessing pair was wearing Jon's good nature thin. "Is that why you came here? To show me this?"

"We want your cooperation," Lowell contained himself.

"To do what?"

"We want to install some recording equipment on your phones and computers."

"We only have one computer."

"Does it have e-mail?"

"Yes. So you want to record Jonathan's conversations with Red, is that it?"

"Yes."

"Is that legal?"

"With your permission, it is."

"What about Red? Are you getting his permission, too?"

"This is a criminal investigation, Mr. Frame."

"What's the crime? Potential sex offender? It doesn't seem right to me. I want to hear how Jonathan feels about it."

"Your son?"

"He's the one making the calls. If it's okay with him, it's okay with me."

"But you know it won't be!"

"I don't know that. We'll have to wait and ask him."

At that moment, the front door opened and Melanie lumbered in bowed by her book bag, a harried strand of hair hanging over her face. Who were these people? Jon introduced them as police detectives. That was the last thing she needed. She smiled wanly and bee-lined for the bedroom.

"She's a teacher in the DISD," he allowed apologetically. "Why don't you give me your number, and I'll have Jonathan call you as soon as he gets home? You can talk to him directly."

"Mr. Frame, Jonathan is a child. This is a decision for a parent to make."

"It's about Jonathan, so he decides."

"Children can't make adult decisions. That's what this is all about. I'm beginning to wonder about the home environment you're creating here with all these kids running wild and the front door hanging open."

"They're Josh's friends, neighborhood kids. They come and go."

"Maybe there's more to this investigation than we thought. I'm beginning to see how a pedophile could take advantage of your permissiveness. Child Protective Services will be interested in our report."

"You can go now," Jon responded coldly.

"Excuse me?" Lowell was not used to having his authority so easily upended.

"This is my house, and it's time for you to go."

"You can have it either way, Mr. Frame. You can cooperate, or you can make it hard for yourself and your son. We don't have to wait for him. If I want to talk to your son, I'll have a uniformed officer escort him out of his classroom."

"Then you can be sure he won't cooperate."

"It's your responsibility to tell him to. That's what fathers are for."

"There are lots of ways to be a father."

"And some of 'em aren't right. Some fathers can lose their kids."

"So you're not asking for my permission. You're threatening me."

"We're asking for one week," Sandra answered in her best negotiating tone. "That should be enough to find out what we want to know. Then we'll remove everything, and you won't hear from us again."

"I doubt that."

"If Mr. Rover is doing anything he shouldn't, the tape will catch it," Lowell continued smugly. "Pedophiles are notoriously careless when they talk to their victims."

"When they think they're having a private conversation that isn't being secretly recorded by the police."

"Exactly. Wouldn't you like to know for sure about him?"

"I already do, but go ahead and bring in your bugs. It won't do you any good."

Lowell called in the technicians. They'd been waiting in the van the entire time.

Red's phone was ringing. They'd found him—not the cops, the media. He didn't answer, but instead sent an e-mail to Alecia:

Dear Ms. Pons:

Here's a freebie for you. At three o'clock tomorrow afternoon, I will meet with a CBN reporter in the studio of your local affiliate here in Dallas for a one-on-one, on-camera interview about the Bull Barnett tape. Your reporter, your questions, your tape. I only ask that you treat this as a pool interview and share the tape and transcripts with your broadcast and print colleagues.

When you agree to these terms, I will put a message on my answering machine referring all media calls to your office. See you at three?

Sincerely,
Red Rover

Her reply was instantaneous: "Done!"

The cavernous black room was draped with lights. Two large cameras moved swiftly and silently about in the shadows on built-in dollies the size of fork-lifts before the brightly lit stage with its two comfy chairs facing each other but cheating out. Coffee table, potted plants, a backdrop of bookshelves, all so brilliantly colorful they looked like a cartoon drawing. The hot seat was warm and homey.

Red sat across from a youngish woman, pretty in the face with long sandy hair cascading to her shoulders, but too skinny, her once soft, girlish features now sharp and her voice low and masculine. TV journalism did this to women. It turned them into skinny men with tits.

"Mr. Rover, where did you get that tape?"

"As a journalist, you no doubt understand the importance of protecting the confidentiality of your sources, Ms. Taylor, but I can tell you that the tape has been verified as authentic. Even more important than the specifics of Bull Barnett's personal behavior, the tape exposes the hypocrisy of the witch-hunt hysteria that has gripped this country for twenty years, destroying the lives of thousands of decent people. I know of one young gay man who was prosecuted for his relationship with his sixteen-year-old lover. They were living together with the parents' knowledge and approval. After his prosecution, he was forced to go to sex offender school and to post a sex offender sign outside his home. As a result, vigilantes burned his house down. To me that's wrong, and I'm speaking out against it."

"Mr. Barnett's people are saying this is a smear campaign cooked up by the international pedophile conspiracy. Are you part of that conspiracy?"

"No, that's nonsense. It doesn't exist. The only conspiracy I know of is the witch-hunt conspiracy that's been going on in this country for twenty years. It's an industry now, based on money and phony science. There's a legitimate study published in the *Journal of the American Society of Psychiatrics* that exposes that phony science for what it is, and the witch-hunt conspiracy is doing everything they can to discredit it, because they don't want people to know that their hysteria is based on a foundation of myths, lies, and hypocrisy. Regarding Mr. Barnett, I wish he'd been more honest with himself about his own boy love feelings and the important role that plays in our culture. Socrates, Michelangelo, Shakespeare, Goethe, and Tchaikovsky were all boy lovers, and I could name you twenty more. Lord Bayden Powell who founded the Boy Scouts. James Barrie who wrote *Peter Pan*. The American writer Horatio Alger, who wrote the famous stories for boys that Richard Nixon used to love so much. Will they still be giving out the Horatio Alger Award after this?"

"How did the tape come into your possession?"

"It was purely by coincidence. After verifying that it was real, I released it to the press, because I want to expose the hypocrisy of the witch-hunt conspiracy. Bull Barnett has been an instrumental force in that conspiracy."

"So you wanted to 'get' Bull Barnett."

"No, I want to expose the web of lies and injustice of which he is a part. Most people don't realize the damage this hysteria has done to our civil rights. Our freedoms of expression, privacy, and due process are being shredded. Our relationships with our own children are being corrupted. Don't think this issue doesn't affect you, the next time you wonder if it's okay to hug your kids. Don't wait until the Justice Department thugs arrest you for taking photos of your kids in the bathtub. The police and prosecutors are very adept at expanding these powers into other areas of law, as well. If drawings are illegal, why not writing? Maybe we'll be burning books next. The witch-hunt hysterics are already advocating that. It's time that we woke up to what's going on, before it's too late." He looked directly into the camera: "Before they knock down your door, and don't be so sure they won't."

"They say your real agenda is to normalize sex between adults and children."

"No, my agenda is truth and justice and common sense. I want to end the insanity of this witch-hunt, so we can look at this sensitive issue with clearer, more reasonable eyes. Other cultures have idealized these kinds of relationships as a blend of devotion and teaching into a higher form of love—the ancient Greeks, medieval Persia, seventeenth-century Japan, and many others. We are the ones who are out of step with a natural phenomenon that has existed throughout human history."

"That sounds like you believe that pedophilia is okay."

"I believe it's a much more complex matter than that, and as long as we are consumed with this witch-hunt mentality that sees everything in black-and-white, we're not going to get anywhere, except to ruin the lives of decent, caring people and shred our own civil rights in the process."

"But haven't you ruined the life of a decent, caring man by releasing this tape?"

"Mr. Barnett ruined his own life by being such a hypocrite. He has led the charge in this witch-hunt, when he himself is a boy lover. That's dishonest, and it's symptomatic of the dishonesty of the entire witch-hunt conspiracy."

She started to ask another question, but he cut her short, "Thanks, Valerie. That ought to be enough. You got some good sound bites there."

"But I have some more questions."

Unclipping the mike, "What could you possibly ask me that I haven't already answered?"

"Are you a member of any pedophile organizations?"

"No, I'm an artist and a citizen concerned about this threat to our constitutional freedoms of thought and expression."

"But you write for a pedophile magazine."

"I write for a magazine that discusses these issues, just as you and I are now."

"Your name appears on an international e-mail list of pedophiles. Isn't that evidence of a conspiracy?"

"No, it's like-minded people sharing their thoughts. You see where this is going? It's thought crime and guilt by association. You're trying to indict people for what they think and who they hang around with. That is the death knell of our constitutional freedoms in America."

"So you write for a pedophile magazine, your name is on a pedophile e-mail list, you speak on pedophile topics, why are you afraid to admit that you are a pedophile?"

Red smiled, "I'm not, but Bull Barnett is. That's what's got him in so much trouble. Thanks, Valerie. I appreciate the opportunity to have my say." With a big grin, he stood up and stepped off the stage.

Jonathan didn't make a fuss when his dad told him about the detectives and showed him the little voice-activated tape recorders attached to the family phone, his private phone, and the external disk drive patched into the computer. He simply waited until everyone was in the living room watching TV and removed the disk and the tapes, storing them in his desk drawer. Then he sent an e-mail to Red: "We've been reading Shakespeare. Oberon is king of the fairies." He hit "Delete" and emptied the trashcan.

Jonathan sat at his desk in science class when the uniformed officer interrupted and had a few quiet words with the teacher. She announced Jonathan's name and excused him to go out with the officer. The kids were abuzz, and the teacher called for order. Jonathan felt more proud than ashamed.

He was driven to a local storefront "cop shop." They parked him in a plain block room with a heavy wooden table and gray metal chairs covered in green plastic and a large square mirror at one end of the room. They were watching him, he thought. So what did he care? Let 'em watch.

The cop brought him a cold Dr. Pepper and left. Sipping the soft drink, Jonathan waited and paced and studied the scratches and marks on the table, chinks in the wall, scuffs on the worn linoleum floor, imagining the thieves and murderers, drug dealers and rapists spilling their guts about their crimes, ratting out their friends, maybe even getting beat up by the cops in this very room. It was almost like a jail cell, except with a door instead of bars. He tried the door. It wasn't locked. "Hell," he thought, "I ain't under arrest. I don't gotta hang around here."

As he opened the door, he was greeted by a pale, skinny woman with mousy brown hair. In a beige skirt and jacket and light blue blouse, no jewelry, no make-up, she was as plain as the room itself. If it weren't for the blue blouse, she might've faded away altogether.

"Jonathan?" she stopped him.

He bowed his head shyly, "Yes, ma'am."

"I'm Detective Simmons, attached to the Mesquite Police Department. You can call me Sandra, if you like," she said sweetly.

"Attached?" he wondered. "Who did she really work for?"

Herding him back inside, "If you have a few minutes, I'd like to ask you a few questions, and then we'll take you back to school. This shouldn't take long. Would you like another Dr. Pepper?" He nodded and she motioned to someone outside. The cop returned with a fresh cold can, and Jonathan innocently sat down across from the detective.

"Jonathan, where are the tapes and the disk that were in those recording devices?" she began gently.

"In my desk drawer at home," he answered in a clear and honest voice.

"Did you remove them?"

With the politeness of a Southern boy, he said, "Yes, ma'am,"

"Why did you do that?"

"I didn't wantcha snoopin' on my phone calls."

"Why? Is there something bad going on that you don't want us to know about?"

"No, I just like my privacy, that's all."

"Have you been in touch with your friend Red, since you disabled the recording devices?"

"No."

"When was the last time you talked to him?"

"Coupla weeks ago."

"Is that typical for you to go two weeks without any word from him?"

"No, we talk all the time, on the phone, on the net, but he told my dad we shouldn't be in communication for a while."

"He told your dad that?"

"Yes, ma'am, that's what I said."

"Why do you think he said that?"

"He said the witch-hunters were after him. Are you a witch-hunter?"

"What is it with this man? Does he have you all brainwashed?" she erupted.

"I don't understand your question."

"How long have you known Red?"

"A year and a half. He's my mentor. I'm his protégé. It means 'protected one.'"

"Yes, we know all about that. Did you know he wrote a story about you?"

"Yeah. He's writin' a book, too."

"He told you about that?"

"Yeah, he read it to me."

She pulled the magazine from her satchel, "He read you this story?"

"Sure, I asked him to."

"Did you know it was published in a pornographic magazine?"

"It ain't pornographic. Lotta famous people write for that magazine."

"It's a magazine for pedophiles. Do you understand what that means?"

"No."

"It means men who like boys. Did you know that Red is a pedophile?"

"No."

"You didn't find it strange that the man in the story has sex with the boy?"

"He doesn't. He just thinks about it."

"He read you that part, too?"

"Sure. Red says that the first thing a writer has to learn is that there are no bad words. You can write anything you want."

"Is the story true?"

"No, it's fiction. Red says that's the fun of writing—you get to make it up however ya want."

"Has he ever touched you?"

"He hugged me once."

"Did he ever touch you down there?"

"Hell, no! Whadaya think he is, some kinda faggot? Oh, yeah, I guess you do." Red had warned him about their tricks, but this was too easy.

"The offices of that magazine were raided by the Boston police. They uncovered an e-mail network of pedophiles around the world. Your friend Red was on that list."

"So?"

"We don't want you to be his next victim."

"I can take care of myself. Can I go now?"

"One or two more questions, and then we'll take you back."

"That's okay. I can walk."

"It's three miles."

He stood up. "It's a nice day. I don't mind."

She placed her hand on his arm. "I can't let you do that."

"Why not? Are you arresting me?"

"We took you out of school. We're responsible for your safety."

"Then take me back. I wanta go back to school now."

"In a few minutes."

"I gotta go to the bathroom." The two Dr. Peppers were having their effect.

"Don't you want to clear your friend's name?"

"I didn't know his name needed clearing. What's he done?"

"Well, nothing yet."

"Then, what's there to clear?"

"The suspicion."

"I'm not suspicious. You're the only one who's suspicious. I want a lawyer."

"You're not in any trouble."

"What about my mom and dad? Shouldn't they be here?"

"We've informed them," she lied.

"Where are they? My dad would be here if he knew."

"Look, we just want you to do this one thing for us."

"What's that?"

"We'd like you to meet with Red."

"He said we shouldn't see each other."

"Why is that?"

"Because of you."

"The 'witch hunters'?"

"Least ya know who you are. Red doesn't wanna see me."

"He will, if you say so."

"And what if he doesn't? Will you stop botherin' us?"

"Okay, fair enough, but if he does agree to meet with you, you have to go along."

"What does that mean?"

"We want to tape record it."

"Ya want me to wear a wire? No way! I don't rat out my friends. I wanna go to the bathroom."

The man with the greasy black hair stormed into the room, "Listen to me, punk, you're in trouble already!"

"Sandra said I wasn't."

"Lowell!" she chided.

"No, this little punk needs to know the score!" In the boy's face, "You've already ratted out your friend. We could arrest him right now just for reading that story to you. And far as you're concerned, did you know it's a crime to interfere with a police investigation? We could arrest you for taking out those tapes. We can send you to juvi jail right now. They'll love your sweet little faggot ass."

"Lowell!" Sandra disapproved.

"Then why dontcha do it?" Jonathan called his bluff.

"Because we'd prefer to have your cooperation," she answered sweetly.

"And you're gonna stay right here, until we get it."

Good cop, bad cop. Red was right, but he hadn't warned him about this piss thing. He had to go real bad. "I gotta go to the bathroom."

"You'll get to go, soon as you call Red." He produced a cell phone. "And you're gonna get to call him right now."

"I don't have the number."

Punching in the numbers, "I do."

"He'll know somethin's wrong."

"Tell him to meet you after school, somewhere public, close by."

"He ain't gonna fall for that."

"Why? Because he thinks he can outsmart the police? Because he has you on his side? That makes you a conspirator."

"In my own abuse? Yeah, that makes sense!"

"You little wise-ass!" He held out the receiver. "Now, do it!"

"I'm gonna piss on the floor."

"Fine, we'll arrest you for that, too."

Jonathan took the phone.

Red picked up immediately, "Hi, this is Red."

"Hi, Red, this is Jonathan."

"Jonathan? Good to hear from you, buddy! How's the Shakespeare comin'?"

"We're still readin' about Oberon and the fairies."

"That's a good play. You'll like it."

"I'm not likin' it so far." Lowell glowered at him. "Red, I gotta talk to you right away."

"Okay, I've got a few minutes. Let's talk."

"No, I mean in person."

"Oh, that kinda talk."

"Yeah, just like ya said. Can you meet me at the A-frame?"

"When?"

Lowell held up four fingers.

"Four o'clock?"

"Okay, I'll see if I can get off early. Are you okay?"

"No. That's what I want to talk about. Meet me at the A-frame at four o'clock."

"I'll be there." Red hung up and hit Caller ID. The number wasn't one he'd seen before.

Jonathan handed back the phone, "Okay, ya got what you wanted. Now, lemme go to the bathroom."

"What's the A-frame?"

"It's a place in the park. Red knows."

"I'll take you to the bathroom," she volunteered, taking the boy's hand.

He pulled it away. "I'm not a little kid. I can find it."

"Someone has to escort you," she explained opening the door for him to follow through. He had no choice. He had to go. As she led him down the hall, her voice was as gentle as a mother's love, "I'm sorry about Lowell. He can be such a jerk sometimes."

"Yeah, right," he said sullenly under his breath.

She showed him a private toilet of fresh, sparkling porcelain and tile, like an oasis in a desert, and waited outside. God, it felt good! He thought he'd never stop pissing. The bastards had it planned from the start, the whole damn drama—the Dr. Peppers, the sweet lady, the fuckhead bustin' in. It was all a setup. That's how they did it, gangin' up on a kid like a buncha bullies!

When they returned to the interrogation room, there was another man wearing a golf shirt and khaki shorts. In his hand was a little disc with a wire like a tail. Jonathan was instructed to remove his shirt, and the adhesive disk was taped to his smooth young skin.

"What am I supposed to say?" he asked.

"Tell him the police have contacted you, and you're scared," Lowell directed. "Then, we'll see what he has to say."

"That ain't gonna work."

"If you're telling the truth, he has nothing to hide."

This is fucked! What right did they have to do this? Mom and Dad don't know. They woulda been here. Jonathan was pissed!

Red left the office early and drove home. He scrambled to box up his computer, disks, and manuscripts. If they tossed the house, they'd find nothing. He dropped by Penny's on the way to Mesquite. Luckily, she was in and opened up her storage locker for his boxes.

Red pulled into the Goose Creek parking lot next to the A-frame. On a weekday afternoon, the site of weekend picnics and late-night teen parties was a deserted slab of concrete lined with barren green picnic tables, except for the lone boy seated on top of one pensively resting his chin on the rim of his skateboard.

What thoughts were going on inside that clever young head? So the cops found him, and in damn short order, too. Red was impressed. How had they abused him in the name of protecting him? His bright and happy life certainly didn't need their protection. But no matter how romantically loyal he wanted to prove himself to be, he was still a kid finding his own way, Red just a blip on his life's radar screen. What a cruel irony that his paean to love should become the engine of love's demise!

Where were the cops? He glanced across the street at a white van parked at the In-and-Out.

Jonathan turned to see Red walking toward him but didn't move. The man sat silently on the tabletop beside him.

"I got a new tattoo," the boy began.

"Temporary, I hope."

Pulling up his shirt to reveal the disc taped to his ivory skin, "Yeah, I call it 'cop-adelic.'"

"Damn, the little fuck made us! I'm gonna arrest that little shit!"

"That's right, arrest the victim. That'll get us what we want."

"We've already got the perv. I'll arrest 'em both."

"Shut up, you guys. They're still talkin'."

". . .they got your name offa some e-mail list."

"Prob'ly when they raided *PAN*."

"That's what she said."

"She?"

"One of 'em's a chick. A guy and a gal. Bad cop, good cop, just like you told me. They poured Dr. Pepper's down me and wouldn't let me piss, till I called you. I asked for a lawyer. I asked for my mom and dad, too, but all they did was lie." Talking to his chest, "So take that, you Big Brotha Muthafucka! Red is my best friend in the world, and I love him, and you can go fuck yourself! How's that?" It felt good to tell 'em how he really felt and show Red he could do it.

"I love you."

"They tried to record our e-mails and phone calls, too, but I disconnected 'em."

"You're free now. You're your own man, Jonathan."

"Listen to that perv. That's how they do it. That's how they work 'em. He's got that poor kid completely brainwashed."

"Why'd ya do it, Red? Why'd ya have to tell everybody?"

"Cause I'm sick of it. Somebody had to speak out."

"But everything was cool before. Now everybody thinks I'm queer."

"I thought nobody saw the show."

"That was last week. Now word is gettin' around. A cop haulin' my ass out of class didn't help."

"I'm sorry."

"It ain't you, it's them." He pointed to himself but meant the wire. "They take something great and make it ugly."

"They don't know shit about us. They're responding to a work of fiction. They're not cops. They're literary critics."

The boy smiled then shook his head, "I don't wanta do it anymore."

"I thought you wanted to be immortalized in lit'ra-chah."

"Look at me, dude! I'm wired up like the phone company! They locked me in a room till I almost pissed my pants. My mom has to drive me to school and pick me up now, because I might get beat up on the way home."

"What about your homies?"

"It's my problem, not theirs. It's different, Red. It's different in a really bad way. I hope that book never gets published!"

"Don't worry. It's a tough sell."

"I mean I don't want us to be together anymore."

"I thought we already agreed on that."

"No, I mean forever."

"That's a pretty long time. Is this your mom and dad talking?"

"My mom and dad, my posse, my school, my church, the cops, and the whole damn rest of the world!"

"But is it you?"

"No."

"You could go to another school. The Arts Magnet School would welcome you with open arms."

"I ain't runnin' away!"

"You wouldn't be. You'd be going to a place where you're appreciated for who you are, instead of being condemned for it." The boy was silent. Red sighed with sadness, "As I've told you before, my commitment to you is unequivocal and lifelong."

"Yeah, I know, *pas question*."

"Have I worn it out already? Maybe you're right. Maybe this is a good time to say goodbye, while we have it on police record."

"Ya gonna put this in the book?"

"Of course!"

They laughed. The boy gazed up at Red with blue eyes and golden rims. The mike sputtered between skin and fabric crushed in their embrace.

"I love you, Red. I don't wantcha to go."

"Don't worry. I'll be around."

"Are they kissing? Can you see?"

"I can't make it out."

"Never mind. We got it all on tape."

"Audio tape, dummass! What are we gonna see on audio tape?"

"Wait, they're talking again."

"Remember that song by the Cure?" Red continued. "No matter how far away, I will always love you.' Instead of 'good-bye,' let's just say 'au revoir,' until we meet again."

"Au revoir, okay, but it won't be like it was."

"It never is." Red pressed his cheek against the boy's own and walked away. Jonathan watched the strange, solitary man trudging through the blanket of broken flowers toward the old red Mustang. At the door, Red turned back and waved, then climbed in and drove away.

Speaking to his chest, eyes welling up, "There you go, pigs! You wanted to wreck my life? Okay, ya did it. Ya succeeded. Are you happy now?" His voice cracked with a sob, as he tore the bug from his skin and slammed it on the picnic table. He dropped his board to the concrete and pushed off.

"Ow! Damn little fuck!" Roger threw off the earphones in pain and anger.

"You've wrecked your own life, buster!" Lowell angrily declared. "And if you've messed up that equipment, you're gonna pay. Go get the wire, Roger." Roger climbed out of the van and ran across the street. "We're not through with this little punk."

"Yes, we are."

"Sandra, need I remind you yet again—?"

"Look, Lowell, we thought we could get the boy and the parents to cooperate. They didn't. Do you think that kid is going to testify in court against Rover? There's no case here. We're not even sure if there's a crime."

"Give me a break! Look at this guy. Look at his background. You think he's hanging around that kid to give him writing lessons? You heard it. Of course, there's somethin' goin' on. They talk like lovers!"

"There's no law against talking."

"So what do you suggest? We go back empty-handed?"

"No, we do what you said. It's Rover we're after, so let's take a closer look at his background, dig a little deeper. If he's done it with one boy, there's bound to be others."

As Red walked in the door, the phone rang. The other boy, now a man, was calling.

"I'm gonna do it, Red. I'm goin' to the cops."

"If you haven't already."

"Hell, no! Why wouldja say that?"

"That's the way they play it. Whatever you tell them, they need corroboration, so they make you call and to get me to say something incriminating over the phone. Are they recording this conversation right now?"

"Shit, Red! I wouldn't do that to you!"

"Then why did you call?"

"To warn you."

"Of what? That you're about to stab me in the back? I appreciate your sincerity, if not your moral confusion."

"I guess I'll have to take that as a thanks. Sometimes it's hard to tell with you."

"It's too late anyway. The statute of limitations has run out. I told you that."

"No, it ain't. The law says ten years from my eighteenth birthday. That's three more years from now."

"That's Ohio, not Texas."

"I'm talkin' about Texas! Tammy checked it out with a lawyer."

"So Tammy's got a lawyer now! What does she want? Money?"

"Worse. She's Catholic."

"*Cherchez la papiste!*"

"Huh?"

"Nothing. It's French. Do you have any idea the coals of fire you'll be heaping on your head?"

"I do. She don't. You know me, Red. I hate cops."

"Then don't do it."

"I have to."

"The old pussy whip, huh?"

"No!"

"Then why? Do you agree with her? Do you think I abused you?"

"I was fourteen, dude! I didn't know what I was doin'."

"That sounds like a yes."

"You know I don't think about shit like that. That's you and Tammy. You two are a lot alike."

"I doubt that."

"You know what I mean."

"So think now. Did knowing me hurt you or help you?"

"It helped me. You were the only one I could rely on. As bad as it got, I knew ol' Red would be there, even when I was. . . I knew you loved me. You loved me more than anyone, till Tammy, I mean."

"So that's why you're turning me in."

"She said a straight man would do it. Only another fag would try to protect you."

"She's holding your masculinity hostage."

"She's my wife, dude! She's the most important person in my life. I don't want to fuck that up."

"In the immortal words of Ken Kesey, 'Fuck the wife!'"

Mark laughed. "That's funny!"

"Yeah, funny and true. It won't work. They have to have corroboration, and if they toss my house, they won't find anything. There's nothing that would prove we even knew each other."

"What about the Mark box? What about all the photos and letters you kept?"

"They're gone. I threw them all out."

"No, you couldn't do that!" Red could hear the shock and hurt in the young man's voice. "All the photos? Everything?"

"Everything. I destroyed it all." Long silence. "Mark? Are you there?"

"Why? Why did you do that?" He was in tears.

"You threatened me. You betrayed my trust. I told you then you had no idea of the damage you were doing to yourself and everyone around you, but I knew that telling you would make no difference."

"That was my life, dude! It's like you erased a whole piece of my life!"

"Mine, too. Do you think I did it with pleasure? It ripped my heart out!"

"I know you, Red. You keep everything. You could never do that."

"Then you know how much it hurt."

"Like it hurts me now, even worse."

"I'm sorry."

"I'm angry with you, Red. I'm angry with you for doing that." His voice grew cold. "You've made it easy for me now."

"What'd you expect me to do? Break out the bubbly? What we had together was unique in both our lives. That's why we're talking now. They did this to us. The self-righteous, self-hating bigots of the world did this to us. We could've gotten through it, except for them. Of course, you would've gone on anyway. I was cool with that. Sometimes I thought that's why you did what you did, to tear yourself loose from me."

"So you could start on someone new."

"That's what I do, and I love every one of you. I would have scrubbed your hairy fat back in the tub at age fifty, if you'd let me."

"Yeah, and you at age eighty. You'd be lucky to wipe your own ass."

"Point taken, bitch!" They laughed together. Mark whistled at his bon mot. "Poor Mark. I honestly believe your heart is generous, but you have never understood how the things you do and say have consequences. It made you sweetly naïve as a boy, full of confidence in the life that lay before you, but it's a terrible deficiency in a man. I was hoping we could be friends again someday. That's why I answer the phone when you call, but it hasn't worked out."

"Ya mean I can't call you anymore?"

"That's exactly what I mean. If you do, I'll hang up."

"Then we can't talk at all?"

"Yes, that's right."

"This is it, huh?"

"I'm sorry, but going to the police is the one thing we never did to each other. Adieu, forever."

"Wait!"

Red hung up the receiver and wept for the second time that day. The phone rang again. He turned off the machine and let it ring until it stopped. By then, he was already packing suitcases. Two hours later, the Mustang roared out of the bat cave and headed for Penny's high-rise.

She opened the door in her housecoat, not expecting guests, but her face lit up to see him. "Richard! Twice in one day?"

The Moralist

"Mon cherie! Quel plaisir tu voir!" He gave her a big hug.

She invited him, chiding, "Suelement, il faut que telephoner premier."

"Je ne peux pas se mon telephone servir."

"Que'est-ce que se passé?"

"C'avait ete un dur jour. Allumer le TV. Je pense que je serai au journal televise. Tout que tu disais alle se passé."

"Avais-tu des ennuis?"

"Pas encore. In the past two weeks, I've been on national television, fired from my job, said good-bye to Jonathan, gotten my hands on some money, and Mark just called to say he's turning me in to the cops, not to mention the huge scandal that's erupting with Bull Barnett."

"Bull Barnett? The voice of Moral America?"

"Watch the news. You'll catch the whole thing. There are no more reasons for me to stay here, and several good reasons to go. Veux-tu encore d'aller au Paris?"

"Ce train-ci se partit de station, baby. En voiture!"

"Justement que je voudrais entendre. Quand tu te partas?"

"D'aujourd'hui en huit."

"Je me retrouvais tu la. Je volai aller demain."

"Demain?! Tu avais des ennuis!"

"Not if I leave tomorrow. Can you get that condo opened a week early?"

27

A year later, *The Moralist* was published in Paris, in both French and English editions. The critical response was a mixture of praise and outrage:

"*The Moralist* is an in-your-face apology for pederasty."

"The perfect example of Joseph Campbell's 'didactic pornography.' *The Moralist* gives a whole new meaning to the phrase 'aesthetic arrest.'"

"A political document disguised as a novel. Red Rover is America's 'underground man.'"

"In Paris, they call him 'the new American Gide,' but Red Rover can't touch Gide. His moral message is that child sexual abuse is a good thing."

"Pederasty as a metaphor for the chaotic nature of love."

"Tie down your totems before you read *The Moralist*. This 'novel' depicts a Kafka-esque vision of totalitarian America. A black comedy, it is also a *roman a clef* by the author's own admission that he had to fictionalize the story to protect himself from the police."

"Rover's moral mysticism examines the moral self beyond moral principle. He is a preacher and propagandist."

"We first heard Rover's brand of moral relativism back in the sixties: 'If it feels good, do it.' *The Moralist* is the same mushy moral sentimentality delivered with a stick of dynamite, a letter bomb filled with oatmeal."

"Through his persona "Red Ryder" ("read writer"—get it?), Red Rover strips his moral self bare, which also by the way, includes his thought, experience, and sexuality. You can't take the thought without the man or the man without the thought. As *The Moralist* says, 'Now you see it, now you don't.' His moral legerdemain more resembles Genet than Gide."

"In our age of Jerry, *Survivor*, and Internet web cameras, it was inevitable that our literature would turn exhibitionist."

"You may want to condemn *The Moralist*, but those who have lived it know that it's true."

"The literary sophistication of a chat room."

"A new voice for the new millennium, Red Rover has put the twentieth century to bed."

"The title is a deception. Make no mistake, *The Moralist* is a demonic book."

From their vantage on the North Ridge, New Harbour was a pretty little town nestled among a patchwork quilt of green, yellow, red, and orange. New England was the most beautiful place in the world in the fall, but this day was overcast and cold. A sharp wind cutting through their jackets, Red and Malcolm walked along a wooded path, Red in a loose nylon parka of neon orange, yellow, and red like the leaves, Malcolm in a rugged suede windbreaker. The wind blew through his dark hair, his sharp features fit for the sharp wind like the Great Stone Face itself. He looked like an academic Sam Waterston, but put her in a leather jacket, and she turned butch.

"Penny was insufferable. That is one high-maintenance gal! She had this vision of herself as a mad bohemian. She was mad all right, the kind of mad everyone else had to put up with—a horny, neurotic drama queen who drank too much."

"How many have we known!"

"But she got the job done. I think Dr. Flo convinced her."

"She saw your performance."

"She saw the reaction to it. She'd read some of the book. She knew where I was coming from, but it wasn't until she saw how people reacted that she realized its potential as cutting-edge art."

"With a little help from your golden tongue."

"You flatter me, Dr. Bransom, you who can talk yourself into a full professorship at Harbour from the nuthouse! What better way to establish her bohemian credentials than to be the Paris agent for *le nouveau Gide de siecle vingt et un*? Anyway, once she bought into it, Penny was hell bent on our success and damn near drove me crazy in the process. I was trying to finish the book, in between her bouts of boozy self-pity and the social calendar. She dragged me everywhere. That was part of the plan, exposure. She was showing me off. It was fun. We were always 'on,' sometimes a team, sometimes apart, two old flaks workin' the room. At first, she called on her old contacts in the city, the same kind of boring yuppies she knew in Dallas, but pretty soon, the parties started getting gayer. Penny knew where the action was. And we were untouchable. I had no sexual interest in these queens, nor they in her. So they had no choice but to love us. Many were boy lovers themselves and understood what I was doing. Others were appalled and fascinated. Long ago in Dallas, it was fun to make our entrance at the Wildcatter's Club filled with Texas oilmen drooling over the boobsie blonde babe on my arm, to watch their eyes dart and tongues hang out. But in Europe, Penny wasn't the bait. She was the queen, the queen of queens, and she played it as only a true fag hag can. But there was still that problem. She wanted to get laid. The queens wouldn't fuck her. I wouldn't fuck her. She wanted a Frenchman to fuck her. Enter Luis Cohen, editor for *Pensée Café*. Luis was no pansy, or maybe he was one of those European pansexuals."

"Dontcha love 'em!"

"Not my type, but he came on hard to Penny."

"So to speak."

"She was in paradise. It was the romantic adventure she had dreamed of. Luis completed the equation."

"Was he your publisher?"

"No. Ironically, for all of Penny's hard work promoting me, that lead came from my buddy Eugene from Vermont, who introduced me to a fat old Ali Baba named Karin, or Karen, as he was most often known."

"A boy lover?"

"Yes, he'd read my short stories, and I'm sure he would have much preferred to publish *Seeing Red*, when I was thirty and looked twenty, but he knew *The Moralist* was real, and it knocked his froggy socks off. He couldn't resist delighting the French literary scene with the tale too shocking for the States to tell."

"Why are boy lovers always fat old queens?"

"I beg your pardon."

"Okay, you and Darren and Theo and many others I'm sure, but you know what I mean."

"Age doth make boy lovers of us all."

"Even if the boy I love is eight years older than me."

"Once you were my bright young grad student. Now I'm the professor's catamite. With chemistry like that, no wonder we've stayed together!" Red glanced into the professor's hungry eyes, alight with the same glint he had seen on his birthday twenty-five years ago. "Now that I'm your boy, does that give you a feeling of power?"

Malcolm replied by grabbing a fistful of nylon and spinning Red around, kissing his passionate lips, as full and soft and sweet as a boy.

Malcolm's crib was sparsely furnished with modern multi-colored tulip lamps and Mies sofa (all ordered off the Internet), as austere as his grad student lodgings had been twenty-five years ago. They did whiskey shots just as they'd done then, and Red became the professor's catamite once again.

The following day, they sipped fresh cappuccino and ate buttered croissants at a sidewalk café. It reminded him of Paris. If only Malcolm had been there!

"Where is Penny now?" Malcolm invited Red to continue his tale.

"In Manhattan. She's meeting with Mr. Shakespeare's Books."

"The retail store? Why?"

"Where have you been? Oh, yes, I forgot, your books are published by the university press. Outside of academe, it's the retailers who drive the market. They tell the publishers what to publish. We need a U.S. connection, so last summer, Penny started talking to Mr. Shakespeare. They've got a reputation for shelving controversial stuff. Now that *The Moralist* has the European stamp of approval, that makes it okay."

"America has never been comfortable as a leader in the arts. Our chaotic culture might produce the most cutting-edge stuff in the world, but we still rely on Europe to tell us whether it's any good or not."

"We've got the artists. They've got the critics. That's why I went there."

"Not the only reason, I understand."

"Mark's charges were dropped. They tossed my house and found nothing."

"Especially not you."

"Not me, not a photograph, not a letter, not a shred of evidence that I ever knew him. I threw it all out a long time ago."

"That was smart. He could've put you away for a while."

"It wasn't him. It was his wife, Lady Macbeth. He hates cops, but he's weak when it comes to women. I think she was after money. If they convicted me on a criminal charge, she'd have come after me with a civil suit. So tough shit for Tammy. It didn't happen, but it destroyed what was left of my love for him. I will never speak to him again, and I'm sad about that."

"He'll turn up. What about your journals? I'm sure you didn't destroy those."

"I don't keep a journal, only notes for my creative work that has been published, marketed, and sold."

"I think I'm beginning to understand what you've done. You're writing is so revealing and intensely personal, you have no privacy. With everything you write, there's a cop looking over your shoulder, so you have to fictionalize it the minute you write it down."

"That's the way it is now in the land of the free. You can't tell the truth anymore, not without a mask. No one can. The noose was getting pretty tight after Dr. Flo. I got out just in time. They couldn't get me, so now they go after the book instead."

"Yes, I've read some of the diatribes."

"I couldn't have written them better myself. It's Lenny Bruce! It's *Naked Lunch*! It's the American irony. The more they hate me, the more books fly off the shelves. And right now, I'm the most hated man in America."

"It sounds like that's what you want."

"I'm the Ancient Mariner. I have a story to tell, but it's not what everyone wants to hear."

"You've certainly put your balls on the chopping block."

Red remembered Michael's Boy Tom. "You're not the first to have made that observation."

"Don't be surprised if they chop them off."

"They're still trying."

"At least you have balls. Your book is making a difference, Red. You've said the emperor has no clothes, and people are starting to listen."

"Like one of the reviewers wrote, 'Those who've lived it know that it's true.'"

"But it's those who haven't who will make the difference."

The two lovers finished their coffees and walked toward the Harbour quad, past Reverend Bailey's chapel, home of the scandalous wine and cheese twenty-five years ago.

"Speaking of the naked emperor, what's the latest on Bull Barnett?"

"He's been indicted for indecency with a child."

"Did the nephew testify?"

"It was on CNN. I'm surprised you weren't glued to the set."

"Frankly, Scarlet, I don't give a damn."

"You should. That's why the right wing hates you, even more than your book. You brought down their hero."

"From Europe, it all seemed so tawdry and irrelevant. Not everyone shares in our American insanity."

"The left is laughing up its sleeve, as they wag their fingers at Mr. Moral Authority. The right responded by accusing them of joining the pedophile conspiracy to assassinate Barnett's character, but that didn't fly. That tape is a thorn in their side, so now they're going after the kid, claiming he did it for revenge."

"Which he did, but it's still great television. Barnett'll get off, because he's famous. What we call 'justice' is just another form of myth, revenge, and politics."

"You're famous, too, y'know."

"Not literary fame, I mean real fame, Bull Barnett fame. I've been in this country for two months with complete anonymity. I went to my daughter's wedding in Florida. I visited Jonathan in Dallas. Nobody said a word. Penny even lined up a soiree. Her old 'friends' were falling all over themselves to host the radical new author. I was a guest of honor at an AIDS benefit!"

"Did they ask you about any of this?"

"It's Dallas. The socialites don't follow the news, even the queer ones, especially them. They didn't remember that I was involved. Most of 'em hadn't even read my book. All that mattered was that I was controversial in Europe, and that made me an item. Compared to the charged intellectual climate of Paris, the level of interest and understanding of these issues in Dallas was so banal I would *prefer* to talk about their new Lexus. So would they."

"Not everyone in America is as shallow as Dallas."

"I'll take shallow over stupid and mean. The Christian crazies are already picketing Mr. Shakespeare's across the country. It's good buzz for the tour, I understand that, but—"

"You're doing a tour?"

"Soon as I leave here. That's part of Penny's deal."

"Shouldn't you be in on those negotiations?"

"And miss my only chance to see you? Malcolm, I'm not only married, I'm pussy-whipped. I'm the perv . . . uh, perfect husband. I do what I'm told. Just like Luis was the perfect cock. If she could only get them together in one man. That's the female dilemma. In some cultures, they call manhood 'The Big Impossible.' The Big Impossible for a woman is to find the perfect cock in a man who does what he's told."

Malcolm laughed but continued, "I hope she's making sure you have the proper security. Some of those crazies really are crazy."

"It's on the agenda. Thanks for your concern."

It was almost noon. The campus was alive with fresh-faced youth, the best and the brightest, pouring out of their classes and headed for the dining halls.

"No wonder so many professors are boy lovers," Red observed. "How could you not be with this around you all the time?"

"And they're young forever," Malcolm added, echoing Rupert's observation of two years ago.

As the quadrangle spilled the two men back onto the streets of New Harbour, they stopped at Louie's, immortalized in song for its tables bearing the carved graffiti from two hundred years of college boys. Those tabletops were now mounted on the walls, replaced with the linen-draped variety attended by young men in dinner jackets.

"Tell me about your boy," Malcolm began the conversation again. "You said you've seen him since you've been back. Was it awkward, or did you just pick up where you left off? A year in the life of a teenager can be a very long time."

"We stayed in touch."

"E-mail?"

"ICQ."

ICQ

> School?

> Better.

> Harassed?

> Nah, old news. The kids thought the cop thing was kewl. Everybody askin' questions.

> What say?

> Cops asked about me and the guy who was on TV.

> What about the news?

> Kids don't watch the news. The cops cleared up my rep. Everybody figured if the cops checked it out, it couldn't be true.

> A delicious irony!

> Yeah kewl.

> What rep now?

> Outlaw Man.

> Anyone ask about you and me?

> Sometimes.

> What say?

> One answer: No, we didn't; no, we never did.

> I have a publisher for the book.

> You'll be famous!

> So will you.

> I don't wanna be. gtg

"I brought him to Paris for the millennium. He stayed almost a week."
"His parents allowed that?"
"How could they refuse? It was the opportunity of a lifetime for a fourteen-year-old boy. That's one millennium he won't forget!"
"But after all that happened—"
"What happened? I was out of the picture. Life went on in Mesquite, Texas. Jon and Melanie were excited at my invitation. His sister was jealous and made all sorts of nasty accusations. I was surprised. She was always on his side in the past, but I can't blame her. She knew she would never have such a rare opportunity. I barely recognized him when I met his plane at Orley. He's taller than me now. I used to have to bend down. Now I have to look up. It was hard to imagine that this tall, slender teenager was the same

little boy I'd met at MLK almost three years ago with his freckles and little round babyface. As a youth, he had the perfect frame for fashion, so I dressed him in the coolest French styles. I wanted to show him off, my fresh American boy, eyes wide-open seeing everything, saying nothing, being cool, as Penny gave us the grand tour. What an odd trio we were, like the Addams family on holiday, I in a gray sweater shirt and soft black cotton slacks, Jonathan sportin' shiny red Italian silk, Serengeti's, and purple hair, a continental Blues Brother, Penny in her St. John's knit top with pleated skirt, black stockings, and black Escada loafers. Her crowning touch was the black crushed felt fedora with a three-quarter veil. She looked like a boobsie Texas Marlena.

"Our first stop was the Opera House," Red continued his story, "where she knew the director, who showed us the view from the roof overlooking all of Paris. Then, it was off to the Palais de Monai, a museum of the money of France, the perfect choice for a Dallas gal. The director, whom she also knew, placed in her hand a six-hundred-year old coin, the oldest coin in France. Most rare coins today are sealed in plastic, so I knew what a *rare* moment that was and asked to let Jonathan hold the thick, dark, leaden medallion of uncertain composition and arcane design. 'They must have had some pretty big pockets back then,' he quipped. Penny translated, and the director laughed, explaining that this coin wasn't likely to be exchanged for a cup of coffee or a pack of Galoises. Coins like this were kept in the national treasury as the foundation of the nation's wealth, a fortress filled with metal discs.

"After the Palais de Monai, Penny begged off and returned to the condo. At last I was alone with my boy in Paris. We had lunch at the Café des Deus Magots."

"How do you like it so far?"

"Everything is different."

Theo had once observed that if you want to be alone with your lover, take him where he doesn't speak the language. "Yes, it is. That's the fun of foreign travel. You discover that the rest of the world isn't Mesquite, Texas, and once that happens, you're never quite the same again."

"There's so much color. Since I've been taking art classes, I've been noticin' colors more."

"They don't call it The City of Lights for nothing, and there are colors yet to come, I assure you. What else are you studying? Are you still writing?"

"We have to write a sonnet for English class."

"An English sonnet?"

"Yeah, we've been reading Shakespeare's sonnets."

"My favorites. Most of 'em were written to a boy. Did they teach you that?"

"This isn't another one of your theories, is it?"

"No, it's common knowledge among scholars. Shakespeare wrote 154 sonnets, and the first 126 were written to a boy like you. They include all of the great love sonnets that you are probably reading right now: 'Shall I compare thee to a summer's day/ Thou art more lovely and more temperate. . .' 'When in the sessions of sweet silent thought/ I summon up remembrance of things past. . .' 'Let me not to the marriage of true minds admit impediment. . .'"

"Those are the ones."

"If you read them all, the fact that they are written to a young man is obvious. In the first ten, for example, Shakespeare tells the boy that instead of loving him, he should find a woman who can bear him children and carry on his beauty. The last sonnet #126 starts out, 'O thou, my lovely boy.'"

"Then, why don't they teach us that?"

"It's a cover-up. They don't want you to know that Shakespeare was in love with a boy. It's even worse than that. Your teacher probably doesn't even know it himself."

"But if he's read all the sonnets—"

"He hasn't. He's only read the ones he teaches to you. I once told another boy this same thing. Just like you, he was studying the sonnets in English, so the next day in front of the whole class, he asked his teacher, 'Isn't it true that Shakespeare wrote all these love sonnets to a boy?' She was horrified. 'What makes you say a thing like that?' she demanded. She really didn't know. Then he nailed her with 126, 'Well, what's this one here that starts out "O thou, my lovely boy"? He's talking to his lovely boy, right?'"

"What did she say?"

"She sent him to the principal's office for disrupting the class. Authority is the last refuge of ignorance. That's what concerns me about the education you're getting at Mesquite High. Do you think things will look the same to you when you return from Paris with your photos from the top of the Opera House and holding the oldest coin in all of France in the palm of your hand? They will not. I've told you about the Arts Magnet School. I have friends there. They used to be my classmates in Paul Baker's theater program at the Dallas Theater Center. Mr. Moony has a few connections there, too. He showed them some samples of your work, your poems and sculptures, and of course your award-winning story from the Authors of Tomorrow. They said they'd make a recommendation to the admissions committee, which is a strong first step. When the book comes out this spring, I'll make sure they all get copies. That should tip the scales. You'd get in on your celebrity alone. That's the difference. At Mesquite High, the fact that you're the subject of a radical book is a problem. At Arts Magnet, it's an asset. But I want them to know you first, that you're an artist in your own right, and you deserve to be one of their prize students. The question is, 'Do you want to go?"

He looked down into his coffee and spoke softly, "I don't wanta leave my posse."

Red nodded, "Okay, I'm not asking for an answer now. Just think about it. Tomorrow night, you will witness the turn of the millennium in Paris. It's a memory you will cherish for the rest of your life."

Penny threw a huge bash. From the balcony overlooking the City of Lights, they watched the Eiffel Tower explode with fireworks whose reflection danced on the face of the boy, now blue, now red, now golden and white. Even the too-cool Mr. Frame was gollygeewow once again. Gazing at the spectacle, man and boy held each other close. Red felt the new adolescent frame of his beloved, lean and incomplete, brimming with the joy, hope, and glamour of life before him. He tasted the sweet soft lips of youth.

The old friends continued their tour through the gray New England town, past Theo and Red's old townhouse, their salon where the professors and students from the Drama School and the School of Art and Architecture had gathered for fun and games. It was memory lane with a final destination, The Peacock. Gone were the giant bird over the dance floor and the niches in the wall and the easy sex. Stripped of its seventies flamboyance—even the flame was dropped from its name—The Peacock was now a serviceable gay bar that had a subdued early evening happy hour before the late-night club crowd showed up with plenty of town-and-gown cuties, Malcolm assured him. They sat at a quiet corner booth.

"In the spring, the book came out. The French literary press ate it up. They gloated over stealing me. France is the home of the modern pederastic tradition in literature. Karin was so pleased, he sent us on a tour: Brussels, Amsterdam, Hamburg, and Copenhagen. And sales did very nicely everywhere we went."

"Any backlash?"

"Only in The Netherlands. There were some nasty editorials by a crusading police commissioner. It's a terrible shame what's happening there. A generous and tolerant people are being corrupted by the American poison, but still, it's nothing like here. The beauty of getting published abroad is that you enjoy the cache of being American and the remove of being foreign. It's not the same as when the story takes place in your own backyard."

"Which it is here."

"Exactly, which is why Jonathan got so upset when I told him the book was coming to America."

<u>ICQ</u>

> I don't want 'em comin' after me again.

> They won't.

> How do you know?

> Because they tried once and failed.

> What about when the kids at school hear about it?

> I doubt if my book will be on their reading lists.

> But it's right there on the bookstore shelves. Anybody can get a copy, or maybe somebody's mom or dad will read about it. Then it will start all over again, even worse. What if somebody starts showing the book around school? I don't wanta do it again. I don't wanta go through that again.

> You don't have to. You've been accepted at the Arts Magnet School, if you want to go.

> Because of your book?

> No, because you're the kind of talented young artist they're looking for.

> You said you were going to send them copies.

> I didn't. You got in on the merits of your work.

> You didn't have to. They've probably already heard about you and me and the book. I feel like some kinda freak now.

> I thought freaks ruled.

> Not that kinda freak. Besides, how can I go there? I'm not even in the same school district.

> It's like a private school. You have to pay for it.

> You mean *you* have to pay for it.

> Which I will do with great pleasure. You stood by me. I stand by you. You're not my little dog anymore. You're a young sorcerer now.

> I just don't want everybody thinking I'm a fag.

> That's Mesquite High talking. At the Arts Magnet, girls and boys will be all over you. Take your pick. Try both. See whatcha like?

> You don't care?

> I care very much. That's the point.

Red continued, "Love is humble. Love is a tyrant. One must choose. For the humble lover, the presence of the beloved is enough. The tyrant wants to possess the beloved but only succeeds in driving him away. Yet inexplicably, most choose tyranny over humility. The tragedy of love is the belief that love is its own argument for reciprocation. Truman Capote once said that the beloved would inevitably give in to the lover's devotion. The flattery alone was irresistible. But only the humble lover can accomplish this. When the tyrant emerges to claim his prize, love flies."

"You confuse seduction with conquest. The seducer is humble. The conqueror is the tyrant."

"That's love's challenge: to conquer and remain humble."

"Then, you're always seducing him."

"Yes, the true lover seduces the beloved forever. Like John Lennon said, 'Love is all you need.'"

"Is love all you need?" Malcolm inquired.

"Yes, not only all you need but all you can need. Love is the energy that unites the I and It, that binds consciousness to life. Love is the engine of life itself. Love is the unified field theory. It will be another thousand years before our science understands this."

"You're completely out of your mind, I hope you know that," he laughed.

"Out of mind, out of body, out of space, out of time."

"At least, that's your pose. You want to be a madman like Theo, but unlike Theo, you're sincere. Most people are dishonest but wear the mask of sincerity. You're sincere but wear the mask of dishonesty. You may be the sincerest person I've ever met."

"We all wear the mask of personality, which is a deception by definition."

"Then we are all dishonest."

"All the world's a stage."

"Which gives you the freedom to be sincere unabashedly."

"The truth of masks."

At the wedding, in miniature top hat and tails, little Scottie was the ring bearer at Cindy and Achi's insistence and over Barb's objections. Yaya didn't want the boy anywhere near that dirty old father-in-law, who had written that nasty book, but Scottie couldn't wait to hang with Red, which infuriated her even more. After a few cocktails, she confronted him at the reception.

"I read some of that shocking book you wrote," she began.

"I hope you enjoyed it," he smiled gallantly.

"I did not. I could hardly read fifty pages before I was overcome with disgust!"

"Well, it's not for everyone. I've talked to many people who find it funny and real."

"Is it true? Are you a child molester?"

"No."

"Then, what are you? An alien from another planet? I thought I knew you, Richard. I still remember when we flipped hamburgers together at Achi and Cindy's horse show. What a good time we had that afternoon! Then I read this book! I can't believe the same person I know could have written such filth!"

He shrugged his shoulders. "I was drunk."

"Oh, well, I can understand that!" she cackled mirthfully.

It was a wedding party. Like it or not, he was family now.

Red continued, "If you want to be a moral person, don't ask what is the right thing to do. Instead, think back to when you were five years old and find what made you feel good then. That is your true moral self.

"Look at the great moral heroes of our age—Martin Luther King, Mother Theresa, Gandhi. We praise their courage and compassion, but not their righteousness. There's a reason for that. Instinctively, we know that courage and compassion are an unqualified good, but righteousness is only the social version, "the specious good," as Lionel Trilling calls it. The righteous of the world are immortalized as our Tartuffes, Blifils, and Elmer Gantrys, because we know they are hypocrites. The dirty little secret of moral principle is that all righteousness is self-righteousness.

"The moral struggle is not between good and evil, right and wrong, but self and society. The irony is that society presents itself as right and good, when in reality it is the deal with the devil. Only when the self overcomes society's temptation to 'do the right thing' do compassion and courage triumph. The moralist is an enemy of the people. The moralist must and inevitably does take on society."

"You've certainly done that!" Malcolm laughed.

"At the core of self, we all do. Every one of us takes on the whole of human history and knowledge. We have no choice."

"Double puns!" he smiled thoughtfully. "Social, ethical, epistemological, and existential!"

"Existentialism is Newton's physics in Einstein's universe. It's valid on the local level. But when things get cosmic, when space bends and time slows down, when there is no choice nor time to make one, morality comes alive, not as principle but vital energy. You could call it 'God' or 'the moral self' or whatever. From the cosmic perspective, every act is moral, though tragically we cannot with certainty tell good from evil. We only think we can. It's the Oedipus in all of us.

"For the tragic hero and the ironic comedian—they are the same—moral choice is easy, being and doing at the same time. The refined moral sense is musical. It hears the fine thin chords of beauty and love, the low bass of cruelty and ignorance. Moral principle is deaf. It demands accountability. We cannot dance to the music of the cosmos and account at the same time.

"This is not an argument. It's a path to freedom from the tyranny of principle, the Big Impossible of trying to do the right thing. It frees us to play with our life like a shiny new toy. It does not free us from fear and pain. Like Hamlet says, no proof can put an end to pain.

"Moral principle imposes certainty where there is none. Moral impulse creates unity where there is none."

The old Mustang had been in the garage for a year and a half, but it started right up. His first weekend back in Dallas, Red picked up Jonathan at home, and they headed for the loneliest country road they could find. Red stopped the car, and man and boy hopped out switching sides, Jonathan for the first time in the driver's seat. Red showed him how to work the gears, and soon the car was lurching forward. After about an hour, the boy got the feel of it, and driving down the country road was no longer a challenge.

Red spotted a rock quarry and ordered, "Pull in here!" Jonathan made a sharp turn off the highway into the broad, flat gravel pit, a deserted arena the size of a football field. "There's nothing to run into here, and the only way you can roll this car is to pick it up and turn it over, so knock yourself out."

Without having to ask, Jonathan floored it, and the Mustang took off in an explosion of dust and gravel. Halfway across the plain, he wrenched the wheel, and the car spun a complete 360. The boy laughed and squealed with a Texas "Yee-haw!" By the time they got back to Red's place, the once red car was white with quarry dust.

Leaning back on the futon on opposite sides, shed of their dusty clothes, the man and boy stretched out in their skivvies, Red in his Calvin briefs, long-legged Jonathan in his boxers, now printed with reefer leaves instead of cartoons. They crossed their legs on top of each other in the middle on the coffee table, an arabesque of ankles revealing the barely visible down along the boy's lower legs. His natural strawberry hair cascading forward, he leaned to the side to pick up one of the books arrayed next to him. He flipped it open and read aloud:

> "Let me not to the marriage of true minds
> Admit impediments. Love is not love
> Which alters when it alteration finds,
> Or bends with the remover to remove:
> O, no! it is an ever-fixed mark,
> That looks on tempests and is never shaken. . . ."

He handed the book to Red who flipped to another page and read aloud in turn:

> "Shall I compare thee to a summer's day?
> Thou art more lovely and more temperate:
> Rough winds do shake the darling buds of May,
> And summer's lease hath all too short a date:

> Sometimes too hot the eye of heaven shines,
> And often is his gold complexion dimm'd;
> And every fair from fair sometime declines,
> By chance of nature's changing course untrimm'd;
> But thy eternal summer shall not fade. . . ."

Jonathan picked up a little magazine and read:

Chan squealed and jumped away landing on both feet. He looked around. The sorcerer had vanished. "Old man, where are you?" he cried, but the sorcerer was nowhere to be seen. Suddenly, he realized he could talk. He was no longer a dog, nor had he transformed back into a boy. Chan had grown into a young man.

Chan came upon the emperor's army, who asked him about an old man and a dog. He knew nothing of this.

No trace of the old sorcerer and his dog was ever found, but to this day, there are stories of a young man, who wanders the mountains doing good deeds.

Red smiled at the exquisite beauty of this moment, his beloved boy reading his own story, the story they wrote together. "The boy wants to become a sorcerer, but he becomes a man instead."

"I'm a man now."

"How's that?" Red looked up at his sparkling eyes then down at the substantial hard-on Jonathan had released from his marijuana boxers, swollen and fat, filled out from the slender young boner he remembered from Paris almost a year ago.

"Fourteen years, nine months," he grinned.

Red
An essay by Jonathan Frame

When I was nine or ten, I used to worry about not having anything I was really good at. Everybody else seemed to have some talent or special interest that took up their time, but I didn't feel like I was outstanding at anything. I knew I wasn't stupid, because I was chosen for lots of school programs like TAG and MindQuest, but "Where is my strength?" I wondered.

Then one day, my English teacher told me about a writing contest at my school called Authors of Tomorrow. She said I should submit a story that might be chosen by a published writer, who would help me develop it. Then, at the end of the year, all the stories would be published in a magazine and entered in a competition for the best stories.

I sat down and wrote a little story about a boy who took a magical ginseng pill and turned into a dog. The story came easy to me. The plot just flowed out of me.

A few weeks later, I got called down to the library to meet my new writing coach, Richard Rover. He had chosen my story. He told me to call him "Red."

Red helped me develop my story into a piece of real literature. He taught me all sorts of writing exercises and words that no kid my age could imagine knowing. It was great to have somebody to guide me through the process. Along the way, we became good friends.

At the banquet celebrating the publication of the magazine later that year, the winners were named. I won first prize. Red presented the awards. When he called my name, he could barely keep it together. My heart was so full that someone other than my parents could be pleased with my success. Best of all, I found my calling: I can write.

Red and I still see each other, and he continues to be my mentor, not only in my writing but also in my life. We are very close friends.

Some people have tried to keep us apart. They say he's abusing me and all these awful things. None of it is true. They're scared of the idea that someone his age (Red is 52) would take an interest in a kid like me, but I think they're really scared of themselves. I wish they would just mind their own business and leave us alone.

I like having Red as my friend. He is available to me whenever I need him. He helps me with my writing and my art classes, and he brings me good books. He listens to me when I need to talk. He counsels me from the depth of his experience and out of his heart full of the love we share. I am so thankful for the forces that brought us together, for the inspiration I've gained to write, and for the life-long friend I have found.

Rod Downey is an author, playwright, journalist, and communications consultant. His plays include **Dirty Pictures, The Boy Lover,** and **The Black Orange**. His short stories have appeared in *Gayme* magazine. His articles and critical reviews have appeared in numerous newspapers and magazines.